*From* The Women's Press Ltd
34 Great Sutton Street, London EC1V 0DX

Manny Shirazi was born in Iran and was a teacher there for five years. She first published a feminist short story at the age of twelve. She has had both prose and poetry published in Farsi (Persian) and is the author of the highly successful *Javady Alley* (The Women's Press, 1984). She is a photographer and has held exhibitions on women in Iran. She was part of the Spare Rib collective from 1982 to 1986 and was responsible for the film and fiction pages. She is currently a writer and freelance film critic.

MANNY SHIRAZI

# Siege of
# Azadi Square

The Women's Press

First published by The Women's Press Ltd 1991
A member of the Namara Group
34 Great Sutton Street
London EC1V 0DX

British Library Cataloguing in Publication Data
Shirazi, Manny *1946–*
  Siege of Azadi Square.
  I. Title 823

  ISBN 0-7043-4264-2

Phottypeset by Intype, London
Printed and bound in Great Britain by
BPCC Hazell Books, Member of BPCC Ltd, Aylesbury, Bucks

# Acknowledgments

My thanks to friends – Anna Fairtlough, Penny Henrion, Hilary Lester, Rachel Langton, Zoë Fairbairns and Marla Bishop – who read chapters of the first draft of the manuscript and advised me on it. I am especially indebted to Elizabeth Smith who flew in from Auckland for a month's holiday and spent it in my sitting room typing the manuscript on to the computer.

Many publications, books, journals and pamphlets – including *In the Shadow of Islam* ed. Azar Tabari and Nahid Yeqaneh, *Women in Iran – The Conflict with Fundamentalist Islam*, ed. Farah Azari, *Women's Rights Movements in Iran* by Eliz Sanazarian and *Going to Iran* by Kate Millett – have helped me in the writing of this book. Also many friends' and relatives' personal accounts and the personal testimony of Iranian women exiled since the revolution have been a great source of inspiration for and a challenge to tell this story.

I have in my possession an eleven-minute video of the Iranian women's massive protest march against the imposition of the compulsory veil on the 8th and the 12th of March in 1979, filmed by the French group Des Femmes du Groupe Politique et Psychoanalyse. I am grateful to them for recording some of the deep emotions, personal pain and passion of the women at the time of the event.

I think it is also relevant to mention here that halfway through writing the first draft of the manuscript the beautiful, large Victorian house and garden that I was living in was demolished to build offices and a car park for the local council.

It seemed fitting that I should be writing on destruction amid the destruction.

The first poem in chapter 20 is by the early Iranian feminist activist, Zand Dokht Shirazi. The second poem is by Eshqi Gazvini, the famous radical poet, friend and supporter of Zand Dokht. Zand Dokht founded the Society of Revolutionary Women and the magazine *Women's Liberation*. She lost her sanity and was housebound for fifteen years before her death. Eshqi was assassinated for his radical ideas. (From my article in *The Leveller*, no. 69, 1981.)

This book is dedicated to:

Farideh Bahaie from Ardabiel, who was sentenced to death for adultery in January 1980. Following a summary trial she was executed by a firing squad. In the mortuary it was found that she was still alive. By the order of the Islamic court she was executed there for the second time.

Maryam, Fatemeh and Zahra, three prostitutes who were burned alive when fundamentalists set fire to the old red-light quarter, Shahr No, in Tehran.

Seventeen-year-old Pooneh, who was attacked because she was unveiled. Acid was thrown in her face, and burnt half of it, and her scalp, away.

For their courage and love of life.

# 1

It was International Women's Day, 17 Esphand (8 March). A clear cold day, snow drizzling down, slowly and insistently. It was the last snow of the year, crow snow; spring was late this year.

Zareen looked out from the window of Ziba Style, her hair-dressing salon, to the road. It was early yet. The vendors at the fruit and vegetable market in Seh-Rahe-Jaleh Square opposite were busy unpacking and tidying their stalls. Zareen was waiting for her friend Malihe to come to the shop. They were to set out for the women's march together. She had told her workers and regular customers that she was closing the shop for the day and going to the women's demonstration. She decided to write a note and put it in the window in case a new customer dropped in: 'Closed, gone to International Women's Day.'

Malihe arrived as she was putting it up. 'No,' she said. 'It's too soon to make such an open declaration, especially in this area. Just say "Closed, open tomorrow". There are bad rumours around.'

'Already?' Zareen asked hesitantly, changing the old message and writing a new one, accepting that it was safer.

It was eight o'clock in the morning when they left the house, the streets busier now, snow coming down but too little to settle. Zareen was young, her face and hair well made-up, and she looked cheerful. Malihe was an older woman, small and well built. But not much of them was visible today under long thick coats, woollen hats, scarves and gloves. They set off prepared, with their hot tea in flasks and sandwiches in their bags, huddled together under Malihe's umbrella.

'Which way shall we go? Through Shookofeh or Shahbaz?' Zareen asked. 'Shookofeh would be quieter, Shahbaz more conspicuous.'

They decided to go the Shahbaz way, in the hope of finding more women and joining them. They wondered whether they should take a bus as the weather wasn't on their side, but decided against it. All the fun was in going on foot, meeting other women and talking with them.

Once in the wide arena of Shahbaz they wondered how they would recognise whether the women on the streets were going to the march. Zareen and Malihe weren't carrying a placard. Zareen said she had written a small one; it was in her bag. She would take it out only when she was in the crowd of women, safe. But the street was packed with people, buses, taxis, the pavements crowded, masses of women everywhere.

'Soon we will know if they are coming in our direction,' Malihe said hopefully.

They were heading towards Tehran University in the centre of the city, three miles away from where they lived. Malihe and Zareen were walking up from the south east towards Jaleh Square, which was now called Martyr's Square, towards Phooziyeh, and then Shah-Reza, the long avenue that houses the university at its western end.

A rumour had started a few days before that a leading clergyman had given a private audience to a group of fundamentalist women and that, when the question of the veil was put to him, he warned them that in an Islamic state the veil would be compulsory for women, and that the provisional government was considering bringing out new legislation to enforce this. The news had spread, by word of mouth and women's committees, throughout Tehran and other cities too. This coincided with the preparation for the celebration of International Women's Day at Tehran University, the first open celebration for women by women under the new revolutionary government. The rumour had been confirmed on television the evening before the march. Thousands of women had spent an anxious night and had woken up deeply

2

unsettled. The first doubts since the victory of the revolution were beginning to assail them. Was this a warning? Women started to feel nervous. All their pre-revolutionary uncertainty about an Islamic government was surfacing. Fear of what might come gripped them, although the militancy and the revolutionary spirit were still there, but with a dent or two. For the revolutionary women activists who had never fully trusted a future Islamic government to take care of women's needs, the television announcement, that in a revolutionary Islamic country the veil, and a fully engulfing cover was to become a necessary part of clothing for women, was seen as a danger signal. It added a new vigour and urgency to their march for the celebration of International Women's Day.

They felt angry, outraged and betrayed. So soon, only three weeks after the victory of the revolution that had overthrown the old order, some leaders were bringing out a new old order against women, this time with the sealed approval of God.

The taste of victory was turning sour. They had to move fast, call a meeting, organise, make counter-statements. They thought it all out: spread the news, urge everybody to come, get prepared.

At first the women who had been sympathetic to the revolution (who were mainly from working-class and professional backgrounds) could not believe that such a restriction would be enforced. They paused and wondered what to do. Should they march against it, or take up another form of protest – or wait and see? How best could they resist? They waited.

The fundamentalist women who were devotees of the revolution were pleased. Women had become the focus of attention for the new leaders. It was a good sign. This was good news for the morality of the country. But they were uncertain how it could be enforced. How could legislation force women to become veiled, especially the generation who had never known or worn the veil? Perhaps they could be of help. They must think about that.

The morning after the announcement the city was thronged with women who were planning, acting, thinking protest. From the poor south, where the railway linked Tehran to the other cities, to the northern snow-capped mountains where the rich chalets spread, over the eastern plain of a newly built suburbia, to Meher' Abad airport in the west where the country was linked across the sky to foreign lands, women came out on the road. The vast majority of them poured out into the streets as a spontaneous act of self-defence; a first response to the warning of their instincts. Many were unsure, hanging around, waiting for friends, neighbours, others' reactions. Many talked in doorways, by windows and on phones – talked about what was best to do.

The spirit of defiance and protest that had affected school children, university students and teachers, women in the medical profession, textile workers, industrial carpet weavers, secretaries, women in the oil industry, women in the media, women in telecommunications and heavy engineering in the struggle against the Shah, rose up again, but this time for their own cause.

The early morning snow was light but consistent. It waved and waved down; danced on the gloom of the day. It was cold but the schoolgirls who were the vanguard of this demonstration appeared not to notice. The students from the southern schools of Ameeriyeh, Mokhtari, Nazi-Abad, Javadiyeh, and from the secondary schools of Ebrat, Poorandokht, Sharebanoo, alone or with friends and families, were on their way. These new working-class and rural migrant workers saved to send their kids to school. Education was their salvation from poverty and their hope for a better future. Many girls in these families were educated to be financially independent and future breadwinners. They knew the zeal of the Islamic fanatics; they had tasted it before in their communities. They were walking along the pavements in small groups, isolated, with furled banners under their arms. They were hesitant, nervous, but aware that women would have much to lose from the planned new legislation. They walked through the narrow streets and small lanes until they converged at the main Pahlavi Avenue. They were a sizeable number now and felt safer, strolling, chatting, looking on; snow sitting on their hair and their rolled-up banners.

From the northern areas of Tajrish, Sheemran, Vanak, from the schools of Azadeh, Saba, Alborz, Danesh, came a different

4

kind of anger. These women had never trusted the idea of a religious leadership and their anger had been brewing even before the revolution. This was the area of the upper-middle classes, the professionals and intellectuals of the right and the left who inhabited the neighbourhood of the royal family. The women, from whatever political inclination, were consistent in their demands for equality with men, and they were fervently anti-veil. They were angry, loud and determined to make a strong protest.

They came out with their families, mothers and grandmothers whose generation had been the first anti-veil fighters, and with their young children, firmly holding the girls' hands. As they streamed down the wide avenues lined with tall Tabrizi trees, by the stream from the mountain, they shouted, waved their fists and carried their flags and placards openly and defiantly. The women were in elegant dresses and make-up, wearing their thick red rouge like a banner; their children, in some instances, were equally fashionable, in others deliberately under-dressed, looking like students. Older women, as well as younger ones, carried overtly militant and feminist banners:

'In the dawn of در طلوع صبح آزادی . جای زن خالی
the revolution a place for women is missing', 'Liberation is neither western nor eastern, it is international'. Some of their children's slogans were Marxist: 'Women are workers', 'Workers, national minorities, students unite against reactionary forces'. This section of the demonstration was the most vocal, heated and uncompromising.

The western road to the university was relatively new, with more offices and institutions than houses and homes. Azadi (Freedom) Square and its huge epic central monument, Tehran's Arc de Triomphe, was a symbol for freedom due to its dynamic days during the revolution. It was the grandest square in the whole of the country, and used to be called 'Shahyad', meaning 'In the memory of the Shah'.

Here there was a new middle-class and lower-middle-class area with professional women holding positions in the institutions, hospitals, nursing colleges and various university departments dotted around. The majority of the women were older, modestly dressed, most wearing a scarf, experienced in peaceful protest, graceful and confident. There were some younger student nurses and secretaries who mingled among them too. They were generally quiet, but sharp and fierce at times. Their small placards read: 'If women's bodies excite men, men should put the veil on and be housebound', and 'If women must wear the veil, men must wear the aba' (the surplice). In this way they exposed the basic contradiction. As it was on women alone that the new leadership had imposed the Islamic Hejab, men were free to wear western clothes.

Many male colleagues joined them, even some older men, in sympathy with their cause but also through a deep suspicion that the successful suppression of women would be followed by similar treatment of other groups.

From the east women came from as far away as Tehran-Pars, Narmak and Farah-Abad, from the schools of Esmat, Ayandeh, Jehan, Bahar. They came down to Jaleh, either upwards towards Phooziyeh or downwards to Baharestan Square (Parliament Square) and Shah-Abad – where on the top floors of the buildings women worked on the textile machinery that produced jumpers, stockings, bedding, etc. – through to Laleh-Zar, Ferdosi and Shah-Reza. These women came with their children, in small groups of twos or threes, unsure of themselves and worried that they would be the only demonstrators.

This was the area where women, through some education, small home industries and small businesses had gained financial independence and a comfortable life. They were traditionally conservative but independent, observers of Islam but using its inherent contradictions to adapt it to their needs. They had jobs, a little wealth and the relative security that this provided. They wanted more, not less, and a better future for their children. Now anxiety was seeping through the fragile security they had so carefully built.

Zareen and Malihe were among these women. They had started suspecting the leadership a while ago, but hoped the situation would change for the better. Their friend Fatemeh from Tehran University had told them about the earlier rumour and the demonstration. They were hoping to find her at a bookstall on the campus. As they walked up towards Jaleh Square they eyed the women, the passers-by, the drivers, the shop assistants, and wondered if they would be coming with them. Did they know what was going to happen to them? Didn't they suspect anything? Weren't they afraid? The streets were still marked with the revolution's bruises: the writing on the walls, the closed banks, burned cinemas, broken windows.

Malihe and Zareen reached the square and stopped to decide which way to go: straight up to Phooziyeh Square and then turn into the Shah-Reza or turn into Jaleh Street towards Baharestan Square. They chose the latter route. Fatemeh lived off Jaleh in Khorshid Street. They were familiar with this area; the women here would certainly participate in the demonstration. Besides its schools and institutions, the Shafa Hospital employed hundreds of women whose jobs could now be on the line.

Zareen and Malihe were pleased to see nurses and staff outside the hospital, banners in hands, protests ready, gathering to move on. They joined them, relieved that this was an open demonstration. By the time they got to Shah-Abad which was only a short distance away, they could see a definite, large mass of women. Thousands of students and staff from Shah-Dokht, an infamously militant school, were outside with their energy and fresh fury, mobilised to march on, drops of snow falling on their hot breath.

Full of hope, they approached Shah-Abad with the nurses, talking with them, getting closer and warmer amongst the women. In Baharestan Square more women could be seen – small groups, isolated batches, appearing from various sides of the square. As they walked on their numbers increased. They grew noisier; more banners were unfurled:

‏- آزادی نه شرقی است نه غربی است جهانی است‏

'Liberation is neither eastern or western, it is international', 'We will fight to the death for women's liberation', 'The veil is women's grave'. More were on the march. From inside the shops women cheered them on. Outside on the pavements the growth of the crowd gave the women a new confidence, refreshing their energy and vitality. Shah-Dokht's contingent was on its way.

Zareen sighed deeply, 'Thank God we're not the only women any more. There are thousands of us.' The marchers were moving slowly, on the road, on the pavement, down the ever packed street of Shah-Abad towards the old luxury shopping quarter of Laleh-Zar. It was so good to be walking in a crowd of women rather than alone, scared and uncertain. A small placard proclaimed the women from Mohades, a secondary school in the heartland of fanaticism in Bazar district. A strange and exciting sight.

Snow was settling, sitting on the surfaces, on the edges of the pavements, on the narrow ledges of walls and the corners of the roads. It was a crisp day, but ash coloured, and weighted with the sense of a heavy load: felt in the sky, air, streets and within every woman. Would it clear up later on? Would the sun shine and warm the day? They surged on, as slow, and as multitudinous as snow, noisily shouting:

آزادی آزادی آزادی  'Azadi' – freedom – raising their hands, angry, angry.

The tail end was quiet and relaxed, just gathering force. Some men onlookers weren't sure what it was about. Luckily not all men knew about Women's Day. Some thought it was one of the usual marches of the revolution. Many of them were just puzzled, looking on in amazement. But women onlookers, the shopkeepers, boutique owners, textile workers and some housewives, hanging out of their second or third floor windows with curiosity, were different. They were sympathetic, supportive, excited and friendly. Some waved their hands, some smiled and nodded in support, some made victory signs, some shook their handkerchiefs or scarves from their high-rise blocks, and some just looked, all eyes, amazed. Marchers responded too, clapped, smiled back, invited the watchers to join in, and blew kisses backwards and forwards, left, right and centre, in all directions. Those who were 'anti' were lost among the astonished and the supporters.

The crowd turned into Ferdosi Street. More women, more bodies joined, all surging towards Tehran University, the hotbed of the revolution, not far now. The streets were filling up with women, with loud, outraged, resolute fighters; the first opposition, the first mass opposition, a courageous opposition by women. In some quarters the shouting was becoming fainter and women's voices were getting deeper and coarser, with occasional hitches and knots in their throats. They were getting out of breath, cold, tired, shouting all the way, raising their demands, swallowing flakes of snow, but who would hear? Would the revolutionary government listen? How could it ignore this!

The demonstration was now so packed with women that it was moving slowly, at an ant's pace. They reached Ferdosi roundabout, the convergence of the other women's contingents from the north, the west and the south west. The square was overwhelmed, overspilling with women, all turning to Shah-Reza, just a short space within the vicinity of the university. Everything came to a halt. Nobody could move on. The adjoining and back streets were packed with women. Shah-Reza was occupied. All the roads leading to the university from where the revolution had flourished, were now overflowing with protesting women, the magnificent sight of women out occupying public spaces. This had not happened before, not like this.

The sound of women rang out again; 'Equality and liberty!' shouted thousands of voices from thousands of mouths with a new vigour, force and passion. Banners were everywhere, placards dotted around in between small handwritten rough messages held up by many individual women, personal, bitter and at times humorous: 'The revolution that sends women back to the kitchen sink, stinks.'

The sight of all these women, here, protesting, making a united stand for women's liberation, was powerful. Power to women. Pure passion. Itself a revolution. Dangerous. A speaker with a microphone squeezed through the crowd, informing women that there was no way through to the university. The streets were crowded everywhere. The meeting of the organising committee for the International Women's Day celebration was taking place but it was over-subscribed and impossible to reach. The spontaneity and the sheer volume of women had surprised the small organising body. They were overwhelmed and couldn't do much.

'Please be patient and careful. There have been some threats by the fanatics. Demonstrating men should link up at the edges of the demonstration and be a protective barrier between the women and the fanatics.'

Malihe and Zareen squeezed tight together, cuddled by masses of women and looked at each other in sheer amazement and delight.

'Remember how anxious we were? What do you see now?' Zareen said, amid pushes from the crowd.

'Oh, I love these gentle squeezes!'

Malihe wondered for a bit. 'It is a great sight, a pleasure to the eyes. We are a force to be reckoned with and there's no denying it. We will not be moved,' she said.

'I wish I had a magic carpet. What a sight it would be,' answered Zareen. 'I want to sing. It is a time for singing.' She was joyous.

And they sang: 'We are marching on, for bread, for equality, for liberation, we are marching on . . . '

The snow was coming to its last gasps, having settled on most flat surfaces, narrow edges, women's hair and shoulders. It was shedding its last white feathers on the tightly knit, tired bodies of standing women. Hope rose that it may clear up later and the sun decide to come out.

A loud impatient voice shouted, 'Let's have our meetings and speeches here. I want to speak.' Suddenly, a stool was pulled out of somewhere as if by magic, and the woman stood on it. 'I am a biology teacher from Qum, the city of mullas. We have been under increasing pressure for some time. The veil is now compulsory, even before any legislation comes in. If women refuse to wear it they are thrown out of schools and workplaces. They want to close secondary schools for girls, have some subjects for women censored out of biology books, ban women from some public places . . . '

A few yards further away, another woman speaker stood up, 'I am a scientist at Shiraz University. I have heard a rumour that I could be excluded from working in a laboratory, as mixed scientific work for women could soon be banned . . . '

10

A woman carrying a child, holding her black chador very tightly around her face, stood and shouted, 'My daughter was warned by a male colleague that she should wear the veil, she refused. A few days later she was followed on her way home and beaten up. She is in hospital now. We have complained about him, but nobody cares. It seems nothing will touch him. I have always been a devout Muslim, but I want my daughters to be educated and independent people in their own rights. If this is Islam, their kind of Islam, I forsake my religion.' She was very angry, tense and emotional. Women felt for her and cheered high and loud, and chanted, 'Liberation is neither eastern nor western, it is international.'

'I am a night porter at Rey textile factory, I have been warned that a woman night porter can attract men and that things can happen. Night work leaves women open to suggestions. I have been doing this job for ten years yet it is only now, suddenly, that my suitability is under question . . . '

'I am a music teacher to school children. I have heard that I may lose my job, as teaching music is not essential for school children anymore . . . '

An older woman, gripping her long veil, raised her voice. 'I am here for my granddaughter, she is a brain surgeon at Jondi Shapoor Hospital. I encouraged her to become a brain surgeon, to be what I couldn't be myself. She has been working there successfully for many years. Now she is told that operating on men's brains may excite her. Who has heard such a tale before? Men's brains exciting anybody!'

Women laughed, laughter of fun and laughter of nervousness. They clapped for her and, angry at the implication of what each woman had said, raised their voices in a furious cry, 'Death to reactionaries. Death to historical backtracking. Power to the future.' Their voices rang sharply and loudly into the chill air, filling it with determination, force and warmth – warmth for all the women in danger under this new revolutionary regime.

The snow had stopped now; its last flakes flickered in the air above the women's heads. It was getting brighter, the wintry afternoon light was spreading. Umbrellas were being closed, hats and scarves being taken off, raincoats being

11

shaken. The women's heads were raised, lifted out of the depths of their shoulders, straighter.

Zareen was getting tired, and impatient with standing around all this time. 'Let's have some tea and food. If you hold these I can serve it,' she told Malihe. Malihe suggested they should move towards the wall, where it would be easier. They squeezed on and edged towards the wall, which had an iron fence half-way up. They cleared the snow from the edges, put out the cups and poured out the hot tea. These were handed round, and food went round too. They leaned on the fence drinking and eating. Women relaxed. The hot tea burned their impatient lips but it was welcomed. The slogans, shouts and singing were dying down. The calm atmosphere, food and soft squashes of women's bodies brought about the intimate feel of a woman's kitchen. So chatting began.

'How did you hear of it?' Zareen asked one woman.

'My daughter is a nurse. She's here with her colleagues. She's been so upset about the proposed new nurses' uniform, a white veil to engulf the whole body except the face. Her hospital's medical personnel has been taken over by the mullas, who are not medical staff, and just preach morality and repression. The nurses feel so powerless and depressed now. They don't know what to do. What can you do when you have no choice, and you lose your bread?'

'I know,' Zareen agreed, 'I am a hairdresser and my bread will be affected too. There will be so many restrictions. Soon we won't be able to breathe before asking a mulla for permission.'

'But they can't ignore such a protest,' Malihe said positively. 'That's why we're here. We won't stand for it. This must be the largest demonstration of women I've ever seen, perhaps the largest in our history and in the history of the Middle East.'

'Sure, it's the largest street opposition by women,' another woman commented. 'Don't be so sure they'll take any notice of us though. You either accept Islam or lose your head. It has always been like this and the mullas are not afraid to kill a few million women. They're fanatics – they believe they're right and that they have God on their side.'

'Nothing can change their minds,' another woman added. 'Ah, it is too demoralising.'

'No, we won't let them do what they want!' cried Malihe.

'We won't, over our dead bodies!' another woman's voice chimed in.

'Don't say that. Death is their business. We won't die for them. We will fight them. Yes, we will fight them,' Malihe replied affirmingly.

The crowd was moving now. Zareen suggested they should slip out of the crowd, go to the university to see Fatemeh, their friend who was at a bookstall on the campus. Malihe wasn't sure how easy it would be, but saw no harm in trying, so they said goodbye and good luck to the other women and started to squeeze through the tight lines of women's bodies.

'Let's go through Bobby Sands Road, behind the British Embassy,' Zareen suggested.

'No, that's the long way. Let's go along Palestine, hopefully it'll be quieter and we'll be able to pass,' Malihe replied.

They looked back, a last look at the massive street packed with women, its pavements, windows, walls, and even the roof tops overflowing. Wherever you looked there were women. They turned into a quieter, smaller street and held on to each other as they heard the insults of some fanatics on a balcony.

'Shame. Shame on you, street walkers and anti-revolution-aries, Shah supporters, foreign agents.'

'They don't dare come down,' Zareen said confidently.

They went through a few smaller streets, back alleys, long narrow lanes that led into one another from Farvardin, to the top of Ordibehesht. They were back to Shah-Reza, and the university gate was across the road, barely visible through the impassable barrier of women's bodies. Now for the last hurdle, inching their way through. The university gate was wrought-iron in the shape of a huge open book, each side one half of the book. They passed through it. Just beyond, there was a long line of bookstalls, each belonging to a left-wing group or party. Fatemeh was at the Radical Muslims bookstall.

The stalls were surrounded by people, by discussions and disputes. Was it a celebration of ideas or a war of person-alities? Zareen was baffled. Here the crowd was engaged in a war of words, and through it she saw Fatemeh talking to some women. Zareen waved and shouted, but her voice disappeared in the lines of bodies. She shouted again, 'Fati, Fati . . . ' In the end the voice caught Fatemeh's ear. A few steps and they were face to face exchanging stories about the march. That morning Fatemeh had had to abandon her car, the roads were occupied by women and it had been impossible to drive through.

Zareen looked at the table covered with books, posters and pamphlets. *Women in a Progressive Islamic Society*, she picked it up and ruffled the pages. Fati helped with the Radical Muslim bookstalls every now and then. She agreed with most of their politics but not all, and especially not on the issue of the veil and women's sexuality. She thought they adhered too much to the rigid interpretation of the original Islamic code, which held that women's bodies are inherently sexually attractive to men and that, as men's urges are uncontrollable, even the sight of women's bodies therefore creates disruption in society. Thus women must cover themselves to save men's purity. This was more or less the same view on women's sexuality and the veil that the fanatic Islamic faction, dominant in the present government, wanted to impose on women. Radical Muslims opposed and fought the fanatics on every other issue because they considered their strand of Islam backward and obstructionist; however, their difference with fanatical Muslims over the veil was qualified only in that they did not recommend force but believed that women should be educated to veil themselves voluntarily – but they did not elaborate on what course of action they would take if women refused to wear the veil, or how they would try to 'educate' women if they did not want to be educated. What methods of educational brainwashing would they employ anyway? They were liberal enough to allow women without the veil to join their group and co-operate with them, but on a voluntary basis, not as official members.

Fatemeh was not an official card-carrying member. She had hoped all along that by co-operating with them and discussing the contradictions in their theory and practice, she would be able to persuade them to democratise and modernise their

Islamic interpretation of women's sexuality and rights. Zareen didn't believe in Fatemeh's politics, but their friendship endured. She put down the pamphlet, which was depressing her, and asked about the different people on the stalls.

'I thought you weren't interested in how many ribs the left has got,' said Fatemeh.

'While I'm here I might as well learn about the variety of views in this city of brains,' Zareen replied.

'Here the stalls are the mouth, not the brain,' Fatemeh said.

Malihe interrupted to suggest they press on to the speakers' hall, and as they went Fatemeh described the different groups.

The largest table belonged to the Radical Muslims, then there was the militant left, divided into majority and minority, the centre left, the Iranian Democratic Front, the Socialist Workers' Party, and the Communist Party, all with their own women's sections and women's journals. All the women's groups were there too, each with their own stall, the National Union of Women, the Emancipation of Women, the Society for the Reawakening of Women, the Militant Women, the Women's Rights Defence Committee, the Association of Women Lawyers, the Women's Solidarity Committee, the Revolutionary Union of Militant Women, the Society of Muslim Women, Muslim Women's Movement, and many more.

Zareen was surprised at the number and variety of women's groups.

'The times are changing,' Malihe said. 'It's good to see books and leaflets on the table rather than under the carpet, or rotting away under the floorboards.'

Outside the hall women were standing shoulder to shoulder, barricading the door and the stairs below. Other women were trying to climb over them. There was no room to drop a pin, either in the hall or in many of its entrances, and women were even sitting on the window-sills, but the organisers could be heard through the loudspeakers, so Fatemeh, Zareen and Malihe simply found a corner and sat down to listen.

The speaker was spelling out the danger that the imposition of the veil on women would have on a new revolutionary state which did not respect personal freedom. She was nervous but articulate. She went on to defend a woman's right to choose

15

the veil or not, and outlined women's historical struggle against the compulsory veil, the endless 'veil' wars that women had fought, and how its imposition was against basic human rights.

'However,' she said, 'the issue of veil is now a symbol, the symbol of the path this revolution will take. Will it be democratic, or will it be another form of tyranny? If it is tyrannical it will enforce the veil and this will mean inferiority and subjugation of women at home, in the street and in all other areas of our lives – at work, in society, in law and so on . . . We must resist the veil . . . we must keep up this protest, as demonstrations are our only means of survival.'

She ended with the frequently chanted slogan:

'With veil and without the veil we fought the Shah, with veil and without the veil we will fight for our freedom now.'

The audience roared in noisy appreciation, the clapping enthusiastic, the atmosphere electric. The cheers went on.

The next speaker was introduced as the representative of women made unemployed since the revolution. She was angry but tried to speak calmly and emphatically. She spoke of the discrimination against women at work, the lack of provision for women workers in mixed factories, the dangerous and unhealthy conditions for most women and girl workers.

'We made the revolution to create a better situation for workers. The new revolutionary government, instead of healing wounds, remedying unhealthy working conditions is offering redundancies and unemployment in the name of Islam. In the name of the tradition of women as wives at home, the only social function women can have – as if this revolution is about men's power over women, as if men's might is right.' She finished with a warning: 'Women must resist the bully boys of the revolution, the bouncer militia at the factory gates who are intimidating women. We will not submit. This is the fight for bread and rights.' She got a standing ovation. There was deep feeling for the plight of working-class women.

Zareen sighed with relief, 'Thank God somebody has

spoken about women and work. I wish my bloody union could be exposed.'

Fatemeh smiled at her friend. 'You can speak too if you want to. This demonstration is going to go on until the regime retracts its statement on the veil. Tomorrow we will be here again, and there will be more speakers.'

'Me! Public speaking!' Zareen went shy suddenly.

Malihe was quiet and meditative. She was looking around and listening, not saying much.

The next speaker was announced as a sister from the Workers' Revolutionary Party. She started her talk without much introduction, 'The revolution has achieved victory because women, workers, national minorities, all sections of our society were united against the dictatorship of the Shah and his imperialist supporters. We must keep this unity. Today women are under attack. The left must unite to defend women's rights; tomorrow it could be those of the left, or the workers, or those of toiling women; toiling women or any other group. Our main enemy is international capitalism and imperialism, not the women. Women have been at the forefront of this revolution. Our working-class sisters have been fighting shoulder to shoulder with our working-class brothers. We want revolutionary changes. The new revolutionary government must change the existing laws to benefit working women. Women must have a right to work, and equal pay with men; they must have the right to terminate their pregnancies, and have more and better child-care facilities at work. Compulsory and arranged marriage should be abolished. Women must have the right to enter studies of their choice. These are the basic civil and democratic rights of women. The veil must not be used as a smokescreen to deny women's rights.'

She continued in defence of women's rights and equality. She was rational, logical and impersonal. She spoke in the language and with the authority of a party representative, rather than as a woman for her own cause. She drew chants from women devoted to the left:

'Independence, freedom, ۱- استقلال و آزادی، حقوق نسا ری

۱ - خواہری، برابری، حکومت کارگری

17

equal rights, sisterhood and brotherhood, government of workers and tailors.'

With such an enormous number of women in such a small space, very little air, and the heat and stuffiness, there could have been chaos and panic. But the women present were patient, listening nervously, sometimes shouting approval or disapproval, mostly attentive, involved but worried.

The speeches had come to an end. Next there would be question time, and after that they were going to create a committee for the defence of women's rights. Question time was difficult for the audience, as the microphone couldn't reach each questioner and the audience heard only the answers. After a while, it became frustrating and so Zareen, Malihe and Fatemeh decided to leave, get a breath of fresh air and have a cup of tea outside.

Women and men still surrounded the bookstalls. A woman standing on a chair was declaring her vision of the revolution, her independence and her refusal to obey. Another woman was surrounded by five men who were lecturing her on how the veil, women's clothing and personal freedom was a minor matter. 'Women should see themselves as a whole, part of the success of the revolution,' one of the men stated.

Further on, a group of women were attacking the left, 'If you are not with us today, you are against us. It has always been the case. When women are in need of help, the socialists are too busy overthrowing capitalism. If you ignore such a mass movement of women, you are betraying us.'

Two men and two women were arguing on abortion and sex, 'If you have sex with more than one man, what about the baby?' one man said.

'Oh, so your main worry is your fatherhood, isn't that so?' Malihe was surprised.

'Vaugh! Vaugh!' Zareen replied, also surprised. 'I have seen so much today. I don't know why I should be surprised. It is upheaval. It is the time of fast-changing ideas, quick learning and quick action . . . Revolution has transformed people overnight, look at the expression of energy and vitality, as if everybody is electrified. The pavements are full of arguments, the streets are full of chanting, uproar, statements, women's rebellion. One's senses and sensibilities grow, one grows tall with a revolution.'

Malihe was beaming. The demonstration had lifted her up a few inches. 'People are so full of hope, hope for change, so full of ideas, new ideas. They are growing overnight, brains throbbing with new knowledge and possibilities. So challenging, so determined to change the old order, to build new ones, to create, to make what they have always dreamed of. This uprising is a dream, a dream come true.'

They had gone to another building, found a quiet room on the third floor, and were sitting on the window-sill, looking out of the window to the streets surrounding the university which was still throbbing with women. They drank their old brewed tea, and leaned back, resting and watching. The streets were quieter, but still full of life, colourful banners, movements in and out, shaking hands; so many tired women still moving on. Zareen wished again that she had a magic carpet, so that she could go higher and see more, see all the women.

Fatemeh was remembering how around the stalls there had been all sorts of people discussing all sorts of issues. It had been liberating, issues from Mohammed to Marx, from sex to religion were dissected and scrutinised. 'All the forbidden issues, all the taboos are out in the open now,' she said.

'What do you need to talk about sex for? You just do it, and ignore the rest . . . ' Zareen replied.

'I used to think a bit like that; you don't think about such things, it's private, it's the bedroom job, but I don't agree with that anymore . . . there is much to say about sex, so much to learn. We are so ignorant, especially the men,' Fatemeh insisted.

'Really, how boring! Is this what you do in the university?' Zareen persisted.

'Come on Zari. Why do you underestimate it? It is about the value of our emotions, our physical needs, acknowledging them and being open and honest about them, and talking publicly . . . God . . . public discussion on sex and love . . . our right to question certain taboos, our right to speak openly about these, the whole point behind the veil, monogamy for women, polygamy for men, the issue of women's virginity, heterosexuality, homosexuality, why the university boys want many girlfriends but their girlfriends should have only one boyfriend.'

'I thought one man was more than enough. Who wants more? Honestly Fati, I don't care about sex, I care about the compulsory veil . . . I struggled so that my girl could be decently educated and independent . . . and not wrap herself in a black shroud like a crow,' Malihe said, tired.

'But Malihe, we can now handle many issues together. They are not separate, don't you see? Veil, sex . . . ' Fatemeh was impatient. 'It's just like you digging the books out from under the floorboards, from under the carpets, and dusting them down and putting them on the shelf.'

'If you go on talking about sex so much, you won't have much time to enjoy it,' Zareen was unrepentant.

'Come on Zari, stop joking.' Fatemeh wanted to get into a serious discussion. Zareen and Malihe wanted to enjoy themselves, having had their serious talks all day on the march.

'But why? I want to joke, to laugh, to dance, to celebrate, to paint the town red. When did you move in such a glorious crowd? When did you see so many women in one place, at one time, the best time? I want to take everybody to my shop and make them up beautifully.'

Fatemeh was quiet. Their moods didn't match. She dropped the topic.

They sat there, resting, chatting, joking, debating for a long time, until Zareen decided it was time for her to go home.

'It's getting dark, the old man is hungry, he'll eat the children!' she said. 'How shall we get home? I can't move myself – my legs have given in.'

'What? A ten-hour march and your legs are tired, woman? You need them to work harder for you, like camels'. This is just the beginning,' Malihe reminded her.

'Let's get a cab,' suggested Zareen. 'I've heard that even drivers of private cars give people lifts now, since the revolution, and they don't charge them.'

'Hmm,' said Fatemeh. 'So men are suddenly disregarding

their profits. I wonder.' She offered them a lift in her car and they set off to where it was parked.

They left the university. It was getting dark, navy blue spreading across the sky, as when their mothers used to dye the white sheets with Azur powder. It was possible now to walk without pushing, without the tight squeezes, but people were still occupying every corner of the streets, locked into endless to-ing and fro-ing of words, outside the bookshops, the tobacconists and by the street vendors, selling cassettes and records, in sight and visible. The three women passed them, trying to avoid the main roads, turning into smaller and narrower side roads that led one into another.

They were making their way to Fatemeh's car and even though it was far, it was easy to get there, she said. Malihe was wondering about the left and its support for the women's demonstration.

'All the socialist branches support women's day and women's liberation within the general anti-imperialist strug-gle, but the Socialist Workers' Party is more liberal than the rest,' Malihe said thoughtfully. 'But the Peasants' Party and the Radical Islam were against the women's protest demon-stration. They see the veil as a minor issue compared with other working-class issues. And I didn't have much luck in my arguments with the Radical Islam members. They can be as dogmatic as their Marxist mates. Most of them just want to appeal to women and convert them to their group. I never understood the fundamental frictions between the left, they don't seem real to me.'

'I guess it is in the nature of being students in university, they have to find things to disagree with,' Zareen said.

'You old cynic . . . ' Fatemeh was angry with her.

'Me . . . me? No, just a bit suspicious of such talk.'

A street light came on, shining faintly down on their dark passage. They were going through the long alleys that were now empty, peaceful and mostly dark, in total contrast to the scenes of a few hours ago. Zareen and Malihe complained about the long distance, Fatemeh replying again that they would soon be there. Darkness followed them, their shadows and their silences. Exhausted, they could hear their footsteps, the sound of the dragging of their feet, their breathing loud and deep. The streets were eerie now, some without light.

'Let's sing, it's suddenly so empty here. I'm afraid,' Zareen said. 'La . . . la . . . Women are marching on . . . marching on, come on . . . all of us together.'

'You're right, it's suddenly so quiet, and so dark and people-less,' said Malihe.

Zareen went on, 'Women are marching on . . . marching on . . . ' She started to waltz around on her toes, dancing to the rhythm of the song, on the wet ground, on the tired snow, hugged by the raw night.

This was not a residential area, and they were surrounded by long, empty office blocks. Zareen's song echoed in the narrow alleys, between the walls and returned to them, peter-ing out.

Oh God, let us be out of here soon, Malihe wished inside herself. In the lull of sound, the three women heard a faint cry. They slowed down. Someone was nearby but in which direction they couldn't tell. They moved towards the dark lane on the right, slowly and nervously.

A faint, choked voice called out, as if from the bottom of a well. They stood still. It sounded like the voice of a child, a girl. Their hearts sank to the pits of their stomachs. In the darkness nothing was visible. Zareen shouted fearfully, 'Who is there?' A few seconds later 'help' was heard, the voice sounded drowned. They ran towards the end of the lane. Three large shadows were grappling with a small figure. The forms untangled and, when they heard the sound of running feet, they moved away from the figure and separated. The women realised they had been seen and pulled up short. The sound of a sharp slap rang out, 'Bitch!' The figures contorted, bending, picking up, straightening, holding. Three men in militia army jackets and heavy boots, one hand grasping their guns, the other holding up their trousers.

'Beasts, men . . . ' The three women stood back, guns point-ing at them.

Deadly silence. The men backstepping, the women afraid to move, to open their mouths.

Suddenly the men are gone, running down the lane, Zareen and Fatemeh went after them, 'Beasts, bastards, men!'

Malihe went immediately to the fallen figure, lifted her, tidied her, held her.

Fatemeh and Zareen returned, and squatted down around the figure, not seeing her properly and not recognising her. No light . . . Malihe searched inside her bag for her lighter; it flickered to reveal a young woman's face, battered and bruised, her lips cut, fresh blood spilling, dirt and dampness on her hair and her face, eyes closed, black and blue, cold and half-unconscious. Her blouse was torn, her throat grazed and scratched as if they had been trying to strangle her, trouser zip broken, hair in knots, her hands dirty and bruised.

They sat there, shocked, scared and speechless, each holding a hand, a foot, cradling the head of the battered woman, stroking her brow gently, reassuring her, caressing her, their minds blanked out, their senses in disarray. They whispered safe words, holding her and wondering what to say, what to do next. What do you do? What can you do?

It took them a long time, it seemed light years, to say a word out loud, to utter a full sentence.

'What is your name, woman? Where do you live? Shall we take you home?'

The unknown woman made some noises, formed some rusty words, unrecognisable. They asked again. She moved, held her breasts, turned, hid her face. Long silence again, stroking her, uttering the simple questions, bare words, Are you cold? Are you in pain? Your name? Where do you live?

Still silence. Faint noises. Slow breathing.

'Go . . . li.' Coughing. They waited for the rest impatiently. '3. . .5. . .8. . .Is. . .la. . .mic Rev. . .o. . .lu. . .tion.'

The half chewed words, came out reluctantly, syllable by syllable. The three women could not fathom it until Fatemeh confirmed that was the new name for the old Aryamehr road. The three women got up. They picked Goli up and carried her. The melted snow on the ground stuck to their clothes. They retraced their steps down the lane, to where Zareen's last song hung in the air. They walked, shaken and sad, knees weak, heads bowed, spirits broken, pain in every pore. The carrying of Goli. The rape of Goli.

## 2

### 17 Esphand: Goli's night

        The others had taken her home, entering through the back door because she didn't want anybody to see her. Once she was in the safety of her room they left quickly, not wanting to have to explain their presence in those unfamiliar corridors. All four women went to bed with a day of celebration wiped out by a night of violence.

  Goli threw herself on her bed. She felt heavy: as if a stone slab was pressing upon her. Her body was in pain, her mind numb. She was shaking uncontrollably, her senses displaced. Which limb, what pain? Her memory did not reach her – the threads were disconnected; she was shocked out of her soul. Alive, breathing, all her limbs were there, but she was not. Was she falling asleep, losing consciousness or just dying soundlessly? It mattered little.

  Halfway through the night she jumped up. A horrible nightmare. She was re-enacting the event. She saw herself at the end of the lane, pushed to the wall by the iron gate of a huge garden. The three pasdar (militia) were calling out insults: bourgeois whore. They laughed at her. There was nobody around, no help. They were being threatening, pushing her head around, roughing-up her bare hair.

  'So you want freedom, freedom to choose your own clothes, perhaps to wear nothing.' Pulling her jumper off, her trousers down, poking at her naked legs. 'You want to throw these legs wide, show them to the whole town, you don't like the veil. You know how I feel when I look at these naked legs. I'll show you.' His trousers were down now, she shouted, his mates pushed her against the wall. She bit his hands and, in a second of release, she shouted, 'Help!'

'You want women's liberation so you can have as many boyfriends as you like? One man is not enough for you is it? We'll give it to you, three of us will try our best to satisfy you, won't we?' he called to his mates.

'After you, Mohammed,' one said. 'Bloody university, the toilets are full of foetuses. How many have you aborted so far?' He pushed himself against her, poked at her belly, tore her shirt, grabbed at and bruised her breast.

Violence and hatred were pouring out of their eyes. She struggled against their movements, their language. They held her firm and pushed her back. She struggled again, twisted her body, tightened her muscles, pushed and freed her mouth again, shouted, 'Help!' with as much force as she could muster. Screamed, 'Rapist! Beast!' A hard slap burned her cheek. They were outraged, held her tighter, assaulted her more fiercely. She simply hoped, desperately, for someone to appear from somewhere and save her.

Suddenly the iron gate in the garden opened and two men came out, saw her held down by two men, another ready to rape her. 'Ah . . . um . . . ' they said, 'excuse us for disturbing you, we don't want to interfere in another man's business.' And in they went and closed the gate behind them.

Horrified, she came to with a jump and sat up in her bed. Where was she? Was this her bed? It was late in the morning. Was she asleep? Was she awake now? She tried to move her body, but couldn't feel her limbs, her belly; it felt like they weren't there. It was too much of an effort to move. The sequence of events in that dead-end lane came to her again. Her memory flooded and, although she didn't want to think about it – she was too weak, too drained – her mind was all over the place and she couldn't control it. The dream. The three women who had saved her. If she could only stop her mind from careering chaotically and reaching the pain of remembrance. How had she got there, in that dead-end lane with those three men? The time between being at the university, in the demos and debate, and being there, in the lane, was lost. A bitter taste in her mouth. Had she vomited? Was her body in a state of shock? She touched her belly, her legs, her feet. They were there. She felt the material, leather and cord, of her clothes. How had they come to bed with her? She couldn't make it out. She wasn't even surprised. Her hand touched the material, the leather and passed over her skin lightly, moved further down to between her legs, to the thick warm hair and stayed there. The hand covered, cuddled, the legs drew up and held it. She encircled her body around her centre and remained there.

Goli was twenty-one years old, a second-year student of sociology at Tehran University. She had been brought up in a professional, middle-class family, her mother an art historian, her father a dentist, with two brothers who always competed with each other and bossed her around. Her younger brother was at Tehran University too, in the third year of a geography course. He was left wing and last year had joined a small Trotskyite group at the university, and was very active in it. She was relieved that he was so busy and out of the house at all hours, as it meant he didn't have enough time to watch over her, to control her movements and argue with her about her friends and her absences from home. She had been under pressure from him and the women in the group to join the Trotskyites, but her only involvement with them was in women's issues, focusing mainly on the position of the women workers. She had worked with the university women's groups and the working women's groups during the revolution. Since the victory of the revolution and the mounting attack on the position of women she had continued her work, but only with the university women's groups in defence of women's rights and equality. She was a familiar participant in the long and persistent debates with the men on campus – some even turning into slanging matches – where she was called bourgeois, little rich girl, young and naïve.

Young and independent, Goli had learnt a lot during the dynamic days of the revolution, when she had actively taken up women's issues. She was influenced by her mother and by her mother's mother. As the only daughter and the youngest child, she was loved and cherished to a degree which she found restricting and stifling. Strong willed, she knew what she wanted, and it was hard to influence or to try to change her mind: her mother thought of her as spoilt and stubborn.

She was a sociable and friendly young woman; intelligent, open-minded and radical. Her build was small and she looked, in her own eyes, dark, hairy and ordinary. Her face was too hairy, her eyebrows and eyelashes too thick and black on her almond brown skin crowding her face. But on closer observation, her eyes had a bright shine and her eyebrows formed a definite curve above them, sitting elegantly above her high cheekbones, and when she laughed, the dimple in her chin deepened, and spread smiles all over her face.

## 17 Esphand: Zareen's night

When Zareen got home she quickly made food for the two kids and her husband, made a few excuses and went to bed. She was haunted by the image of Goli. She saw her pushed to the wall, her jacket on the ground, her shirt torn, her trousers half-way down, her pants half-torn and hanging. Her clothes were damp with snow, her arms, her bare breasts and her face were blue with cold, sticky, bruised and damp. Her hair had been roughed up: they must have pulled it around, hit her on the head, saying that her bare head was a deliberate ploy to excite them. Zareen held her own head between her hands, feeling it. Goli's head must have been hurt.

I hugged her, Zareen thought to herself, tied up her hair, wiped mud from her, covered her body, but I didn't hug her head. Her head – the uncovering of it – had caused her trauma, the veil that was absent, the hair that was free and seen, the sin, the holy violence. How has she suffered? How is she now? How could she sleep after her body had been invaded, polluted like that? How could she? Ah, my God, she is too young for such brutality. I wish I had stayed with her. Why didn't I?

Zareen had never seen violence against women on that scale with her own eyes. She had read about it in the newspaper, the honour killings, how brothers, fathers, husbands, uncles

27

had, for one reason or another, killed, maimed, mutilated their sisters, wives, mothers, to protect their honour. But she hadn't seen it herself. Her only experience of violence was in the streets when men pinched her behind, touched her, pushed her or whispered dirty words into her ears. Her husband had forced himself on her a few times when she didn't want sex but she had thought she'd better let him have it. Perhaps she would enjoy it. She never had; but she had learned to do the same to him when she, and not he, wanted sex – and what a pleasure that was: getting what she wanted. She knew that many men battered their wives, the women spoke about it all the time in the salon when she was busy cutting their hair, doing their faces; but she also heard how some women took their revenge, starved their men of food as well as sex, hit them in the balls till they screamed.

Zareen turned around in bed. She was exhausted physically and mentally but couldn't sleep. Images of Goli, battered and bruised, came to her mind. How was she? How could Zareen find out? Was Goli safe now? Oh, the endless questions.

Zareen wasn't sure about the revolution. Most people around her were supporting it, talking about it in terms of progress, of hope, of new development, including the women in her salon. Her husband was for it too. He was dissatisfied with his work in the bazaar, where he had his delicatessen shop, selling dried fruit and nuts. Business was very unstable. Agriculture wasn't improving; home products were suffering in quality and quantity, and so exports were dropping and imports increasing. This, he complained, made everything very expensive. But she thought the bazaar has always had its ups and downs. In the ten years of their marriage she'd never not heard him moan about high costs, low costs, drops or increases in agricultural production; it was all part of the job.

She, however, was not convinced that the revolution would stabilise the market, improve agriculture and stop her husband worrying and, if it did, he'd only worry about other unseen problems. But she did not speak openly against the revolution. She couldn't, so many people were supporting it. Every now and then though in the salon when women had boasted joyfully about their sons burning cinemas or attacking shops she had reminded them gently that if their sons were burning cinemas and shops as school children what would they be burning as grown men? She supported only women's and school children's actions, especially the girls' rebellion, demonstrations, sit-ins, boycotts of classes, but she didn't believe in the motives of the men and boys or in the wisdom of their actions.

The main reason that Zareen had withdrawn her support from the revolution was because of what had happened in her union. The revolution wasn't only in the streets, in the army and in the workplaces, but everywhere; there were changes in her union, brought in without the consultation of its members. The union had always been dominated by women and even though there were male hairdressers and their numbers were growing due to western influence, women's membership had always been three times that of men's. But during the last months of the revolution women members of the union, most notably those in the positions of chair, secretary and treasurer were being pushed out; and unknown men who had never been seen before took their places. With their beards, worry beads and gloomy faces, they didn't look like hairdressers. They were Islamic fundamentalists. They took over the union meetings and instead of dealing with the specific issues relating to work, membership, and other union business, they gave endless lectures on God, women's position in Islam and how undesirable hairdressing, and having your hair done, was for women under Islam, especially if they were vain enough to want to go out looking like that. Make-up and hairdos were only permissible in the home, for their husbands.

She had thought all the lectures meaningless and irrelevant. What woman wanted to do her hair, make her face up and wear beautiful clothes just to stay at home for her husband? How boring. Why did women need to do themselves up for their husbands anyway? Waste of good make-up, she thought. She couldn't believe how a union whose job it was to promote the interests of its members, and lobby for better working conditions and rates of pay could choose male leaders who had no interest in the hairdressing business and were even encouraging members to give up their profession. It was ridiculous; but she had found it impossible either to express her view or to alter the situation. She had left the union and so had many other women.

Come to think of it, this was violence, the violence of fanatical men, to deprive her and many other women of their rights to organise, to improve their working conditions and pay. The invasion of her union, like that of Goli's body, was an act of violence. Like and unlike.

But she had left the union. Was this a way to deal with men's pressure and force? Did this mean that Goli should also leave her university? Her political activity? Her freedom to walk down the street? Was this a solution? No. Too much, too heavy. I could live without a union, how can she stop going to university? She couldn't. She shouldn't. It's unfair. Zareen was getting angrier and angrier. The darkness of the night was breaking. The dawn was visible. She must at least sleep for a couple of hours. She had to work in the morning. She couldn't close the salon again. She couldn't afford it. She shut her eyes and put her hands over them to shut out every flicker of the dawn.

Zareen ran a hairdressing salon from the ground floor of her house. She was thirty years old, with a cheerful personality, and was always well dressed and made-up. She knew how to look after her curly hair, light skin and beautiful body. She had a vivid sense of humour much appreciated by her women friends and customers, and her affectionate and extrovert nature was good for her work: she enjoyed the confidences of many women. She felt sometimes, though, that her other, more reflective self hid behind her work and her home.

## 17 Esphand: Fatemeh's night

Fatemeh went home deep in confused thought. Once there she dismissed the servant – she didn't want any food or drink – and walked through the avenue of carved wooden bannisters to her room. She closed the door and leaned on the thick wooden panel, feeling safe now, but still nervous. How could soldiers of God, the militia of the revolution do that? She paced up and down the large oblong room. From her window the garden, with tall cedars and pines, held an air of menace. She drew the heavy velvet curtains and cut out the view. The room was cast in a light that was dim but peaceful. She went to her mirror; she looked tired and alien to herself. She wiped it. It was still the same. She took off her jumper and threw it in a corner, agitated. How could this happen? How can our revolutionary men be so inhuman? Poor Goli. She paced up and down the room, gazing at the bold patterns of her Tabrizi carpet. Its naturally bright colours and clear patterns and symbols contrasted with her mood. She looked up at the wall.

As the only child she played the part of a son substitute for her father, and he was not keen to marry her off; but her mother – from whom she learned about women, arts and history – was worried that she was getting old at twenty-five, and still had no husband, and her mother no grandchild. She was the pillar of the family, though, the source of energy and excitement. Her parents loved her and were dependent on her presence in the house, and even the servants liked her. Her mother was too busy with the local communities, religious services, the distribution of charity to the local poor and with organising the large household efficiently and smoothly to worry too much about Fati.

They often had religious ceremonies in their garden and it was at one of these that they had met Zareen and that she became their private hairdresser. She would come to their house about once a week to cut or henna their hair and to do their faces. Fatemeh and Zareen enjoyed each other's company and became close friends. Zareen thought Fatemeh's room was magnificent, and found it peaceful to be in. The afternoons spent cutting or hennaing Fatemeh's hair were the most peaceful times in her job; in that room she found tranquillity, comfort, and moments for the private self which she otherwise lacked.

Fatemeh had lived a privileged, sheltered life and believed that those who adhered to Islam, were good natured, reasonable and compassionate men, against violence in any form. Her father abhorred violence, having spent two years in jail for opposing the Shah. Her mother had told her that he had

31

been tortured and that one of his toenails had been pulled out. She had often tried to visualise how one's nail could be pulled out and how one's body could sustain the pain. He had taught her that the history of Islam was full of wars, expansion of empire and blood-baths; but this, he had admitted, was past history. What would his response to Goli's assault be? How would he see it? Should she talk to him? Fatemeh was close to her father but wasn't sure she should talk to him about this.

She began to feel angry and resentful towards those men, full of hatred. Distressed and confused, she remembered Goli's tortured look, as she lay unconscious and powerless. Unable to talk, wrapped in Malihe's chador, stretched out in the back of Fatemeh's car. The memory hurting: she had never seen so much pain concentrated in such a small face. The agony of rape. She tried to imagine Goli's pain, her body's torture, her tomorrow. She realised she had no idea of Goli's pain: the rape of her flesh, the rape of her soul. The ultimate weapon. The real agony of it was beyond her. On her bed she hid under the pillows, hoping that total darkness and sound would muffle her memory. She fell asleep just before a heavy dawn.

Fatemeh was from an upper middle-class religious family, skinny, with short, straight black hair that was usually hidden, large brown eyes and a very soft delicate skin as dark as honey. She had completed a university law degree, and was now unemployed, still spending most of her time at the university, organising, helping her comrades shape the revolution. She was close to her father, an Islamic intellectual, and was influenced by him and his opposition to the system. She dressed modestly, wearing a scarf outside the house, and, in deference to her father who didn't like bright colours on women, she usually wore green clothes with black or white. When her father was away lecturing in other towns, which was often, she wore what she liked. She spoke softly but with confidence, thought more than she said, and looked more serious than she was. She was kind and generous and, at times, unpredictable.

When Malihe got home she was trembling with fear. She had managed to keep herself together until then. But not now. She lit her small Aladdin oil heater and sat by it. She nearly hugged it, although she wasn't cold. She was hungry but she had no appetite. In the dim light of her small square room she was safe, but she didn't feel it. Memories of the past troubled her. She couldn't stop her shivers. She had sat by Goli's feet, massaging them, and meditating and praying for her. Goli had been raped and brutalised, just as she had been threatened with torture and rape when in gaol under the Shah.

Malihe was forty-five years old, strong and dynamic for her age, a largish, typical Iranian middle-aged woman, sometimes in chador, sometimes not. Her round face, crowded with early wrinkles, made her look older than she was, her eyes were keen, her hands rough and hardened with sewing. She lived alone and earned her living as a seamstress. She had moved to Tehran with her husband from her village outside Yazd twenty years ago in search of work. He was a builder and they had two kids. She had given birth to six but only two of them had survived, a boy and a girl. She worked very hard to educate them, her daughter became a nurse and her son a chemist. As there was only a year's difference between them, they were very close friends, regardless of their gender and the restrictions that this imposed upon them.

As students they were socialists and politically active, influenced by their father's union work. After the completion of their education they decided to go abroad for travel and work; because they were blacklisted, they didn't think they would find jobs easily at home. Malihe was heartbroken when she heard this, but they managed to convince her that they were only going for a couple of years, that travelling broadened the mind. She had said the same herself, and they would learn much more and enjoy themselves in another country. Rumour had it they had joined the Palestine Liberation Organisation and she heard from them only through short notes brought to her by strangers. She did not know where they were and could not write to them; they thought this was best.

A year after their departure her husband had an accident at work from which he never recovered, and his death made the absence of her children much more painful. She felt disappointed in them and their independence; they left you, and supported other causes, other struggles, instead of their parents through old age. She was lonely and missed them, especially in cold, desolate winters such as this.

She especially missed the warmth of a daughter's company, until Zareen had partially taken her place. She had originally been friends with Zareen's mother, but since the Ziba Style salon had opened she had visited it frequently and enjoyed the social gatherings there, particularly after her many attempts to form a sewing co-operative with other women seamstresses had been sabotaged.

One day, however, before then, just prior to when the revolution gained momentum, soldiers had burst into her home, taken her to Gasr gaol and locked her up. She had been in solitary confinement for a couple of weeks before they questioned her. Malihe remembered those frightful days. She had been in prison for six weeks, questioned, threatened with torture and rape, beaten up and starved. She could not answer their questions; she didn't know where her children were and knew nothing else about them, other than that they were alive. She was told then that they had both joined the PLO's military faction, that they were engaged in activity against Israel and that they would be arrested the minute they entered the country. She didn't know whether or not to believe her interrogators; but it made no difference, she trusted her children's politics and supported their aims.

Goli reminded her of her torture, of the fear that had lived in her, and that possessed her for months. She had broken down and gone to pieces after those violent weeks in jail, and it was only with the support and help from friends, especially Zareen, that she managed to pull herself together and recover her energy and strength. If her children were fighting for a cause so worthwhile, that she was being tortured for it, she

34

must live to see them alive and victorious. She had to stem her fatalism and gather strength to confront life, and not give in to the torturers. It had taken her months after her release, but she had pulled through remarkably, much wiser, and more resourceful and appreciative of life.

Tonight, however, her defences were down. Goli was so young to be assaulted like that. How would she face tomorrow, the day after the vicious night? Was she as terrified as Malihe had been in gaol when the torturers threatened her with rape? Was she as uncertain about tomorrow as Malihe had been behind those cold, iron bars? How was she now? Was she cold? Was she sleepless? Did she feel guilty? Did she blame herself for walking down that alley? Did she hate her body? Oh . . . no . . . God help her. Help her youth, her precious youth. She wanted to rush to Goli and tell her own prison experiences in detail, to comfort her, to give her hope and to hug her. Goli must not be afraid because of this experience. She must not feel insecure and demoralised. Goli must recover, forget, and build her defences, build them high.

Malihe sat there in the cold solitude of her room and felt a tiny bit warmer. But where was sleep tonight?

Malihe made women's clothes to measure, and enjoyed her job – she was a creator of a different kind – and the shop was a good place for her to meet all kinds of women, potential friends and new customers; some women even used the salon for measuring up and trying on their new clothes.

Her life and needs were simple but she had a very keen eye for injustice; and since the revolution had made Ziba Style a women's 'conference' room, she had become a regular feature there, contributing to the bundling and unbundling of experiences.

## 3

The next morning – a cold, sunless day – Zareen pulled back the curtains and opened the door of Ziba Style. Remnants of snow still patched the square. She turned the heater on and lit the samovar.

Her head was spinning, from lack of sleep and anxiety. She was very worried about Goli: she planned to phone her in the afternoon – Goli would probably sleep in – but meanwhile was impatient for the day to pass.

Her two workers, Muneer and Shabnam, arrived and started to get ready. Zareen hoped it would be a quiet day. Early customers had arrived to have their faces done. Muneer started on band-andazi. Shabnam was getting another customer's hair ready for a wash. Zareen switched on the radio for some news, but it was prayers and she turned down the volume.

She couldn't stop thinking about Goli. A customer observed that she was not her usual chirpy self, and she made an excuse, saying she had a headache. She hoped nobody would ask her about the demonstration. What could she say? The revolution has turned into the rape of women? Oh no, spare me, she thought. She apologised to another customer who was waiting. The woman replied that she didn't mind, that it was relaxing to watch Muneer at work on band-andazi, she had nothing exciting to do anyway, and that when the samovar had boiled, she would make some tea.

Ziba Style was a small, women only hairdressing and beauty shop. The modest room in which it was situated was medium sized with three hairdryers, three long-mirrored dressing tables, two sinks and a few trolley trays containing all sorts of hairpins, tweezers, cuticle removers, scissors, toenail clippers, nailfiles and so on. In one corner of the room a fitted cupboard was filled with shelves partly for stock and partly for brooms, brushes, dusters and cleaning materials. There were also some hooks for hanging overalls, aprons and so on. The room was decorated plainly with various newspaper and magazine cuttings of hairstyles, large posters and a frame containing a quotation from the Quran. The window to the street opened on to the small square in which there was a lively little fruit and vegetable market.

The window was covered with a white lace curtain which shut out the gaze of outsiders, and a colourful cotton over-curtain which was drawn when the shop was closed. Sometimes you could hear the hubbub of the market and the shouts of the street sellers, and see the delightful mountains of water-melons, colourful grapes and peppers. The position of the shop was handy for women on their way home from shopping or taking the kids to school.

Before the revolution Zareen had had a roaring business, with four assistants and many customers, often working late into the night. Now it was dwindling little by little: the funda-mentalists advice against hairdressers, beauty salons, make-up and fashion was proving effective. She might not be able to keep Shabnam on that much longer.

Zareen felt as though she were sleep-walking through the morning. She managed to get through it somehow, living half in the anxiety of the previous night, half in her present troubled state. Fatemeh rang; she too had had a dreadful night, and she was going to see Goli.

Malihe arrived after lunch, just as the women in the shop were talking about the demonstration. Zareen took her to the sitting room and offered her a cup of tea. They sat cross-legged, leaning on the heavy poshti, tea tumblers in hand, faces steeped in worry and exhaustion, sipping quietly and thoughtfully.

'I could hardly sleep last night, it all crushed in on me,' Malihe confessed.

'I know, I didn't get a wink. I couldn't work this morning either, my head is spinning like a ball. I haven't told anybody yet . . . don't know what to say . . . ' Zareen fiddled with her hair.

'A terrible night . . . I couldn't stop thinking about Goli, and worse, it brought back all my prison experiences so clearly.'

Zareen touched her with affection. 'Oh Mali, you should have come here. You shouldn't have stayed alone.'

'I know,' she replied, 'we shouldn't have just left. I felt as if I'd been put into iced water for hours . . . just shivering.'

Zareen rubbed her hands and shoulders. 'Do you feel better now?' she asked, holding Malihe's hand. 'Do you need anything? I'm going to ring Goli later, I'll pass on your love. Fati rang this morning, she wanted to go and see her today.'

'That's good. She's too far away for us. Any news from Fati?'

'She's going to the university, another full day of demonstration . . . '

'I don't know what's going on. What's going to happen to us? I'm afraid for the women,' Malihe said, tidying her chador.

' . . . Well, it could be just the one isolated incident,' Zareen suggested.

'There is never only one incident where women are concerned.' Malihe was definite.

Everyone waited anxiously that day for the evening news, but the eight o'clock radio news and an hour later the news on television remained silent on the events of the previous two days. What had been a major event for women in every town and city had not deserved a mention. Why had some of the largest women's demonstrations ever in many cities not been considered newsworthy? Later in the evening there was a short radio news item about a small group of women supporters of the Shah who had threatened the Minister of Justice with guns. Perhaps some of the dailies would have a bit more tomorrow.

The next day the dailies did indeed have more, but only a

few lines in obscure corners about a couple of thousand women demonstrating at the university – nothing about their reasons or demands, nothing about the attacks on them, no pictures, and no response from the authorities. What was this? A news black-out on women! It was infuriating.

A few days later when Zareen spoke to Goli she heard that she was feeling better, had been to the university and had lots of news. They arranged to meet at Zareen's house for lunch, to which Malihe and Fatemeh were invited too. That afternoon, during a long-lunch-break, Zareen made a simple, popular, nourishing stew, aash-reshteh, so that they could spend most of their time talking. The food was ready; she had left it to keep hot and was sitting by the window when she saw Goli arrive.

She was a bit pale, and looked nervous. Some scratches still remained on her throat, but her lip had almost healed and she was standing on her own two feet, smiling and talking. As the others arrived there were long greetings between Goli and the three friends. They each hugged her, kissed her on the face and neck, shook her hand, made sure they felt her properly and that she was all right. They were so pleased to see her smiling and greeting them, in such constrast with that other night.

She had come in person to thank the women who had saved her. They were so pleased to be with her, to talk to her and see her talk. They couldn't stop questioning her: 'How do you feel?', 'How long did you sleep? Did you tell your mother? Did you tell anybody? Have you seen your attackers? What has happened at the university?'

Goli sat cross-legged under the korsi, Zareen apologised that with the long winter this year she hadn't yet packed it away, but Goli had already sunk under it, she needed it's heat. She leaned against the poshti, took a long relieved breath and began to speak.

'I slept that night – perhaps it wasn't sleep but a continuation of unconsciousness – and most of the day after. I had lots of bad dreams, nightmares. I kept waking up, jumping up and then trying to sleep again. The day after was hell; I spent all day vomiting . . . thought my body filthy, hated it, was in and out of the bath. I was alone in the house, which at first I preferred . . . but then in the evening when I felt a bit better and I wanted to talk to somebody, there wasn't anybody. My mother would have been the wrong person. She would worry herself sick every time I come home late. My brothers, oh God, no, they'd take it as an excuse to keep me under their control and be very self-righteous that they had told me so, that the streets are dangerous for women, that I should stay at home and only go out with them. Or they'd seek revenge for honour. I couldn't trust them. In the end I told a friend at the university. I'll tell my mother later on, when it's quite safe. My friend's been very supportive. We had a long chat. She's wiser than me. Apart from that, there's a lot happening in the university, and everywhere else. We have so much to do. I don't want to lose touch, so I've been out on the demos again, but only in the safe quarters.'

As Malihe and Fatemeh were not newcomers to the house, they knew where things were kept, and they got the food ready while listening to Goli. The lunch was brought in and put on the sofreh, which was spread on the korsi, and the four women sat around bending into their bowls, heads towards the centre as if sharing an intimate secret. Goli was worried that the strong taste and smell of garlic might be anti-social, but Zareen assured her that etiquette should be the least of her worries. They laughed.

Tea followed, and they leaned on the poshti, drinking while Goli broke the silence and started to tell them about events at the university.

'There's so much happening, some small events, some major ones . . . small gangs of men going around stopping women getting into their classes, especially agricultural students and those in mining, oil and gas engineering, and maths and physics . . . Harassing them, telling them they should be doing humanities and domestic science. Some women heads of institutions, factories and colleges are being harassed to give up their jobs and return home to their homes and children. In one area a respectable headmistress was kidnapped by two boys and interrogated for five hours. She was abused, beaten up and threatened that if she didn't make the veil compulsory for all seven hundred girls in her secondary school she would see the boys again. She's resigned. There's chaos at her school because the teachers are intimidated, afraid that one of them will be next.

'News like this goes round every day. We have so many demonstrations and pickets to go to . . . leafleting to do, and because of all these pressures we can't organise ourselves effectively.'

'What I don't understand is why such news, news about women, is not reported,' said Zareen. 'Is there a news black-out on women's demonstrations?'

'The new revolutionary head of television is adamant that no women's demonstrations should be shown,' Goli replied.

'Is he afraid that women's news is bad for women and could incite more women to protest or is he worried that women demonstrators would incite sexual urges in him . . . and his mates?' Malihe asked.

'Perhaps both!' Fatemeh laughed.

'And it would show women's real demands and aims, which would no longer leave room for rumours and misinterpretation,' Zareen went on. 'For five days now women have been in occupation of every important institution – the Ministry of Justice, the law courts, television and radio stations, the Prime Minister's office – and it's going to continue. It's not just the compulsory veil or the sacking of women from television and radio, or the segregation of students, it's everything, and the issues are growing and expanding all the time. So much is happening now . . . the sacking of women lawyers because under Islamic rule women are said to be incapable of being rational, school books are changing, Darwin's theory is being taken out, biology books are being rewritten . . . so much non-sense that we must fight against.'

'I was there at the sit-in at the Ministry of Justice,' said Fatemeh. 'Seven thousand women packed the law courts. The building was shaking with chants for the reinstatement of the women lawyers. Well, I have no prospect of a job now,' she finished.

'They are advising you to take up secretarial jobs,' said

Goli. 'They hope women will quietly make more sacrifices for the revolution. They'll be lucky.'

'But even the secretaries of the Ministry of Defence are being sacked . . . ' Fatemeh responded.

'What?' Malihe yelled. 'So the Ministry can't decide whether or not they'd even be good spies now.'

'No, they'd incite sexual urges in foreign diplomats and imperialism would become doubly dirty,' answered Zareen. 'Anyway, how do they manage to report all this as only a "handful of the Shah's supporters"?'

'I don't know,' said Fatemeh, 'but they do. Discrediting women could be one reason why they're doing it.'

'So they can begin the repression,' added Malihe.

'It's already here, I can feel it.' Zareen admitted. 'I'm frightened and it takes a lot to frighten me.'

'I feel frightened too,' said Malihe, 'but we can do something about it. There is always something to be done; even in prison, in solitary confinement, we created a language by tapping on the brick walls to communicate with the other women prisoners.'

'Have you been in gaol?' asked Goli. Malihe nodded her head.

'Incredible. Tell me about it.'

'Another time – it's not very helpful at the moment.'

'My father told me he saw women in dreadful states in prison, women who had been tortured horribly, raped, given electric shocks.' Fatemeh said.

'Please, please, let's not talk about the horrible past,' cried Zareen.

'It may not be just the past,' Malihe whispered.

'It *is* the past,' Fatemeh reassured her. 'There's no comparison. What we have seen so far, the loss of women's jobs, the attempt to impose the veil, and the violence, are not the acts of this government, only of some individual male zealots or groups doing it in their own names. We're still protected by the law.'

'You've studied law, tell us what we can do now,' asked Zareen.

'I don't think we should rely on the law,' Malihe interjected.

'The revolution has broken down law and order and the old structure. We are not protected by anything or anybody.'

'I thought you supported the revolution all along Malihe; the Shah's system was corrupt and brutal, as well as foreign. Have you changed your mind?' Zareen asked her, sensing deep unrest in her friend.

'Not yet,' Malihe replied. 'I'm still assessing the new regime. I'm not yet convinced this is the system I want or need.'

'Give it a chance Malihe,' Fatemeh told her, 'it's too early to make such a judgment.'

'Maybe,' Goli said, 'but . . . this is a fine start for a new government. It doesn't take much imagination to guess what is mapped out for us, the women.'

Each woman was feeling the pressure of violence, the fear of what might await them on the streets, remembering Goli in the alley, yet reluctant to anticipate their fear with self-restriction and self-censorship, and thereby do the zealots' dirty work for them. Was it only a small group of hooligans abusing the uncertainty and chaos of a revolutionary period, or was it the beginning of a new future for women? Should they wait and see, or start doing something now? These questions continued to occupy the mind of each of them. They could neither think of an answer nor search for a solution. Uncertainty, confusion and fear paralysed the four women as they sat, Malihe gasping into her chador, Zareen clasping her hands together, squeezing them hard, Goli leaning on the poshti, head thrust back, looking up at the ceiling, and Fatemeh appearing as calm as the hoze in the absence of a pebble tossed in it. The comforting heat of the korsi served not to relax but to heighten the tension inside them.

4

Another large demonstration was planned for the following Monday, to protest against the government's silence on the fundamentalists' attacks on women's rights. It was going to be a large, organised march, with demands and resolutions to be handed in to the leaders of the revolution, unlike the massive spontaneous demonstrations of 17 Esphand. The marchers were to gather outside the university and walk to Azadi Square, an open space symbolic of the revolution, where a rally would be held.

On Sunday, the day before the march, there was a meeting to decide how best to organise the event. Goli was very concerned about the women's safety and decided that she would raise the issue.

The meeting was packed, as she had expected, and the speakers, each from a different left-wing or women's group were making political statements, discussing their slogans, their banners, their contingency plans, the carrying of microphones, stewarding and every other related issue except that of women's safety.

Goli was impatient. Safety was the most important item and it was, apparently, absent from their agenda. She waited for question time. When it came a sea of hands went up and in order to make herself heard she had to stand up and shout till she was seen.

She was nervous, her voice slow and shaky, as she began her question. 'I am very worried that we haven't said anything about the safety of women on the road. We know that the fundamentalists have started systematic attacks on women's demonstrations, and on individual women and that this is getting worse. How are we going to organise for the safety of women on the streets during and after the march?'

She sat down breathless and exhausted. Silence. Who was going to answer her question?

The chair stood up and elaborated on Goli's question, describing some of the new tactics used recently on women. She compared the situation with the times the workers had gone on strike under the old regime, when the police and plainclothes security agents would follow them, threaten them and beat them up if they didn't give themselves up. She suggested the women could learn a few of the same lessons, namely, not to go out alone, but to move in groups, especially at night, to avoid alleys, small roads and the empty streets between office blocks. She explained how the workers had learnt to keep to main roads and residential areas, to carry torches as deterrents to flash into the face of an assailant.

Goli was restless. She wasn't satisfied with these answers, they didn't seem enough. Another speaker stood up with more suggestions. If a woman was near water or earth, she should throw it at an attacker's face. Women should be alert at all times, they should carry some kind of defensive tool with them, such as an umbrella – particularly in winter, the sort with a sharp end – a bunch of keys, nail-file, anything small and metallic, but nothing dangerous like a knife or scissors unless they could use them expertly, because if they fell into an attacker's hands, he could always say he used them in self-defence.

While she paused, another speaker quickly put in a few words. If women had cars they should organise giving lifts to other women, and most important of all they should wear easy shoes and loose, comfortable trousers, in which you could run for your life. If a woman was wearing a scarf, this was useful for throwing in the face of an attacker, like the torch, so long, of course, as she didn't mind him seeing her hair. The audience laughed.

Another speaker announced that they were asking all the men from the left-wing groups to come to the march to support women and to protect them. If the left agreed to put all its force behind women's demands and women's right to demonstrate safely, then the women would be safe she believed.

What had been said was very useful and Goli agreed that such defensive measures were helpful, but somehow she still felt this wasn't enough. She wasn't sure the left would support the women; some of them might, but she still had doubts. Outside the meeting a woman was talking about karate classes which were being held at the university but which were not open to women. One of them suggested that they approach the tutor and ask him for lessons. It was generally agreed that the women should learn self-defence and make themselves strong. Goli joined in and it was decided that those who were interested would meet later on the campus to discuss it further. Goli found that she had been so keen to follow this discussion that she had missed the security details for the next day.

Later that day, Goli arrived at the circle of enthusiastic, excited women with Marjan, the friend who had become her confidante and chaperone since the night of her rape. Marjan had a car, an old Beetle, and as she lived not far from Goli she regularly gave her lifts to the university. Marjan was a year older than Goli, tall and slim with long black hair that curled around her shoulders and big brown eyes that changed colour in the sun to a light green and yellow, honey-eyed. Goli was envious of Marjan's height; she saw herself as small and chubby. They would tease one another about their different shapes: 'Why have you grown up straight like a ladder, when the rest of us all grow sideways and chubby?' 'Don't say "ladder", say "Sarv Shiraz" [cypress] instead. I don't know how I got this way, perhaps my mother did it at the right moment of the new moon. If you insist I'll get her recipe for you.' Their laughter was a point of departure, and a change of subject.

They disagreed on some political issues: Marjan was a member of the militant left and worked with their women's section and on their paper; while Goli had been put off joining any of the left-wing groups by their lack of understanding of women's everyday issues, such as the daily violence and its causes. She preferred to be independent and non-aligned and, although Marjan criticised her for sitting on the fence, Goli argued that she was not prepared to commit herself to any one group until she was sure of its politics – theoretical, practical and personal.

Some of the women at the meeting were already involved in a sport, running, throwing the discus or playing ping-pong, and they recommended that the other women follow their example for building up strong legs, arms and fists. They agreed that on the day of the next karate lesson they would send a delegation of three women to see the trainer while the rest of them waited in the canteen.

Goli was pleased with this; things were moving and she felt optimistic about dealing with her fear of the fanatics in the future. Armed with this new sense of strength, she felt better about Monday's demonstration. As the meeting broke up she and Marjan decided to go to one of the cafés across Shah-Reza Avenue for a short break before Goli went to print some posters for the next day.

The café was small and cosy. Marjan brought over the black teas and sandwiches and sat down. She wanted to know how Goli had been, how she felt.

'I'm trying to get over it fast,' Goli told her, 'I must. So much is happening these days that I need my energy, my mind and body to be active, to work alongside other women. I can't stop thinking about it though. I hate my body, all the bits that were manhandled. I have several baths a day, to wash their dirty touch from my skin. I don't know how long it will take for me to recover fully. Perhaps I never will. Does anyone recover from an invasion – from an assault? I must. I need my energy.'

Goli was holding on to the table. 'The thought of coming to the university made me shaky. Because it was dark and I couldn't see them properly that night, sometimes I think every man that I see is one of them. I don't know what to do or how to handle it. If I saw them again . . . the thought of it makes my stomach churn.'

'You have to get this out of your system somehow,' Marjan told her. 'Shall we – a few of us – walk to that alley, so that you can see it again, confront it, and try to come to terms with it – that you've come out of it safely? Shall we?' Marjan was insistent.

'No! Are you crazy?' Goli was frightened. 'It's too early. Not now . . . maybe later . . . after I've come through it completely. It's a good idea, Marjan, but I'm so afraid that I may see them again.'

Marjan put an arm around her waist and held her. 'You won't see them, it's not possible. Have you told anybody else yet?' she asked.

'No,' Goli answered.

'You could tell your brothers and their comrades,' her friend went on; 'or tell the university militia for whatever use that is . . .'

But Goli was adamant. 'No, I don't want to tell my brothers, I don't think they can help, and the militia would just question and interrogate me. That's not what I want, or need.'

'I assure you, you won't see the men,' Marjan said. 'They'll be afraid of seeing you.'

'But they have guns, I don't . . . ' Goli replied.

'Listen to me, Goli, they were caught by three women, four women can testify against them. They would be very nervous about appearing around here again . . .'

'But that doesn't mean they won't go on doing it somewhere else. I want to hurt them . . . to hurt them badly.' Goli was squeezing her fists.

'But . . . ' Marjan stopped. Pain was spread across Goli's face, all over the newly-healed scars on her lips and throat. She was not listening to her; she was somewhere else.

The two women sat there looking at each other and their half-empty tea glasses and half-eaten sandwiches.

*To hurt them badly*, Marjan thought, and wanted to say something, but she didn't. They sat there, silence soaked in like upset tea on a white sofreh cloth.

Goli couldn't believe her ears when she heard the news that night. She had arrived home exhausted and hungry after delivering twenty rounds of posters and distributing four thousand leaflets. According to the radio announcement, the government, which had ignored the women's protest since it had begun was now warning women not to take part in the planned demonstration on Monday. The statement, which was apparently being broadcast on radio and television, told women that they should not march to Azadi Square, there was no reason for the women to march because the prime minister of the provisional government of the revolution had stated that the veil was not compulsory, and that there had been a misunderstanding. Women had nothing to fear, their rights were safe and respected by the revolution. This march was therefore unnecessary, and anti-revolutionary. The statement continued that if women ignored this warning the government could not ensure their safety.

Goli was afraid and angry. She immediately telephoned the other organisers. What did it mean? A statement had been broadcast nationally at last, it had acknowledged that a demonstration by women could exist. However there was anger that the government's response had been virtually to ban any further demonstration. There was anxiety at the thought that women might be intimidated and stay away the next day. A low turn-out would mean defeat. It would create division among the women where until now there had been a high degree of unity.

It was agreed that the organisers would arrive early at the university in order to call a meeting to discuss what to do.

Goli and Marjan set off together the next morning. They arrived to find a group of women standing in the cold outside the locked main gates. The two open pages of the book were chained together. The women couldn't believe their eyes.

They became furious and started shouting, 'Open the gate, open the gate,' but the guard didn't move. So they increased their chanting, and a few women started to climb up onto the gate and over to the other side, encouraging the others to do the same. 'Shame, shame, the chain belongs to the Shah, is this a new revolutionary chain?' they shouted. The guards, who were moved either by the women's climb over the gate, or by their shouts, unchained the gate and let the women through.

The meeting started noisily. Two conflicting views flew back and forth across the hall. Some women felt strongly that the government's words were not to be trusted, they had given no guarantee. They wanted to march on and hand over their resolution to the prime minister and demand an answer. Others were against the march. They insisted that since the government had at least made a statement declaring that the veil was not compulsory, they should wait. A march at this time would be provocative.

A heated discussion followed. Would the left honour its agreement to march in support of the women and protect them? Some women were very nervous of the possible retaliation if they were left without the support and protection of the left. Goli, Marjan and their group were very impatient; they wanted to march. Behind them, another group began to chant 'Rahpaymai', 'to march,' 'to march'. It was said that a section of the militant left and Radical Islam were against the march.

'Typical,' Goli said, 'our revolutionaries choose the most unrevolutionary option.' Another section had agreed to support and protect the women, however. Finally, to avoid further disarray, it was suggested that a vote be taken. Again chaos reigned. Where to march to? Some women only wanted to march within the university boundaries, not beyond. Many insisted that their plan for a rally in Azadi Square should go ahead. As soon as the raised hands declared the intention of the majority to march, they were moving on and towards the gate, singing, 'We have made a revolution so that we can march on,' and, 'Women are marching on, to Azadi Square, we are coming on.'

They sang themselves out of the gate, past two platforms of speakers, devotees who were advising them to obey the government, not demonstrate, warning that the government would not be on their side if things turned violent. The women surged on into Shah-Reza Avenue.

These days the university no longer functioned as an academic institution; before the revolution it had been occupied by groups working to overthrow the Shah. Now it had been taken over by the revolutionary activities of various left-wing groups, and during the past week by women.

In the past year, Goli thought, she had learned more about

life, about struggle, about the history of other struggles in the world, and about women's interminable struggle, than in all her years of study put together. And she had learned fast. The university really was a seat of learning for her. The sound of women's cheers interrupted her thoughts.

They were on the road, in the open, in the public sphere, among all the other people in the centre of Tehran, demonstrating, making a public appearance, a public protest directly to the people. The people their witness.

'Oh God,' Goli sighed with relief, a small, first victory. What effort it takes to have the right to protest openly in public. They streamed down the long road, gathering strength and momentum. Goli stood within a circle of friends, well protected, a bit tense and worried, but thrilled to be out on the long march to Azadi Square, a stretch of about six miles. She was not going to venture out of this safe women's circle. Images of the 17 Esphand and the previous demo were with her. The crowd was smaller than she had expected. The organisers had hoped that this demonstration would be twice as large as the previous one, especially as they knew that women in other cities – Isfehan, Shiraz, Tabriz and Ahvaz were coming out simultaneously. The radio warning must have put women off, must have divided them.

The colourful banners sailed above the heads of the women in the pale sun of the open street. In bold blocked letters their messages demanded equal rights, civil rights and dignity for women:

'No to Islam's slavery of women', استبداد در هر شکل محکوم است –
'Iranian women will not ارتجاع در هر شکل نابود است –
remain in bondage', 'Assault on women is assault on the revolution', 'Down with censorship'. Some of the posters were handwritten pieces of papers, a slogan on each side: 'Women's liberation is the measure of the whole of society's liberation', 'Dictatorship in any form is condemned, reaction in any form is unacceptable', 'We are not window breakers, we are idol breakers'. Personal one-liners on slips of paper read, 'Put the veil on the clergy', 'Don't leave us alone with the mullas'.

The crowd moved on and grew in size and emotion. Latecomers must have overcome their hesitation and decided to join the protest rather than put their trust in the government statement. The dominant mood was one of mistrust, a sense of betrayal. The rhythm of the women's anger, the force of their frustration and disappointment rang out in the songs of protest: 'Minute by minute, here and there and everywhere, under the torture, we said it, we will say it, either death or liberation . . . minute by minute . . . '

The passion rose, the air was thick with protest. The mass of women slowed the pace every now and then, and the men from the left – comrades, colleagues, friends, cousins, husbands and fathers – held hands on each side of the road, keeping the women in and the hostile crowd out, presenting a protective chain, solidarity with their women comrades. Bystanders on the pavement were growing in number too, either saluting or insulting the women, the fanatics in groups shouting: یا روسری یا تو سری 'Prostitutes . . . only prostitutes will go in public bare headed . . . either put on the veil or we will break your heads.' Their voices were hard and merciless. They looked incensed, their faces closed and knotted, hating the women. Their jeering, self-righteous contempt infuriated the women.

The sight of the women's hair, open faces and colourful garments had caused this open hostility, this ferocious enmity. Women had made a point of dressing colourfully and beautifully, their make-up bright, their hair striking: now that the snow had stopped, the air was dry and crisp and the women's dark, shining, living hair streamed out behind the wide banners. Many had taken particular care with their hair that day, pleased and proud of its power, celebrating its exposure. Their hair, a passport to freedom or a mark of captivity . . . the outcome of this revolution would determine which it was to be.

The pavements held nervous women supporters of the government, some with placards which read 'We are Muslims, we should support the government.' The placards of the passive left on the government's side read, 'Don't divide the revolution.' But the protesters did not take kindly to such slogans and responded by chanting 'Unity not at my expense', 'I am my own God', 'Reaction in any form is condemned',

'Repression in any shape is condemned ', 'Independence, equality, liberty!' در طلوع صبح آزادی جای زن خالی

'In the dawn of freedom – women have no freedom'.

Goli was a bit shaky. Every now and then a fanatic's face would frighten her. Would she see her assailants here? Would she recognise them? She would definitely recognise their voices. What could she do if she did see them? She was chanting, but her thoughts were going backwards and forwards between the march and that terrible night. She hung on to Marjan and tried to fix her mind on the present struggle.

The pavements were growing as crowded as the street. The hearty shouts of freedom slogans had brought out the shopkeepers, housewives and workers, who lined up to greet or simply to watch the women. The huge nine-storey Shafa Hospital had its balconies lined with nurses, medical workers and women kitchen staff, who blew kisses, or raised fists in support of the marchers. And in response the women shouted:

درود بر پرستار درود بر پرستار
*Dorood bar parastar*! *Dorood bar parastar*!' 'Greetings to the nurses!'

'They will not have those nursing uniforms on for long,' Marjan commented. 'They'll soon be issued with long, head-to-toe kafan.'

'So that instead of nursing the patients they can pray for them,' Goli replied.

The march went on smoothly, slowly and powerfully. It was militantly non-violent, peaceful except for some recently sacked television workers who were furiously chanting against the Islamic fanatics and reactionaries, 'We will not surrender', 'Either death or freedom'. Their voices were dry. They were presenters, announcers, newscasters, programme planners and producers and had been sacked for being women. They would be given jobs on a lower scale, so long as they remained invisible and worked behind the scenes. They had defied the new Islamic head of television. Their open faces, their defiant presence on the screen, were an affront to the manhood of the fundamentalists. And now they were retaliating. 'Prostitutes, supporters of the Shah, foreign agents!' The words were uttered like bullets, spat out to injure them. The ferocity of feeling, the extent of the hatred was hair-raising.

The independent feminist section of the march was restful. They were slowing down, tired but joyous and challenged, celebrating their power to protest so forcefully and continually for a week now against the anti-women revolutionary regime. '*Azadi, azadi*,' they chanted.

لحظه به لحظه ميگه . . . درشكته گفته ايگرد آزادى . . . .

'Wherever we are, we sing *azadi, azadi*, under the Shah, *azadi, azadi*, under Islam, under the mullas, *azadi, azadi*.'

Two older women in full black chadors were dancing on the hostile pavement to the rhythm of '*Azadi*', holding their veils tight around their faces with one hand and moving their fists and bodies to the harmony of the lines, 'Under the Shah, under the mullas, *azadi, azadi, azadi* . . .'

A foreign camera crew was shooting away, its women friends stood around them, guarding them, minding their work. They were zooming, witnessing, recording. An elegant young woman in the march saw the lens, took out her lipstick and applied it thickly to her lips. A woman in a colourful veil called out to a woman in the crew, 'Madam, madam, listen to me . . . tell the world . . . we are here for freedom.' The microphone was held in front of her. 'For our children's freedom, we want freedom for them, our children are not free. Is this freedom? We marched against the Shah, we have given martyrs for this revolution too. We fought for the whole of society before, now we are here for our rights. Madam, my daughter is in hospital, the fanatics have broken her nose, her lips have had twelve stitches. Nobody listens to us, nobody protects us. Is this Islam, this atrocity? Tell the world, thank you.' The lens framed her, the microphone memorised her voice, immortalised her words.

There was a sudden halt, panic rose, but quickly the organisers reassured the women through their microphones that everything was all right, that they had come to a large junction, and were joining up with the northern contingent which had blocked the surrounding streets.

Goli and Marjan stopped.

'You know, it seems the new government is only lashing

out against the professional, independent, career women right now. The ones with education and some power and social status,' Goli said. 'If they break them, then the rest – the women workers, women in the service industries, the farm workers and the carpet weavers, could all follow rapidly.'

Marjan agreed, nodding seriously. 'It seems this revolutionary government thinks it would be cheaper to run a country with no university, no education, no science, no hospitals, no entertainment – just prayers, basic food, wars and martyrdom, and eyes fixed on heaven.' Goli continued.

'Don't be such a cynic,' Marjan riposted. 'They want hospitals, universities and television but only for men and under men's control.'

'Still, it would be a cheaper way to run a country: provide for only half of the population at the expense of the other half and, when they protest, just bump them off.' Goli argued, reasoning along the lines of Islamic fatalism.

'If you think that's the way things would develop then we're wasting our time here,' retorted Marjan, unhappy with the simplification.

'Perhaps we are,' Goli's voice and mood were low.

'Come on. Goli, please be a bit more positive. Don't underestimate this show of strength. Let's soldier on and enjoy it. It's not everyday that we see such a gathering of women.'

After a while they started moving again slowly and resolutely under the pale winter sun. This was one of the last days of the year, soon the new year would be here. In any other year women would be out shopping, baking cakes and sweets, spring-cleaning their houses, soaking grains and planting new seeds, making new clothes and buying gifts for their children, preparing for the arrival of Nu-Rooz.

This New Year though the women were too busy defending their existence to think of preparation and celebration. The old year was hanging on tenaciously and its end seemed no nearer. In any case, there was a rumour that celebrations for the New Year should be banned because of their pre-Islamic and secular associations.

Exhaustion was overtaking the women. They must have walked over five miles. Fatigue was sitting between their shoulder blades, pain bit deep into the soles of their feet. The massive Azadi Square monument was in sight, a plain, white and blue marble arch, its simple geometry was magnificent. The Shah had had it built to commemorate his fortieth birthday, but the massive square in which it stood was now the site of numerous revolutionary gatherings.

The women saw it in the distance and relaxed, a brief moment of rest from chanting, saving their energy for the crucial rally in the square and the conclusive hours of the day. The pavement now had new occupants – women and children, young girls just out of school, looking on, pleased, astonished, laughing, hanging on to their mothers, with the bright, wide smiles of youth. The new generation.

The women were nearly there. They had made it. An organised peaceful march, resolute, non-violent, was reaching its destination. A sigh of relief, a few light jokes, hopeful anticipation, men giving water to thirsty women.

'We're nearly there, Azadi Square,' Goli said.

'The tall, elegant statue looks beautiful. Proud though reaching into the sky. We'll rest there, in its bosom,' said Marjan.

A surge of women went on towards the entrance to the square. This was history, young, energetic, in the making. The loosening of tensions, the peace, the rest, the cool breeze off the fountains. The anticipation of a cold splash, a wash, the wiping away of sweat, the wetting of hair. And the excitement, of reaching the destination. Delighted, the stream of women at the front of the march glided into the square.

A pause, murmurs, ripples of doubt. Stalled. Slight panic. The stewards' quick movements. A small hitch. Orders came to sit, to squat down. As if flags were folding, the waves of women sat. Squatting, they could see the roof-tops better, women on the roof-tops, waving, the mountains behind them, snow-capped, tall, circling those in the square. Amazement, fear, silence.

Suddenly Goli heard a familiar voice.

'Oh, thank God we've found you. We've been looking for you, in a crowd of thirty thousand!' Malihe and Fatemeh greeted Goli.

'Where is Zari?' she asked them, looking around.

'She couldn't take another day off. She said there are going to be many demonstrations; she'll join more later on. It's a pity she's not here,' Fatemeh said.

From where they stood, just outside the square, while the rest sat, they looked out on a sea of colourful women extending from one end of Shah-Reza to the next. A heart-warming sight, bright and beautiful like a Persian carpet, woven in pain.

The murmuring grew, ripples of movement in the crowd as the women stood. There were loud shouts, angry voices, men's threats. Women rose, chanting furiously. Fear gripped Goli. No. What is happening? Why don't we go in? She couldn't see what was happening from where they stood, which was still quite a way from the entrance to the square. 'What's happening?' frightened women were asking.

Goli felt a deep sense of danger. 'Please take me home, Marjan, I'm afraid,' she begged.

Her friends encircled her. 'Leaving is difficult, more dangerous,' they told her.

'My stomach is in turmoil, I can't stand it, I feel sick, I'm going to shit myself,' she said. She was shaking, her hands slippery in her grip on their arms. They started to squeeze their way out of the nervous crowd, apologising, explaining, trying to find a way through to a cab, or a safe place to hide.

Malihe and Marjan decided they would go with Goli, but Fatemeh wanted to stay, so she helped the others out to the pavement and when they had disappeared among the bystanders she returned to her friends. The square was blocked by large numbers of angry men, shouting, warning the women to return, to obey the revolution, to go home. Behind them, the square was packed with green buses, cordoning off the open space.

Women stood their ground, protesting:

'We will not submit.    - با حجاب بدی حجاب علیه شما میجنگیم

With the veil and

without the veil we    - با حجاب بدی حجاب آزادیها باید اد

overthrew the Shah, and with the veil and without the veil we fight for our freedom', and 'We want a rally, we want a rally'. The women's chanting made the men angrier. Their numbers were growing in size and fury; they were moving in, towards the women, trying to encircle them. They were rough, ragged, poor. They were armed, concealed weapons bulging inside their jackets. They were under the orders of a few well-dressed bourgeois-looking leaders.

Women looked about for the militia, the armed guard of the revolution. Where were they? Why were there so few of them? Why didn't they keep the fanatics away? Panic caught the women like fire does dry wood. There were screams for help from some women, while others went on chanting, their only defence. The fanatics were everywhere now, for the first time outnumbering the women, trying to encircle them. But the women outside the square were determined to make a way through, to get into the square. Push and force, the smell of tear-gas, canisters thrown into the crowd. It burned their eyes, making them cough, their eyes streaming. Men were charging the women's lines, and breaking them up.

The chain of male protectors was broken. They were trying to keep the women in and the fanatics out, but once they came under attack, they were forced to defend themselves. Lines were broken. The concealed weapons were out, the march was invaded, women were being pushed around and beaten up. They tried to run, looking for safety, but all was confusion and turmoil. The fear of the women had added to the self-righteous violence of the men and they went all the way as nobody was standing up to them, neither the militia, nor the bystanders. Here was a chance to crush the women, to force them into submission once and for all. The women, unarmed and unprepared for hand-to-hand combat felt their resistance crumble. Next to Fatemeh a veiled woman was being clubbed, caught up in and trapped by her chador. Fatemeh rushed to help her and was immediately grabbed. A brass knuckle went straight into her eye. Blood blinded her and she fell to the ground. Above her, the battle continued. It was a long, pitched battle. The women had been caught, unarmed. It was a siege.

By evening, when the fanatics had left in their Islamic green-coloured coaches, Azadi Square was quiet, abandoned in a blanket of darkness and silence. The oblong slabs of white marble that paved it were littered with tufts of variously coloured hair, hairpins, torn scarves, blood, empty handbags, make-up and broken mirrors. A child's shoe was floating in the fountain. Papers, placards everywhere, and there, on the ground, a small handwritten note, crumpled and trodden, read:

'Don't leave us alone with مارا با آخوندها تنا نگذارید the mullas.' A satchel on the lawn. The silent remnants. Hope's precious shrine.

... ... ... expression with ... ... Se ... ... ... ...
... ... personality ...

## 5

When Zareen was told, that same night, that Fatemeh had been hit in the eye and taken to hospital, she was shocked and immediately wanted to rush to her friend's bedside. But her husband reminded her that between their house and the hospital she would have to pass at least six komiteh checkpoints and answer numerous questions which would only mean more trouble; she should wait until tomorrow. So she lay in her bed gazing into the night, her mind crowded with images of torn, bleeding flesh, of Fatemeh, helpless and wounded, perhaps even to blindness.

Zareen could not sleep. The thought of Fatemeh's pain and potential blindness pinched her heart. She got up and paced about the house, swearing revenge on the men who had done this. Towards dawn she cried herself to sleep. Zareen was very close to Fatemeh. They had been friends for a couple of years and Zareen felt that Fatemeh was the closest and most intimate friend she had. She loved her.

Goli had arrived home safely but the next day she felt anxious and unwell. She had been told about the battle in Azadi Square and the attack on Fatemeh and, even though she had not witnessed the events in the square, she felt as if the whole trauma of her personal assault had been repeated on a mass scale.

She couldn't get rid of a dreadful vision that all the women in the demonstration had faced her own vicious assailants. The tension in her stomach was so great that she had been sick and had the runs throughout the night and the day after. She was surprised by her capacity to shit interminably. She could hardly sleep. Her mother sat at her bedside and Goli talked to her for a long time about the demonstration and the zealots' attack, and about her fears for the future. She had not confided in her mother about the full extent of her attack but her mother was warm and sympathetic and told her about her own similar experiences. She told her that this was not the first time that women had been systematically intimidated and that it wouldn't be the last time; she told her about her own schooldays and their demonstrations and how police had run through the crowd with truncheons.

Her mother had her own worries. She was anxious for her job and for those of her colleagues at the School of Fine Art. Clearly the last thing this revolution needed was fine art.

Goli made a few enquiries about Fatemeh, but she didn't have the heart to visit her. She decided to stay at home for a few days until her shattered confidence had healed. She heard that the intimidation and violence of the men had worked and that the women's demonstrations had dwindled. The organising body in defence of women's rights had decided to stop demonstrating and instead put all its effort into creating a solid organisation, to find an office and write a constitution.

It was frustrating and demoralising to stay at home when all the action was outside, when all her friends were involved in rebuilding and protecting the women's movement from the organised vandalism of the government and its allies, but she knew she had very little choice in the state she was in, and so she tried to make the best of it.

Marjan took on the job of bringing news and messages from her friends. She brought her piles of library books and Goli began to make notes for articles. She concentrated on historical and analytical books on the struggles of people in Iran and in other countries. It seemed that women everywhere had fought hard for the little they had achieved, and even harder to maintain these achievements, as every political system seemed to be ready to exploit women – Pakistan, India and Egypt for instance, and the west was as bad, particularly when it came to sexual violence against women.

Some of the ideas and strategies of these struggles caught Goli's imagination. Nineteenth-century Iran was interesting. The people had used simple and ingenious tactics, like sit-ins in the telegraph buildings, so that when the authorities didn't move quickly to deal with their issues they could use the wireless to spread the news and ask for help. This had been extraordinarily effective. Or women had dressed as men and used horse-drawn stage-coaches to travel around spreading the news and gathering support from other towns and cities. How clever, she thought. They could use some of these tactics, wearing men's clothes perhaps, maybe even using coaches and horses if the media continued with its black-out. Goli found it heart-warming to read such tales of struggle and endurance. It gave her new strength, hope and visions on her horizon.

Every now and then she tried to find some news and entertainment on the radio and television, but it was hopeless. The news was simply strings of newly inflated slogans against America and Israel. What boredom, she couldn't even hear music. Folk songs and classical music were no longer broadcast; in their place were prayers, sermons, and the didactic voices and faces of the clergy. No wonder the television was called the bearded glass.

After three days at home she was utterly bored and impatient, desperate to go to the university, and be active again. She wanted to see Fatemeh, to go to Ziba Style and to see all her friends again.

Marjan brought news that Mr Hamidi, the karate teacher, was sympathetic. He had heard about the attacks on women and wanted to help, but he was afraid of losing his job as the university was being taken over by clergy. According to his job description he was only allowed to train men. He couldn't change this, but he would think of something, would talk to other sympathetic lecturers and would let the women know.

A few days later news came that he was willing to take the risk and train the women and he that he had even booked a session for them. Goli couldn't wait to get going, her excitement tinged with apprehension. It felt good to have the confidence to return to the old battlefield, to be prepared to face the scars of the war and to see them healing.

Marjan gave her a lift to their first lesson. In the car they were both quiet. Goli looked out of the window and noticed changes in the scenery. The walls, the windows of offices, and even the parks and open spaces were taking on the shapes and colours of a fanatical Islam – the thick lines of the slogans, gloomy pictures of martyrs painted on the walls, black and white banners, the atmosphere of death, depression and destruction, black and white, nothing in between, no other colour or shade.

She picked up a paper from the back of the car: a large picture of some SAVAK men, tied and hooded, and shot, a bloody image. The SAVAKs had been the Shah's most infamous secret police, responsible for the torture of countless numbers of political prisoners. They had been arrested and tried behind closed doors, denied an open trial or the right to legal defence, and subsequently executed, the truth buried with them. A group of young, unemployed men arresting the most high-ranking army and police personnel, tying them up, beating them and putting bullets in their heads. I wonder what kind of pleasure they get out of this reversal of power, how violence tastes to them? The whole of our male population gets off on violence. What a sick state, Goli thought, utterly depressed. The streets went by fast but she could not help seeing the walls and their galleries of black pictures of martyrs. She looked back inside the car, picked up another of the pamphlets from the pile that Marjan carried with her for delivery. She looked through it, reading the headlines and looking at the pictures.

She turned to Marjan. 'Why does your paper not cover news of violence against women?'

Marjan was taken by surprise, and hesitated for a few seconds before replying. 'You're right,' she said. 'I hadn't thought about that . . . we don't cover the increasing attacks on women as a social issue—'

'Perhaps because it's not a women workers' issue?' Goli was teasing.

'It isn't, but it's still a women's issue,' Marjan replied.

'You cover shortages of food, agricultural problems and the ways in which they affect women, violence against women at work, but not domestic violence, rape, street attacks. Why are you silent on these issues? Doesn't the left care about what happens at home, where people spend most of their time, their personal relationships?'

'Be reasonable, it's only recently we have started our open political activity after years of repression and underground work, and of course there are thousands of other women's issues that we haven't covered or we haven't thought about. Give us a chance.'

'I don't think this is about chances. This is the most crippling and crucial issue for women today and the left has no position on it; it tries to ignore it, to slight it. Since I was attacked, I've thought a lot about it while reading papers and listening to the news, and I've sensed this inadequacy and neglect. I fear that you patronise women by having issues like women's work, wages, nurseries at the top of your list and issues that are uncomfortable, like physical violence, at the bottom. Perhaps you don't want to offend your male leaders and workers?'

'If you're insinuating that we are deliberately ignoring issues so as not to offend our male membership, you're wrong. We always debate with them; they're very open and sympathetic. Anyway, it you care about these issues, why don't you join the group and fight to put it right?'

'That's not fair, every time I criticise my brothers about their lack of commitment to women's issues, they say the same thing, "why don't you join the group and fight to put it right?", as if each member has to pay an entrance fee so as to absolve the group of its duties and responsibilities. I have my own problems as a sympathiser with your politics and your group. I'm telling you what is lacking and you should take my suggestions and those of others like me as feedback and act on them. Bloody hell! If every time I suggested something to a group it meant I had to join them to put it right for them, I'd be holding a hundred cards to a hundred parties.'

'No need to be so angry. I get your point, woman. But I still think you would be good in our party.'

'Much better outside it. Come on, you can't recruit me now, in your car, when I'm at a low ebb and need you. Save your energy for looking after me. And now, more than anything else I need to go to the loo. Can you come with me, and wait outside for me?'

'After all you've said about my lack of commitment to women's issues, I'll have to think about that . . . All right then, I'll continue to do my duty by women's liberation, and chaperone you to the loo and back, with pleasure.'

Goli was annoyed and disappointed, but not seriously; it wasn't the first time they had disagreed. She was nervous, and she realised that Marjan was trying to cheer her up, and responded in kind:

'This is my chance of a lifetime – a chaperone – and I'm going to make the most of it.' She held Marjan's hand, touching the soft skin and feeling the connection like a silk string. She was not in danger alone. She was safe. It was a warm feeling.

The university area was quiet. It didn't have the buzz and excitement of the days of the women's gatherings, though there were still large groups of people around. Goli and Marjan walked around the knots of discussion, the bookstalls and placards, the street politics of the revolution. Street politics had been the pulse of the pre-revolutionary days and the major force that created the explosive moments of victory. This was the power that had overthrown the three thousand-year-old monarchy and oligarchy. Now the power was shifting, like sand, back into the hands of the institutions, the army, the government and militia and the media. Was this scene merely ritual then? The ritual of street politics? Goli felt she too was on shifting sand. These streets no longer hold power, even the power to give information and ideas. Their movements are just reflex actions now. They don't intend to revolt; they don't have the capacity for it anymore; they've lost the heart of the revolution, Goli thought to herself as they passed by.

Mr Hamidi and nine women were talking in the corner of the sports hall when they arrived. Mr Hamidi started by giving them a short introduction, explaining first that the most basic requirement was common-sense. To begin with they must be fit and agile, and must therefore take up some form of sport. They must be very observant and aware of their surroundings at all times, avoiding dark streets, not going alone to demonstrations, or wearing impractical and dangerous clothes such as high-heeled shoes or tight trousers. If threatened with an attack they must keep cool, act confidently and swiftly, and be ready to defend themselves. They must avoid fear and nervousness, as fear is a sure sign of defeat. He told them about the vulnerable points in the body at which the women should aim: the knees, throat, eyes, testicles, the hollow beneath the Adam's apple, the nose, fingers and the joints of elbows, and how to strike at them effectively. Finally he handed round books and photographs demonstrating karate. It was a short session. He told the women to take away the books, to study them and to try to practise on each other during the university break. He would see them again in the new term when they would begin the practical lessons.

The women went together to a quiet corner on the lawn to look at the books and photos. The figures of grappling men, kicking and throwing each other about, looked so strenuous and demanding of physical strength that the women felt intimidated. The emphasis on individual fitness, speed and keeping cool at the time of an attack astonished them.

They divided the books between them and agreed to meet again during the New Year break.

As they left Goli complained to Marjan, 'How can we do all these movements, and get fit and agile when we've never done any physical exercise for fear of losing our bloody virginity? It'll take ages to get used to.'

'Why are you so depressed – we've only just started doing it?' replied Marjan. 'Of course it's a slow process, and we're not used to it . . . And this bloody virginity is a problem too – I must get rid of it . . . but don't be so down.'

Goli couldn't help herself though. She had missed Fatemeh too. Would she be able to join them at the next lesson? She began to sink back into depression. She had come face to face with her physical weakness. How could she throw her attacker on the floor like that, or keep him at bay and run off? Lack of confidence overtook her. Fear came back. A cold, merciless fear, icicle-like, trapped her. How could she fight it off? Doubt hung in the air like the hangman's rope.

## 6

It was less than a week to the New Year. A new spring. The university was officially closed but the activists still kept up their bookstalls and their pavement debates. Women and arguments about women's rights were absent though, other than as the subjects of side talk at the bookstalls. Most women were intimidated and the remnants of their resistance movement were now concentrated in their workplaces, colleges and nurseries, their focus on practical issues.

They were still picketing their workplaces against the wholesale sackings and redundancies, and there were sit-ins at the mixed technical and religious colleges from which women were going to be barred. Mothers occupied factory floors because their nurseries were closing down and they were being encouraged to give up their jobs for unemployed men.

In Kashan women in the education corps who were denied employment as teachers held the official in charge hostage until their demands had been dealt with and they had been promised employment. Unemployed women organised the occupation of the Ministry of Kar (work) for a few days until their proposals had been accepted. These pockets of resistance were sporadic and unconnected, and the news coming in about them was distorted, and often manipulated by the media; but it kept a little hope alive.

The pasdars had quickly moved into the factories and workplaces and barred any outside solidarity with the workers. They isolated the women inside and stopped their news spreading. The university women's demonstration had dwindled, like the milk that boiled and boiled and finally spilled over; only drops remained in isolated pockets around the university – the old boiling pot of the revolution.

Traditionally the weeks before the New Year are devoted to spring cleaning, buying new clothes for the children, baking the annual cakes and sweets whose scents sweeten the streets. The Islamic fanatics, in search of further restrictions on the people, had claimed that the New Year was not Islamic and decreed that celebrations should be stopped, but the public outcry was so great that they recanted.

Zareen was a keen believer in celebrating the New Year. She had put her grains and green lentils in water by the window and their new green shoots were an inch tall. She had packed away the korsi, the symbol of winter and had done her spring cleaning and bought material with which Malihe was going to sew new clothes for her and the kids. She had bought her haft-seen, the seven 's's – seven items starting with the letter 's' – seer, serkeh, samovar, sabazi, somagh, seeb, samano, that is, garlic, vinegar, samovar, a vegetable, a herb, an apple and a sweet grain dish. She had set these out on a white lace sofreh, along with a fish bowl, and a plate containing a few coins and some traditional sweets and dried fruits and nuts. She wasn't going to miss her Nu Rooz (New Year) for anything.

She was celebrating it with her customers too. She was going to have a festive day, a hanna-bandan, a whole day spent in hennaing her customers' hair.

Hanna-bandan was originally her mother's idea: she had suggested it for older women who wanted to hide their white hair, and to colour their hands and feet. Zareen had started it for her mother and her friends, on one day a month, but a year before the revolution it had become fashionable for the middle- and upper-class women to henna their hair in various shades, from a light shining bronze to the dark matt shineless colour of old copper. Zareen wasn't sure about hanna-bandan day at first: it was a long, hard day, and the work was messy; but as it was the fashion demand increased and she got to enjoy it, until, at one point, it became a fortnightly fixture and quite a social occasion. The customers brought fruit, dried nuts and raisins and roasted seeds of all kinds – pumpkin seeds, watermelon and sunflower seeds. Zareen would get the samovar going all day and make a plain dish, addasi, and somebody would buy hot, newly baked bread and bring fresh cakes for tea. Malihe came to the hanna-bandan day not only to have her hair hennaed but also to meet her customers and do some measuring, trying on during the long hours that they sat waiting for the henna to set in their hair. This hanna-bandan day was the special New Year one. She had invited Goli and Malihe, but Fatemeh was too ill to come, although she had left hospital and was resting at home.

Goli had been to the hospital and seen Fatemeh. Her stitches stretched from beneath one eye to the top of the eyebrow. Her mother was very upset, worried that Fatemeh had lost a lot of weight. She was encouraging Fatemeh to have plastic surgery to hide all trace of the wound, but Fatemeh didn't like the idea. When Goli saw her friend she was in a good mood and pleased to see her. They talked about themselves and their friends, exchanged news of the latest events, and discussed the politics of their daily life. Goli was, however, disturbed at the sight of Fatemeh in hospital, bandaged and helpless, and could not bear to stay for very long. She excused herself and left.

Zareen and Malihe had been to see her many times, both separately and together. Whenever Zareen went to see her, she took a handmade present, cakes, sweets or a nourishing soup. They had spent hours together and Fatemeh made sure that neither her mother nor any other visitor came at the same time. Zareen wanted her out and fully recovered as quickly as possible; she was reluctant to have her New Year party without Fatemeh, but Fati insisted that she mustn't let her friends and customers down, nor should she give in to the anti-New Year lobby. So Zareen carried on with the preparations.

On hanna-bandan day Goli and Malihe came one after the other at lunchtime. Zareen had planned that they could all eat together in the shop and that after lunch while the others were resting they could retire to her sitting room for a private chat. Goli was surprised to see the shop so neat. On the floor were the samovar, tumblers of tea, sweets, pistachios, dried figs, and roasted pumpkin seeds. All the usual objects, chairs, hairdryers, were pushed back to one side against the wall. It didn't look so much like a hairdresser's as a women's meeting in the changing room of a hammam. Didn't they used to have political meetings in the hammam, seventy or eighty years ago during the constitutional revolution?

As they gathered around the plain sofreh, Goli was a bit dazed. She took to the place and the women, even though she didn't know them. She felt intimacy and warmth here. The seated women, the plain food, the cracking sound of sunflower and watermelon seeds, the homeliness of it all touched her. It was unlike any other hairdresser's she had been to. She had been feeling low when she had arrived, but now she felt lifted. She was wearing a short green jacket and a pair of jeans with a matching top. She sat down, squatting, found it a bit difficult and wriggled in her jeans. She was introducing herself when suddenly Zareen ran to the radio which had been on very low. It was the lunchtime news. All the women turned to it as the broadcaster announced the minister of education's statement about the new Islamicisation of schools and universities and their curricula. The headlines continued. The ministry of art had announced the Islamicisation of all areas of fine art, music, theatre and cinema. A leading mulla had added his voice to the compulsory veil and accused women who resisted it of being anti-God and anti-Islam. The government had announced that the birthday of Fatemeh, daughter of the prophet would be a Women's Day and a national holiday. A statement by the Women for Islam organisation had declared that they were planning demonstrations against unveiled women and all forms of corrupt imperialist influence.

A young woman, Azadeh, who was a friend of Zareen's assistant Muneer, was sitting in a corner reading her women's magazine. She said quietly, 'Under the Shah, his wife and sister were the patrons of the women's organisation, now our new patron is the prophet's daughter.'

Goli wanted to follow this up, but another woman turned to her and asked, 'What is this rumour about masses of women not wanting to wear the veil?'

Goli was surprised that nobody had responded to the rest

of the news or to what Azadeh had said. Perhaps they hadn't heard it. She didn't know what to say, but luckily Zareen intervened to suggest that they begin their lunch. she was upset by the news and wanted to talk about it. She didn't want the veil to be yet again the central issue.

The women made a large circle and the oblong sofreh was soon covered with addasi, bowls and spoons. Muneer brought in the freshly baked hot sangak. The sound of eating dominated.

Goli was preoccupied with the news and wanted to talk about it, but she didn't know how to begin. Did she look like a student agitator? What were these women's politics? Could she trust them?

'It's more than two weeks now since those women at the university protested against Hejab, isn't it?' The question was addressed to Goli. It was the same woman as before.

'Yes, I think so,' Goli replied.

'They're all rich women who have never worn the chador, who fear that now they may have to, and don't like its discomfort, is that it?' the woman continued.

Azadeh replied, 'Of course, it is uncomfortable, why should the rich have to be uncomfortable as well as the poor . . . and anyway, I don't think it's anything to do with being rich or poor.'

'Poor women must have the same degree of choice as rich women about whether or not to wear the veil,' Goli said. 'Lots of rich, older women wear it because they want to . . . at a certain age they start thinking about going to heaven . . . '

Another woman joined in, 'Heaven or earth, this is our chosen Islamic government and we must listen to what is required of us, we must be prepared to make sacrifices for our country, for our leaders . . . '

'It's for your own good,' the first woman continued. 'When it comes to sex, men are wild animals and you must put on the veil to protect yourselves from their gaze and their dirty hands. I don't understand why women have become so obstinate, so insubordinate. What is a little personal discomfort for the sake of personal safety in difficult times like these?'

'So you think Hejab will eradicate sexual crimes, male violence, family problems, all the other social ills? That women should just sit at home and obey the government?' Goli asked her.

'Yes,' the woman retorted. 'Life would be so much easier for everyone. Why do women want to go out, to work, I think they're crazy. Surely there's already enough work at home for women without wanting to go out to an office to work too. They give their wages to the men anyway. No, thank you, one job is enough for me, my husband must earn my living for me.'

Malihe, who had known some of these women for years, came to Goli's aid. 'But why use force, guns and knives, to beat up women in the streets and in their workplaces? Why?' she asked.

'Who does that?' Zareen's mother said, looking horrified.

'Pasdars, young boys, everyone has a gun these days,' Malihe replied.

Zareen's mother was shocked. 'God forbid, no, this is lawlessness. Why don't the authorities confiscate the guns?'

'But our young men and young boys are the keepers of the revolution and of the country,' the second woman told her. 'They have given so many martyrs for the revolution, and Hejab is for our protection. God be with these men,' she finished.

'They think they are God themselves,' Goli said quietly.

'Aren't we big enough or capable enough to protect ourselves?' asked Azadeh.

'It's not protection if it's forced on us, especially with violence, is it?' Zareen asked. 'And you wouldn't want to be afraid of going out because armed men might attack you.'

The second woman took up the challenge. 'I don't go out; I have no business outside my home alone at night. I have always been afraid to be out on my own. Fear is nothing new to me.'

'Ah, never mind the veil now . . . Did you hear the news? It's so depressing,' interrupted Azadeh.

Goli looked up, relieved that the subject was changing. It was incredible. The very woman who was defending the role of the gun-toting boys and bandits had to be the one to say, 'fear is nothing new to me'.

'Why shoud we live in fear?' Goli asked. 'Why?' She was nervously cracking pumpkin seeds from their shells.

An elderly woman who was sitting silently in the corner, knitting peacefully, raised her head and said authoritatively, 'You can't question the unquestionable my girl, because we can't challenge the system. People change, but the system remains the same, and the system hasn't changed for as long as I can remember, and for as long as my mother and grand-mother could remember.'

The two women defenders of the regime were getting upset, they hadn't seen sufficient support for the men and Islamic virtues. They said they were surprised that women had become so selfish and didn't want to submit to the government: what was wrong with a little submission for one's own country? Muneer, who often wore the veil herself, listened and shook her head in support of Azadeh, who was still busy being challenging, openly and bravely. She was sixteen years old, a student, fashion and image conscious. She was passionate about her freedom and so opposed to restrictions on women that she didn't notice the risks she was taking.

The afternoon rest interrupted all that and Zareen, Malihe and Goli went into Zareen's sitting room. There they were at last able to discuss the days news and their reactions to the discussion in the salon freely. Goli was still thinking about the way women here viewed the recent events. It was good to listen to the opinions of people other than the university crowd. She hadn't thought about the way women in the south of Tehran perceived the situation, the diversity of their views and, of course, of how the class division played a part in all this. When she expressed how she felt to Zareen, her friend told her that she was welcome to come and join in whenever she wanted as such debates were part of the daily life at the salon.

'I worry though,' complained Zareen, 'that often women change their position too easily – they're always influenced by the dominant line.'

74

'But that's good, it shows that women are flexible rather than sticking rigidly to one argument,' Malihe argued.

Zareen was not convinced. 'Hmm . . . I'm always careful what I say, and to whom, when I'm in the salon. A couple of those women are outright reactionaries.'

Goli consoled her. 'It was really friendly today – I've seen much worse than that in the university.' Silence for a few moments.

'Islamicisation. What does it really mean to have an Islamic Iranian cinema?' Goli sighed deeply.

'No women in it, of course,' came Zareen's reply.

'Or an Islamic education,' continued Goli. 'No science or biology, back to God making babies, and sending them down the chimney.' She sighed again. 'Orders from above, clergy censorship of everything, no chance of opposing God and his representatives on earth, a rapid descent into medievalism, total submission is what's required from all good Muslims: Islam *is* submission. Well, goodbye decent education, art, entertainment.'

'We never had it, only a shadow of it, so we won't miss much,' Malihe was rueful.

Goli then mentioned the rumour she had heard about mothers being instructed by Ayatollah Gillani to warn their children against theft, any child caught stealing, he had proclaimed, must be warned three times, and the fourth time have the tips of their fingers chopped off. Thereafter their fingers should continue to be mutilated each time they were caught.

'I've been dreading this for a year, I've had an intuitive feeling about it,' said Zareen.

'So the Women for Islam organisation is going to protest against the unveiled, naughty children who pinch apples, and the reds . . . ' Malihe observed.

'And for the first time in their lives they will taste power . . . the social and political power they've never had before,' Goli replied.

'I'm worried,' said Zareen.

'It's a worrying time,' Malihe told her. 'You're not alone. There are at least five million women worrying with you.

Could the women teachers, headmistresses, lecturers, artists, musicians and actors go on a mass strike and demand a hearing with the ministers for the arts and education?'

'No, none of those traditional methods of protest will be effective anymore,' Goli said. 'They would simply sack them wholesale, just like the women lawyers, and employ fanatics in their place. Lawlessness is becoming law, and our worst fears are coming true. We can no longer say that the government is not part of the violence against women.'

'It's becoming systematic,' Malihe agreed. 'It's not just a group of men who have gone crazy, is it?'

'I wonder what Fatemeh thinks now,' Goli said. 'Does she still defend the government's responsibility for the protection of women? And her revered, precious law?'

But Zareen defended her. 'I don't think she should be thinking about any of this now, she must simply try to get better. Mind you, she would like having Women's Day named after her!'

'Yes, and now every Iranian woman will be expected to be like the prophet's daughter. There'll soon be competitions for the best model Fatemeh,' Malihe said bitterly.

A depressed silence fell among the women. Only the sounds of the sunflower seeds, the shifting of the cold tea glasses remained.

Goli's attention wandered to the framed text on the wall. It read 'Bes-Mel-Lahe-Rahmane-Raheem' (In the name of God who is generous and forgiving); she thought of Fatemeh's wound – had that man called upon the name of God when he ripped into Fati's skin with his brass knuckles? It was beautifully embroidered in Arabic, delicately stitched and colourfully decorated. The letters were intricately woven, each letter curling into the next, forming an amalgamation of shapes and symbols that was both fascinating and mysterious. She didn't know what style of calligraphy it was – Kofi or Nastalegh? She looked at it for a good while, admiring its artistic innovation and the beauty of the decorated words. The words were a vehicle for sacred meaning, idols for worship and, the irony of it all, it was a foreign language that was the object of this worship. Since when had art become so alien?

She would have to learn to hate the art that is dangerous to and violates women even though it may be difficult to resist its visual beauty, she thought to herself, turning her gaze back upon the others. They looked sad and felt hopeless. Hope was distant like a white handkerchief on the barrel of a gun.

The New Year holiday was going to be a far cry from the usual scene of festivity. Everything came under the severe scrutiny of the militia: women's and children's clothes, gifts, even the traditional family visits during the first twelve days of the holiday.

Zareen felt the pressure of the restrictions. She lengthened her daughter Parvaneh's New Year dress, which was plain and dark, she took off a shade or two of her make-up; only later did she realise that she had 'censored' herself.

She heard rumours that people were being arrested for visiting the wrong relations at the wrong time. Many women were arrested and taken for questioning for travelling in a car with a man who was not an immediate relation, even if other members of their family were also present. Each family visit meant negotiating militia checkpoints at which both male and female members of the family were cross-examined according to the latest family visit rule book that each militia group had created.

Eating in a restaurant had become a major adventure, sausages were declared impure and banned, wine was served under the table or out of a teapot, music was censored and war marches alone were broadcast. And as for those who failed to calculate correctly the number of checkpoints and were still in the street after curfew . . . By the end of the holiday Zareen wondered whether the New Year celebration had been banned after all. She was glad to have the holiday behind her, and looked forward to the meeting she had planned at the salon with her friends.

Fatemeh looked recovered, but a long line of stitches marked her face. The raw line from beneath her eye curved round her cheekbone and cut through her eyebrow, and there were other, smaller, marks around it. Fatemeh had left hospital during

New Year and had been visited by Zareen and Goli, but this was the first time they had all been together since the siege of Azadi Square.

The samovar was clean and shiny. As Zareen poured out the tea, they could see her hands distorted surreally in its bright bronze panel. The restrictions of the New Year and Fatemeh's presence among them again set off a discussion about ways in which they might protect themselves. Fatemeh, who had made herself comfortable on the cushions, said that she had thought a lot about starting a women's vigilante group.

'It would just be a start,' she said, 'there must be so much happening out there that we don't know about . . . and there must be so much we could do, but to begin with we should get out and observe . . . '

'What you're suggesting sounds very dangerous, Fati . . . ' said Zareen.

But Malihe interrupted her, 'Fati is right, we should do something; we can't just sit around passively and allow this brutality . . . we have to act, to resist . . . '

'Look, it's easy for you to want to be militants,' Zareen said. 'You're single women. I have a family, a husband who is all right really, two kids who are all right too. I don't want to jeopardise their lives . . . nor do I want to die . . . or to be arrested and put in gaol for nothing.'

'But Zari, what are you suggesting?' Fatemeh asked her.

'I'm not suggesting anything . . . ' Zareen said quietly. 'I'm just afraid. This system is popular, it has many supporters among women, you know what our sex is like, and it has the army, the militia, the courts, the mosques, the police, the judiciary, the secret service and now the revolutionary guard behind it. Who do we have?'

'So what? Women are like that, eternally patient, waiting, waiting . . . but they will come around, they have to,' Malihe said confidently.

'After how many women's deaths?' Zareen persisted.

'I don't mind going out to patrol the streets, but only if it's in men's clothes,' said Goli suddenly.

'What?' Zareen yelled. 'First you don't want to go out at

all, the streets demoralise you, and now you want to go out in men's clothes . . . my God.' She wasn't the only one to be surprised by Goli's declaration.

'I think it's a good idea,' said Malihe, in Goli's defence. 'Take it as a lesson in street life under an Islamic governed state. It'll be a new experience for us; to see the way the men control the streets; the way they intimidate simply with their presence, with their body language . . . I don't want to do it myself, I'm too old, but the three of you could do it.'

Encouraged, Goli continued, 'I've tried a few self-defence tactics, some moves to overpower an attacker. I'm practising at home on my brothers . . . and . . . '

'I want to join you,' said Fatemeh. 'I've always been slow in learning physical activities, that's why I prefer chess, sitting down and beating a king's army without moving a leg, but I must join you . . . when I feel stronger.'

The others looked at her stitches, at the patched flesh, slowly healing.

'You wouldn't have any difficulty wearing men's clothes I reckon,' Goli told her. 'But how will I find men's clothes to fit me?' She looked at Malihe who had just put down a piece of sewing.

'I could sew you an aba,' she said. 'It's easier to hide under it. You're too short for a man's suit.'

'If you're determined to do it, yes, I agree with Mali, it would be difficult to get men's clothes that would fit you,' said Zareen.

'Not that difficult,' replied Malihe. 'I could try to get something for her in the second-hand market, the one in Parke-Shahr.'

'And what would you say to the shopkeeper? That it was for an absent son? They'd think you wanted it for a terrorist.'

Suddenly a cloud of sadness and pain settled on Malihe's face, and she froze. Zareen, unaware of what she had said, saw Malihe's expression and only then, a few seconds later, realised. What a stupid thing to have said. With her left hand she covered her face, bending down.

'Is it any use to apologise?' The words stumbled out. Goli

looked at Fatemeh and shook her head enquiringly. They made some gestures. Silence fell.

Malihe, feeling the eyes of the others on her, said, '*No*, it's not your fault . . . I still get upset. I know I shouldn't . . . I don't know. Why didn't they return after the revolution? They sent a message to say that they would. What's keeping them there? What is more important than their mother? It was their best opportunity to return . . . '

Fatemeh tried to comfort her, 'Well . . . it's wiser that they didn't; they would have been arrested, perhaps not immediately, but eventually for sure.'

'Mali, I'm sorry for saying such a stupid thing,' Zareen repeated. 'Honestly . . . it is much safer for them that they are not here. I know you want them here next to you, but think of their future . . . think of our future, if we have any.'

In an attempt to lift the tension, Zareen made fresh tea, but the atmosphere of anxiety remained.

Malihe, tea glass in her hand, sipping it slowly and gazing fixedly at it as if looking through a crystal ball, turned to Goli, who had remained silent and confused, and said, 'You don't know the full story of my life, do you?' She began a brief account; they all listened. 'Sometimes I can accept that people have causes to fight for which come before everything else, even their family ties and relationships, but at other times I get very angry and upset. When I see other mothers with their grown-up children, when I see old friends and the changes they have gone through, I want to know about my children too. I want to witness their lives and be part of them. Sometimes, when I feel my body ageing, when I'm lonely, I feel bitter, I feel very strongly then that for my children there should be no cause worthier than me. I know I'm being selfish, but I tell myself, why not? I'm much better now; I was much worse during the first few years of their absence.'

They were all sad and meditative. Zareen was moved. She said, 'We are here, we are together and we care.'

Goli was overwhelmed by Malihe's life, by her resilience, her depth of feeling, and her pain. She went to her and gave her a big hug, and as she lost herself in Malihe's deep bosom she said, 'You are a very courageous woman. Courage is not recognised in women, is it?'

There was silence until Zareen said, 'No, I won't let you leave like this; we need some music to cheer us up. I know, I'll get my dayereh and play a tune for you.' She ran out of the room. In response Fatemeh dug into her bag and brought out a small, shining harmonica.

'You play that?' asked Goli, surprised.

'When I'm lonely at home,' Fatemeh told her. 'It's not so nice to be the only child. I have this little companion and I like its music. I'm not allowed to play it when my father's in, but he usually comes home late so I often play it at dusk, when our house sinks into a deadly silence.'

Zareen returned with her dayereh, a large hand-drum with lots of jingles around the sides. Fatemeh put the harmonica to her mouth, her long, stretched fingers curved around its tiny body and blew into it, a breath like a ripe pomegranate bursting open and the red juice pouring out.

Zareen held the dayereh between her hands above her left shoulder, her fingers resting firmly on the edges of the bright skin, waiting to begin. Fatemeh played an old folksong with low, melancholy notes. Zareen accompanied her with sharp, slow beats of her fingertips. The notes touched all of them under their skin, and moved them.

Zareen started beating faster, hitting the jingles and shaking them hard. The sharp rhythm of the dayereh no longer fitted with the delicate notes of the folksong that Fatemeh had started, so she changed her tune and harmonised with Zareen's fast, loud music. Their mood was changing, smiles set on their lips, their feet tapped gently. Goli hummed the songs. Malihe looked at her, her lips and throat were healed. She thought, young women's wounds heal quickly. Malihe joined in, whistled, shaking her head and shaping the tune with her fingers. The drum beat went on hard and persistent, the harmonica sharp and smooth. Goli clapped and snapped her fingers and Malihe started to move in the small rhythms of dance.

'Come on Goli, you too, dance,' shouted Zareen, encouraging.

Two small heads came through the door, 'You're too noisy, we can't do our homework. Can we come in?' Zareen slowed down.

'No, go back and finish your homework. I'll come and see you in a minute,' she told them. The heads disappeared and she resumed her high tempo. As their mood was rising with the beat of the drum, the sound of a knock at the door interrupted them.

'Those kids, honestly,' she said and ran outside, her dayereh in her hand.

Fatemeh slowed her harmonica; their movements and whistling stopped. Serious words could be heard outside. It sounded as if a man were talking to Zareen. They listened hard. After a moment she came back into the room, shoulders hunched, her hands empty and her face blank.

'My dayereh has been confiscated . . . an immoral and dangerous tool for pleasure. Music is against the law. The militia have taken away my dayereh . . . it's been arrested,' she repeated. They looked at one another, speechless and Fatemeh instantly hid her harmonica.

## 7

Goli was haunted by Malihe's story and by her pain. The other events of the day gripped her, their private musical soirée and the confiscation of Zareen's dayereh. Soon they will come to arrest our smiles, she thought. What would legislation forbidding music say? In Islam music enhances pleasure, pleasure rots the mind, corrupts the soul. Are no pleasures allowed to us, not even a little hand-drum? What next?

She thought about Malihe, about the difficult and painful life she had had, a lonely, older woman, her children away, maybe even lost; and then having been imprisoned under the Shah in solitary confinement, threatened with torture. And she thought about her courageous survival. She thought of her with affection, for her fortitude, her graceful patience and her good sense, and she felt uplifted.

She tried to imagine Malihe's children. They must have been just a bit older than Goli was now when they made their decision to leave. She tried to understand them. They must have been clear about what they wanted to do and how to go about it. There must be very few people who make such decisions, who fight for other people's causes. She had difficulty understanding them. She thought of Marjan, of her work and commitment, and began to see her in a new light. Goli felt vaguely guilty and inadequate for not having a more collective purpose, a more international perspective.

On her way home from the university with Marjan she tried to decide whether or not to tell her Malihe's story. Goli hadn't told Marjan or her other friends about her meetings at Ziba Style. She wasn't sure how they would react, what they would say about her regular visits to a hairdresser's salon in the poor south of the city, near the famous, or rather infamous, beggars' cemetery, Mesgar Abad. She didn't know what would come out of all their meetings, or what she wanted from them.

She started to tell Marjan about Malihe and her children, but in a general way. Marjan expressed sympathy with her as a mother but was not much in favour of people going to fight in Palestine, or anywhere else. She had her doubts and expressed them openly. She said she wasn't sure whether such involvement was an act of courage or simply flight from responsibility. Men and women who chose to leave their own country in turmoil and disaster to go to distant lands and fight for others' rights were meddling in Utopian heroism. Her attitude was stiff, and her words were cold and harsh.

Goli was very surprised at the strength of Marjan's dismissal; she realised she had expected Marjan's support, and was disappointed.

'Palestinians don't need a bunch of Iranian novices to go and help them, Marjan said. 'They're fine fighting for themselves. Why aren't these people here to join the revolution, to fight this disastrous backlash? Huh?'

'I don't know, you don't know. But for God's sake don't jump to the conclusion that because they are not here with us they are doing less, or that they're escaping from their "real" commitment.' Goli replied, angry now.

'But look at our state, we are more in need of help and support than the Palestinians today. Why didn't they bring a brigade of Palestinians to fight for us, a brigade of their women to show us how to hit back at the fundamentalists?' Marjan continued.

Goli smiled. Marjan looked at her and smiled too.

'It's not fair to judge people like this, you of all people,' Goli said. 'They couldn't have just dropped everything to hop over here. You're not being realistic. They have their own lives too, you know.'

'What I mean is that sometimes it is easier and more prestigious to fight for someone else's cause, for a distant cause, rather than the small, daily struggles here at home.'

'And I mean that sometimes it is hard, even for socialists, to make the link between what you are fighting for and other people in other places. Some people can't see further than the end of their nose or their wage packet; it's a good thing that other people are taking the kinds of chance that very few of us would.'

'Anyway, who is this woman?' Marjan asked. 'How do you know her?'

Goli was startled. The question brought her back to earth, from her world of ideas and of taking up positions, correct positions. 'It's not important. I don't know her myself,' she said, deciding not to tell Marjan after all.

Mr Hamidi had let the women know that the best time for him to give them a lesson was on the afternoon of the following Wednesday. Due to a protest meeting outside Parliament, most lecturers and students, especially the fundamentalists, would be away. The university would be quiet, and nobody would be using the gym.

This was good news, although the number of women would drop to six, as the rest were joining the protest. Marjan managed cautiously to inform some other women who might be interested and by Wednesday there were eight women who didn't mind taking the risk of being seen with a man in the gym when the university was so quiet. They had all read the photocopied sheets and had tried to memorise the positions.

Mr Hamidi was not a big man but he looked strong. Because of the women, he kept on his tracksuit, which covered his legs and arms. He had advised them to dress sensibly and comfortably, no tight jeans or skirts. He did not want to risk touching the women so he had brought along a colleague with whom he could pair up. He lined up the women and started with warm-up exercises.

Before pairing them off to begin the lesson proper, he expressed sympathy with women and said he had heard that the attacks, especially on single women at night, were growing. He thought it was important that women should learn to defend themselves. He stressed the importance of being fit and strong, and of using the best and fastest methods of self-defence in a given situation. For instance, he pointed out, there is no use shouting for help if a woman is grabbed in a dark road surrounded by office blocks. She would simply be wasting her precious energy. At this, Goli thought back to that horrible night and her knees shook. She held on to Marjan.

Mr Hamidi was continuing, 'If you're in a crowded bus or street and you feel a man is pestering or molesting you, then shout. He'll be startled and embarrassed and will leave you in peace. Again your energy is very important. Don't waste it. If you're trapped in a park or an empty office, don't scream. Avoid getting tangled up with him, wasting your energy. Think fast, be very calm, and act fast too. Then you can surprise him. Don't be afraid of a big man, or a muscley, sporty type. They fall down just as quickly if you know the tactics.'

He then showed them a few moves with his colleague, who became the attacker, as he was the larger of the two. As he grabbed Mr Hamidi's hands from behind, Mr Hamidi very calmly and strongly pushed his assailant's hands down and, with one fast push, he freed his own hands. Then he turned and hit the other man in the balls before he'd straightened up. It was simple but very effective. He demonstrated it a couple of times and then asked the women to try it with their partners. He went round to each of them, correcting their positions.

Another move he showed them was with the victim down on the ground and the attacker holding her with one hand while taking off her trousers or skirt with his other hand. He demonstrated this with his partner. Calmly, he lifted up his head and made as if to bite his assailant's neck, a big bite. 'Bite as hard as you can,' he told them. In another example the attacker was on top trying to take off his trousers. Mr Hamidi pushed his feet into the attacker's belly and toppled him off.

At first the women practised nervously, frightened of hurting one another, but they soon got the hang of it and at the end of the lesson they were exhausted but eager to go on. Mr

Hamidi promised that he would get in touch with them if an opportunity arose for another lesson.

As they were leaving Goli approached him and asked if it was possible for him to give private tuition at her house or at Marjan's house. He told her that he would think about it and let them know. Goli was delighted that he hadn't rejected it outright, as was Marjan, and they thought of asking one or two other women. In the meantime they agreed to exercise regularly, Goli cycling, Marjan running.

It was a long way from Goli's house to Zareen's, but when Malihe phoned her to say that her suit was ready, Goli immediately got a cab to Seh-Rahe-Jaleh. When she arrived they were all there, a lovely clean sofreh, beautifully embroidered, spread out and the samovar steaming away surrounded by cut-glass tumblers and colourful sweets.

'Oh, such preparation, so elaborate. What's happening? Who's celebrating?' Goli cried out.

'We are,' Zareen replied. 'We're celebrating your entry into manhood.' They all laughed.

'Oh, sohan! What a treat . . . I love it,' cried Goli. 'Who's been visiting the mullas' home town?'

'We were given it, or rather my father was by one of his colleagues. It's especially good,' said Fatemeh taking some.

Goli didn't wait for the tea, instead took a piece of the sohan, 'Oommm, oommm, so nutty and crunchy, delicious. Pity these lovely sweets come from that sick hole of a town.'

Fatemeh was quick to reply, 'It's not a hole of a town, it's a nice place – the shrine of Masomeh is supposed to predate Islam. Anyway it's good for all these men, going to her shrine and falling at Masomeh's feet. I've heard that one of the columns of her shrine is in the form of a naked woman who holds a sprig of wheat between her breasts.'

'I bet the mullas love that!' cried Goli. They all laughed. The tea went round.

'When are you going to try your suit on Goli?' asked Zareen. 'Come on, stop moving from foot to foot!'

Goli went behind the curtain to put on the trousers, and then slipped into the jacket. She emerged a new person. The others stared, their mouths open. Goli walked up and down, up and down, in front of them, her shoulders straight, head up, firm steps, while they watched her unblinking.

'You've finished off all the sohan! I've been cheated!' Goli said it in her new, deep voice, and sat down.

'What if they find out?' she asked.

'I've checked that,' Fatemeh said. There's nothing in the law that says wearing men's clothes is illegal.'

'Who listens to the law?' Zareen replied.

'The fundamentalists are a law unto themselves,' said Malihe. 'But the news says that they're going to change it all anyway. I bet they're getting ready to do it now.'

'Well, it doesn't need much changing. Our law is already based on the Quran.' Fatemeh said.

'Revolutions are supposed to be a means of moving forward, but ours is moving backwards, and proud of it too,' Malihe commented.

'What's the plan? Who are we going to catch?' Zareen turned to Goli.

'I don't know. You see when I suggested it, I thought it was a good idea, but to go out like this, my God . . . I'm nervous now,' Goli admitted.

'I'd have to ask my old man to mind the kids but I don't mind going with you, once or twice . . . Fati, can we borrow your car? Do you mind?' Zareen queried.

'No, take the car, as long as I can have it back the next day.'

'You can drive?' Goli asked, surprised.

'What is this?' cried Zareen. 'Whether I can drive, whether Fati can play the harmonica; you northerners . . . '. She was angry. 'Soon you'll be asking if I can understand your language, or read the papers. What is all this prejudice from you middle-class university prats?'

'I didn't mean it.' Goli was embarrassed.

'You bloody did mean it. Your eyes speak better than your mouth.'

Goli was silenced. She began to chew her fingernails. The faint sound of crunching and chewing turned everybody's heads towards her but she was looking at the cotton rug on the floor, her eyes fixed on the geometrical pattern.

After a few moments she looked up at Zareen. 'You're right,' she said. 'I was surprised at you being able to drive. I was surprised at Fati playing the harmonica the other day. It's true . . . I admit it. As you said, we middle-class university prats have a very narrow, limited, stereotypical idea of other people, of everyone who's not like us.'

'Which reflects more on you than on us,' Malihe murmured, thoughtfully.

'Yes, it does. It's more exposure of my narrow-mindedness . . . but that's not an excuse not to do something about it. I have learnt a lot since I met you and I'm still learning, not just about politics, the horror of the new revolutionary government, but also about my own personal shortcomings as a woman. But I *am* learning, you are my friends now . . . please be patient with me.' She was humble, ill at ease, in a minority of one and in need of acceptance.

'Come on, you are my friend,' Zareen started.

'Let's get back to what we were saying,' Fatemeh suggested.

'Yes, we all have faults . . . and will all be exposing ourselves sooner or later, so let's get back to our plan,' Malihe agreed.

And so it was arranged that Zareen would call Goli once she had settled a night on which she could leave her children with their father.

'I wonder how you will charm your old man to agree to that,' Malihe said.

'If you want to know, stay behind after these girls have gone, and I'll tell you,' Zareen replied, looking at Malihe mischievously.

Taking Goli's hand, Fatemeh told them, 'Don't you corrupt her. She's our brain and strategist . . . You married women! It's no wonder we've been warned not to associate with you!'

'I'll corrupt you too, if you stay on,' Zareen replied, laughing.

'I'm going, and taking Goli with me.' Fatemeh stood up. 'Haven't you heard about all the things these hairdressers do with their clients?' she said to Goli jokingly.

'No, tell me,' Goli said, playing the innocent.

'Oh, I will. Come on.'

# 8

In the thickening evening Zareen and Goli, well
covered in their chadors, checked the streets from behind the
heavy curtain of Ziba Style. There was no one about and all
the heavy cotton curtains in the other houses were drawn.
They left the salon quickly and tiptoed to where Fatemeh had
left her car for them earlier that evening. They drove off
quietly.

'We mustn't drive slowly or cautiously,' Goli said. 'Be as
reckless and as inconsiderate as the other drivers.' She was
excited and nervous.

'I will. Give me a chance,' Zareen told her. 'I'm just getting
used to the car.'

The plan was that they would stop when they found a quiet
spot, take off their chadors and become a man and a woman
driving to visit friends.

'Somehow it's more relaxed in this area,' Goli commented.
'Although there are more soldiers and pasdars, there's less
surveillance, less guarding of the women; it's not as vicious
and thorough as the north of the city.'

'Well, here women guard themselves,' Zareen replied.
'Their sense of danger is much stronger, they can smell it
coming a year in advance.'

'Are you condoning them? excusing their collaboration with
this system and their cowardice?' asked Goli.

'I am not. Let's turn off here, it looks empty and safe. We
can take off our chadors.'

She turned into a narrow lane, they got changed and after

a minute or two they joined the traffic on the main road. Suddenly Goli, who had been looking through the side mirror, trying to catch a glimpse of herself, realised that the car behind seemed to be edging closer.

'Here they come,' said Zareen, who had slowed down. 'They're laughing their heads off. Keep cool, don't look up.'

Coming bumper to bumper with them, the car behind suddenly passed them, its occupants shouting, 'Can we borrow your wife?'

Goli was half-frozen with fear, and Zareen was nervous too, her hands and legs trembling. She quickly turned into a side road and stopped for a second. They turned on the light, looked in the mirror and straightened their clothes. They put their hands over their hearts, which were pounding, as a waterfall beats down on to rocks.

'We'll be all right in a minute . . .' said Goli.

'I'm weak. God help us, imagine if they had crashed into us and . . .' Zareen replied. She looked at Goli. 'But you look convincing, except that your hair is too long and you don't have a moustache. Shall we park the car and walk?'

But Goli wasn't ready for that. 'Not yet,' she said. 'I haven't got my breath back. Let's drive around a bit more. Luckily, the darker it gets, the fewer cars there will be on the road.'

'And the more men,' said Zareen.

They started driving up into the district of Shahbaz, towards Jaleh Square where shooting during a peaceful demonstration had marked a turning point in the revolution. The walls were still covered with red slogans. Burned-out cinemas still stood in this bastion of fundamentalism. In this district the middle and working classes lived on different sides of the roads.

In the residential area men were still returning from work, slow and hunched into themselves. Some were carrying shopping, some had only their empty lunchboxes under their arms. Women and children were still queuing at the bakery, the fresh smell of baking bread wafted through the car. Groups of youths hung around the corners of dark alleys, chatting, showing off their verbal strength, displaying their claim to their territory, or boasting about their day's achievements.

'Men going home after work look so tired, so hunchbacked, so preoccupied . . . revolution makes people tired, doesn't it?' Goli said.

'Very tired, it seems it takes so much out of them that when the revolution goes wrong they don't have the energy to put it right,' Zareen replied joylessly.

To Goli who had not been to this part of the city before, this was a different world from that of her quiet, green sub-urban home in the north of it. She was watching the streets, the narrow treeless side alleys, the crowd, the noise, the tired men, poorly dressed children, glimpses of women in veils and the lightless, airless, small houses packed up against one another. She wondered at so much deprivation and at all the hope the revolution had dashed. Zareen told her that women in this area would not usually go out at night although if they did, the militia would not harass them in their own locality.

'We're coming into another quarter now,' she said. It was behind the Parliament and Sepah-Salar Mosque, still on the poor side.

Zareen turned into the large Parliament Square.

On the top of the wrought-iron gates to the Parliament building hung a perfectly balanced set of scales, a symbol of the constitutional revolution.

'Symbols live a long time,' Zareen commented as they passed by.

'They're very small scales, more for weighing gold or pearls; they should be in a shop, not hanging there so precariously in mid-air,' said Goli.

'The shopkeepers' revolution ends in government by the mullas,' Zareen murmured.

There were a lot of men in the square, all crowding around the coloured fountains. As well as the pasdars, shopkeepers and workers, there were crowds of armed and uniformed men: soldiers with their guns; militia with their Kalashnikovs, guards with their machine-guns and pistols; police with their batons and their guns; gendarmes with their revolvers and knives; and finally traffic wardens armed only with whistles.

'So many weapons – how will we cope with them?' Zareen asked Goli.

'With karate, I hope,' Goli replied.

'I hope so too,' Zareen said. 'Let's get out of here. The sight of all these uniforms frightens me.'

Further on they went down into Shah-Abad where the Shah-Dokht secondary school dominated the square.

'I went to that school,' said Goli, 'Isn't it huge and impressive – it's named after the princess. You know the zealots are demanding that a large girls' school so near to Parliament has too much prominence, and that it should be a boys' school – the girls would be moved into a smaller building in the back streets.'

'I guess we should be thankful that they didn't set it on fire,' Zareen said.

'Yes,' Goli replied. 'I heard once a historian friend of my father say that the toilets in the school are full of foetuses and candles . . . bloody men! Just because it has a long militant history.'

'Well, how else do women go down in oral history . . .' Zareen sounded depressed. She turned sharply into Ameer Kabeer towards Toopkhaneh Square (named after the cannon house), which was now called Sepah Square. They drove round the square, passing the Ministry of Culture. The Ministry of Justice, with its magnificent neo-classical front pillars caught Goli's eyes, spectacular in their contrast to the crowded street market below. Zareen was interested in the Ministry of Justice and the court of law which, like the gates to the Parliament building, had a pair of scales, but they were larger and were held by a statue of a woman. Goli wondered about the empty scales hanging in mid-air. What was the history of the symbol, its use, and abuse? How much weighing and loading had gone on? Who had invented it and where and why?

They drove back, in the vicinity of Bazar, towards Shah-Abad, passing the Ministry of Education. It seemed to Goli that there was a distance of only about forty metres between Sepah and Shah-Abad squares, and apparently not much difference in terms of the mixture of class composition. Both places were hectic, buzzing with people, most of them men. Each place had a shopping area centred around a large square with historical connections, and each had its own civil buildings. Sepah Square was a larger, older, dustier and more varied place than Shah-Abad, which was a smaller, newer, and clearly more upwardly mobile place. Parliament Square and the adjoining Shah-Abad was full of cafés – including the large, well-known cake and tea restaurant called Khayyam, which the zealots were demanding be closed down because it was the meeting place for many young women and men – snack bars, ice-cream parlours, photographic shops, small family textile workshops where women worked, and small passages containing boutiques. The street sellers in Shah-Abad sold Marlboro and Winston cigarettes, photo albums and lighters and so on.

Sepah was one of the gates of old Tehran, and the area around it was full of offices, institutions, printers and bookshops. The Tehran telecom office was there (where nearly all the workers were women), the main post office and the famous Dar-Ol Foonoon boys' college, surrounded by a large army barracks. The square itself was adorned with fountains and statues of leaders on galloping horses. The street sellers sold fruit, cooked food for quick lunches or suppers for the workers, and also sold men's secondhand clothes. Secondhand books were spread all over the pavement and up the walls – people looked through these more than they bought them, and poor men leaned on the wall and read them. On the long Persepolis style stairs of the post office male translators sat, illiterate women crouching down beside them, having their letters read and written for them, and around them stamp collectors were spread out like a small market.

Goli saw a world of difference between the men in the two squares. Shah-Abad, the newer place, was like its occupants – the various armed men: younger, brasher, more eager. The men were also students, street sellers, businessmen, and even though they were from different parts of Iran and from different classes, they looked the same: city animals. Not many wore the colourful traditional costumes or headgear or spoke their regional languages. They were fashionable, urbane, and did not openly harass women. They rushed around, going backwards and forwards, using the pavement for standing around but not for sitting. They wore a different style of shirt. The women in Shah-Abad moved around more easily. They made eye contact more readily with men, wore fewer veils, more make-up.

The men in Sepah were older, more resigned; they were poorer and from rural and tribal parts of Iran. Some wore their own colourful national costumes, spoke their own languages and looked either like aimless tourists or hopelessly in search of work. They were more sedentary, sitting around, eating, resting or just looking and waiting. While the older men in Sepah were humbler and gentler, the younger ones in Shah-Abad were louder, rougher and on the make. Continuous bargaining gave the atmosphere a weary and shifting aspect. There were fewer women around in Sepah and a definite class line was drawn between the telecom workers and the veiled shoppers. Here women were more often physically molested.

Goli thought about the men in the two squares and the differences between them while Zareen was driving carefully up towards Sepah-Salar. She suddenly turned to Zareen and asked, 'Which men do you think are more violent to women, the men in Sepah Square or the men in Shah-Abad?'

'I hadn't thought about that, I was thinking about the Ministry of Education and what people do in that huge office. What difference does it make anyway? Seeing those scales has given me ideas about weighing things up.'

'I just thought there may be a bit of a difference,' Goli continued.

'Yes, I guess there is. One assumes men in poorer areas are more violent, but it isn't true, is it? Middle-class men hide it better. The men in Shah-Abad do look more confident, better dressed—'

'—and they do have more buying power,' interrupted Goli. 'They objectify women more; I think they feel more alienated and gender-bound. But I agree, violence isn't class-bound. Look at Sepah-Salar Mosque, isn't it amazing? Is it Oajar?

'I'm off religious monuments, even the old artistic ones,' said Zareen. 'I'll stop somewhere in the residential area, park the car and we'll get out and start walking. Pluck up as much courage as you can in the next two or three minutes.'

The area between Jaleh and Shah-Abad was lower middle-class and mostly residential. It was like a maze – full of alleys: small, long, wide, short, narrow and tiny, some leading to each other, some leading to dead-ends. Wall to wall unlit alleys, each black with slogans, printed, handwritten, painted over and rewritten: 'Death to . . . '; crossed out and 'Long live . . . ' added, over and over.

'We're looking for a number 30, Mr and Mrs Golhari,' said Zareen as they got out of the car, 'in case we look suspicious and somebody asks us what we're doing here; so off we go.' They set off down a well-built road which soon led to a grim alley.

'As a man and a woman you should be going first, act masculine and talk it,' Zareen said, but she wasn't convinced that Goli could carry it off, especially as she herself was taller and bigger, and this fact didn't inspire confidence in Goli. However, they walked together, and didn't speak, just looked around. A single passer-by went past, fast, and they realised that they were too slow and casual. They walked faster and the alleys suddenly got darker, echoing with low sounds, voices, faint music or the sounds of TVs filtering out from the houses. They heard some loud arguments, women's voices raised, talking to their kids. The dark alleys went on and on, without end. It was a moonless night, ominous, with a dull sky, hardly a star. They went on, wondering if they would see anyone: there had been only a few passers-by. Doors, windows – with heavy curtains which imprisoned the light inside – they passed them all. Most of the doors to the houses were the grotesque, iron gates that had replaced the lovely old carved wooden doors. They went from one dark alley to the next, quiet, ghostlike. What incidents, tensions, traumas and uncertainties went on behind the walls? Every sound that broke the silence gave Zareen and Goli a start; each knock, each opening of a door, each time a curtain was drawn or a voice raised. Each was a menace to them. But still they saw few people and no militia, guards or vigilante zealots.

They walked nervously into another alley which was darker

than usual, walking by the wall. No tiny ray of light escaped from any window here. They groped along into the unknown territory, the weightless dark enveloping them. Suddenly a noise came from the distance.

Goli was startled. 'What was that?'

'Keep calm, and walk normally,' Zareen tried to reassure her. The faint noise grew louder, it was the sound of a chain, a rusty, creaking chain. Goli stopped breathing, grabbed Zareen. A tiny moving light appeared from nowhere and moved towards them faster and faster, making a hole in the thick barricade of darkness. The chain noises came closer, the light grew stronger, a shadow of a figure on a bicycle was riding in their path. Zareen stopped and leaned flat against the wall as there was not enough space for pedestrians and cyclists in the narrow lane. Goli, horrified to see a young man on a bicycle coming towards them, hid behind Zareen. The cyclist passed, stopped further up the lane by a door and, before turning the bike lights off, looked back at them. There was not enough light for him to see the women clearly. Zareen tried to pull Goli from behind her. After pausing for a few moments the cyclist opened the front door, turned off the lights of the bicycle and pulled it inside the house. With the return of darkness and quietness, Zareen sighed with great relief, grabbed Goli's hand angrily and walked on without saying a word, passing the cyclist's house and turning into another lane.

Once they were safely three or four lanes away, she released Goli's hand and hissed in her face. 'Woman . . . why did you hide behind me, like a lost fish? We looked so suspicious, so damned suspicious. You're a man . . . trying to catch a few militia and teach them a lesson or two . . . you gooseberry!'

'All right, all right, be bloody high and mighty . . . I just lost my nerve. I'm sorry, but it's my first time . . . you don't have to be so insulting.' Goli walked off, offended. Zareen followed, intending to go back to the car in a roundabout way so that they wouldn't go through the same alleys and lanes and hopefully would not meet the same cyclist again.

They went on through the night in silence, without a word, or a sign, keeping their distance and ignoring one another.

Light and noise, were signs warning them of people, but they hardly saw anybody, and especially no pasdars, no armed fanatics, no dangerous men lurking about. Perhaps these alleys, being residential, were secure enough for the women who lived there, and also for women who walked there. Zareen seemed to know where she was going, she didn't hesitate much or look back, possibly she was still angry with Goli. Goli just followed her, having no clue where they were going, waiting in anticipation of the safety of the car. Zareen slowed down and waited for Goli to reach her. She put her hand around her waist and whispered an apology for the careless things she had said. Goli took her arm and nodded. 'You are dreadful sometimes.'

Suddenly at the turn of a corner they heard noises, coming from the adjoining alley, lit only by a dim light from the balcony of a house. They crept on, the noises becoming more audible, voices of a woman, a man, children. They found the house where the voices came from and moved to the window. They could not see anything. The voice of the woman was crying, pleading, and an angry voice of a man was shouting. Goli stuck her ears to the window.

'My son is bleeding! Heartless woman!' Lace curtains and another heavy thick curtain shielded the view, and only the sound of heavy feet, slaps, a struggle, his scream, 'Leave, it is my fault for letting you work, you should sit at home, look after my son, I pay you.' And her response, pleading, 'No, . . . just a few days . . . the nursery will open . . . four days they said . . . '

'I don't care. I don't need your money.' The woman was now crying, sobbing incessantly. They tried to find a crack behind the white lace and the heavy material behind it, to look into the room and see what was happening, but they could see nothing except for the shine of a faint light. They stood there together listening to the sounds of crying, sobs, anger, moans, insults. The woman's voice was faint now, 'No, I can't, I don't want to . . . '

Goli turned to Zareen and made a gesture as if to knock. Zareen gestured back, no. Goli insisted, moved her hand angrily. Zareen took her hand, moved it down and shook her head

Why, Goli asked, her hands moving up again, her fingers opening out. Zareen moved her fingers and pointed them to her head, signalling to Goli that she must be crazy. Nobody was around, nobody from the other houses came out or drew their curtains to see or to enquire. It must be a familiar event. The last sounds were dying down. As the sounds faded Zareen took Goli's hand, worrying that she would after all knock on the door, and pulled her away. Goli was reluctant and resisted, but Zareen walked fast, dragging her on.

'Thank God the car is here. Our box of safety,' Zareen sighed as she got in and threw herself into the driving seat.

'Yes, safe, relatively.' Goli got in on the other side. 'Why on earth didn't we knock on that door and question the man?'

'Because she is his wife, and he could tell us to go to hell,' Zareen countered.

'He might not have done. Perhaps he would have been surprised that we bothered to enquire and he would have calmed down and stopped it,' Goli suggested.

'Yes, perhaps he would have stopped now but there'd be a repeat performance tomorrow.'

'But we are here tonight and we could have interrupted his violence.' Goli was insistent.

'. . . Look,' said Zareen, 'you're not being sensible at all. We can't interfere in the domestic life of other people, not like this. And anyway, you wouldn't have knocked on that door yourself – you wanted me to interfere while you hid behind me . . . But that's not the point . . . Domestic violence is happening, has always been happening: *we* can't change it.'

'We could have done, perhaps in this instance – if we had tried.'

'I would feel much better doing that sort of thing around my house, and not in a strange area,' said Zareen wearily. 'Have you forgotten why we're here? We're not here to reform individual husbands. What can we gain by that? He could have turned against us, and what would we have done then, if he had attacked us? You can't save individual men or women.'

'We're talking about domestic violence here,' hissed Goli. 'I don't know where your sympathies lie.'

'I'm tired, shattered,' was Zareen's answer. 'My sympathy is now with me and you, and with making sure we get home safe tonight.'

Goli squirmed in her seat, drawing up her knees and squaring them off with her arms. She was very upset.

,'Perhaps this is why we are warned about and prohibited from being out in the streets at night. The danger is in our knowing these things go on.'

'Of course everything has to do with knowing and not knowing,' Zareen replied. 'Just when we thought we hadn't seen a pasdar, a member of the armed militia, fanatics waiting to catch women, just when you think streets can be safer for women, those very unsafe streets are shown to be safer – than women are in their homes . . . how very safe, safe, safe,' she mumbled to herself.

She started the engine. They were going to return home via main streets as Zareen wanted to take Goli through another part of her district. She drove very cautiously although the roads were nearly empty. They passed the large grounds of the palace which had belonged to Ashraf, the twin sister of the Shah. The place was dark and lifeless – what a contrast to its heyday. There were many guards walking around here, in twos and threes, roaming the area, guns hanging from their shoulders. Goli wondered about their over-sized green jackets: were they real army jackets, so fashionable at the time in the university? Being green, of course, the Islamic colour, they were doubly sacrosanct.

Zareen's eyes checked the road as they cruised along it. On the pavement in front she saw a suspicious figure, hazy in the distance, a woman who looked lost. She slowed down and told Goli to watch the woman. She was wrapped in her chador and was looking back after every few steps.

'Let's follow her,' Zareen said. She parked the car just as the woman went into a dark alley. They got out and looked around carefully before they also turned into it. They walked slowly behind her in the dark empty alley. Her black chador mingled with the darkness, and sometimes she disappeared into it like a ghost. Finally, at a turning she stopped and hid in the shadows. They approached her cautiously. She was a young woman and she was leaning against the wall casually, but when she saw them she panicked.

'Who are you?' Her voice was high, nervous.

'Who are *you*? Why are you standing here alone like this?' Goli asked.

'Look, these streets are very dangerous,' added Zareen. 'Can we help. You must go home . . . we can give you a lift if you need one . . . you can't stand here like this—'

Goli went towards the young woman and reached for her hands to pull her away, but caught the edge of her chador. It fell open and she saw, a barely visible blur in the dark, her white body nearly naked underneath it. Goli was stunned.

'I'm okay,' snapped the young woman. 'You go away, don't touch me, you are—'

'We won't hurt you. It's too dangerous for you here, please be sensible . . . the armed militia are everywhere . . . they might hurt you.' Zareen tried to reason with her, but already suspected something strange was up.

'You go! Nobody will hurt me. I am waiting for some friends, and they won't come here if they see you. Please go . . . you are harassing me!'

'Are you expecting a man, perhaps one of the militia here? Now?' Zareen decided to confront the young woman with her worst suspicion.

'You're being a nuisance. The pasdars are all right, they are my friends. They know me. Please, I beg of you, go! They won't come if they see you here.'

'But what about the neighbours?' Goli was still agitated. 'What if somebody sees you? Will you be all right?'

'Go!' cried the young woman, trying to get rid of them as quickly as possible.

Zareen grabbed Goli's hand, 'Let's go, we're no help here. She knows what she's doing. Come on.'

Reluctantly they returned in a rush to the car, hoping not to bump into any pasdars. They left the unknown woman in the belly of that mysterious night and at the mercy of the militia. They got into the car and Zareen moved it to a shadowed spot under a huge tree. They waited to see what would happen. Soon two young pasdars appeared. One stood outside the alley, guarding it, and the other went in. After a few minutes he came out, looking self-consciously about him, straightening his jacket, and then he stood on guard while his mate went into the alley. He too returned after a few minutes and continued on their patrol.

The young woman came out, wrapped tightly in a black chador, hidden and anonymous, and walked in the opposite direction. It had all happened in about ten minutes.

Their bodies stiff with concentration, they relaxed and sat back in their seats. Goli held her head in her hands, distressed, nervous and silent. Zareen was sad and subdued, but not shocked. She sat still and looked at Goli. The two women stayed separated, distant, each wrapped in their own emotions and thoughts for a while. Neither tried to console the other. They didn't know what to say. This was not what they had expected.

'Come on, we must move,' said Zareen. 'The night has come to a close for us . . . What an end . . . hmm.'

'I know.'

'Is this what happens in the dead of night? How women are swallowed up in the vicious belly of this deadly night,' Zareen thought of all the things that befall women at night.

'Yeah,' said Goli.

'Say *something* please.' Zareen turned to Goli. 'Why are you speechless? Come on . . . Haven't you seen a prostitute before?'

'I have—' Goli was still holding her head in her hands, as if squeezing her skull would push her troubles out of her mind.

'Are you so naïve and out of touch with the reality of women's lives, are you so hidden in the walls of the university and among the tons of books, that by seeing one prostitute you have lost your mind, shocked to speechlessness. Are you?' Zareen was impatient and angry. She started the car. 'I'm taking you home.'

'No, don't, just take me to the Dar-vazeh-Sheemran. I'll get a cab from there. I am not naïve, it's not about being out of touch with the reality of women's lives in this vicious city. It's not that. It is something else . . . something different.'

'Don't you want to tell me now? All right. Let's go – we

can talk about it later with the others.' Zareen gave up, feeling suddenly exhausted. She wanted to go home.

Goli was resigned now. They drove up Shahbaz towards Dar-vazeh-Sheemran.

'I'll give you a lift,' Zareen insisted. She didn't want to let Goli go by public transport.

'Thank you. I feel safe in this car,' Goli said quietly.

Zareen touched her shoulder, and then the soft and naked part of her neck. Goli was warm, the moment was intimate, Zareen smiled. Goli smiled back. On the long wide road to Sheemran Zareen drove beneath the tall, leafy umbrellas of the Tabrizi trees, which offered them some protection from the night.

# 9

Zareen had put the samovar on in the back room, and had tidied the salon. Her husband usually came home after eight, and the salon closed at six, so there would be two hours to talk. Malihe was already there stitching up a dress that she had cut out that afternoon. She was complaining about the colour and the pattern of what she was making: 'There's no more joy in making made-to-measure clothes for anybody any more, I can't influence them to choose the fashion that suits their body best because the regulations only allow dull materials, uniform styles, and plain shapes and lengths. Something to depress and denigrate women as if they hadn't had enough already. The authorities are afraid of a few nice stitches, some colour, soft delicate cotton, delightful style, something new to be pleased about, and proud to have on. And for me the pleasure in making something beautiful and the pride in seeing it worn – there's none of that in these straight, long, dark sacks I'm told to sew up . . . Imagine, an order from above telling women what to wear . . . ' Malihe went on, talking mostly to herself.

The radio droned on. It was Mulla Haj Ali with his special praise for women. Whenever Zareen heard the word 'women' she turned the radio up hoping it would be about something useful: 'You dear and brave sisters who alongside men secured the victory of Islam—'

'Nonsense!' Zareen went to turn it off.

'No, Zareen, don't! It's not nonsense. It's a very calculated and effective piece of political oratory. Let's hear him – after all, a lot of women could fall for it.'

Zareen stopped and looked at Malihe. 'It still is nonsense,' she muttered.

'I thank you women of Iran and Qum. You came to the streets with your little children and supported Islam with your enthusiastic demonstrations. You heroic women were pioneers in this victory. You encouraged the men, we are all indebted to the braveries of you lion-hearted women. Islam has a special view of women – you have more rights than men over this movement, you foster great men in your lap. Tomorrow is the birthday of our lady Fatemeh Zahra – Women's Day for the brave women in this country. She was a heavenly woman, a human being in the full sense of the word, a total reflection of it, a total reality of it, a total reality of humanity. She was not an ordinary woman. All characteristics that can be thought of as pertaining to humanity and to women are manifested in this woman: a woman of morality, divine – angelic – appearance, of a heavenly chasteness; all are assembled in this woman. A woman who embodies all the wishes of the prophet. A woman who obeyed all the desires of the prophet, a woman who – had she been a man – would have been a prophet, the prophet of the God, Muhammad. You honourable women, you are free to do the correct things, to go to universities, and the like. Everyone is free to do these things. But if anyone wants to do something against chastity, or that is harmful to the nation, a stop will be put to that. This is progress. You honourable women wake up, be careful, do not be deceived. Do not be deceived by these devils who want you to come out on the street. Women of Iran! You are such courageous beings! With limitless power you can defeat the Satanic power—'

Goli and Fatemeh were standing at the door to the back room listening, when Zareen noticed them and turned off the radio.

'We have had enough praise for one day.'

'How right he is,' said Goli. 'We need to recover our power and courage.'

'Of course they don't want women on the street any more, unless it's on their behalf.' Fatemeh followed Goli in.

'You didn't hear the half of it,' said Zareen. 'You missed the precious points about chastity, obedience and all the heavenly bits – I felt quite angelic myself.'

She welcomed them in and offered them comfortable places next to herself and Malihe. She offered them tea and they warmed their hands around the glasses, looking at each other with hesitation for a while, impatient for each other's news. Who was going to start? And with what? The sound of hot tea being drunk – faint whistles and sucks – went on until Goli said, 'Last night, when Zareen and I were driving around, we saw a young prostitute who was waiting for two boy soldiers, and they just did it in the corner of the alley. We talked to her before it happened, we tried to send her home. But she begged us to go and leave her alone. Because we were wasting her time, being a nuisance to her and meddling in her business.'

'It's nothing new to see women in dark streets making money,' said Malihe. 'Don't think just because red-light districts like Shahre-Nu exist that all women prostitutes are gathered there. That's just one small centre. And then there are lots of women who have their own flats and rich clients, they don't need to do it on street corners. Let's not assume that the revolution has eradicated prostitution, or is going to do so.'

'It is shocking, but we mustn't be shocked, mustn't see the women as guilty,' added Fatemeh, 'we must see the cause—'

'I think she knows all that,' interrupted Zareen. 'There's something else. What is it that's bothering you? Why should such an everyday incident affect you so much?' She addressed Goli, assuming that Goli was not bothered by the prostitute herself or by the morality of the situation. Goli heard her, nodded her head, but did not answer. They were all silent, waiting for Goli to speak. She looked at the samovar, the glasses of tea, and then around the room.

'You're right.' Goli lingered over the word 'right', and then continued, 'It's not that young prostitute. It's me, I'm shocked and confused. After what happened that night, I don't know when violence isn't violence any more. If some women accept it, give in to it, profit by it, is it still violence? I don't know any more. I have been looking for a way to avenge the pasdars, their violence to women, their power over them, their endless harassment and intimidation, and now that incident has put a damper on me, has shaken my logic.'

'But why? I don't understand you.' Fatemeh had no idea what Goli was on about.

'If a woman needs money and allows her body to be violated, isn't that violence?' Goli asked. 'But we couldn't take up her case, punish the pasdars, beat the hell out of them, take their money and give it to her, because she didn't want us to.'

'Of course she didn't want us to.' Zareen said. 'That's her regular bread – beating up the pasdars wouldn't have done anything for her.'

'Well, when is violence not violence then? What is the difference between what happened to me and what happens to that young woman?'

'Miles of difference – you were forced against your will—' cried Fatemeh.

'But I have no will,' interrupted Goli. 'The state doesn't allow me a will, a choice, a right to protest. So my rape is not violence against me, and therefore neither is prostitution a violence against women.'

'But we don't accept that,' answered Zareen, 'we say it *is* violence and we will not accept it. We will not obey.'

'But obedience comes in many forms,' insisted Goli. 'Women have to obey for financial reasons, for moral and social obligations—'

'Like their responsibility to their children,' Malihe interrupted. 'Women obey for love – they don't want to but life is much easier if they do. So where do you start from?' Malihe sometimes took her time to get round to saying something and then made a statement that threw everybody back to where they had started.

'We start from ourselves, from our own experience, that is what I think,' Fatemeh said.

'I don't know what we can do,' Goli persisted. 'It is not so simple any more—'

'It's simple enough – an eye for an eye!' All eyes turned to Fatemeh and her injured eye for a couple of seconds. She stopped talking and looked down, embarrassed.

Goli thought, an obvious wound doesn't need explaining, but inner wounds are not so easy to talk about. How can you talk about rape? But I have to. I have to break its invisibility, its silence. Malihe's voice nudged her out of her personal entanglement and back to the group discussion.

'You can't just take revenge like that – punish one man, or two, or even a battalion of them – there must be a better way than that.'

'I want to,' said Goli.

'How?' Zareen leant forward.

'If I knew that, I wouldn't be sitting here and agonising – gazing at the samovar.'

'We have to focus our intentions and limit our targets – we can't attempt to fight against all violence in our society: physical and mental abuse, rape, wife-battering, prostitution, harassment at work, you name it – and even the suffering of childbirth—'

'Since when is childbirth violence against women?' Zareen cut in on Fatemeh.

'It's painful and dangerous for women, a depressing and unnecessary experience. And this country's birth rate is exploding. It's a burden for life, but women still want children,' finished Fatemeh.

'I disagree with that. Goli is only attacking men and wants to punish them, but you are putting down the nature of womanhood, the base of human history.' Malihe said it to Fatemeh's face while pointing at Goli.

'I don't want only to punish a *few* men, no, that won't be enough. I feel so strongly about it that I haven't set myself a limit!' cried Goli, jumping to her own defence.

'Don't tell me you're plotting it all in here, in Ziba Style, are you?' Zareen struck a light note and they all laughed. 'Of course women collude in their own oppression, they're accomplices,' she continued. 'I will support you – within limits

– I'll even be your chauffeur.' Another light note, but nobody laughed this time.

'I disagree with you,' Goli turned to Fatemeh. 'But it would be good to have your support. I want to do *something*. But I don't want to die, to be a martyr, or rot in gaol, not for any cause, not even for my cause. I want to fight back though, to attack, and live to tell the tale.'

'That's good – life is worth living, even in a den of mullas.' Zareen was suddenly aglow with optimism.

'Why don't you go out more at night, see more for yourselves, learn about the street life, its menaces, its potential, and learn how to fight best,' Malihe suggested.

'That would only make me more depressed and more demoralised. I don't want that,' replied Goli.

'I would actually like to follow a few of these boy soldiers into a dark alley, and beat the hell out of them.' Zareen sounded vehement.

'Didn't know you approved of child battering,' commented Malihe.

'Oh, I do. These kids, these gun-toting kids, preaching Islamic morality when they don't know their arses from their elbows—'

The sound of a door opening startled the women. Zareen looked at the clock.

'God, it's past eight o'clock. Jalal's here. You must all go now, I've got to go. Let yourselves out. See you soon, perhaps tomorrow?'

'Zareen, are you still in the salon?' A man's voice called, and everybody swallowed their breath. She went back into the house and left the women there.

'We must go . . . We were just in the middle of a discussion, perhaps coming up to a kind of conclusion. But we are going to have to wait till next time. God, how did the time pass so quickly? What am I going to eat tonight? Not another omelette.' Malihe murmured the last few words to herself, as they left rapidly, burdened with dangerous new ideas, only half articulated.

# 10

Goli had not seen Marjan much in the past few weeks except at their regular self-defence sessions, which now took place in Goli's house, and which were going very well. She felt sometimes that they were going in their own different directions. Marjan was occupied with the problems of her comrades as the divisions among the left groups were widening and attacks on them growing. Goli had also been busy with her women's group and with the opening of their new women's office in the new premises outside the university.

To start with they had had to do a lot of basic cleaning, painting, washing the windows, getting hold of tables, chairs, typewriters, stationery and also of some very heavy secure locks. All of this took time and energy, especially because it had to be done very secretively. Luckily, though, there were many of them around and with a good, tight rota and the commitment of strong women they had finished the elementary preparation fast and now had a nice little office to themselves. They were very proud of it but sadly they could not put their beautiful photos and posters of and about women in Iran on the walls, nor could they put their name – the Organisation of the Women's Liberation Movement – on the door.

As soon as they started planning for their future political work and activities, creating a rota for job sharing and guarding the office, new problems which they had not envisaged upset their schedule. Every day one worker or even two were late, some arriving after five hours, having been arrested and taken to the Komiteh for questioning, to be released four hours later, if they were lucky enough not to have any political or women's literature with them. This went on nearly every day. Goli was arrested twice on two different days. The experience was frustrating and humiliating. There seemed to be a semi-official no-go area for some people, especially if they looked like students, women's liberation activists, or just like non-fundamentalists.

They began to wonder how long it would be before passes would be instituted in order to restrict their movements, and they began to find ways of avoiding arrest and questioning, to prevent so much of their time and energy going to waste. They produced a detailed street and route plan for each woman, evolved a system of giving lifts, and learned how best to disguise themselves. Some even adopted the disguise of a harassed housewife in a veil carrying tons of groceries.

At about this time Goli asked the group if one of their first papers to come out could be an analysis of the issue of violence, and its diverse manifestation in our society. But, as things were, it looked as if writing and gathering material for publication, and printing it on the premises, was going to be a very slow process. However, Goli felt she had to do some preparatory work for it, and since she had been preoccupied with the prostitution aspect of violence against women, which she had not considered before, she decided to focus on it. She tried to talk to a few people about it but was soon disappointed with their views.

Marjan's response was that women's issues were not anybody's priority any more. Goli reluctantly asked her brothers for their opinions, and first they scorned her for not helping them on their stall as she had done in the past, and then their most useful contribution was to say that it was not separate from class issues and she should read Trotsky on women and the family. She told them to stuff themselves.

She then went to the university and did some research in the social studies faculty, in sociology, on gender relationships, rural women, family relationships, femininity and masculinity. But there was nothing on violence against women under any of these categories, not even any statistics on wife-battering and honour killings. She went to the librarian and complained, and then he had done a search too; but no, he was sorry, titles on such a subject didn't exist. Goli had shouted, 'It does exist! Why isn't it filed and kept here?' As she walked out of the library a bookworm raised his head only to say loudly, 'Another hysterical woman.' Goli heard it and was pleased – great, so you know other ones too, she thought.

She went and bought a load of women's magazines, both secondhand and new and took them home to study. In the women's magazines most of the articles were written by men and men's photos were splattered all over them, even on their covers. What was in them for women? They were addressed only as people who needed to be advised, directed, told to follow the path of the clergy; religious leaders wrote most of these articles. One interesting article caught her attention. It was written by a respected member of the clergy and it was on the subject of care and respect for women in an Islamic society. In it he contradicted the Quran's directive – that if your women don't obey you, beat them – focusing instead on the pride and dignity of women, as *mothers*; and how their sons, potentially the great leaders of the nation, were brought up on their laps, and how 'paradise was beneath their feet', in the words of the Iranian proverb. Goli was infuriated that women were only accorded values and respect if they were mothers to sons, and that only then were they free from violence. Such writers were even more dangerous than husbands. Goli decided to abandon her study and went to see Fatemeh, whose eye was healed now.

They met on the campus and walked out through the concrete book gates.

'Perhaps soon they'll take them down and we'll have a concrete gun, or tank for gates,' commented Goli. 'Once, we the students had control over our movements, our activities, our expression of ideas in this place; there was room to struggle, to debate. Now everything is forced on us, by zealots, down the barrel of a gun. So depressing.' She suggested to Fatemeh that they go through Villa Street into Boulevard, to a quiet coffee shop for a long chat. Fatemeh protested that it was a bit of a walk.

'It's worth it, though,' Goli said. 'The streets are quite nice and the poplars are tall and full – if we can manage to avoid the pasdars, it's a pleasant walk. The university crowd don't go there; but perhaps you don't have any old boyfriends to hide from?'

'No,' Fatemeh said.

Goli was silent, not knowing how to go on from here. Worried about what Goli might be thinking, Fatemeh continued, 'It isn't because of my father or my religious background. I never fancied having one; men don't excite me. I don't see why I should have a boyfriend or get married.'

'Doesn't your mother or your father insist on it?'

'My father doesn't but my mother does, but then I am the only child and they don't want to lose me. What they really want is a grandchild, but apart from that, they're not bothered about the marriage itself. And I always tell them, there is still time to bear children. I think they are divided. They don't want to be alone in their old age and yet they also want grandchildren. So I think I will be all right for a while.'

'Still, they must be quite liberal.'

'Yes. Look, you have to get rid of your idea of what a clergyman's daughter is. I'm not the closed, conservative, orthodox woman that you think I am. I am some of those things, not all . . . '

In the tiny coffee shop they sat around small wooden tables and benches with their hot black coffee at their elbows.

'You know, since that night I've been haunted by the range of violence against women, the forms it takes: rape, wife battering, prostitution, child abuse, incest, street harassment – all, in short, that happens in a 'happy' home and on the mean streets of Tehran. But I can't find anything that explains the reasons, the causes, the effects . . . Why are men violent? Why do they commit such atrocities against women? Don't they get guilty consciences? Don't men have an average human conscience? Where does it come from? Is it in their nature? Is it hormonal? Is it hereditary? Is it a social disease particular to religious societies? Or what? So huge a problem . . . How can we combat it?' Goli sounded exasperated.

'I hope you don't mean you and me?' said Fatemeh.

'No . . . '

'What does Marjan say about it?'

'She says it's a class issue, that radical legislation and public teaching are the ways to solve it. But I don't think I'm going to live another five hundred years – or that many women will be left around by then if it all continues at this rate . . . '

'I don't think we can solve it through intellectual debate now – it's a bit too late for these questions—'

'But I want to know . . . What do you think?'

'Oh, I think the answers are in our history, our type of Islamic patriarchy, in being a vanishing empire, in our social psychology, in the structure of masculinity – and don't ask me what I can do about it, because I don't have that answer.'

'But that doesn't explain fully the attack on you, or on me. I think it's to do with power and control too. Men enjoy having power over women, just as factory owners have over their workers, they like controlling them, they get pleasure from it. But Fatemeh,' Goli continued after a pause, 'why do women submit? Why do they put up with all this brutality?'

'I am very unpopular for what I think—'

Goli went on regardless, 'I don't believe it is just for economic reasons, because of financial dependency on men, or anything like that. I think that's all a cover.'

'I agree.'

'If women wanted to they can live by begging, and anyway most women earn their keep. Why have women allowed this to continue so long? Why have they not dealt with it before, so that we can live in peace and safety?'

'I told you I am unpopular for my views. I think it is—'

'Not love,' Goli leapt in as Fatemeh spoke.

'Children—' Her words got lost in Goli's anticipation.

'That—'

' . . . not alone . . . and emotional needs . . . ' Fatemeh tailed off.

'So what? If women give up their children and their emotional needs they—'

Fatemeh was into her stride now, 'That's not possible, it's a very long term struggle. What would have been possible,

114

now, for us, is if our government took a stand against violence and took measures to protect women and girls.'

'I don't think that would be enough. I thought that out of the revolution would spring so many alternative ways of living, being, loving, having children. That women would be confronted with alternatives, would learn about choice and that there are freer ways of interaction – if they don't like a situation they can move out of it, and create a better one; and that they would have hopes, dreams, desires – and those the wildest of desires; that they would know they are not alone, and don't have to be.

'For me it was all that and more, an Islamic society that put humanity first, people and their needs first. It was going to be humble and generous, a kind and unselfish society, holy and unmaterialistic, like the Zand period, but progressive and loving peace. A caring country, not misogynistic, not manipulative and not tyrannical.'

'We thought, we hoped the revolution would bring it all about . . . '

'We hoped . . . '

'And look at what we have got,' Goli said sadly. 'Is this the only revolution in the world that has retreated totally from its original aims and inspirations?'

'I don't think so,' said Fatemeh wryly, giving a quick glance at her watch and looking worried. 'I must go. I love sitting here and talking with you like this, and questioning the miserable state of this revolution. So many of my comrades have disappeared, you know. They are going underground, because of the vicious attacks on them, because they don't want to give up their arms.'

'Will you go with them?'

'I don't know. I am not sure.' They left the coffee shop and walked back down the boulevard under the heavenly height of the poplar trees, by the noisy cold current of the small stream, with the white-capped mountains behind them. Goli told Fatemeh of her nostalgia for the good old days when she had walked along here with a handsome man, holding hands, hearts beating up like trapped sparrows, feeling passionate and in love. The best moments in her life had been and would be those spent indulging in such sweet feelings for as long as they lasted. Fatemeh whispered to her, as if afraid to say it aloud, 'Do you miss it?'

'I don't know, I guess so.' Fatemeh slipped her arm through Goli's, holding her.

'I think there is something very attractive and seductive about love. Isn't there?' Goli appealed. 'It radiates warmth, intimacy and passion. I don't know why there should be one kind of love, and why one gets that intensity, passion, that sense of walking on the side of the moon only by being in love with another person. I don't know. Yes. I do miss it.'

# 11

That day the streets around Zareen's house were heavily patrolled as a result of a shooting incident between some 'counter-revolutionaries' and the revolutionary guards early that morning, so they heard. The women had a meeting in the salon scheduled for that night and Zareen had been worried all day. She had dimmed the lights in the salon and drawn both the curtains, and was keeping an eye on the street outside impatiently. Soldiers and militia were everywhere and the streets would be more fearsome tonight than on any other previous occasion. She looked through the crack in the curtains every now and then to check who was out there and how they looked. It was difficult to see the faces of the guards but they looked unfamiliar, as if they didn't fit in, not from this district. In twos, or threes, close together, they walked on guard, disappearing from view for a while and then reappearing. They had walkie-talkies which they muttered into occasionally, while keeping a very close watch on the surrounding buildings and gesturing to the men positioned on the surrounding roof tops. The area was obviously under siege.

Zareen wished that they had not arranged to meet at the salon this evening. She even tried to inform everybody but could not get hold of any of them. She sent her son with a message to Malihe not to come and told him, 'If anybody stops you, say you are just going to a friend's house, don't say anything else.'

The child was playful and happy to go out, unaware of the tension in the street. Zareen thought it possible that he could be stopped, but he was obviously harmless and if he were stopped, it would be all right, as he didn't have anything suspicious on him.

She sat down, to wait anxiously for Goli and Fatemeh. She put out a few bottles of shampoo, her scissors and comb, in order to look as if she was going to do their hair or nails when they arrived, but to her the salon still looked suspicious: dimly lit, empty but expectant at that time of night.

There were few cars or cabs around on the street – the sight of the militia was scaring people and cars off the road, although there were still some people out, shoppers, home-going men and children doing errands. But everybody was frightened. Zareen was afraid that if Goli or Fatemeh were stopped, if they were questioned, if the boot of their car was searched, if they had some women's pamphlets or 'un-Islamic' books with them, that they would certainly – especially Goli – go down for a couple of years, and God knew what would happen to them there. She was sick with worry and paced the shop up and down, up and down, stopping, twiddling with her hair, pulling a few stray ones out, peering out of the window.

Suddenly she saw a cab draw up outside the salon and Goli, without wasting a second, flew inside.

'Oh, Zari! Where are you? Such a dim light! What's happening? There are so many pasdars around.'

'I've been wishing you wouldn't come, or would at least ring before . . . we must ring in future before coming over . . . it's so stupid to meet here tonight . . . '

'You think the phone is safe?' was Goli's answer.

'I know, but today has been especially bad. This area is surrounded by police and militia. There was a dawn raid further up the road.' Zareen was still pacing up and down, peering out of the window, awaiting Fatemeh.

'What happened?'

'They say a 'counter-revolutionary' safe-house full of ammu-nition and anti-government publications has been found but I think also that the disagreements between the government and other Islamic groups, possibly including Radical Islam, has come to a head. So it must be an opposition house with their publications and guns. There were shoot-outs as well.'

'Does Fatemeh know? Is she all right? Could they be her comrades?' Goli's anxious questions tumbled out. 'But thank God some people are saying no to the dictatorship of the mullas,' she continued.

'It's not so much that – it's a conflict over power sharing and territorial struggle; but I didn't think it would come to the residential areas so soon.' Zareen did not stop her pacing.

'It had to sooner or later – if the streets are unsafe for dissent, people move back home, to the centre of protection and organisation. Do you know for sure that it's Radical Islam or could it just be a house with some bottles of wine, or a few arty magazines, with some bare hands or legs showing?'

'I'm not sure. These days it's so difficult to know the right news. Why isn't Fatemeh here?' Zareen crouched down by the crack in the curtain, wary of her shadow being spotted from the street outside.

'Ah, I hope she is safe. In my area the house-searching is so bad. Every day a different house becomes suspect, is surrounded, searched, and the people taken away. My mother comes home with horror stories: some of the rich families have been visited by the Komiteh, their homes searched, their family videos and photographs in swimsuits confiscated – in one house they even read out a woman's old love letters, and her husband was furious.'

'God, the reign of terror has arrived: real, cold, merciless terror,' said Zareen, thinking sadly of the confiscation of her dayereh.

'Poor, illiterate, deprived men and women who never had anything themselves, now trying to make sure nobody else has anything either,' Goli went on. 'My mother says some of her friends have started purging their houses even before the Komiteh's visit. They've started to burn family photos, their wedding videos, their games and cards, old love letters and to keep nothing that is personal or private.'

'To the Komiteh, privacy for women means whoring – like when they burst into this woman's luxurious villa and demanded to know why she lived alone with her child. She appealed to them, saying that her husband had died recently, but no, they couldn't accept it: a woman alone meant she was a whore, especially a rich woman,' Zareen concluded.

'Since the revolution I have felt more in sympathy with the rich than the poor,' said Goli. 'I think the middle classes are being oppressed and that they must revolt. I worry for my socialist principles now – how will they survive?'

'Where the hell is she? I hope she is safe. Sit here, Goli. I am going to do your nails and calm my nerves. I'll turn this side-light on to see what I am doing, although somebody may knock any minute,' Zareen said while sitting Goli down on a chair. She began to fiddle with scissors, tweezers, nail polish, her fear and tension continuing to simmer in her belly.

A knock on the door startled both women, and they shot out of their seats.

'Oh my God! Who can it be? I didn't hear Fati's car, did you?' cried Goli. But Zareen sat down with relief.

'Oh, relax, it's my son back from Malihe's. She went out and, while letting him in, had a good look around the street and roof tops. Nothing was visible, Malihe had got the message, had given some food and drink to Bahram and walked back part of the way with him. That was one problem solved. Now there was only Fatemeh.

Then some vague noises, the sound of a car as it slowly and quietly stopped outside the window. With their hearts in their mouths they lifted the curtain edge. It was Fatemeh.

Cautiously and noiselessly she came in.

'Ah, Fatemeh! Where have you been? I am *so* pleased to see you!' Zareen hugged and kissed her.

'I've had a hell of a day. Some of our comrades were in the house nearby, the raided one; somebody – either a friend or a neighbour has betrayed them. They were three sisters and one brother, they were armed and were planning to move out to the countryside and become part of the new underground armed struggle. But it's dreadful, the two sisters were killed in the shoot-out, the others are badly injured. I've been running around all day, taking messages, warning others, giving people lifts, doing a bit of spying. I'm shattered. Let me sit down.' She collapsed onto a chair.

120

'But . . . the armed struggle in a residential area? This is crazy.' Goli's mouth gaped.

'What a tragedy,' said Zareen. 'Did you know them personally?'

'No, not really, just by sight in meetings. But I heard they were good combatants. This is devastating for our group.' Fatemeh's face was drawn.

'I must go home now. If I'm late my mother will worry herself sick.' Goli got up.

'I'll take you,' said Fatemeh, 'but let's wait for a while till it gets quieter and I can get a bit of rest. I shouldn't have come, it was very risky, but I wanted to know how you all are and see you and reassure you that I was all right.' This sentence was directed at Zareen who was too confused to respond.

They kept an eye on the state of the street outside, waiting for the best moment to leave, perhaps until there were other cars on the road, so it would look less suspicious.

Goli lifted the corner of the inner lace curtain, making the crack between that and the outer, heavier curtain wider, and watched the streets getting emptier and more peopleless. She was disturbed by what she saw, by what she had heard and her nervousness about getting home increased. The empty streets, the darkness, the invisible lurking soldiers summoned up her fear and brought back painful memories. She shuddered. How many occupied streets did she have to walk through and be passive and accepting when what she actually wanted was to be angry, confrontational, offensive, to do something dreadful . . .

A couple of cars and some passers-by began to people the streets at last and Fatemeh and Goli said goodbye to Zareen and dashed out of the house. Zareen crouched by the crack in the curtains. Cautiously they started the car and drove off, tortoise-like. Zareen did not move from her vantage point, but soon they passed beyond her vision. She wanted to go out onto the road, and follow them with her eyes. But she didn't dare, and continued to stare out at the blank darkness.

Suddenly she heard a loud 'Stop!' A car screeched and a few running steps pattered in the distance. Zareen's heart sank. She sat down and waited. Was it them? Or somebody else? What would happen now? Would the guards burst in any minute? She felt as agitated as if pounds of salt were boiling away within her. After a while she got up, and to calm herself down she went to see to the kids and dinner, still with that salty feeling inside her.

Zareen carried the salty feeling on into the next day, but she didn't think it was safe to ring. She wondered how long she should wait for news. A couple of hours? The morning? The afternoon? A whole day? Two days? Impossible, far too long. The next day there was a hanna-bandan and Fatemeh had been invited. Would Zareen know by then? How long was an average time to wait for news of the safety of a friend? The morning passed but there was no news. Perhaps no news is good news, she thought. A difficult afternoon wore away. And still she waited with increasing uncertainty. Every phone call, every turn of the doorhandle, every greeting in the salon gave her a jump. She kept her eyes on the door, on the phone, and her ears were tuned to the sounds of the road as she continued working.

In the late afternoon when the salon was nearly empty and Muneer was clearing up the place, Zareen was doing a customer's face, her head bent down, the cotton string between her thumbs pulling the hair on the upper lip of the woman, she heard Fatemeh's sweet voice, 'Salaam.' The string pulled the woman's lip hard and she twitched; Zareen twitched too, but caught herself in time.

'Hi, Fatemeh, are you well?'

'Yes, thanks, very well.'

'I'm nearly finished. If you don't mind waiting for a few minutes I'll be with you soon.'

'All right. I can wait.'

Zareen relaxed. She didn't hurry the customer, finished the job smoothly and told her workers she would lock up, that they could go if they wanted to.

When the salon was empty, she looked at Fatemeh and sighed her relief, like drinking cool water down her dry thirsty throat.

'I have lived with tension in my stomach all day. Tell me what happened.'

'We had passed your house and I had gathered speed and really didn't want to stop, when the militia appeared, and so I had to do a noisy emergency stop. Goli nearly fainted. But by the time the militia got to the car we were prepared. They searched the boot thoroughly without a word, then in my handbag and Goli's and, because they couldn't find anything suspicious, two of them got us out of the car for questioning. I gave them my name, he wanted proof, I showed them my driving licence. They each scrutinised the name in turn, and after a good while they apologised and became very polite and humble and didn't ask any questions of Goli or me and then let us go.'

'How lucky. So they didn't find anything in the car or on either of you. How come? Goli usually carries lots of university books and women's papers.'

'Well . . . I emptied my car in the afternoon because of what had happened and Goli . . . well . . . she didn't want you to know, but she left them here before we went. She said she put them in the cupboard, under her suit, when you were out of the room.'

'Oh my God!' Zareen pulled the cupboard open and pushed the brooms, the overalls, the broken hairdryer aside. And yes, there were the books on women in history, revolution and women's role in it, leaflets on meetings, women's newsletters, they were all there rolled up in Goli's suit.

'The cheek of her! I could be gaoled for harbouring anti-revolutionary material!'

'Come on . . . She didn't want you to worry. I guess she just did it on impulse. She didn't have much time to think about it. You wouldn't have said no, would you?'

'No, of course not. But I'm glad that I didn't know.'

'It's late. I had better go,' said Fatemeh. 'I can still taste my fear from yesterday, but it's eroding slowly – feels good to have got away.' She went and Zareen locked up.

Preparing for the hanna-bandan the next morning, Zareen thought about the shooting incident. It would be interesting to know what her customers thought about it and she planned to raise a few questions and find out if the women knew anything more.

The customers and neighbours began to trickle in one by one, Fatemeh too. Zareen busied herself preparing the tea and turned the radio on.

Azadeh, a young woman who wanted her hair to have a henna treatment lasting for ten hours, giving it the colour of polished copper, was the first customer. Zareen knew why she was early. She was Muneer's friend and they always had a good time when she was having her hair hennaed, chatting, laughing, and exchanging music and fashion tips.

Muneer had washed Azadeh's hair and was applying henna to it when Shamsi arrived, a large veiled woman with a lot of gold at her neck and wrists. Zareen started on her hair. Maral was an older, bony woman who had her hair, her hands and her feet hennaed. She believed henna was a heavenly plant and that its colour and smell would lead her through the gates of heaven. Sima was one of the local teachers and Wednesday was her day off, the only day on which she could come in. She knew a lot of parents in the area and often dropped in on them for a chat. She came to have her hair removed from her legs, arms and face. It took Muneer and Zareen hours to pluck her, and therefore she had to wait till they had finished hennaing the others, but she didn't mind. Narges was a young woman with three small children, who always looked haggard and lifeless. Women thought it was because of her children but she had confessed to a close neighbour and Zareen that it was because her husband was a writer. He didn't do anything for himself or the children and exhausted her with his strange lifestyle – sleeping during the day, writing at night, expecting his food ready at odd hours and needing more care and attention than a sick baby. She spent the day of henna as a rest and took the opportunity to get her cares off her chest, as she sat knitting her baby clothes. Sometimes Zareen would joke with her,

'What you need is a new husband. Why don't you change him, at the local greengrocer? Who ever heard of a useful writer husband?'

124

After Muneer had hennaed Azadeh's hair, she started on Fatemeh. She knew her and they had a nice little chat which saved Fatemeh from feeling like an outsider.

Once everyone had been hennaed Zareen made fresh tea from the boiling samovar and started pouring it out. The radio was quietly preaching in the background before Shamsi went over and turned it up, giving their ears no choice but to hear it.

' . . . This is not all. The family is the foundation of our new revolutionary constitution that we are creating at present. The family is the main focus for the growth of humanity. With such an understanding of the family, women have been saved from objectification, the labour market, from being tools at the service of the consumer society, and from exploitation – and can regain the elevated valuable duty of motherhood to rear the vanguard fighters of humanity . . . '

'Do we have to listen to these pathetic excuses for all they have done to women?' Sima was very angry. Zareen made as if to turn it off, but Shamsi requested, 'Please! It is important. Let's hear him. Now he is talking about suckling – that's a concern of all of us. Let's just hear this bit. It's useful.'

They couldn't protest at that, except for Azadeh, who said quietly, 'What a big jump from the family to breast feeding – what powers of association the mullas have.'

' . . . milk . . . mother's milk helps a healthier and stronger child to grow, it creates a warmer and more human relationship between mother and child. It is cheaper and always available. It is nourishing and clean and easily digestable. Feeding their children on their own milk makes mothers healthier and less in danger of cancer. They would feel more affectionate and attached to their children . . . '

'Honestly, Shamsi, have mercy on our tired ears and brains. I have learned enough, haven't you? You know how to feed your kids, don't you?'

'It is very important to listen to our leaders. I can learn a lot from the radio – I can't read like you lot. Anyway, it's good to know men have ideas about things like breast feeding.'

'They have ideas all right,' said Narges. 'They're full of them. It's a good excuse to push us about.'

'Shall we leave off discussing the radio?' Zareen seized her opportunity. 'I want to know about the shoot-out and arrest in our street a few nights ago.'

Everybody went quiet. What was there to say? To make it easier Zareen started refilling their glasses with tea and having a small chat with each woman as she did it. They began to relax again. Azadeh started reading her magazine, Shamsi took up her crocheting, Sima her tapestry, and Narges resumed her knitting. Fatemeh waited, hoping to hear something. But nobody volunteered to talk about it.

Zareen handed a glass of tea to Shamsi and, as she pushed the sugar cubes towards her, asked, 'Did you see any of the pasdars around your area before the shooting? What did actually happen?'

Azadeh stopped turning the pages of her magazine, Sima's needle got stuck, Narges dropped her knitting onto her lap, Maral, who had just got herself comfortable on her cushion in readiness for a nap, sat upright, Shamsi dropped her hook. The way Zareen put the question surprised them. It wasn't in the usual informal chatting manner that came naturally and spontaneously; it was precise and determined. Zareen wanted answers.

'Are you asking me?' Shamsi was twitchy.

'Yes. It was next to your house, wasn't it?'

'Yes, it was. Well . . . but we didn't see much. We were too afraid to come out. We had heard things, rumours.' She looked around her at the women, one by one, and lowered her voice.

'I don't know exactly but they said that the children were members of Radical Islam, and had illegal arms, and were plotting against the government. Three young women, who always looked very pious and well veiled, and their brother. They were plotting to assassinate a well-known member of the clergy. That is what we heard. Their poor mother nearly died of grief. They had guns and some papers and printing machines and—'

'Having papers and guns, and belonging to a group is not a crime yet. It's revolutionary still,' interrupted Azadeh. Maral joined in.

126

'I heard they had arrested some of them in another area, just like this incident.'

'My husband says the government has started to clamp down on the opposition, that it is only the beginning,' added Narges.

'I don't believe such a baseless accusation against the government. They should have handed their guns over. Why didn't they?' asked Shamsi.

'Did you see when the militia arrived? How many they were and how they stationed themselves?' Fatemeh was frustrated that she could not get any precise information out of Shamsi.

'No. It was very early in the morning.'

Fatemeh tried again. 'Did you speak to anybody who saw anything?'

'Nothing more than I have just said, just lots of rumours.'

Fatemeh thought that possibly Shamsi knew more than she wanted to give away.

'I don't care about any of those Islamic groupings,' Azadeh broke in. 'They are as bad as the mullas, so gloomy all of them. Their women always look like they have walked out of a religious ceremony. They're no fun, preaching at us all the time.'

Zareen looked at Fatemeh. She didn't like Azadeh's comment.

'Don't generalise,' she said.

'I'm not. Their line on women, the veil, on sex is exactly the same as the mullas. So I say to them, radical or unradical, if you don't like to see our hair, or our legs, then you should bloody well close your eyes or put the veil on yourselves.'

'Aren't you ashamed?' cried Shamsi. 'We have made sacrifices, our young and dear ones were killed for the revolution – and all you care about is to take a bit more off your skirt or let your hair dance in the wind. It's an insult to the revolution.'

'You think we didn't make sacrifices for this revolution?' retorted Azadeh. 'We are still making them, women always are! . . . '

'Don't lose your tempers,' interjected Zareen. 'Here we are talking. We are a group of women, none of us are in the paid service of the government. We are just talking about the way we think, and the way we would like the government to act for us. Of course we don't all agree with each other.' She was more conciliatory than usual, not wanting the day spoiled. Her calm words had their effect. The women cooled down a bit.

'It is stupid to use arms against the government, of course they won't win.' Shamsi said. 'We are a new government and we have to protect ourselves.'

'Who is protecting whom?' asked Sima. 'They say the same thing about the veil – teachers must wear the veil, it protects women: I don't want the government to protect me, the veil is not a protection for me. Even if I'm chained to the parliament railings I still won't wear it, I don't want to be bothered by the weight of those clothes. This is a hot country and I want to have as little as possible on and still go out all the time, be visible.'

'And the veil is such a pain, honestly.' Narges agreed. 'If you had to carry three kids, hold the veil *and* carry the shopping . . . '

'If the clergy and their men are so weak below the belly that each time they see a bare leg they have an orgasm on the street,' said Azadeh, 'don't you think *they* should stay at home and mind their virtues?'

Muneer was the first to laugh and the rest followed her and they all rolled around with laughter except Shamsi, who saw it as an affront and was angry.

'But men are like that even if you cover yourself up in a tent. The *name* of a woman makes them drip.'

Shamsi laughed. It was the casual way that Maral had said it.

'This doesn't bode well for men,' Narges extended the argument, 'if they are so weak and have so little self-control over their sexual energy, then they should stay home and get busy with their four wives and five thousand concubines. They have no place in the government.'

'Yes, I always said mullas should be in the mosque,' Maral nodded. 'If they're in the parliament now, they shouldn't stay there long. They should appoint their trusted delegates and get out of it fast. Politics don't go with religion.'

'It makes it doubly corrupt,' Sima said. 'One corruption for one class is enough.'

Zareen was exasperated. The veil, yet again, dominated everything else. Women were so preoccupied by it. Fatemeh too had a hopeless look on her face. She wanted to divert the talk back to the shoot-out and get the women's views on that.

'Why are we so stuck on the veil? This shoot-out in our residential area is much more disturbing. What is happening? Who is fighting whom and why? What does all this mean for us, and for our future?'

Maral was the first to answer. 'I think we should be cautious as always—'

Sima interrupted. 'Obviously the dominant fundamentalist group in the government is trying to consolidate its power and if they can subdue women, Radical Islam, and the other guerrilla forces one by one, then I think they will create another dictatorship, one directed by the mullas. It seems we don't get away from our past easily.'

'You're rushing too fast. This is an emergency period. Always after a revolution there is upheaval, there are times of confusion, chaos, rapid change. This doesn't mean it's leading to a dictatorship. It will get better – once it's clear who are the enemies and who are the friends. The dawn gives a good idea of what kind of a day it will bring,' said Narges.

'Then Sima, you are saying that the consolidation of power necessitates a clamp-down on the opposition.' said Zareen. 'But Radical Islam is stronger, better trained and more experienced than the government forces. Why can't they be assimilated? That would make better sense.'

'You said it, for the same reasons, assimilation would mean democratic procedures.'

'No, not necessarily,' Zareen countered. 'They have been co-operating so far. But the government could go over the head of people, couldn't it?'

'I think it is really foolish to try to fight a government, however strong and well trained you may be,' said Narges. 'It is death and killing and more death. Useless.'

'I don't think it's useless; it's just that no urban guerrilla group has won, however courageous they may be they cannot win against the system,' Sima said.

'This is not true,' Fatemeh said, but was sorry immediately and didn't pursue it.

'Well, I think it is.' Sima was surer than her.

'What bothers me is,' Azadeh's face was wrinkled with anger and impatience, and she pointed her finger at Shamsi, 'what is wrong with wanting to be fashionable, putting on make-up, red lipstick, blue mascara, yes, take a few inches off the bottom of my skirt, yes, show off my legs – what's wrong with this? It makes me feel good.'

'Shame on you!' cried Shamsi. 'The country is upside down and all you think of is to show more of your legs and catch a few hungry men's glances.'

'I'm not responsible for their hunger. Don't you shift that on to me.'

'Oh, my girl. Is that all you want from life, to be fashionable and pretty?' Maral sighed as if only she knew of the weariness of the world.

'What little you are satisfied with,' Sima commented.

'It's not little at all. It's just the beginning and if you,' Azadeh's finger was pointing at Shamsi again, 'and your supporters, the fanatics, can't tolerate red lipstick and blue mascara, it won't be little, not little at all.'

Zareen felt frustrated. Tempers were high between Shamsi and Azadeh. She didn't want any confrontation between the two women. There was the rest of the day to get through, it was her salon, and although she didn't mind the anger and a bit of a hot debate, she did not want an open conflict or a personal fight between her customers.

'Look, I don't want a confrontation, or any bad feelings between any of you. After all we are here, friends and neighbours, having our hands and hair done together. We are changing the colour of our head, sorry, hair, and our faces, taking lots of unnecessary, bothersome hair off our bodies. We want to know what colour government we like, in what shades, with what make-up of forces, what image and what style best suits our mood, our thoughts, our tomorrows. We don't want to fight each other, it's not necessary, we're just exchanging our views. I'm not running a parliamentary debate, and women fighting in my salon is not good for business!'

'Enough of this politics nonsense, it always makes people quarrel. Let's talk about something else,' Maral butted in.

The women looked at her and silence followed. Zareen's heart sank. She hadn't meant to shut everybody up. She began to get the lunch ready. The other women resumed their activities, and Fatemeh took a book out of her bag. The needles clicked and stitched until the sound of plates arriving on the sofreh drowned them out.

Zareen wondered why, since the revolution, more and more women had taken up tapestry, crochet and knitting. The silence was more forboding than the confrontation. Hoping that eating would break it and usher in a new atmosphere, more engaging and enlightening, she began to serve the food.

12

It was a week or so after the hanna-bandan when Fatemeh invited Goli to her house because she had something – she didn't say what – to talk about. A servant opened the door and led Goli through the courtyard. She was taken aback by its beauty, by the traditional Persian garden with a beautiful marble hoze in the middle. They walked under trellised grapevines and on to the verandah. Goli paused, feeling the smoothness and oldness of the carved wood, smelling the potted jasmine, shamdani, shahpasand sitting side by side on the edges of the verandah, while the maid went to call Fatemeh.

She came out radiant with pleasure at seeing Goli, and led her through a dark carpeted corridor with antique Persian paintings on the wall to her room. Goli felt herself drowning in the shapes, colours and textures of the things around her on the walls and under her feet on the floor.

Fatemeh's room was dim, filled with strong dark colours: sapphire, green and lighter shades too, turquoise. The large oblong Tabrizi carpet covered the floor of the room, and on it was a small, bright silk rug from Qum by her bed. Her bed was a mattress on the floor, with a heavy velvet spread covering it, and thick, stiff rug cushions lined up around it. They sat down and leaned back on them. Goli ran her hand over the rich texture of the carpet, unable to keep her eyes off it.

'When you've had enough of the objects around you, perhaps you can look at me, the mortal one, and say what you'd like to drink,' laughed Fatemeh, and waited for a reply.

Goli looked at her then, glancing at the line of scarred tissue around her right eye, only to say: 'I can't think about that now. Tell me, what an exquisitely beautiful room – where is this carpet from? The silk rug? The bed cover? This book by that man Shariyati – I really, really disagree with him. He was the epitome of a mediocre romantic Muslim intellectual. I'm sorry, but I find his writing lacks any modern intelligence.'

'Come on Goli, I disagree with you – and him too – however, he is a very important figure in our modern ideology and we can't deny it.' Fatemeh was embarrassed. 'I like my room, despite its ancient flavour. What kind of a place do you live in?'

'My place, our place, is modern – moquette floors, wooden chairs, posters of famous Western painters, some modern Iranian paintings – all light and bright colours and political posters and pictures – nothing to envy.'

'Sounds fashionable. This is all traditional and out of fashion, steeped in the beauty and art of the past. My mother's choice, really. And my father, a mulla to your horror, travels and lectures in other cities, and brings back many art objects, on my mother's orders. They get on. He is not a reactionary fundamentalist, and doesn't interfere much with us. You could say he is a Muslim liberal intellectual. However, I have not asked you over to discuss my father, or to show you the *objets d'art* in here—'

'Has Zareen been here? Does she like it?' interrupted Goli.

'Yes, she enjoys being here.'

'Does she visit you often?'

'Yes. She's our family hairdresser. My mother and our servants and myself invite her over for a day when we need our hair and faces doing. She enjoys coming here and spending a few hours in my room. We are very close.'

'What an unlikely match.' Goli didn't mind showing her surprise to Fatemeh now. She felt more at ease with her.

'You have an incurably stereotypical mind you know, full of straight lines and corners and—'

'How did you meet? I feel there's something strong between you two, I can't put a name to it. I'd love to know. Tell me.'

133

'No. I don't want to.'

'Please Fati, why not?'

'No, why should I tell you? It is too personal.'

'I feel such an outsider among you all. You have known each other for so long, meet up with each other more frequently, and now you want to keep a secret from me. Won't you let me in?'

'It's not like that. You're our friend, and a comrade, I don't want a secret to come between us, it's . . . just . . . difficult . . . you would be more surprised . . . and more stereotypical . . .'

'No, I won't. I promise. I like surprises. Don't be mean.'

'Well . . . well . . . it started with her coming to do my mother's and the servants' hair . . . and one day I asked her to do mine. She cut my hair and bandandakht my legs. She liked this room, liked being here and resting for a few hours. She liked my harmonica and I played for her. I liked her.'

'Interesting . . . What do you like about her?'

'Many things. I like her touch, when she cuts my hair, her eye for detail, her mouth when she talks, her gentle hand on my neck.' Fatemeh lowered her eyes, and was looking at the carpet, drawing on it with her finger. 'She has an incredible eye for detail, things we always miss.' She lifted her head up high, looking at Goli and asserting her words. 'The first time she came into this room she sat down and closed her eyes and said she loved the peace, the absence of sound in this room. When she opened her eyes she took this glass pot in her hand and, with her fingers, wandered about the curves of the neck, mouth and bottom and counted how many curves it had and said it was like currents, waves upon waves. Interesting, no?'

'Yes. But she's not like that at Ziba Style.'

'She's not her private self there.'

'So, I am fascinated and . . .'

'And . . .?'

'Jealous. Tell me more.'

'There is not much more to say and anyway, why should I give you the pleasure of my experience? I prefer women, I don't need men.'

'Well . . .'

134

'But I love my father and he is a good father. One man is enough, no?'

'Not for many women.'

'Well, perhaps they don't have much choice.'

'Perhaps. Oh God, I am embarrassed. I feel so innocent. Here I am, a second-year university student, one of the handful of women in the whole country who have such a privilege, with professional parents who go abroad often and I thought I knew so much. And I know so little. You are great, Fati. Your dignified patience saves me. I am glad you treat me like a real friend.'

Fatemeh was blushing now. Goli went to her and gave her a bear hug.

'When you've finished,' Fatemeh laughed and hugged her back, 'I have a piece of news for you and I want your full attention.'

She ordered some tea, remembering her good manners towards her guest. Goli welcomed it, she was thirsty.

While they drank Fatemeh passed a newspaper cutting to Goli. Two brothers, who had suspected that their sister was in love with a man in another neighbourhood, were so outraged at her that they planned and executed her murder. They killed her in her sleep, and gave themselves up to the police the day after. But they walked out free men, because they had defended their honour. Fatemeh was evidently very angry and sad about the incident. She admitted that such incidents were not new, but that atrocities against women like this one were on the increase – such as the burning of prostitutes, the throwing of acid on unveiled women's faces, the lynching of women by their male relatives. She could not bear it, and felt so strongly about it to want to do something to the brothers. She wanted to know if Goli felt the same. Goli was furious at the small amount of coverage the incident had received: more space had been given to the brothers' photographs.

They had a few moments of silence for the dead woman, and then began to discuss what action they would take.

What could they do, how could they protest at such murders? How could they bring these murderers to justice? If the law supports honour killers, in what way could they avenge the death? They discussed some of the options open to them: throwing Molotov cocktails into the shop, thus destroying their livelihood; making threatening phone calls to disrupt their lives; throwing acid at them. None of these options had the effect of taking a life away, because they were not yet sure that they wanted to commit themselves to the ultimate revenge. Fatemeh confessed her present disillusionment with armed struggle as an effective way to fight against a tyrannical state.

'After a few unsuccessful battles between my comrades and the army, I have lost my faith in it. Some of our best comrades have been killed, or have had to kill themselves so as not to be captured alive, for fear of torture in gaol. It has been very destructive for my group, they have lost some of their best women and men. I think if this government has decided to destroy all our democratic rights so soon after the revolution, then it has to rely on very vicious tactics to continue its reign of terror. And when a government decides to use all means available to suppress a people then no armed struggle can succeed. Because no group is stronger than a state, no one group can combat effectively all the brutal force of a state. So I don't want to use any deadly methods. I want to live and continue living and fighting. But I still want to avenge her death in some way.'

Goli agreed with her, 'Women engaging in armed struggle use violent methods advocated by men and thus even in struggle they remain subordinate to them. Also it's very elitist – many ordinary people don't really sympathise with armed struggle and won't support it. We can't afford to adopt such unpopular tactics.'

Fatemeh remembered the talk in the salon at the hanna-bandan and what the women had said then about resistance. Women . . . especially ordinary women don't like such violence.

Finally they agreed that they needed to talk to the others about it and get their agreement too.

However, when the four of them met, they didn't discuss

whether or not they should take revenge because Fatemeh and Goli felt very strongly that they should. The only question was what kind and what degree of revenge. Zareen agreed nervously to join them; but Malihe declined – she wasn't ready for it, but didn't mind helping them to prepare for the action.

In the meantime, Fatemeh had done some detective work. She had posed as a freelance journalist and found out that the two men were carpenters who made expensive wooden furniture, and that they lived and worked in Tehran-Pars, a suburb in the north-west. Now that they had their address, they decided that the best plan was to go there, disguised in men's suits, kidnap the brothers and teach them a lesson.

Goli already had her suit. Zareen thought she could borrow one of her husband's, and Malihe managed to find a second-hand suit for Fatemeh, which made her look like a worker boy. Fatemeh said she didn't mind being a king in ragged clothes for a night.

They had a few dress rehearsals at Ziba Style and Malihe coached them in their new roles. Fatemeh was the tallest and looked best in her suit, although the jacket and trousers were loose on her. Malihe thought the best way to disguise her slightness would be to wear more clothes underneath, but Fatemeh said she would feel uncomfortable, and decided instead to wear an overcoat to bulk out her narrow frame.

Goli was smaller than both Fatemeh and Zareen, and made a convincing boy. As she had already had a dress rehearsal she didn't need to be scrutinised by Malihe, and watched the others.

Malihe sat in a corner and asked them to move around, to walk, to sit down, to shake hands, to talk as if they were men. Goli and Zareen had had a few tries at it before and it was Fatemeh who was the real novice to manhood. She was hopeless at first, with a bent head, dropped shoulders, hands flopped at her sides, eyes lowered to the ground as if going to the mosque, a result of her present fear, nervousness and lack of confidence. She rehearsed hard, determined to get it right. She soon learned to stride with open legs instead of just walking, to look up and around as if she were controlling her surroundings with her eyes.

Zareen's mannerisms were casual, flighty and uncertain. Malihe told her to stop joking, take it seriously, and to inscribe that seriousness in her body language.

'You can't move as if you're learning dance steps!' Malihe showed her how to move, patiently going through it with her, straightening a shoulder here, giving a swing to the arm there.

'Because you crochet, and bend over women at your work you must now try to get out of that posture.' Zareen went on trying until she was firmer, surer in posture and manners, more assertive with every step.

Goli looked boyish in her suit. Her size wasn't the problem. She had to learn how to hold herself. 'Imagine you're standing on a street corner, like any young man,' said Malihe. 'Look the girls up and down and smile at them,' she continued. They all smiled. 'Act as if you're aware of your presence and sure of your place.'

She then made them all go through their karate moves, and following Goli's example they accustomed themselves to moving swiftly into attack positions in their new cumbersome clothes.

Shoes and hair were the other problems. None of their shoes were manly. They discussed in detail the possibility of obtaining men's shoes for their small feet. In the end it was agreed that each was responsible for borrowing a pair of shoes which were comfortable and convincing from within their own family and circle of friends. Their hair was left in Zareen's hands, even though she protested that she liked doing women's hair styles and not men's. She cut Goli's hair short like her husband's, and made her own a bit shorter. Malihe supplied her with a small chapeau (a hat that most Iranian men wear), and Fatemeh would shorten her father's amameh and try it with an aba.

Finally they practised speaking, turning their feminine voices into deep, commanding and authoritive masculine voices.

The night of the action arrived and they met as planned at

Ziba Style, although Malihe could not make it as she was working late. It was the early part of the evening, and a few people were going to the mosque for early evening prayers before going home for their evening meal – Zareen's husband included. The streets were not empty therefore, which was good, as it would make them less conspicuous.

They got dressed and acted out their parts in front of the mirror for the last time. Fatemeh had put on a modified version of her father's aba over the suit, and an amameh around her head, which helped to make her look larger, a younger, smaller version of her father, and she also had his driving licence. She was a mulla for the night.

Zareen thought she cut an awkward figure as her husband, not a proper man at all. Fatemeh had given her a gun which she had 'borrowed' from her father, and its presence, tucked into the inner pocket of the jacket, was making her feel even more awkward. Goli went round and straightened their collars and sleeves, assuring them that they looked fine, she would fall for any of them, any time. Once they were ready they laughed, marvelling at each other. They looked like different people.

Outside they walked to the car, trembling a little but gaining confidence with every move. What if they were stopped by the militia – even though they had chosen the longest, most tortuous of back street routes? They would have to rely on Fatemeh's father's driving licence, Goli's karate and their own sheer resolution. Fatemeh only hoped that having a mulla in the car would deflect any suspicion.

They drove through the back streets of Jaleh, a long troubled drive.

'Can I just be an observer? I feel such a novice as a man.' Zareen's doubt was gaining on her.

'No, you're the largest body among us. No.' Fatemeh would not have it.

According to the plan the car was to stop a little way along from the brothers' shop and Zareen would go in and ask them to come out and meet the reverend Mulla Haj Ali who wanted very much to meet them and ask them a few questions. Then she would show them the car with, of course, Fatemeh sitting by the window with her aba on and amameh, looking convincing.

There was a bit of a panic when Fatemeh thought that she had missed the shop, but soon she saw the familiar street signs and they regained their calmness. The shop loomed out from the dusk and Fatemeh drove slowly, looking for a good place to park. Outside the shop were two chairs, on each side of the door. As is usual with such family businesses, they were still open at this late hour.

Zareen left the car and walked across the road. The others' eyes followed her, she looked taller than usual, her back straighter. She went into the shop. After a few seconds one of the men came out and looked in their direction, at which moment Fatemeh held her head high to make the amameh more visible. He went in and the two brothers then came out, and both looked in the women's direction again. They closed and bolted the shop, and walked behind Zareen towards the car. Fatemeh started the car, they got in and said a revered hello to Fatemeh, she returning their respect with a certain assured pride and dignity. They settled themselves in the back with Goli, while Zareen got into the front. Once seated she leaned over and said, 'We're going to the police station in upper Tehran-Pars.'

'But we gave ourselves up in our local police station just behind here,' said the elder brother.

'Yes, we know, we have your file,' bluffed Zareen, 'but Haj himself,' pointing to Fatemeh, 'works in this police station. I know that's far from you, but we'll give you a lift back, don't worry.' Zareen detected nervousness in them, but she was calm, calculated and in control. They drove on, Zareen and Goli keeping the small talk going.

They were leaving the outskirts of Tehran-Pars when the doubt began to appear on the men's faces.

'Surely the police station isn't as far as this?' queried the elder brother.

'Yes, it is. It's in the village of Ali-Abad, four miles away. Don't worry.'

But when the car started turning on to dirt roads with no

lights, no buildings and no other people around, they began to suspect something.

'Are we going to a police station? Can't see anything around here. Where are you taking us?'

Zareen looked about outside the car to check that they were alone in the darkness, turned round in her seat and then calmly took her hand out from her jacket pocket and pointed the gun that had been nestling there at the brothers.

'Sit still and don't do anything stupid, otherwise I will blow your brains out.'

Startled, their eyes stuck to the gun, they started stammering.

'Who are you? Where are you taking us?' The younger brother spoke for the first time. He had been very quiet until then and was obviously more confused than his older brother, who cried at the same time, 'What is the meaning of this?'

'We're here to avenge your sister's murder. You deserve to be killed too. How did you kill her? You cut her up in pieces, didn't you? We want to learn how you did it and then use the same technique on you. Tell us how you cut her up in pieces.'

'No! Please, not me, she still comes to me in my dreams. I didn't want to . . . cu— c—' The younger brother began to whimper.

'It's none of your business! It's a family affair,' the elder brother cut in. Under the faint light inside the car, which Fatemeh had parked on the side of the road which ran through a deserted orchard, he looked from one woman to the next rubbing his hands slowly. Fatemeh kept an eye on them, nervously checking that they weren't about to open the car door and run away.

'Who sent you anyway?' asked the elder brother. 'Him? That bastard who interferes with other men's sisters? I knew I should have killed him too.'

'Yes, why didn't you kill him?' asked Fatemeh.

'He is not part of our honour, we are not responsible for him,' said the younger brother.

'No. That's not it. If you had killed him, you would have been persecuted. You're clever as well as being zealots.

141

'Rubbish! She was our sister, she behaved atrociously, ungratefully towards us. She was disobedient, ignoring our family respect and honour in our neighbourhood, all the years we cared for her and protected her, she deserved death.' The elder brother was angry now. Hatred flashed in his eyes.

'We warned her not to see this man,' added the younger brother. 'She saw him though, she spoke with him, held his hand and laughed with him.' He held his forehead as if with the shame of mentioning it. 'We heard about it. We didn't see it ourselves.'

'So,' said Fatemeh, 'she didn't sleep around – she wasn't pregnant or anything like that?'

'Oh, good God! No,' exclaimed the elder brother. 'Look, who are you? You're not Nakeer or Monker?'

'No. What would you have done if she warned you not to see the woman you love?' asked Fatemeh.

'What nonsense!' The brothers both said at the same time.

'She was our sister.' The younger brother was self-righteous.

'Is a sister a human being?' Fatemeh retorted.

'We were ashamed of a loose and uncontrollable sister,' the younger brother snapped back.

'We're ashamed of men like you walking around free. You're a danger to all women . . . and men.' Fatemeh said.

'We are no danger to anybody. We want only to maintain our honour.' The elder brother insisted.

'Your honour . . . ' said Zareen, disgusted.

' . . . her life,' Fatemeh added, sadly.

'Why does your honour need women's sacrificial blood?' Goli asked.

'Are you not men yourselves? You would do the same.'

'Don't you look at that door handle! You've nowhere to escape to. And anyway, she,' pointing to Goli, 'is a black belt expert. If you move she'll break your neck, and save me dirtying my gun,' Zareen said.

'No, we are not men, thank goodness,' Goli said. 'We are three women, part of a women's army. We're going to avenge your sister and defend many other women like her. We believe she has the right to do what she wants and with whichever man she chooses. The fact that you feed her is irrelevant to her and her life.'

'She was our sister, too.' said Zareen.

'So you are women. I thought you looked strange.' The brothers looked closely at the women.

'What a disguise. You fooled me,' said the younger brother.

Goli hit the first blow – she couldn't take their arrogance any more. Out of the blue she grabbed the younger brother's arm, twisted it with one hand and with the other hand chopped his neck hard. He bent over with pain, but the elder brother quickly came to his defence, hit Goli on the head. Goli's anger overcame her pain and she got hold of his fingers, twisting them as hard as she could until she heard them cracking. Zareen pointed the gun at his hand and warned him.

'I'll blow your hand off if you raise it again, and my friend, the karate expert, will deal with your brother.'

Fatemeh opened the car door and went to the boot, returning with some heavy ropes. The three women tied the men up, binding their hands and feet, stuffed their mouths with old material, and carried them, kicking and struggling, to the side of the road and dropped them there, under a tree. They then began to hit them with all their power and hatred. With each strike, each woman said, 'This is for the knife that you pushed into her back, this is for the knife that you pushed into her arm, this is for the knife that you pushed into her womb.' They left when the men were unconscious.

Back in the car they collapsed, trying to get their breath back. Anger and hatred were exhausting, Zareen concluded; Goli conceded that revenge was bitter sweet. They straightened themselves, tidied their jackets and trousers and drove away. Pleased and proud with their success so far, they talked about being hungry, about wanting to eat barbecued fresh rainbow trout, by the river Levizan and drink the best of Ghazvine wines. They hoped that the brothers would not be found for many days. Perhaps they had managed to break a few of their bones. The car surfed on through the dark, and they wished all the way from there to home that all the pasdars were dead.

## 13

Fatemeh was overwhelmed by the revenge they had carried out the night before. Having been part of the planning and the execution of the attack, she was now not so sure about her action. She felt guilty and confused. This was the first time in her life that she had been violent, that she had inflicted pain premeditatively on somebody. Her generous heart, her sensitivity and tendency towards non-violence were in conflict with her sense of duty and responsibility to women. And then there was her religious duty and her position as a lawyer to think of. Throughout the attack itself she was not as involved as Zareen and Goli: she had constant images of brass knuckles hitting her eye flashing through her mind when she was hitting them, which made her hesitate to inflict pain on them. Even though she had agreed that they had to suffer for the murder of their sister, and that this was the mildest revenge, she was not happy about being the executioner of such justice. How could she be a lawyer and make her own law? How could she abhor violence, suffer from it herself and then be violent? What was happening to her? All the years of studying law, hoping to practise it, looking forward to defending human rights and justice – had it all been a waste of time? Useless? If she was barred from practising her profession because she was a woman, was she going to practise it anyway, outside the law? What about her religious beliefs: thou shalt not hurt anyone – her father's precious motto. All was falling to pieces, all had been falling to pieces for quite a while. What was happening to her? She touched the scar around her eye.

She was changing, becoming a different person. How far would she change? Could she consciously choose her future direction or was she going to be overpowered by the events around her? She was afraid to ask herself such questions. Where was her harmonica? She found it. But damn, her father was in. No music.

She remembered the last conversation she had had with Zareen and Goli.

'I was so angry when I was hitting them, I really wanted them to be conscious and feel my every blow, not like when they killed her, in her sleep. Revenge was sweet after all,' Goli had said, pleased with herself.

'I didn't do much, but I don't feel happy. What is the purpose of beating up a few men? So what? The country is still full of them,' Fatemeh had said. The other two didn't respond for a while to what she had said.

'Yes . . . I guess in a country full of wild men, each a little dictator in his home, a little dictator at work and a big dictator in the street, it achieves little,' Zareen had said after a long pause.

A wall of silence later Goli had said, 'We had to do something. You don't mean that we should have just sat wringing our hands at all these murders but doing nothing.'

'I don't mean that. We can't remain passive victims forever, I know, but we have to do something more effective, something different . . . '

'I think what we have done tonight is good, not because it's the answer, the cure or a practice to follow, but because it is something that *we* could do, something small for a sister.' Goli had said. 'And we are learning. We will find something more powerful, more effective to do. We're just beginners in this dirty trade.'

'That's right. You know we are only learning about our capabilities, and, of course, we make mistakes—' Zareen had added.

'But then we live in this land,' Goli had said, 'a land that is constantly shifting and sinking beneath our feet . . . '

' . . . and we just have to lift ourselves an inch or two, every now and then, to escape sinking.' Zareen had finished for her.

A sense of dismay, disillusionment and self-scrutiny had set in among them. But just before they parted, Zareen had said, 'Don't forget we are gradually losing our fear, this monstrous disabling fear. That must be good.'

True, Fatemeh *was* losing her fear, was becoming more critical, less forgiving and was gaining more strength. But she was gaining more confusion and doubts too. They had decided not to meet for a while so she could not even confide in Zareen. She picked up her harmonica and, regardless of her father, started to play a tune to herself.

Only three days later the front pages of the newspapers were blazoned with the news of the attack and large pictures of the two brothers. The headlines were sensational.

'Women in Turbans and Surplices,' 'The Imposter Men', 'The She-Devils Strike', 'The Women Terrorists in the Guise of Men', 'The Revenge of the Women', 'The Phoney Men', 'The Karate Women Kick Back'.

Each of the women read the headlines in her home with shaky fingers, a tight throat and weak knees. A mixture of excitement, fear and deep pleasure accompanied their reading of the news.

The papers from the conservative right to the centre left were all terrified, angry and very offensive. Their news described the beatings, the bruises, the pain and sufferings of the two brothers in detail. They were found after two days by a gardener who worked at the orchards. They were taken to a hospital and their condition was not serious. They had even been provided with full-time police protection. Some of the editorials went over the top: warning men to be careful of their fellow men, to suspect them, and especially all strangers approaching them at night. The streets were no longer safe for men! The police and pasdars were to stop and search all men. The government warned that it was the action of a well-organised gang, possibly directed by foreign agents.

The socialist newspapers had a different view of it. They presented it as women taking revenge, giving details – unlike the mainstream papers – of how the brothers had killed their sister and won their freedom. They elaborated on the fact that the brothers had said they felt an eternal shame at having been beaten up by women: they couldn't resume work, they couldn't face family or friends.

The women's newspapers, which came out later than all of them, were more sympathetic and had printed statistics citing the number of women killed through domestic violence and honour killings, with some terrible pictures of mutilated and raped women, concluding that enough is enough. The law must now give women human rights and abolish adultery punishments, honour killings and all other discrimination against women. Women are angry and getting angrier, said their editorials. Women activists everywhere, in each town, college, workplace and every home were nervously pleased and inspired by the news. It had become the talk of every meeting, school room, the topic of conversation at every bus-stop, shop queue, hospital waiting room. Women were talking – it was food for thought, and gave them strength and ideas.

The friends were unable to understand how, with so much censorship in the media, the news was published in the first place and given so much coverage. Was it to warn men? Was it to inspire a backlash against women? Was it an excuse to implement further restrictions on them?

They had hit the media in the eye and put a bit of fear and awe into the men who normally wrote or read news about crimes against women with indifference or just slight discomfort. Perhaps now they would question the nature of the crime, the criminals and how they were represented. Only when men were directly threatened themselves did they start thinking about the implications of their actions. They were itching to meet up and discuss the news and excitement that they had created, that enormous shared pleasure.

That morning Zareen waited for her customers in nervous anticipation. She had turned the radio on and left it on to hear the news. She hoped it would be a busy day and that different women would come to the salon, women who would take up the news and make abundant comment on it.

As she was tidying and laying things out, Muneer walked in, her face pain-stricken.

'It's incredible,' she said slowly. 'Azadeh is missing. Can't believe it. She's just disappeared. Missing.' She sat down, petrified. So did Zareen. Azadeh wasn't a political woman, in the sense of being an activist. She was just a good-time girl, a young, jolly, sixteen-year-old woman. What could have happened to her? Zareen just held Muneer, and comforted her quietly.

Muneer went on, 'She was just walking with another friend after school, going to a coffee shop, but just before they reached the café they were stopped by a couple of young men. She was smoking, she had lipstick on, her skirt was a bit short – this all infuriated them. You see, everybody has to wear the veil at school, but many girls take it off as soon as they've left school for the day, put it in their bags and put it back on again before they go home. Azadeh often did this. The two young boys questioned her, but she didn't realise they were off-duty pasdars and she didn't take them seriously, just joked about it, lifted her skirt even higher, was silly, said stupid things. "What's wrong with my thighs? Pity to hide them under a black garment. Is it because you can't control yourselves. Because my leg makes you feel sexy? Let's see it then." Stupid things like that. She made fun of them. Her mind must have gone soft or something. How could she treat a pasdar so slightly? They just took her away, for more questioning, they said. Her friend saw her being taken away, and then ran away as fast as she could. Nobody knows who they were, or where she could have been taken. She is just gone, like water that falls on the dry earth. Oh, Zareen, what am I going to do? How can a friend disappear like this? Her family are in agony, they have tried everything, searched everywhere, gone to the most likely places – the police stations, enquired at all the interrogation centres, visited all the prisons, what more can they do? What can I do? How do you find a missing friend?'

The first customer entered, so Zareen took Muneer to the back room. She was crying, tears dropped slowly and soundlessly down her cheeks, she brushed them away with her fingers, Zareen sat with her until her tears had dried and she was quieter, when she left her and returned to the salon.

She apologised to the customer, said that Muneer wasn't feeling well, and got on with the customer's face and eyebrows, which she wanted done before she went shopping. Zareen's heart wasn't in it. Muneer was her only other worker, she couldn't afford to employ anybody else. Soraya, a nurse who lived nearby came in for a hair cut, looking haggard and pale, because of her long working hours and unsociable shifts. She looked like she needed a nurse herself. Another customer brought in her granddaughter, Susan, for a hair cut. The older woman held her hand as if Susan was about to run away. The girl didn't like having her hair cut, she wanted it to be left alone, but her mother insisted on her looking neat and tidy. Zareen often joked with her to make it easier.

Muneer returned to the shop, with red eyes. She apologised for being late and looked for her apron. Zareen was washing Soraya's hair, when she heard the nine o'clock news come on the radio.

'The two brothers who were seriously beaten by a gang of women have been deemed well enough to be discharged from hospital. Three women dressed as men kidnapped Mr Akbarian and his brother, and beat them up until they were unconscious. The pasdars are on the look-out everywhere.'

Susan made the first excited exclamation, 'Oh good! Girls wearing boys' clothes. Can I do it too?'

Her grandmother shook her head and said, 'Oh my God. What is the world coming to? No, of course you can't do that! What next? What else?' She tapped her knee as she said it with a mixture of horror and disapproval.

The radio went on '. . . minister for home affairs, in replying to questions from journalists, admitted that the law has to be changed so that dress codes would become much stricter. It will be made illegal for women to wear men's clothes.'

'Damn!' Zareen gasped involuntarily, but bit back any further comment quickly.

'God,' said Soraya, 'what a fuss they're making about the injuries to a couple of men! You don't know what we see in hospitals these days, so many battered, knived, bleeding women, some even miscarrying because of their husbands. They beat their wives up right inside the hospital now, if they give birth to a girl, or have twins, or their baby son dies prematurely or something. It seems all classes of men have become more vicious, more misogynist than ever before. And with the shortage of nurses – they sack us for not wearing the veil – it's hard work. I think those brothers deserved it.' Soraya seemed to have witnessed worse.

'It takes a lot of courage to do something like that. I wish I had a bit of that, it would be very handy, very handy, especially these days,' said Muneer, plucking her customer's eyebrows. She looked calm and busy with her work. She must be in turmoil inside, Zareen thought.

'So it's giving you ideas, is it? I tell you nothing is keeping women down. Who do you want to beat up, I'd like to know?' Susan's grandmother asked.

'Oh, don't put your hand on my belly . . . a few . . . a few.' Muneer sighed deeply but wasn't giving anything away.

'How did they do it? Where did they get the men's clothes? Imagine having a turban and a surplice on!' said Mina who had had her face done and was getting her bag ready for her shopping trip. 'How funny, I would have laughed myself silly. What a picture!' A couple of the women laughed with her.

But Zareen was unhappy. She wanted to listen to the women and concentrate on their discussion, to know their views and feelings, but her heart was too heavy for rational debate. Another customer, Simeen, a neighbour, walked in and sat down.

'Are you talking about these three women gangsters? The latest in the organised kidnapping warfare.' She tried to make herself comfortable in the chair.

'It doesn't take much organising, just putting on some men's clothes, acting like one of them, and beating them up,' said the grandmother.

'They've taken a great risk and I wish more women would follow their path.' Mina sat down again, keener on participating in the discussion than doing her shopping.

'It sounds like a joke, not quite real,' said Afroz, a new customer who had just come in.

'It's a serious joke, very real. How can it do any good for

anyone – the government will just put more restrictions on women now.'

'Incredible, isn't it? If they bring out a law to forbid women to wear trousers and jackets, it just confirms how much each sex's identity and personality is embodied in what they wear,' said Soraya. 'We have to wear a uniform, a veil, like prisoners, like nurses. We wear our identity cards on our bodies, saving the intelligence service the job.'

'Yes,' agreed Zareen eagerly, 'there's power in men's clothes, strength, freedom.'

'Who cares about wearing trousers? Why isn't there power in skirts?' asked Afroz.

'I prefer my comfortable skirt and chador,' added Simeen.

'I don't. I can't play in them,' cried Susan.

'It's a complex problem, why is Islamic doctrine based on the absence of women's body, voice, founded on her immobility—'

Soraya was interrupted by Simeen. 'That's not true! You're a queen in your own house, within your family, among your relations. You have a strong presence and an audible voice there. God, you should have seen my mother!'

'But what if you don't want to have a family, you don't want to be like your mother and grandmothers, you want to be somebody very different?' asked Mina.

'If you ask me,' the grandmother faced the rest, 'you can't be, and it's senseless to try, a waste of time and energy. You can't fight the government and you won't get anywhere with an eye for an eye.'

'It can never be an eye for an eye. It is only ever a single eyelash for an eye,' Muneer said.

'You must admit though, those women have been very courageous. Bravo to them.' Mina obviously couldn't postpone the shopping any longer and left.

'Bravo to being brainless,' commented Simeen.

'Yes, it's okay for some women to act crazy, but we must be wise and think about the future and protect ourselves. Well, I'm going to make sure my granddaughters are well protected – don't you stray Susan. You must catch them young. Haven't you heard the wise Mulla Nasredin's tale? I'll tell you anyway, Susan should hear it. One day Mulla Nasredin set out on a journey with his donkey and her foal, carrying a load. Halfway through their journey the mother donkey ran away. Mulla ran off in hot pursuit and tried hard to catch it but the donkey disappeared. So Mulla returned to the foal, got hold of a big stick and beat the hell out of it. Some passersby who saw him and his cruel act were dismayed, interrupted him and asked: "Mulla, why are you so mad at this poor foal? The mother has run away, why are you hitting the child?" Mulla replied, "You don't know anything. If I let this foal free, it would run faster than the mother." '

This was an old fable. Most of them knew it, but they still laughed at the way the grandmother had told it. Susan didn't laugh.

'It wasn't fair, the poor baby donkey.'

'Of course it's not right, but don't worry, it's an old story,' Zareen said to her as she led her to a seat to have her hair cut, away from the grasp of her granny.

The uneasy conversation continued. Zareen listened and tried to concentrate on what each woman was saying while she worked. She could not draw any conclusions about how the women viewed the action as a whole. Their conversation was so inconclusive and vague, their desires often unclear, uncertain. She wanted more definite and reassuring responses. But she also knew that what people could say in a public place, a hairdresser's salon was limited. But how else would she know if such actions were supported or approved of by women she knew, women like her from her background? She needed to know that. She didn't want to be an isolated figure, to live and work in a vacuum, separated from the women of her class. The only way she could have got a definite answer would have been to participate in the debate herself, equally, to question them, confront them and present them with situations; but that was too risky. And now she was confused, frustrated and uncertain like everybody else.

She couldn't wait any longer: she needed to meet and talk to somebody, however unsafe it was. She decided to send her son with a message to Malihe, asking to meet her in the local mosque.

They arrived separately. Malihe got there first and, when Zareen arrived, was sitting in a dark corner with some neighbours. Zareen went in well wrapped up in her chador and said hello to a few familiar faces, before sitting down quietly by Malihe.

They were surrounded by Malihe's neighbours, who talked about the children, the shops, the high price of food. It was early evening and women were coming in gradually and filling the place up, which gave Malihe and Zareen a chance to move further away to a quieter corner between two groups of praying women. They each took a Quran, rested them on a wooden holder in front of them and started reading with a slow hum. After a while they stopped to rest and interpret it to each other, whispering quietly, as was customary in such a place.

'You have read the news? Great, isn't it?' asked Zareen.

'Yes, but still, we have to wait, it's too early yet to see.'

'In the salon they were talking about it, they have such mixed feelings, it's killing me. Only two women were definitely in favour of our action . . . actually two and a half,' she added with a smile, thinking of Susan.

'What did you expect?'

'More support from women, more approval. Is it too much to expect?'

Malihe coughed a little and straightened herself, having a good look round. Everything looked normal. 'That's not possible. You can't expect that. It isn't so simple.'

'If we don't have women's support, why should we do it?'

'You're not just doing it for other women, are you?'

'No! But I'm not doing it for myself alone either.' These last words were loud enough to turn a few heads, which Malihe managed to reassure with a professionally wise look and a pious nod of the head.

Don't expect any praise,' she said. 'You don't want to be a hero. Women distrust heroes.'

'I don't want any praise. I just want to know what women like me think or want one way or another.'

'Women are divided, their attention and energy is all over

the place, it's least with what they want or need. We have to rely on our own judgment now.'

'Are we alone in this then?'

'Maybe, for the time being. But don't lose heart – two and a half isn't bad at all, don't underestimate that half.'

The women were finishing off their prayers, their reading of the Quran, and were packing away their prayer mats and sitting down to rest. The tea woman walked in carrying a tray full of steaming tea and a jar of huge unevenly cut sugar cubes. Zareen and Malihe each got a glass of tea and a few sugars and set the tea down to cool next to their folded Quran holders.

Zareen remembered Muneer's story and told Malihe about Azadeh's disappearance, and suggested that Muneer go and see Malihe, as she was good at giving advice. Malihe said she would try her best, but that 'her eyes don't drink water'.

Zareen felt lighter for speaking to Malihe. Her uncertainty was not any less, but it was a state of being she could now accept. She hoped secretly that she would one day be able to rally women's support openly, and hear them speak their mind and ideas clearly. That she would receive their approval and blessing on newer and more daring actions against the anti-women state. And better still, that these women would join them. She looked around at the hundreds of women. Women who looked the same, behaved the same, but were they the same as her? Women sitting and meditating under the high blue arches of this old mosque. A holy shrine for many women, a holy place of worship, a holy gathering – revered, impressive and subdued.

## 14

Only a few days later each of the women got a message from Malihe, asking to meet them urgently, because there was something she wanted to talk about. They were reluctant to meet at Ziba Style, as the area was still under surveillance. They thought about alternative venues – perhaps a mosque, or a visit to a shrine. It seemed that a meeting in public, with lots of people around, would be safer these days than one held in your own place. Then Fatemeh suggested her house. They were having a rozeh, a private sermon, there and it would be a good pretext under which to meet. Malihe wasn't very keen on the idea initially, as she didn't want to see crowds of people, especially as she might know some of them. However, Fatemeh said they could stay in her room, the rozeh would be in the garden and they could listen to it through the window, if they wanted to, which reassured Malihe.

They arrived there one by one before the rozeh started. Fatemeh had left the window open, and it looked as if they were listening to the rozeh going on and to her father's sermon. Goli wanted to hear Fatemeh's father, but Malihe didn't want to, saying that it would disturb her. Everybody was surprised, she sounded strange. But she explained that it was part of the reason why she wanted to talk to them. So they left the window ajar.

The maid brought in some tea and sweets and they closed the door behind her. Zareen and Goli were dying to talk about the reactions of the newspapers and were already engaged in discussing it between themselves when Malihe interrupted them, impatient and uncomfortable with their chit-chat.

'You won't believe what I have to say, I can't believe it myself. I don't know how to say it . . . I feel better now, but my God, I couldn't see straight for two days, it has . . . ' Malihe couldn't finish her sentence. Nobody else offered to finish it for her. No one uttered a word. They were still frozen in their surprise. They waited for her to continue.

'One early evening my neighbour Gohar came to me and said, "Mali, let's go to the large mosque in Shookofeh. There's a new mulla and people say he's very good." So I said, "All right, I haven't got much to do in the evenings these days." So we went. We had a good chat and a cup of tea and sweets in the women's section. Then he came to the pulpit and started off in a slow, soft and appealing voice. Then, when he began another sermon, crying out loud, shouting, the walls of my heart shook. Something familiar in his voice, that tone that I will never forget, trembled me. As he went on I was more disturbed. I had to find a way to see his face so I wriggled around, you know how difficult it is to find a hole through the black tent if you want to see through to the other side and the pulpit. So I wriggled around, Gohar was surprised, asked me what was wrong, told me to sit in one place and don't make a show of myself. But I couldn't. I moved around, peeped into the men's section till I found a corner where I could see his face. But the face was not familiar, not at all, lots of hair and a moustache, a turban and surplice and the mulla's usual long, tight-necked white robe, made recognition very difficult for me. But his voice I couldn't doubt. So I sat there in that far corner of the black tent, gazing at him, through the narrow gap, and asking myself with a broken voice inside me, "Is this really the man who tortured me in Evin?" I couldn't believe it. I wasn't sure. I couldn't recognise his face. The heavy moustache and the beard confused me. But the eyes, the eyes were the same. But how could he be here? How could this happen? I knew that a lot of people joke about the boom in jobs for mullas, that it's the only job going with good bread in it. But this? I thought, I have to try and see him close-up. I waited with my heart in my mouth until his sermon was finished. Then I left the women's section to go out and see him. Gohar thought I had gone potty. I told her to wait for me, I was just going out for a few minutes. So I went out and waited on a corner of the street, pretending I had a question to ask him. I covered my face well behind the chador with only my eyes showing. He came out. I wanted to say something, to ask him a question, to stop him for a second, to look at him, to see his eyes close-up, but I had lost my voice – I opened my mouth, my mouth stayed open, but no words came out. He disappeared off into an alley, taking my peace of mind with him. That night and the day after I spent with my head between my shaking knees, asking myself if it was the man who had tortured me. How could that be? Am I mistaken? But I could not have mistaken that voice and those great ugly eyes.'

Malihe was squatting with her knees held tight between her arms and her chin resting on her knees, looking down.

'I began to remember him coming to my cell, threatening, waving his baton at me, shouting, pacing up and down my cell, insulting me. That brutal look, that brutal uniform with its leather strap going round twice from his belt to his shoulder. The leather so clean, straight and tough. I had to look at that leather for so long. It shined like his eyes, that glassy cruel shine. I felt that leather strap on my heart, in the daytime and in my dreams long after he had left. I have hated leather ever since – I can't see a leather belt, I can't touch a leather bag. I hate leather.'

Malihe stopped, she sounded exhausted, consumed with the pain of retelling that memory. She stopped and the three women sank into their seats, as if they had put all their flesh and soul into listening to her, and were dried out now.

The initial stillness was followed by exclamations.

'No! Impossible! Horrible! No! Dreadful!'

The melancholy sound of the sermon outside was rising. Zareen moved herself a bit to get some life back into her limbs and quickly went over to Malihe and hugged her close, keeping her in her arms.

'What can I say? What can anybody say?' Goli gasped out.

'Let's have some strong tea that will knock some life into us and then think and talk,' Zareen said gently.

Fatemeh felt numb. The sound of the servant's approach was heard, Fatemeh asked for fresh tea, it was brought in.

The strong Lahijani tea, with its delicate sweet taste and gentle aroma, dampened their mouths, soothed their throats, warmed them back to their thoughts. They drank three or four cups of tea one after another and, when the teapot and glasses sat empty next to the half-consumed sweets, they started to form their response to the horror of the event.

'What do you feel now?' asked Fatemeh.

'I don't know, I guess a bit better,' Malihe replied.

'I can't believe that one government's torturer can be the next government's priest,' said Goli. 'On the other hand,' she continued, 'there is a common misconception that all the political prisoners came from the rich northern middle-class families, so he could have thought he was safe in the south.'

'How dare he come out in public like this, though? So openly?' puzzled Zareen.

'Perhaps he's protected by somebody high up, somebody he has done favours for in his former role,' Goli said.

'Ya, right, perhaps a member of the clergy or an ayatollah?' agreed Malihe.

'Well, we knocked out two men a few days ago,' said Zareen. 'Do you want us to take him to no man's land and knock him out too?'

'No! We can't do this. We are not the bully boys, the law enforcers of society.' Fatemeh was vehement.

'It's a waste of our time,' Malihe added. 'I don't want him beaten up. I want to know who put him in that position. I want to kill him. But no, I don't know . . . '

'We can find out for sure if it really is him,' said Fatemeh. 'Do you want me to ask my father to help us find out his real identity?'

'Yes, let's be absolutely sure,' Malihe said. 'I want to kill them all off,' she added suddenly after a pause. 'One won't be enough.'

'This is mad,' Fatemeh said quietly.

'All those men who reinstate yesterday's torturers as today's mullas, the men who listen to them, the higher echelons of the present hierarchy,' Malihe continued.

'But Malihe, how can we touch these men?' asked Goli.

'We can't just gather together all the men who we think are responsible in one room and carry out our kind of justice . . . ' Fatemeh argued.

'Why not?' Malihe turned to her.

'Just kill off the whole bloody brutal lot of them?' Zareen was incredulous.

'Yes, why not?' Malihe answered. 'There must be a way and I must find it. Men move around in one circle, the family of men, they trade professions, the connection between physical torture and religious piety. How can they link up and be interchangeable? God, I am going to find out.'

'Shall I ask my father?' Fatemeh asked again.

'No.' Goli was adamant. 'We don't know how to do this yet or whether he would be on our side.'

'He might . . . '

'No mulla can.' Goli retorted.

'He is not a mulla.'

'Please don't be offended, Fati. Please don't tell anybody. Only we should know. Trust is difficult to come by these days,' Malihe said.

'So how can we find out anything?' asked Zareen.

'Well, we can do some homework ourselves, find out who runs the mosques, which mulla controls what locality, who they are answerable to. Whether they know who is at the head and how each chain is connected to the next, how the establishment works from the Ayatollah to the common mulla, the lowest of the hierarchy,' answered Malihe.

'We'd be no nearer to a solution with that kind of searching – I did that when I was looking for the causes of violence against women and the reasons why men commit it. I didn't get anywhere,' Goli said.

'I still think it would be a good idea to learn about the mechanisms of this new establishment, its nuts and bolts and how it's screwed together,' said Zareen.

'Rather its ingredients – how this bitter cake is made, what proportions of flour, and from where, and how much water from which stream, what kind of sugar – white, brown, home produced, or bitter, where the milk comes from and the butter, what kind of temperature, the shape and size of the pots, who are the cooks and who gets what share.' Malihe countered.

'The ingredients of the establishment? Hmm.' Goli shook her head.

'It's getting airless in here,' said Fatemeh and pushed the window wide open. The sermon sailed into her room.

' . . . No. Nothing like that. With force we won't gain a true Islamic society, a free human society. Our Imam Hussain, God's grace on him, said himself if you can't accept Islam, remain free. I am asked how women should be in our Islamic republic. I say free, strong and educated. Mrs Gandhi is a woman too. We want women like her – she always has a scarf on her head, and nobody forces her. I am asked how our new Islamic republic should treat the Jews, the Baha'is, the Zoroastrians and their holy places. I say with respect and brotherly love, with charity – love your brothers is my slogan. We hear of attacks on the holy shrines of the Zoroastrians, and on the Christians' hospital for the blind in Esfehan. Brothers, this is a shame, shame on our faith. And the killings of the Baha'is, it is unacceptable. We want a humane society. All these recent pictures of the Baha'i women in the papers, in full Islamic dress, denouncing their faith. It's very disturbing. It is a dishonour to us. Brothers and sisters, we have some real social problems like alcoholism, poverty, drug-taking among our youth, prostitution. We must deal with them as social diseases. Burning of prostitutes is inhuman, brothers – sixty young women, some with their children, were burned alive at the hands of some ignorant young men. This is inhuman. This is lawlessness. This is a bad example of an Islamic society. Banning alcoholism, gambling, etc., won't solve our problems. Our first deputies in the parliament after the constitutional revolution of 1905–1911, our brothers in the clergy refused the banning of alcohol and drugs then. I argue against it now. If people need them, they will get them. We must get rid of the need for such intoxication . . . get rid of the need that seeks refuge in such intoxication. We must seek the root . . . '

# 15

It was a difficult time for everybody. The political situation was worsening. Just when they needed each other's company and friendship the most, they were having to work in lonely isolation.

Work for Zareen was becoming more repressive. Women had become quieter, more conservative, less expressive. It was harder for her to speak her mind, and to know the other customers' minds. The atmosphere in her salon had changed: it was boring and subdued, as if all the women were suffering from a heavy depression.

Heavier pressure was being put on women's hairdressing salons. One brand of zealots condemned them as sinful, insisting that they should be banned and closed down. Another group of fanatics wanted them open, but only for weddings and other ceremonies: they argued that women needed hairdressing and beauty salons, but only for wedding ceremonies, or to look good for their husbands. Every now and then the government debated the issue and passed some more legislation to curtail their business even further.

Zareen was still in touch with some of her union friends. The union was allocated the work of rationing, distributing and selling lipsticks, nail polish, hair colourings, shampoos and various other hairdressing materials. It was hard for Zareen to obtain them, in spite of her contacts. You had to have ration coupons for your allowance, and you were only allowed small amounts, accompanied by 'advice' as to whom it should be used on. No nail polish or lipstick on single women or students, for example; meaning that hairdressers had to check the age of their clients and the reason for their visit.

She was frustrated by the continuous pressures in her job, the conservative tolerance of the women around her and her isolation from her friends. She felt dislocated at work and at home. Her family and work suffered, her usual efficient, sociable manner slipped. Her constant monologue of dissatisfaction that she could share only with herself added to her sense of impotence.

It was one of those days when Goli rang her suddenly, saying she was coming over. She arrived in no time, and before Zareen had even ushered her into the sitting room, Goli exploded.

'It's the office, it's been set on fire, arson, just before the publication of our first pamphlet – the one on violence against women! The typewriters, the stencil machine, all roasted, singed . . . The papers all set on fire, reduced to ashes . . . The desk and chairs . . . It's gutted. The window frames are broken, glass shattered everywhere. And then the graffiti all over the walls – "Women's place is at home", "This is a corruption cell", "We will be back", hateful, hateful!'

They hugged each other, taking refuge in each other. Goli said she didn't know what to do next, whom to go to for shelter for their women's office? What could their women's group do now? The two women didn't know what to say to each other, words failed them. Goli departed on a note of hopelessness.

After that meeting Zareen wanted desperately to see Fatemeh: she needed to: she would take the risk. If Goli had, why not her? She rang Fatemeh up to rearrange her mother's hairdressing date, bringing it forward to that day.

At Fatemeh's house, she took Zareen to her mother's quarters, and waited for her to finish there. The minute she had finished they went to Fatemeh's room. Once there, with the door closed behind them, alone together in that dim and cosy space, she was much calmer. They sat close, leaning on the cushions and on each other, shoulders touching, drinking tea which, like a warm sea washed through their bodies and soothed them. They sat quietly for a while, absorbed each in the presence of the other.

'I feel better already, just being here with you. I have been so confused and anxious. I wish the excitement of hitting the headlines had lasted a bit longer. I detest this waiting in fear and impotence. I feel trapped, even though we are free and have not been caught.' She went on, telling Fatemeh about the arson attack, and how it meant the end of the women's group and any hopes of publishing something. She wondered aloud about Malihe and Goli, what were they going through, were they coping; and about her sense of dislocation, how she couldn't help them much, she felt so low herself.

Fatemeh was disturbed by what she heard. Zareen was usually the optimist, the active, clear-minded doer, not so self-doubting and disorientated. Fatemeh tried to console her, speaking about her own self-doubt, guilt and her fear of losing her identity after the revenge against the brothers.

'Why are you so down? We should be positive and more hopeful now that we have decided we are going to act? To do something constructive about the mullas and their power.'

Fatemeh put her hands on Zareen's bowed shoulders. Her chador had fallen down to her waist and Fatemeh could feel her shoulder bones, the softness of her upper arms. Zareen was deep in thought and did not reply.

'*You* need a hair cut now,' Fatemeh coaxed, 'especially if you're going to wear that suit again. You looked so handsome and graceful in it.'

'Kiss that goodbye. We can't now, under all these new restrictions. You liked me in it though? Graceful and handsome in that suit?' Zareen looked questioningly into Fatemeh's face with a tiny smile playing at the corner of her mouth.

'Not just in that suit, you know.'

'No, really!' Zareen was smiling fully now. 'I'm surprised, as I'm the one to make other women up and compliment them. I don't get such a treat myself, to be made up or be complimented. It's in the nature of being a wife, and a hairdresser. Who wants to be a wife to a wife?'

'I would. I would be a wife to you.'

'You would? Why don't you buy a house next door to me, so we could meet every minute of the day,' Zareen joked.

'The day I could buy or rent a place of my own and live in it safely, that day, the consciousness of this land will have risen so high, high above the heavens! Till then I can only dream of it.' Fatemeh's burst of feeling surprised Zareen.

'I dream too. We *can* dream – they can't deprive us of our dreams.'

'Let's get out of this country, go somewhere where nobody can touch us and live happily together . . . Shall we?' Fatemeh asked urgently.

'Not that again – we've talked about it already, you know it's not possible, my children and so on . . . '

'All right, sorry, I shouldn't have said it. You know I love the children too . . . I will begin to miss them if I can't come and visit any longer.'

'The other day Parvaneh and Bahram said they hadn't seen you for a long time. I said you were busy going to the university every day. Jalal asked if you had a job now. I said, fat chance of that. The law doesn't need women any more, male lawyers only can practise justice. He asked why your father doesn't put his power behind the opposition and stop the extremists. I had cooked ash reshteh, lots of garlic and mint on top and the children were eating and complaining that it was burning their mouths; Jalal was worried he would stink out the bazaar.

'He has work problems too, the production of dried fruit and nuts has fallen and the quality is not as good. He said he opened a sack of pistachios the other day and a pack of moths flew out at him. And the religious power struggles in the bazaar are getting more vicious as each member of the clergy tries to gain a larger patch . . .

'Mum was in the other day and I did her hair. She said henna was making her look older, could I use black colouring instead. I told her hair colour is rationed by the union, and it's too expensive on the black market, but that I'd try to get hold of some. She looked exhausted, she is ageing, everybody is ageing prematurely. And, of course, the children rush to her and complain about the television . . .

'I was so angry the other night, you see, because all the bloody programmes had endless moustache after moustache, then beard after beard, then ties after ties. I just got fed up, especially when I heard the minister for employment claiming proudly that he could account for the sacking of a hundred thousand women for refusing to wear the veil. I banged so hard on the television that I nearly broke it. So I wrapped it up and took it down to the basement and hid it in a dusty old cupboard. But since then I have a battle with the children every day now. They've been crying endlessly for it and I have refused to give in. I say to them, you can't watch man after man, boy after boy on the screen, you'll get blind. It isn't like that in the real world – there are women and girls too. But they don't care about such things. They just want the box. They say it's their only entertainment, that they're bored. I tend to agree, but I still say better bored than brainwashed. Well, they get enough of it at school anyway . . .

'I went to the market the other day in my summer sandals. I was in such a hurry I had forgotten to put on my socks. The bloody greengrocer says, sister! Your feet. I say, what about my feet? He says, they're naked. I say, so what? He shakes his head in disgust. I say, are my toes too sexy for you? What sexy toes I have – I'm going to get them insured for millions, and I just walked away, didn't wait for his reply. You know now in the bazaar and at some of the markets, stall-holders won't sell to unveiled women. It's a total siege declared on women. Ah, what am I talking about? Why am I rattling on in this way? What is happening to me?'

'Nothing, you're just talking to me. It's fine. We're all under siege, but we will break it. We're going to strike our blows too, one day . . .'

'Are we? When?'

'Soon,' soothed Fatemeh. 'I heard this joke yesterday, let me tell you, it will cheer you up. There are so many jokes going around the university these days. This great member of the clergy dies and, of course, expects to arrive at Heaven's gate. But the Angel of Hell welcomes him and directs him towards his punishments. He protests that he has been a very chaste man, he has obeyed all his religious duties, he has prayed all his life and, above all, he has created a massive Islamic revolution on earth and many people have followed him, so on, so forth. The Angel of Hell says to him, stop, stop all that. We know what you have done on earth, don't brag on about yourself. You have done some good and some terrible things, and because of that we allow you to choose your own punishment. He tries to change the Angel's mind, but to no avail, so he reluctantly agrees. In one corner he sees people that are burning in fire. He says, no, that's too hard for me. In another corner people are being flogged. He says, no, that's too hard for me, and so on. Until he comes to a huge, square swimming pool with many people standing in it, holding their noses. A man is standing on the poolside with a whistle in his hand. This grandee asks, what is this. The Angel explains that the swimming pool is full of shit and that this is the punishment for those people standing in it. He thinks, well, that's not bad, after a while I'll get used to the smell. So he agrees to that punishment and jumps in. A few minutes later the man with the whistle blows it, shouting, "The break's over, heads under!" ' Fatemeh laughed; but Zareen only smiled.

'There are some funny ones made up in my union too,' she said. 'But right now, I am worried. I'm still preoccupied with what my customers think of our action. I've spoken to many of them and feel more frustrated with their lack of empathy with other women, their lack of interest and absence of ideas for alternative actions, their general acceptance of the situation. I can't even be sure of those who have supported us in the past. Would they change their minds? Or will they grow stronger, more militant? I wonder. They just don't think in terms of justice, truth, equal rights for women, as you do. They don't think such principles apply to women.'

'No, you're wrong. Women do want justice, equal rights. I talk to women too, hundreds of them pass through this house every month. Why, even our pious maid thinks what is being done to women is unjust, un-Islamic and inhuman. She complains about the latest bus segregation, men in the front, women in the back, separate entrances, separate seats. She thinks it divides the families and the children.'

'But we have no rights anyway. What rights do we have?'

'We're equal under the law – our civil law grants equality to all citizens. And we're equal under God's eyes – even in the Quran there are many passages where women and men are equal.'

'What's the use of that?' cried Zareen. 'In practice we are not equal. What are we doing about it? The black Americans reached the point when they stopped using the buses and walked everywhere, walked on and on, they defied segregation. Why aren't women doing the same here? We too have been segregated for centuries.'

'You didn't see the siege of Azadi Square. We tried to "walk" then, and more – but it's difficult, because we have children. Our children bind us to our men.'

'It isn't that alone. It isn't that simple. It can't be – I have children.'

'Okay, it isn't that simple. Obviously we can't agree on that. I think children have a lot to do with it, though. You know the Greek story, I don't remember it very well, but at a time of war, women decided that it was an unjust war, and that they didn't want their children to be killed, so they went on a no-reproduction strike – they wouldn't have sex with men, wouldn't bear children, until the war stopped. I dream of our women doing that too. But will they?'

'Never.'

'We must have hope, though, Zari. I don't know, the complexity of patriarchy is beyond me.'

'We have to understand it if we mean to fight it.'

'We will. I've been talking to my father, and reading a lot of books on Islamic history, especially battles. They're pretty gruesome war stories, but they give you an idea of the ideology of war. What men do to gain power. We can learn about their determination, zeal and the force of their convictions and use that for our own ends.'

'It makes me sick to think of their zeal and motives.' Zareen looked uninterested. 'We don't want any of that. We have to find our own way.'

'Out of thin air?'

'Perhaps that's all we've got. We want power, but to hold up ourselves, not to hold down others.'

'But how do you free yourself from being held down for so long? Do you think we can just ask for our human rights, demand them, and men will just say, yes, here's the freedom to walk in the streets, have the right to earn your living, have the right to love?'

'Why can't we have these basic rights anyway? It's our birthright! What's stopping us?'

'Women themselves.'

'You would say that, wouldn't you?'

'I wouldn't be totally wrong. But it is the system too.'

'But where is this system? Is it in the parliament, the government offices, in the army, the law books, the media?'

'It's in the way our houses are built, in the air, in the back alleys, in our neighbours' homes, in the children's memory . . .'

'So is there no hope? Of knowing where our enemy hides? And how to fight him?'

'Yes, and no. But we must still engage him in battle.'

'What? Dismantle the system?'

'Why not?' Fatemeh watched Zareen slide down onto the floor, and throw up her hands in exasperation. Her mind was a battlefield of questions, ideas, arguments and dead ends. She wanted just a sign of hope.

'Let me play you a tune,' said Fatemeh, bending to kiss Zareen's head, her hair and her bare neck. The warmth of that touch zoomed through Zareen's blood: more, more of that deep intimacy she wanted.

Fatemeh leaned back on the cushion, Zareen shifted a bit and put her heavy head on Fatemeh's lap. Fatemeh began to play her harmonica. A delicate, yet passionate melody fountained up to hang above the velvet curtains, the turquoise glass jar, the silvery tapestries and the satin hangings. Zareen stretched her body out on the carpet, looking up at the sequins of light, glittering by the thousand: the small chandelier above was dancing to the music, to a tune that left her battled mind behind. How, she wondered, could such a small instrument make such hanging magic?

# 16

The four women did not meet up for some time.

Goli returned to the university scene. After the arson attack on the women's group she felt at a loss, and spent her time talking with friends, not knowing what was best to do. Political life on campus was now very turbulent. Goli walked straight back into the uproar of debates, the heat of noise, the passion of hands, mouths, words, ideas, books, posters and bodies. The grass could not be seen for the moving figures and their body talk.

Looking for Marjan, she pushed through the unveiled, hard and steaming male bodies, squeezed through the walls of body politics, assailed by fragments, half-heard sentences, distorted faces and puffs of cigarette smoke exhaled with moving words:

'The revolutionary Islam . . . '
'You betrayed Gonabad . . . '
'But what about the Azerbaijanies?'
'What about the Kurds . . . '
'How can Islamic religious principles . . . '
'Civil war . . . '
'Revolution . . . '
'Anti-imperialism . . . '
'You're an idealist . . . ' Push, squeeze. 'Sorry.' 'Pardon.'
Goli listened, watched and went on.

The university was still an explosive place, after so many battles, defeats and so much repression. She was pleased: what human dynamite, energy, what a beautiful explosion of ideas, challenges, dissent, an agreement of difference! All the diverse political groups were here, standing and moving around the stalls, among the posters and banners, pouring out years of suppressed, unchallenged ideas, theories, thoughts and concepts. Pouring them out with feeling, passion, anger, hatred and, most of all, with impatience – washing their ideas, hanging them on the clothes lines, in the unsettling wind, still steaming. But, although she was exhilarated at hearing this marketplace of dialogue, of ideas, she was angry that nowhere was the plight of women prioritised – even though they were under constant and vicious attack.

Marjan waved from a flight of stone steps, having spotted Goli pushing her way through the arguments. Afsar, one of the women from the women's group, was with her. They sat on the grass, away from the debating groups. They talked for a while about the cost of the damage to the office and then they exchanged news and gossip about work, home and their karate classes.

Marjan then told them about her dilemma, of being in a Marxist group which had allied itself with the government in the hope that they could influence it, all the time believing that the government was still revolutionary because it had mass support, because it claimed to be anti-imperialist. The group was on the point of splitting because one faction believed that the Islamic government couldn't be trusted and that the option of armed struggle should still be kept open. Marjan's personal loyalty was with the main group – her friends were there – but her political sympathy was with the other faction. They were still committed to bringing out a women's magazine and she was still enjoying working on it. Afsar pointed out that if the split were definite, which it looked to be, the women's section would suffer as they wouldn't be able to carry the cost of running the women's magazine alone. It would have to go. How typical, Goli thought, her plans were sabotaged by the enemy outside, Marjan's from friends within.

Goli sympathised with her and, as an outsider to the group, tried to put the issues into perspective and offer some help. Obviously the left was divided and getting more so. The political climate was turbulent, confusing and dangerous, the government's anti-imperialist stance towards the west, the demands from women for human rights, the demands of the national minorities for autonomy. The left was caught by surprise, it was a testing time for them, they needed to be clear, honest, united, true to their politics and to the people.

'Will they manage it?' Goli asked.

'Afsar butted in. 'They have to, at critical times like this they have to.'

Marjan protested. 'You seem to sit on the periphery and only shout at the combatants – knock him out, knock him out!'

'But look at the record of the left so far,' insisted Afsar, 'its disasters, for instance, only three weeks after the victory of the revolution women were attacked for demonstrating in favour of their human rights. The left said it was secondary contradiction and that women should obey the Islamic theocracy. A couple of months later when the peasants of Gonabad had an uprising to create a council of co-operatives for the right to confiscate land from absentee landlords, the clergy said no, private property must be respected, and the left said, the peasants are the agents of the old regime! Again, two months later when the Azerbaijanies rose against the central government for their ethnic right to choose their own governor general, the left united with the government forces against them – they called this basic right "divisive", they who are permanently divisive.'

'I agree with you on women's rights and I have fought against my group on that,' argued Marjan, defending her group, 'but the peasant uprising, the call for self-determination, autonomy on the part of the Azerbaijanies was ill timed, right issues at the wrong time, when the left and the radicals are all so nervous about an imminent foreign invasion.'

'But Marj, you're being unfair. When is the right time to rise up for your rights? Who chooses the right time? You, me, the central government, the Azerbaijanies?' Goli was reluctant to just listen and not contradict Marjan even though she felt for her.

171

'Was it the right time to summarily execute the Shah's ministers without a proper trial and therefore kill the truth with them? Was it right to call so vengefully for the return and execution of the Shah? When Nasser took over in Egypt with a military coup, he let the king and his family go to America. It just shows how backward we are,' finished Afsar.

'Egypt didn't have that CIA-engineered coup in the summer of 1953 so close to its history and to its people's hearts. But we have,' Marjan countered.

'That's no excuse for a retreat to retaliation and a miserable catalogue of pathetic, defensive revenge and bloodshed,' Goli retorted.

'You seem to forget that when people have been denied power they can't be suddenly rational and wise and plan a good future soberly – anyway you're implying that women's liberation can be autonomous, without the left, without a government, without any alliances and strategies. No movement can last that way,' said Marjan.

'What kind of a left? One with such an aptitude for miscalculation, opportunism, sectarianism *and* betrayal?' asked Afsar. 'Women don't have to be part of that – they must not be part of it.'

'According to you, what will you do alone and isolated?' Marjan questioned.

'We may not be allowed to function openly and freely – after all we are considered to be the most subversive of dissidents – but we will not be deterred, we will think of something, find other ways . . . '

Goli welcomed Afsar's answer, and smiled. Marjan probably wasn't feeling any better, though, and no constructive suggestion had been offered to her. Goli felt sorry for her, but couldn't blame Afsar either. Goli looked around at the crowds of male debaters who were still going strong. From this distance she could see only their gestures, hands sketching in the air, cigarettes waving and smoking and, most of all, the force with which their bodies moved. They looked certain of their views, self-assured and powerful. The hands looked especially forceful. Was there violence in them? she wondered. In their convictions, in their passion for converting? Would they strike each other to prove their point? Or worse, would they betray each other? And the women?

After her meeting with Fatemeh, Zareen decided she would live her daily life differently: she would listen, think and question with a new zeal for understanding. The parts of her daily life that she had never taken seriously or considered important, she lifted out of context and dwelt on them, studied them carefully. As her work was depressing and the shop was getting quieter, she had more time to ponder.

She noticed how customers, neighbours and workers spoke about their lives, their politics and the government passively, as if they were outsiders, uninvolved in these events. They told the news, the local stories and gossip as if they were resigned to their situation. The women complained about their husbands, lack of food, lack of washing-up liquid, changes at the schools, with the sound of submission to a will of higher authority. A pale fear rooted itself in their very posture. And these were the same women that had lifted this town and turned it upside down. Where did the energy, imagination and defiance go? Where did it dissipate to? How was it done? Who did it?

From the shop window Zareen watched the world outside. The life of the square used to be focused on shopping, transport and had a general air of occupation. Now food shortage queues and the demoralised hopelessness they caused, attended by numerous pasdars enjoying their newly gained guns and power filled the square.

These young men looked so scruffy and unshaven. They used to pride themselves on being cleanly shaven and well dressed on a Friday night. Their rags and beards represented the resurrection of hippiedom – Muslim hippies. The beards must add a full pound of hair and holiness; looking pale and exhausted – the fatigue of exercising power – must give them job satisfaction. This new appearance gave them power and dignity, but of a higher quality, a heavenly righteousness. Boy soldiers, thought Zareen scathingly, who felt so mighty and heavenly, yet went home to their mothers for their dinners and clean trousers.

The school children came and went. They seemed to be shrinking, the girls disappearing under the weight of the heavy veil, and both boys and girls weighed down by their new syllabus: they had to be good, to be virtuous, a smile was bad, desire was bad, self was bad.

The market in the square was sometimes bare. There was a lack of fresh fruits and vegetables, washing-up liquid and powder and make-up. The latter was considered a luxury: it was a foreign import and as such should stop being used. Women waited in long lines, in queues that grew longer and longer outside the bread, meat, milk shops. There was no clear reason given to the women why baking the bread or milking the cows took so much longer under a revolutionary regime. Sometimes the blame was put on bad transport, sometimes on the ban on imports, but none of these reasons felt like real issues to anybody.

Other foreign imports that were being banned concerned Zareen and her friends especially: medicine and contraceptives. Soghra, one of Zareen's customers, had always complained that the side effects of the contraceptive she used made sex hell for her. But now that they were banned daily life was hell for her. She was afraid of getting pregnant with yet another unwanted baby – she had six already. Leili, another customer, was forty-five, pregnant and sick with worry, as abortion was now against the law and she hated herself for bearing a child at such a late stage in her life. Hating yourself was fine and encouraged under the new regime but she didn't like it. She was embarrassed to be pregnant in front of her grown-up children and she was trying everything to get rid of the foetus. She didn't want to be a living martyr, but it seemed there was no choice.

Previously, wherever Zareen went, and whoever she spoke with, family and friends, she heard disturbing news of local dissent, protests and clashes with the government forces. It had not been only women who were dissatisfied; men had followed in the women's footsteps. But now women's power to protest was greatly reduced by the sheer repressive force of the militia. Zareen observed, listened and asked endless questions, piecing together fragments of information from daily life in the square, the radio news, the constant images of men on the television screen: the evidence all pointed to the deliberate repression of women in work and personal life. She hated what she was witnessing and going through in her daily life.

Her work, her family, her children were no longer enough. How long was she going to be a proper woman for the shop-keepers, the mullas, the pasdars? What about being a woman for herself for a change? Having a self, a distinct personality with likes and dislikes? The self that she hadn't had time to consider took her by surprise. Zareen had to admit that now she might have to fight bitterly for her self, her identity and the life she wanted. She might have to make sacrifices, go beyond the point of no return, even jeopardise her family – if she were to say no to the government and to this forced life, if she wanted change. And the worst thing about this government was that it didn't like change. Well, she thought, they will have to like it.

Fatemeh had been spending time talking to her father, getting the latest news about the clergy. She had heard that there were murmurs of dissent among some of them and wanted to find out more. Her father explained in detail the composition of the various clerical groupings behind the political parties, their stand on a political Islam, their leaders' backgrounds and their possible alliances and tactics for the future.

Dissent was growing among some of the prominent Ulama, the higher-ranking clergy, with the political style of the government. They were varied in their methods and the degree of their opposition to the leadership of the Islamic republic. This opposition had sprung up among the regional and national minorities in the Azerbaijan in the west and was consolidated by that of the Kurds in the south west and in the eastern province of Khorassan. Her father explained the concerns of these leaders and the risks they had taken, and how not all of these dissenting senior clerics agreed with each other but that they all acknowledged the fact that a tyrannical government was being pushed forward in the name of Islam. One of these leading Ulama actually went as far as to state that it was not the clergy's job to govern: religion should stay separate from the state. 'Return to your mosques and seminaries and leave politics to professional statesmen.'

Another dissenting Ulama had stated that with power came responsibility and accountability. 'The fundamental role of the Shia clergy is the moral and spiritual leadership of the Islamic community.' The clergy should not concentrate political power in their own hands, but should be accountable to the people, allowing them the choice and freedom to criticise them.

Fatemeh's father hinted that his friendship and close ties with some of the dissenting Ulama had put him in a difficult position. He was now suspect too. He was not sure if he wanted to be associated with these Ulama, even though he agreed with a lot of their arguments. He wanted more time to wait and see, to give the Islamic government a bit more of a chance.

Fatemeh summed up her father's description and analysis of the situation in her own mind: there were two levels of criticism being directed at the government. One was about the issues of the social and economic welfare of the nation and the other was on theological grounds. The empty promises of the revolution, of free housing, of a share of the ruling classes' wealth and the eradication of poverty, had brought many peasants and villagers to the capital and to other major cities, turning them into unemployed and under-employed consumers rather than producers. The economic crisis made the management of the factories even worse. The nationalised industries, the education system, foreign trade, all were in chaos and confusion because the local Islamic committees repeatedly interfered in the existing working structures and in the appointment of governors and managers in these areas.

The liberal clergy articulated these criticisms to their large congregation through sermons, leaflets and Friday prayers. There were also other classes, besides the Ulama, who were disaffected and dissatisfied at work in the community with the government's policies. The Turks, Kurds, Arabs, Baluchis and the Turkemens were just some of the many national and ethnic minorities of the country who were already at war with the autocracy and theocracy of the regime. Their demands for autonomy and self-determination had been rejected and their parties and leaders were being harrassed, and their members arrested and executed.

This diverse opposition, including groups on the left, nationalist and ethnic minorities and radical Muslims, had their newspapers banned, offices attacked and burned down, their members arrested while their houses were bombed and their leaders were summarily executed. Free speech, freedom of organisation and meeting and of publication were all sweet liberties remembered from the good old days early on in the revolution. Dissent was seen as treason and no other competing centre of power was allowed. The prisons were fuller than ever before. Some put the number of executions at ten thousand. The newspapers were plastered with headlines about executions, demolished homes, faction fighting and, most of all, hysterical, religious self-righteousness – a catalogue of destructive, hopeless and miserable images.

And, amid all this despair, a large and dedicated band of zealots were always at hand to pour into the streets and defend the regime with their chains, clubs and guns. They were beyond criticism, symbols of truth and right and saw themselves the true representatives of God on earth.

Fatemeh began to read, in the hope that she would understand better the situation she found herself in. She started by reading theoretical and analytical writings which unfortunately had little relevance to her and the opposition's political struggle: theories on working-class revolution, bourgeois revolution, the rise of National Socialism, and so on. She enjoyed the reading, the theories and experiences gleaned from thinkers from the USSR to Spain, and found similarities in particular between National Socialism and the present situation, remembering the brass knuckles swinging, swinging, coming down, crushing her eyes.

She tried to read something else, something nearer to her experience. It was the first time she had read law books critically, from a woman's point of view, relating it to what was going terribly wrong around her. In dismay she thought of the years she had spent learning them as law, as something to correct, abide by. It was a new experience for her. The law books were nearly all based on the Quran and Islamic doctrine, and much of the text she found was inconsistent within its own logic, full of loopholes, contradictions, gaps and inadequacies, when brought to bear upon the present situation.

However, it was evident that under this regime the contradictions could be exploited and used against women and against any liberal practices. The civil law, for example, based on Islamic law, stated that all people, regardless of their colour, creed, gender and ethnic origin, are equal in the eyes of God; but in another text it stated that when witnesses are required if one male witness is not available, then two female witnesses could be used. And there was no sub-clause to explain why two female witnesses were equal to one male witness – had Islam discovered something lacking in women's eyesight or hearing?

Luckily for her, and for other women, not all of the Islamic interpretation was the same; the liberal clergy were progressive. How numerous were they? How much power and influence did they have? It would be good to know how the opposition is constituted. She sat in the middle of her room with all her papers and journals around her, and began to draw a diagram of the forces opposing and supporting the state. It was important to assess them properly.

She got out her chess board and all the pieces. The white king she set down opposite her – what an irony, having got rid of one king, to acquire another so quickly, and all the forces supporting him. She put the queen next to the king to represent the 'yes clergy', those who blindly follow the king. Then on the right-hand side of the king she put a rook – the army, the militia. Next came the bishop – representing the 'club wielder', the mob, the professional demonstrators. Then next to the queen another rook standing for the female spies who are the nation's moral squad, the pasdars' right hands.

On the other side she put all the black pieces, the numerous opposing forces of the left: women, nationalists and the liberal clergy; pawns, knights, rooks and, of course, the king. She sat there gazing at them. For the sake of convenience she called them the left and the right, but some forces on the left were co-operating with the state, so she added a few black pawns to the white king's forces; and took some of the white pieces, who were very critical of the state, the nationalist parties, and put them on the black side.

The forces of the state now looked smaller but still more organised and powerful – the army, the militia and the spies. The forces of the left were now more numerous; so why were they so scattered? So weak? Why did the small forces of the state have control over the majority? How? She looked at them: the rook, bishop, king, queen, knight and pawns, numerous pawns. They are a multitude. Could the left really get such a force together? Such unity of action against the state? Why not? What was stopping them? If the forces of the left were able to unite, then there would be a civil war and the left would win because the army's loyalty to the state is not yet established.

But was there any chance of unity amongst all the forces of the left? Their ideological differences and their mutual enmity were the barriers. But was it a question of the correctness of ideology or one of leadership? Or perhaps the more complex one, the question of a particular leadership? What would be the gain of ideological supremacy? If these ideological and leadership differences keep the forces of the left apart, what hope is there for any change? Would sections of the left betray each other to the state? The thought of that crumpled Fatemeh's heart, friends giving each other away. Her friends being betrayed first because they had consistently and openly criticised the state when the Marxist left had not been prepared to do so. The thought of such an inhuman action filled her with pain and sorrow. What makes a man name another man to his enemy? What would be the personal and political gain of such a betrayal?

This was all too depressing. She got up, left the chess pieces in their place, and went to make herself a cup of tea. She sat leaning on the hard cushions, away from the chess pieces, sipping her tea, thinking about the changes that were needed. The changes that she wanted. The left could go on being as fragmented and ineffectual as it liked, articulate and combatant maybe, its rhetoric ideologically sound, sure, but still politically impotent.

And what hope can there be for women? Women have never been, and never will be, a priority of their struggle. If they are at each others' throats, if they stab each other in the back, what wouldn't they do to women? She was alone. Women were alone. What she could do was return to the campus, meet up with her Radical Islam friends and try to learn from their strategies and plans for urban resistance against the state. Even though she was still opposed to the idea of armed struggle. Her head was with them, but not her heart. And there was little hope that they would be different from the fundamentalists in their views on women's rights and sexual politics. Also, they lacked imagination – a vivid revolutionary imagination. She felt that if they gained power, they too would not change the status of women. And possibly she would be one of the women in front of their firing squad if they decided to continue to implement the Islamic sexual code. But they were the only friends she had, her only allies. They could help her and she needed them now.

Malihe tried to go on as usual with her daily work, talking to the neighbours, shopping and housework. But she continued to feel depressed and confused, and could not stop thinking about Ali Zangeer 'The Chain', her torturer, and her days in gaol. As the days passed she tried to concentrate on her work, reminding herself that her bread lay there. But everything seemed to take her much longer to do these days, and her monologues went on for longer too: it was a lonely job working away in your own bedsit.

As she went on spreading the patterns, slower than usual, placing her haberdashery, pins, needles and cottons around her on the floor memories of the past crowded in on her. The crowded, noisy days. The days when it wasn't safe for safety pins to be around. The days when her children Sahar and Syrus crawled around over everything – the patterns, the sewing machine and herself. One day she had just gone to fetch some water from the yard and when she returned all her patterns had turned into a tent and they were playing under it, sitting cross-legged, pretending it was their home. Syrus liked to turn the handle of the sewing machine and watching the wheel go round, laughing at its noise. Sahar used to gather up the cotton reels and build towers with them. Malihe used to wonder what she was fascinated with most, their colours or the structure she made from them. The way she occupied herself Malihe thought she would either be a bricklayer or a designer. She ended up as a nurse. How did she change? She had said that she wanted to be with her friends.

Her own childhood days in the dry and sunny village had been so different from those of her kids. Most of her time was spent outdoors by the river, up the trees, or with the animals in the fields. What a different world, open, free, expansive, full of light, trees and work that involved nature; unlike her children's world, bound by alley, school and homework. Here one is so isolated. The older people so friendless. No wonder so many women want only to be grannies and to live with their grandchildren. Was this a barren life for her? She put the scissors sharply through the pattern. The cutting sound sliced her thought. She hated these Islamic uniforms. The dark blue sacks for women. She shouldn't make them. She shouldn't be party to this art-less, lifeless uniform for women. She shouldn't. But it isn't possible, it's not worth it, it would only antagonise the women. It would be brainless. She should preserve her anger for a better plan. The tailor's chalk continued on its journey, marking the outlines of the other half of the pattern.

She missed the village, she wanted to go back there to meet all her old friends and neighbours. It must have changed a lot, like her and her life. Would she be able to recognise it? Would they recognise her? Perhaps not many of them lived there any more. She couldn't stop thinking about the past. Why? So much of her memory was bound up in the happy days of the past and the bitter prison days. The past dominated her and she tried to just work without thought or talk; but the images and the monologues went on faster than her patterns, hemming and neatening.

The coldness, the fear and the pain of the prison days swamped her. How unknown everything had been. How she was kept in the dark. What had she done? Why was she interrogated? Stuck in a cell, alone, waiting for her inquisitors and torturers to come in and keep her company. They were men, they were very special men, tough-looking, hard, quiet and, at first, patient. Loud and obnoxious later. Men in uniform. They always started with harmless questions, comfortably posed questions that relieved you for a second, but soon hit you in the guts, and ended in violence. The violence tore her to shreds, she was slapped again and again, until she felt her head going round and round, as if boiling oil were being poured into her skull.

Ali Zangeer didn't look especially frightening, on a normal visit he looked like an ordinary man. He was middle-aged, of medium size, with auburn hair and a moustache. He was the head of interrogation in her section. He was always accompanied by two men, one on each side of him. They wrote things on paper, perhaps described her reactions and fears as well as her answers. But when he was angry or, more conveniently, got angry and paced up and down the cell, or worse, when he took off his leather strap and lashed it against the wall so that it sounded like the sharp shriek of chains crashing on the concrete – then he looked like a torturer. That frightened her and she couldn't help shuddering, cold sweat sitting on her body. The terrifying sound of his strap and the power unleashed by it, gave him his name, Ali Zangeer. How would it have sounded on her skin? She was spared that. Not many were.

Her solitary confinement period was as horrendous, when she was kept tied to a chair by her hands and feet, with little food or drink, in constant darkness, and with the threat of intermittent interrogation. When she was freed she thought her hands had dried up for good, like lifeless winter branches. She placed them on the dress spread out on the floor and moved them in a circle over the seams of the skirt. So good to have them still with her, healthy, unbroken. Without hands how can you work? How can you take what is yours? How can you strike back? Ah, it is so good to have them.

'I just can't believe that he can walk around and be a mulla, a mulla. Anybody can be a mulla these days. The mulla population is growing sky high. No farmers, no artisans, no bricklayers, but everybody can be a mulla. Where are the pins? Yes, not straight. Not bad though. Torturer turned mulla. Perhaps mullas were torturers before. This dress is dreadful, looks like a shroud, would fit a dead woman well, very well. Coffins for the living. The new coffin makers. They're on the increase too. Dead bodies are growing, the living dead are on the up and up. Scissors . . . my Syrus . . . Who makes your shirts now? How much taller are you now? My precious Sahar. Have you got friends? Are you lonely like me? Why am I left here? Why have I been abandoned like this?' Tears welled around her eyelashes but did not fall. The needle stuck in the hem. Malihe stopped and looked around, at the mantelpiece, at the pictures. She couldn't work anymore. She made herself some tea. It took her a long time to drink a cup and then a few more. She looked at the work spread around her, untidy, jumbled and chaotic; and went for a bit of fresh air in the yard. She walked around and sat by the hoze. But the sounds of the children and neighbours annoyed her and she came back in to finish off the last few stitches.

'I won't let you rest. I won't. How dare you? I will spread the story. Expose you. I hate you, bloody torturers. I hope your house is blown up with you in it. I won't rest till you have been punished. Where is justice? Where is all we fought for? God give me help. Friends help. Women help! Help . . . '

As if the weight of the world was on her head and nothing could lift it off, she buried herself in her work, tailoring, stitching away, thinking and planning. The days passed and she cocooned herself in her work, finding inspiration in it. It was no surprise that so many women were seamstresses: the job was one of survival – of tactics, strategies, peacemaking, planning, building. She was thinking and connecting.

## 17

It was Malihe who thought it was time to meet again. She got in touch with the others to arrange a meeting. But where? Zareen was afraid to use Ziba Style. They needed a safer place to meet. Goli suggested a picnic at a shrine in Pas-Ghaleh in the north, a small and pretty place tucked away in the mountains overlooking Tehran and, although Malihe thought that the north of Tehran, the living quarters of the middle and upper classes was an even more suspect area, they agreed that the idea of meeting at a shrine – if not that particular one – was a good idea. Fatemeh was given the job of choosing another location and she, in consultation with her mother, came up with the shrine of Abu-Abdullah in Rey City, not far from Shah-Abdul-Azeem, south of the city. Each would bring some food, rugs and prayer books, except Goli who would just bring herself and her thoughts, because she was travelling such a long distance, from up north to deep south. Zareen decided to bring her children and Malihe brought the landlady's daughter of whom she was fond. They thought it would be much safer to have children around and treat it as a real picnic with lots of food and drink. It would be on a Friday, the Muslim rest day, at a shrine where they would be just a few anonymous women among a thousand others.

On the day of the picnic they arrived separately at Shush Square, all clad in black chadors, like most women around them. The square was jammed with people and it took them a while to find each other and then for Fatemeh to find the three of them huddled together with their heavy loads behind the bus stop. She had parked the car away from the square, and they followed her through the traffic of bodies. They managed to pack all their stuff and themselves in the car, the three children taking it in turns to sit by the windows. They set off, each murmuring a prayer under her breath, out of habit and fear, wishing for a good and safe day for all of them. The children quickly became absorbed in looking out of the windows at the passing of life on each side of the street. This kept them busy and quiet.

'How is it that children always want to sit by the window, in cars, in the train, in buses? What is there that's so exciting to see?' Malihe commented when she saw them looking out so intently.

'There's so much going on, Aunt Mali,' Leila, the land-lady's girl said. 'Everything that goes past fast is more exciting, it's the impression of things, not their reality.'

Fatemeh said, 'I think that's why I enjoy driving, passing by and leaving people, objects, streets behind.'

'I think it's more to do with the speed, and the children's fascination with it and the dream-like world it creates.' Malihe put it differently. Zareen sat quietly. She did not like the speed, which fragmented the world outside: it seemed unreal and disturbing. She preferred things in one piece, static.

They were leaving Tehran and coming to the suburbs that, only a few years ago, had been used as agricultural land for fresh vegetables and fruit, famous for its good quality and abundance. But now this land was being turned into a new housing development for rural migrant workers who had abandoned their farms or sold them off and come to the capital to benefit from the promises of the revolution.

'Well, this must be part of the agricultural expansion that the government is planning – to feed the country, to be self-reliant and cut down on imported food,' Zareen said ruefully.

Later, as they rode through the central square of Shah-Abdul-Azeem, the children saw the kebab houses and suddenly got hungry, wanting kebabs. Goli said that she would take them to one of the famous kebab houses later in the afternoon, if they were extremely good. The children cheered with happiness: 'Yes, kebabs, kebabs please!'

They decided to park near the main shrine in Shah-Abdul-Azeem and have a look around, as they knew that the revolution had changed the area, and the children would enjoy seeing a new, different place.

They walked under the dark arches towards the spacious courtyard of Shah-Abdul-Azeem, which buzzed with men and women, pilgrims and visitors. The golden minarets rose proudly and elegantly above them. The pond was surrounded by abluting men. Men, men and very few women without men. They hung on to the children as tight as they could, symbols of their absent men and a powerful shield to deflect the interest of the pasdars. In places like these children were precious passports to safety and respect, ensuring the entry of women without men to such a place of worship. Single women, unless they were old, would be under suspicion here. They went in for a short prayer to the shrine, where male pilgrims exhibited their religious zeal, openly crying and begging forgiveness.

The brick arches were most beautifully decorated with blue, turquoise and black patterned tiles, leading through to the plain stone and gravel of the inner courtyard. But the hall of the Qajar kings was not in its place. It had disappeared. They knew that it had been attacked in the revolution and that its statues, pictures and marble-headed tombs were broken but they didn't know that the hall had vanished. They asked a cleaner who directed them towards a large adjacent room in the main shrine and told them that there another room had been built in its place.

The tombs of the kings had been destroyed by the revolutionaries and this room had been built in its stead. A huge square room, its high ceiling covered with hacked-up mirrors, its spacious floor laid with precious Persian carpets. A magnificent room. But it was a men's prayer room.

'Kings' tombs were demolished so that men could pray? A public monument becomes an exclusive men's prayer room?' Goli asked in wonder, gazing into the space and the decoration of the room.

186

'I want to know who took the loot, the precious antique chandeliers, the silver-framed old paintings, the rest?' Malihe said with a sense of melancholy.

'Perhaps they were demolished too. You can't expect art appreciation from revolutionary men,' Goli added.

'Men who are shamed of their imperial history, but found it easy enough to claim bits of it and abandon the rest; or sit on it as they are doing now and pray for forgiveness,' Zareen tailed off bitterly.

The children were impatient with such talk and prodded and pulled on their chadors.

'All right, let's see what's left of the mausoleum of Raza-Shah,' Goli said. 'It too has been demolished. They were planning to build public toilets in its place. Let's see if they have.'

They moved on and after a bit of a walk came to a huge pair of hollow bronze boots, thigh high, stuck in the ground. That was all that was left of the huge and fierce status of the founder of the Pahlavi dynasty. They had not been able to demolish them, the might of the populace couldn't pull them out, they were told. Nearby there were new public lavatories for men built where the mausoleum had once stood.

'One generation's mausoleum, is the next generation's lavatories,' Goli remarked. They went back to the car and drove on.

They stopped briefly in Cheshme-Ali because the children were keen to know what the crowds of women were doing by the river. The women were washing carpets and rugs on the stony shore and stretching them out to dry on the rocks. This place had become the traditional place for the ceremonial washing of Persian carpets. From there it was only a short drive to the shrine of Abu-Abdullah. Fatemeh found a safe parking place, well hidden from the sun under trees and heavy bushes. They unloaded the car and carried the stuff through the gate to where they would settle and picnic for the day. The children disappeared to play under the mulberry trees. The shrine itself was a small round minaretted structure built on a square platform high above the ground. Four sets of steps led to it from different directions. The grounds were covered with small mulberry trees, their branches overflowing backwards, umbrella like, and hung with large red mulberries. Once ripe they would go black and juicy, sweet and sour, making your lips, tongue and fingers reddish black too.

They put down their rugs and settled somewhere between the mass tomb to youth and a young unknown woman's grave who had been executed in the uprising of 1953. They spread the rugs and put the food and plates around them. The children were famished again and wandered back from their play. They sat by the gravestones, laying flowers on it and putting their second finger on the stone, as was the tradition, and saying a prayer for the dead.

'God, travelling is tiring, I'm exhausted, how about you?' Zareen said.

'I'm tired too, I'll get the samovar going,' said Malihe.

'I'll get some water.' Fatemeh went off with a jar in her hand.

'I'll just have a rest. I like to watch everybody else working around me,' Goli said lazily.

'Don't worry, there'll be work to do later on, and we'll make sure you get your fair share of it,' Zareen laughed.

They sat at rest to wait for the tea and watched the children climbing up the mulberry trees. There were all the local children around and many other visitors to the graves, families dotted around, but the place wasn't crowded.

'What a trial it's been not meeting,' Malihe said looking round at her friends.

Fatemeh returned with the water and they made tea and drank while keeping a vigilant look out. A gardener was weeding the flowers, further away the shrine attendant was talking with some pilgrims. Was he really a gardener? What else did he do as well as being a shrine attendant? thought Goli. Any man was suspect. They would have to be careful. The tea sweated the tiredness of the long journey out of their bodies. Once they had had a few cups they took it in turns to visit the shrine, taking the kids with them. They were searched thoroughly before entering the shrine. Back at the picnic spot, the children spread the sofreh and put the cutlery and plates out, the girls forcing the boy to do it like them.

188

'Do you feel better after your prayers?' Goli asked Malihe and Fatemeh.

'I just complained to God for landing us in this mess,' said Malihe.

'I warned God that if he doesn't do anything soon, I will,' added Fatemeh.

'Poor God, God and America,' said Goli. It's good to blame them for our mistakes. It makes us feel better.'

'That's not fair,' said Fatemeh. 'Don't underestimate the Americans' role.'

'Don't underestimate our own people's role. This is definitely our mess. A quality Persian mess.' Goli sounded cross.

'Sure, but we're not the only people in the world to make mistakes!' retorted Fatemeh.

'You'll lose your appetite, getting angry like that, and my lovely rice will be wasted. Let's eat now.' Zareen said, worried in case they started arguing in front of the children.

The children were served first.

The sofreh looked colourful with the fresh green vegetables decorated with large red radishes, the fresh yoghurt from Rey City with raisins, walnuts and mint in it and the delicious looking rice cooked with carrots, tomatoes, fresh green beans and meat.

'This is a nice meal Auntie, but can we go to the kebab house?' Leila asked again.

'Oh, yes, we'll get hungry again by then, especially if you run around and play all afternoon.' Malihe reassured them.

'We will, if only to eat kebabs,' Leila said.

'The mulberries are nice too,' Bahram said.

'They're not ripe, you mustn't eat them or you'll get belly ache.' Malihe warned them.

The children finished and soon disappeared off among the graves looking at the inscriptions, and then behind the mulberry trees.

'I need some more tea,' said Fatemeh. Goli jumped up. 'I'll get the water.' She took the jar and went off, returning after a few minutes.

'Tea after a meal, followed by an afternoon siesta is like

what Khayyam says, "A drink, a book, a lover, the shade of a tree, is a heaven for me".' Zareen said.

'Ah, Khayyam and all those romantic poems,' Fatemeh's voice was disapproving.

'Don't be rotten. I like him. I'm only beginning to like Hafiz,' Goli said.

'Oh, only now are you beginning to understand him and his anti-Shia determinist philosophy?' mocked Fatemeh.

'Shall we leave the discussion of male literary figures for another time?' Malihe was impatient.

'Yes,' agreed Zareen. 'And I want to say something that's been giving me belly ache for a few days now. Azadeh came to the shop the other day. Her mother brought her in. You wouldn't believe what I saw. I was petrified. Mali, you remember her – the jolly, chatty good-time girl who was just full of energy and life? She was into make-up, fashion, music, dancing and being with women. She'd disappeared for a while, the pasdars had taken her away for some questioning. Apparently her skirt was too short and she wound them up, lifting it up further and showing them her bare legs – a silly joke like that. She's back now. Crippled. Her right eye has half disappeared under the burned skin around it, the eyebrow, the skin, all red now, crumpled and deformed. She said they were joking with her, had a bottle of acid in their hands, just poured it on her skin, it ate it away. She just screamed. Her left leg has a limp, some kind of electric shock, she didn't know what, she had lost consciousness. And she was pregnant. No doctor would perform an abortion. She's been kept all this time in a private prison by some pasdars, nobody knew where. You should have seen her, all in black, covered from head to toe, only her eyes showing, her hand in her mother's like a child. I just shook with pain. I managed to hold myself in until after I had cut her hair, but after they'd gone I went to the back room and broke down. I couldn't stop crying, for a wasted young life, I can't stop thinking about what they have done to her . . . ' There was a pause.

'She is now an ideal Muslim woman in a just, true Islamic Republic.' Goli broke in, her voice harsh. 'That is the kind of woman they want – either total submission to our will or we forge you, and deform you, in our own image. Of course, she has to be fully veiled now, to hide the inhumanity of men. My heart is so heavy . . . ' The others were quiet. They didn't know what else to say.

'Well, we can't save Azadeh, but perhaps we can save the future generation from being destroyed, perhaps.' Malihe broke the silence tentatively.

'I want to punish all the men who have brutalised me, Azadeh, Fati and countless other women, and challenge the fact that they think they have a right to do so.' Goli's voice was clear and firm.

'I want something different and better.' said Fatemeh. 'A better way of fighting what is wrong. I think we should go underground and do something offensive and effective.'

'Something very well planned,' added Goli. 'Meticulously executed.'

'I don't know,' said Zareen. 'I don't want any suicide attacks or anything like that. I want a better, an easier way of dismantling the system.'

How can we set up an organisation which is capable of delivering such a blow to the system?' pondered Fatemeh, ignoring what Zareen had said.

'I think I have the beginnings of an answer.' Malihe said in her usual calm manner.

'Let us in on the secret,' said Zareen.

'Yes,' said Goli, 'I'm dying to know how you can dismantle this rotten fundamentalist, misogynist system!'

'I can't do that, I don't think any one thing can dismantle this system. I can only knock down one of its pillars,' said Malihe. 'In my village, I know an older woman who was our village wise woman, our herbalist, our midwife, our nurse. She knew a lot about plants that cured and plants that did anything but cure – dangerous plants. I have heard that she's still alive, at the age of 92, and I want to visit her and study with her, apprentice myself to her secrets, and perhaps learn about the most powerful remedies – those which can be *very* effective, fatally so, in a *very* short time. This would be my contribution to any action we plan. I want to go away soon. I might be gone some time.'

'And while you are gone we will start to explore other avenues of action, other possibilities for attack—' cried Goli.

'You're making me feel nervous,' Fatemeh interrupted. 'I don't know what you're up to. I don't want to be part of any killing, not least in the mass killing of men. There must be other means of taking action.'

'You mean printing pamphlets, writing slogans on walls, going on strike, picketing, throwing bombs at empty buildings, armed struggle in the streets?' asked Goli. 'Which one of those over-used, under-effective methods are you advocating? You know yourself that the government forces know about all those tactics – they were using them themselves after all, and not so long ago, against the Shah's lot.'

'I know. I don't agree with killing though,' said Fatemeh.

'We should think about it, though, Fati,' Zareen said.

'Couldn't we make contact with other women in other countries, especially with those who are more experienced than us, and have the same interests? For a kind of joint operation?' Fatemeh suggested.

'It would make it too complicated,' said Goli. 'But,' she added thoughtfully, 'we will need help from outside, weapons, ammunition, technical expertise. And there are women on the outside who could help us, the early flight of women exiles, we need to establish contact . . . '

'Yes, it's a start,' said Zareen. 'Something we can be going on with when Malihe leaves.'

'The prospect of killing still worries me,' said Fatemeh.

'I share your doubts,' Malihe said earnestly, taking Fatemeh's hands in her own. 'It's not the only way. And perhaps it's not even an effective way, as well as being morally and socially wrong. It could mean no end to revenge and bloodshed. But Fati, you haven't suggested anything else. We've been thinking, debating, meeting, planning for months now, and we haven't done anything yet. And there is still plenty of time – we haven't decided on anything. You can all meet up and think of alternatives in my absence. I am still open to suggestions.' Fatemeh was silent. Zareen moved to her side and tried to console her. 'We are going to fight for something better,' she said, 'for a better view, like sitting by the river, eating pomegranates and no mullas around for centuries.'

The children were nowhere to be seen and Malihe and Goli got up and went off to look for them. They returned a few moments later with the children to find Fatemeh and Zareen looking agitated.

'Those four men over in that corner have been eyeing us for a while. I don't know how long they've been watching us and whether they were there when we were talking,' Zareen said nervously.

'I don't think they were,' said Malihe without looking round. She sat down on the rug. 'Let's just go on as usual. Children, do you want a drink or some food?'

'No, we want kebabs.' The three of them said together.

'Don't worry,' said Goli. 'We will go to the kebab shop later on, but now we just want some snacks and a drink.'

'I don't. I want to keep all the rooms empty in my belly for the kebabs,' Leila said, distrustfully.

Zareen sat the children down and forced them to engage reluctantly in a late afternoon picnic ceremony for the benefit of the men. They speculated who they might be – plainclothes policemen? Moral squad? Or just local men in search of a few manless women? Would they be followed? They got the kids ready, cautiously and slowly cleared up the picnic and left together. The men did not follow.

In the dark archway adjacent to the main shrine of Shah-Abul-Azeem, many kebab houses, each next to the other, competed for customers. They chose a small quiet one and sat down at a corner table.

A young man came to take their orders, an older man was at the charcoal grill fanning the blazing coal. It was good to be served by men for a change, and not to have to prepare the food. They were very hungry. The young waiter looked shy, and he had no pencil or paper with which to take their orders down. How religious was he? How misogynist? Did he know, could he guess whom he was serving? The four most ordinary looking women . . .

## 18

Malihe began to get ready to go away. She wanted to finish off all her orders for clothes that were due to her customers, apart from anything she needed the money. She was filled with a sense of urgency and speed, conscious of time as never before. She stopped accepting new orders and waited for her payments, delayed as usual because women depended on their husbands' income. It was a period of tension; her work had taken over her life when she thought that she worked in order to live. Now, though, she had a sense of purpose and she was excited at the thought of going away, travelling, after such a long time of staying in one place.

She felt relieved now, determination gripped her: finally she was going to do something about her anxiety and fear, her pain and misery. Anger and sorrow had handicapped her for a long time, but now they were dissipated by her decision, avenues of struggle and action opened up. She was not going to be haunted by the image of her torturer-turned-mulla: she was going to do something about it. Just as Zareen had said, she wanted to eat watermelons – she didn't like pomegranates – by the river, with no mullas around for centuries.

Her landlady, neighbours and customers were surprised by her sudden decision to go away. But they all felt for her, a lonely older woman, fending for herself, and sympathised with and understood her desire to return to her village and her friends there.

As the time to leave grew near she had to say goodbye to

everybody, friends and customers. Hardest of all, though was saying goodbye to Fatemeh, Goli and Zareen.

They met over early evening tea. Zareen tried to make a few jokes and keep the atmosphere light, but it was hard. Malihe's departure weighed heavily on them all: perhaps it was the last meeting the four of them would have together. Each woman brooded internally while Zareen chatted on to ease the heaviness.

'You must write regularly, don't forget our code. And do send us some lovely silk Yazdi scarves . . . '

At last Fatemeh voiced the unspoken feeling they shared.

'It's awful seeing you go, not knowing when we will be together, if we ever will be together again . . . ' she tailed off. Goli felt especially sad about Malihe leaving. They were all trying to see beyond their personal sadness: this was a leave-taking for hope, for action, love, strength, and courage to fight the apathy and tyranny, a leave-taking for a warmer home coming, a better life: they tried to say goodbye in such a spirit. But it still felt like the longest summer day, after which the days would be shorter, the light scarcer, with only coldness on the horizon.

Mali had bought her ticket in advance. On the day she checked that it was safely in her bag. She tidied her room with a sinking heart, her belly a tight fist. She put the sewing machine away, shaking its cover before putting it on. Drew the curtains, emptied the water jars and gave away the fresh food and bread that was left, swept the floor and dusted the mantelpiece, took the children's photos down and put them in her bag. She gave the plants to a neighbour to water. Put the rubbish out and locked her room carefully and lovingly, putting the key in her purse. Straightened her chador, holding it with one hand and with the other carried her travelling bag, bulging with clothes and presents she had got for her family and neighbours back in the village. She crossed the yard, said a few prayers quietly and left.

The first step, small but significant.

'In the name of God,' she murmured to herself, 'in the name of justice, justice for women.'

She walked through her lane to the main road and waited at the bus stop, looking round, checking other people. Everybody was on the move, all going somewhere, ordinary people like her. Suspicion grabbed her. Would anybody guess her purpose, where she was going and why? She was a lone woman traveller – wasn't that dangerous in itself? A crammed bus stopped before her next thought came along. Men pushed in and jumped up. She followed and squeezed herself into a tiny space among the tightly knitted bodies.

The bus ride was slow and airless but, luckily, it wasn't long to the coach station. Malihe felt small ripples of anxiety in the bottom of her belly when they got there.

On the coach she sat by the window next to an older tribal man with his special Farsi hat and shawl on. There were some women and children in the coach. It was a bit noisy but she was pleased that there were other women passengers. She looked outside, conscious of a crick in her neck but enjoying the moving images passing them. Letters, food, television aerials whizzed by, only the blueness, the speed and the outlines of the images remained.

Once the coach had left the crowded, dirty streets of Tehran she began to feel better, lighter. She was on her way. The route was through Qum and Malihe was looking forward to the scenery. She had purposely decided to travel during the day so she could see the new face of the country. The road was straight and bare on both sides except for small houses and patches of green land in the distance and, by a house, a shady tree or two shaking in the wind.

The more distant views disturbed her. Among the red hills further off she could see lines of ant-like soldiers training, long lines of uniformed men, and women in black veils. The land, hills and mountains for miles around were marked with signs: ARMY TRAINING GROUNDS KEEP OUT NO PHOTOGRAPHY. Women were being trained. It must be voluntary, she thought. She hadn't heard of it being compulsory. Volunteers to martyrdom. What a choice, what a meagre, dead-end choice. Pity about those beautiful hills and that red earth under army occupation like this. How much more of this land is under occupation, denied to its citizens?

Perhaps this is my last journey through my country, she thought. Perhaps I should stop and visit all the interesting places I've always wanted to see. I could stop at Qum and look at the handmade pottery shops and the clay works, and at Esfehan to see its beautiful Islamic architecture, and in Damghan to walk through orchard upon orchard of the best pistachios, and gaze at the carpet shops in Kashan, the lime orchards in Natanz, and, lastly, a prayer at the shrine of Masomeh in Qum. She could just observe it all, have the pleasure of seeing, noting. There might not be another chance.

Some people write down the things they see but I just want to appreciate them with my eyes and remember them. Women's eyes are not usually for seeing and appreciating; they are for watching, minding, caring. They are closed eyes, for looking away, lowered out of modesty, screwed up red from crying.

But no, she thought, I must not think of failure, defeat and death. I must not be fatalistic. This is just the beginning. And although she longed to make other journeys, she would have to wait. When she had accomplished the work she had to do she would have all the time and concentration in the world to reclaim this land for herself, to walk over it step by step, if she wanted to, and to enjoy its dry earth, shining trees and ancient rocks.

The colour of the hills in the distance distracted her again. They still looked red, like wine. How fantastic the desolate, barren land was, changing from flat and smooth to rough and hilly. And then the red earth of the hills turned into mild green rocks. The landscape changed its colours layer by layer, cherry red turning into sandy yellow, light brown to bright grey, apple green, grass green, pistachio, maroon. The earthen rainbow, a permanent rainbow, so beautiful, so intense, bewitched her.

On the left now, in the far distance, at the foot of some hazy mountains, a massive white circle shone. The salt lake, it silvery surface, pure bright whiteness, was hung about with dark clouds, rising perhaps from the burning gases which abounded in the surrounding oil-rich desert. Oh God, she thought, this landscape is so rich, so varied, so diverse in history, in people, in culture. Why have we now landed ourselves with this single tribe of men? Malihe sank deep into gloom; her book, a history of Yazd, remained untouched on her lap. She closed her eyes and tried to sleep.

When Malihe got to Yazd, where her sister lived, it was dark. As she knocked on her sister's door her heart was beating fast. Her youngest niece opened the door and soon there were cheers of welcome as the family crowded round, bursting with excitement and pleasure at seeing her. The children got some food and drink together, while the sisters hugged and talked exuberantly after so many years of separation.

Soon the husband and children went to bed and left them alone. They talked well into that night.

Malihe stayed with her sister for a few days and then caught another coach to Anarak. The village was fresh and lively in the mid-morning sun when she arrived. People were out and about, working, toiling on the land in the crisp air. It brought back memories of her younger days. Although, yes, there were more clay and mud houses built, more cars around and less greenery.

She arrived at her aunt's house. News of her arrival there was spread by the children as if by a broadcast and brought her a great welcome. Later, she went visiting. Banoo was the elder of the village so Malihe went to see her first. Banoo had aged so much. Her face was layered with wrinkles, a book of experience in every fold. Her bony hands felt dry and sandy. She was bent over and looked much smaller – Malihe hardly recognised her; however, she assured Mali that she was in good health.

Malihe decided to tell Banoo the purpose of her visit gradually and carefully. She was in no hurry and had all the time in the world now – but did Banoo? She hoped so. They talked about family and friends, city and village life, jobs and money. Although Banoo was bony and frail she still had a good memory and was physically strong for her age. She did the housework, visited people and kept herself busy. Malihe said that she was going to visit her daily from now on.

Malihe was invited by the families in the village one by one for tea and talk, a customary tradition; and for a meal every night by a different relative – everybody was related to everybody else in this village. After a couple of weeks when she had had tea and a meal with nearly everybody in the village, had been introduced to the newborns and learnt of the fates of the dead and the migrated ones, she settled down to a quieter life.

She told her relatives and friends that she was tired of big city life and had come to rest in the village for a while, to take it easy. She enjoyed the freshness and purity of the basic foods: she had free-range eggs for breakfast and took sandwiches of homemade bread and butter and cheese with her when she went for long walks by the river.

The narrow stream, which dried up in the summer, was beyond the cluster of mud houses and narrow alleys that linked them together, and led to the river. Further outside the village there were small patches of agricultural land where the villagers worked on their own small plots. She enjoyed the walks, sometimes in the company of the children, but she spent most of her time concentrating on how to get closer to Banoo.

Everybody wanted to know about the political climate in Tehran. The centre for political discussion in the village was the tea house where the men gathered every night – no women went there – and over a cup of tea and a water pipe each they hammered out their views. Malihe spoke about the situation in Tehran with women only but even so she was very selective and careful about what and how much she said. Banoo asked Malihe if the situation in Tehran was as bad as the men in the village were making it out to be. Malihe explained that generally, the people's expectations had not been met, shortages were beginning to bite, government promises of eradicating poverty had been turned into the promotion of equality in poverty, and that women were getting a raw deal.

'Each time a new shah or a new leader takes over it's the same,' said Banoo. 'I have seen four kings and three revolutions. This is another era, another kingdom, and not much has changed for us villagers, except that it's getting harder to make ends meet. All their promises, as usual, bloom like flowers and die soon due to lack of water. It always falls on us, on working people, the poor farmers, to work harder, to produce more and to water their promises. But we are tired too. I am too old, old and dying, and can't water any promises. I need to be looked after, to be taken care of, I'm not getting any younger.'

'But Banoo, you're not old – age is in ability and health. I tell you, you're younger than many women I know who are half your age. You're healthy and you've seen so much. You should be proud. You must teach us, your children and friends, your knowledge. I want to know how life in this village over the years has changed, and what changes you have made to it.'

'Well, I didn't do much. I just worked, had children, helped women in labour, collected medicines, treated sick babies and other people, things like that, not much, you know. Us poor people have to get on with our lives, no one helps us and we shouldn't waste our time expecting it or listening to empty promises.'

Malihe visited Banoo daily and, after hours of conversation during which she became close to Banoo, Malihe told her that she wanted to be taught about her medicinal knowledge. She wanted her to show her the herbs and plants that she used for her cures. Banoo was reluctant to take on the responsibility, saying she didn't have the strength that she used to have, her eyes couldn't see properly, she couldn't walk well and generally trying to discourage Malihe. But Malihe didn't give up, she went to see her regularly and helped her in the house, fed her chickens, washed, mended and cooked for her and kept her company, talking to her about anything and everything.

This was a relief to the grandchildren, and great-grand-children of Banoo, who were then freed to devote more time to work on the land or at carpet-weaving. Carpet-weaving was the only source of cash income in their village. The young girls of the village – including Banoo's great-grandchildren, ranging from five to thirteen – were engaged in carpet-weaving. Malihe's help and company enabled them to weave more carpets and increase the family income. The two women grew closer.

Malihe began to take special care of Banoo's health. She took her to Yazd to see an optician and encouraged her to wear glasses. She gave her regular massages, taught her how best to sit and work, to stop crouching and slouching, and put her on a specially nourishing and healthy diet, which she prepared for her. It was time that some of those life-enhancing herbs Banoo had prescribed for others for so long were used for her own health. Her care and dedication made Banoo tease her: why didn't she find a nice man to take care of, who would take care of her in the future? How could she repay Malihe? Malihe replied that the days when women could rely on men were over and that she'd be back to live in the village and Banoo could take care of her then. Yes, when I return from the dead, Banoo had said sarcastically.

In the meantime Malihe was enjoying her stay, although sometimes she missed her friends terribly. Life here was much more humane and simple, with less emotional and financial problems. The villagers had a sense of collectiveness and of belonging to a community which was lost in life in a large city.

It was peaceful here: no television, no telephone, not even a radio; news came with travellers or the odd visitor from Yazd or Tehran.

Banoo began to come round. She rode around the village on a donkey. Malihe had forgotten how to ride one but learned again quickly. The two women rode around together and Banoo took her to the outskirts of the village beyond the farming plots and showed her where some of the herbs grew and why and when were the best times to pick them and how to dry and preserve them. As Banoo couldn't see very well, she used her memory to search out the places and described the plants to Malihe who looked for and discovered them. She was tempted to write down all the information but decided not to, trying instead to teach herself how to memorise it. She was a little worried in case her memory should fail her, but didn't know what else to do – her memory was now her only safe place.

Both women enjoyed their excursions, and Malihe hoped they could do more. However, she was not satisfied. She did not want to learn only about the uses of the plants that cured – and the local herbs – but also those of the plants that killed – the secrets that the desert held. But she had to be patient and allow time to run its course.

As they spent more time together Banoo opened up and began to talk about her medicinal knowledge. Malihe validated her work, instilled confidence in her and, as trust grew between them, Banoo spoke freely of her younger days, her lush garden and her trips to the desert, of the cases she had taken on, the people she had treated, the times she had saved lives and of her moments of desperation.

At last Malihe felt able to ask Banoo about the plants and herbs of the desert. Banoo was curious to know what Malihe was driving at and asked what kind of plant and how much of it Malihe was interested in. It was difficult, but in response Malihe turned the question back to Banoo.

'If you wanted to put a group of men to sleep for a while . . . '

'For how long a while?' Banoo asked nervously.

'I'm not sure, a day or two, perhaps longer, perhaps for ever.'

'Hmmm . . . there's a big difference between a day and for ever,' Banoo said wryly. 'What are you going to do when all these men are "asleep"?'

'I'm not sure, I haven't thought beyond that moment yet. But perhaps we can do something magical and fantastic.'

'Like what?'

'Like . . . singing in the streets . . . girls dancing in the park . . . '

'You're not very ambitious. If that's all you want then return to the village, city life is hostile and miserable. God will see to your wishes. They are simple human desires. I like singing and dancing myself. You should have seen me when I was young, in my twenties. This village couldn't take the sound of my songs and the beat of my feet.'

They dropped the conversation at that point. They each understood the palpable silence that grew up between them and it drew them closer together rather than further apart. Banoo guessed Malihe was up to something. She wanted to know, but at the same time she preferred not to know. She did want to help her, however, for she knew about her children and her imprisonment. She felt deeply for her and agreed to take her on a journey into the desert. A deep, satisfying ripple of joy and excitement welled up in Malihe. Banoo had finally come round.

## 19

At last the day came when they were ready to set off. Malihe had prepared everything according to Banoo's advice – warm blankets, a tent, freshly baked sweet buns, cheese, lots of dried fruit and nuts and, the most important items of all, water casks and Malihe's maps, books and compass.

Banoo had not made a journey like this for more than twenty years and it would take all the strength she could muster. For Malihe this was another step towards achieving her goal, making it at last look feasible, bringing into the realm of the possible what before had just sounded like a dream.

She was going to a land of sun, sand, earth and space: a nomadic life. Hope had suddenly burst open within her, like a dam bursting its bounds and overflowing with water. This was the journey of her life, the turning point.

They awoke at four and loaded up two donkeys with their packs and both donned the heavy clothing and headscarves necessary to protect them from the sun and sand. They had said goodbye to the families and other relations in the village the night before, Banoo having told everybody that she wanted to go and see her grandchildren in the hamlet of Jandagh and was taking Malihe with her to keep her company.

They set off on the slow-moving donkeys, along the narrow alleys and low mud houses of the village which were still in slumber except for a few early rising farmers who were off to their plots of land. They went through the village with slightly heavy hearts, but soon outside under the pale morning light with a vast horizon before them, they felt free, exhilarated to be on their way.

A few miles outside the village the countryside still had an ordered air, with small agricultural patches and plots creating a pattern, part green, part earth-coloured, a few trees here and there and dotted with mud houses. After the first hour of their journey, they would reach the first caravanserai, where they would rest for a while and exchange their donkeys for camels. They would then be on the edge of the desert.

The donkeys jolted along the path. The last signs of village life, green trees, mud houses, plots of cultivated land fast disappeared and the rough gravel path with vast empty space on each side extended in front of them. The morning sun rose higher and higher and Malihe thought, this is the beginning, the exciting, unsure beginning. Banoo rode in front of Malihe and they were quiet, each in her own world centred on this journey. The sun got hotter, the air drier and the earth darker. There were only a few signs of life around them – their movements, their shadows riding along in front of them, small dry bushes growing out of the rocks and sand, a few animals grazing on them and the odd abandoned well.

The long, monotonous ride was tiring for Malihe, unused to such starkness, relentless heat, the hostility of the landscape. It hurt her eyes. They were alone, at the mercy of this land. The heat overpowered and confused the mind, blinding the eyes and weighing down the body. It was too much for Malihe. She saw a scraggy tree that gave a little shade in the distance, and asked if they could stop there for a while.

The patch of shade was just big enough for her but she shared it with Banoo. They fed the donkey after a short rest and set off hoping to complete the first 'house' and have a longer rest at the caravanserai.

They reached it around noon feeling half-scorched. Malihe felt as if she were baking in her skin, sweat was rolling from her every pore down her belly, back and legs, and she wished for the shade of a tree and cold water for a bath. The dilapidated caravanserai still had cool, clean quarters in which they could rest. There was only one other traveller, resting at the other end of the building. An old man, presumably the keeper, appeared. They passed the animals over to him to groom and stable, and made enquiries about hiring camels, which he said he would see to. They had a wash, cooled themselves, ate bread and cheese with dry nuts, fruits, including dates, then spread the mats and fell asleep, the best state to be in, under the shade of the cool birch and mud wall in the 120 degree heat of the afternoon.

When they woke up it was a little cooler but the sun still blazed on. Malihe helped Banoo to pack her bedding, got her water to wash and made her some tea. They drank their tea, leaning against the wall, watching the sun blaze away on the sand and the bushes. The thought of riding under the sun again exhausted Malihe, but she tried to push it out of her mind. The old man came over to them and said that the camels were ready. Banoo suggested that Malihe tried one of them out, to get used to riding it before they set off.

Malihe began to feel frightened in case she would not be able to remember how to ride, or the animal disliked her, and she felt her confidence slipping away as the old man brought the camel to her and couched it. She looked around: nobody was there except the three of them. She looked at Banoo who was as cool and serene as ever. The old man was patient. The camels groaned and gurgled but soon calmed down. Malihe gathered herself together, got up, straightened her long skirt, fixed her heavy shawl and took a few shaky steps towards the camel. She touched its furry skin. It was soft and warm. The brown curls were thick and bunchy. She caressed its head and ears, its huge black eyes were beautiful and friendly. She could trust it. The keeper showed her the saddle, a small, well-made platform of tufted wool with a thick black sheepskin on the top. It sat in front of the hump of the camel and he showed her the ways that she could sit and hold the strap. She could sit with her feet both forward on the camel's neck, or sit sideways with both feet on one side, or cross-legged with her feet under her thighs, or just the most natural way – with each foot hanging down on either side.

Banoo encouraged her, saying she would manage it just fine. Malihe leaned with one hand on the side of the camel and the other on the keeper, and nervously put one foot in the foot strap and threw the other across the saddle. The camel jerked and half rose, the old man lifted her up and she threw herself half on the poor animal's neck, half on the saddle. But she was on and she soon gathered herself together, held the reins and rode slowly and gently with the keeper at her side patting the animal. She rode around trying hard to remember how she had managed it before, would it all come back to her? She felt strange, half in the air, not sure whether she was doing the riding or whether the camel was taking her for a ride. After a few rounds, with the help and advice of the keeper, she felt a bit more in control. She was ready.

They set off. The old man was accompanying them to the next village on his donkey. High above the ground on the soft saddle of sheepskin sat Banoo, dressed in black, with a long heavy cotton skirt, and a thick black scarf covering her head, face and shoulders. Malihe, on the contrary, wore white, in spite of Banoo's advice; she was tired of black. They were much higher now than when they had been riding the donkeys, and the ride was smoother although it had its own jolting rhythm. The dimensions of the views were much wider and more impressive. The composition of the country was beginning to change. There was a range of mountains in the distance on the right and pebbled knolls on the left. Banoo told her that they would have completed the second 'house' of the journey when they reached these mountains. The early afternoon heat was still burning as they rode along the narrow, sandy road of the desert. The vast space before them had no obvious signs, no visible route. In this wilderness how did the camels know where to tread? They were at the mercy of these animals. Malihe was getting used to the camel's movements, shifts and sounds, and began to like them. They were patient, long-suffering animals, and could stand long days without food and water, and were also known for being very loyal, graceful and gregarious beings.

Banoo began to reminisce about the heyday of the salt kavier before the advent of cars and trains. This was the trade route along which the merchants with their caravans of camels took Indian spices and Chinese silks from the Persian Gulf through to the northern ports, and from the Caspian Sea ports brought European and Russian luxury goods through to the south. She went on, giving a bit of a shout, as they crossed a bumpy path, saying that, 'The whole of this salt kavier was a sea bed in some ancient time.'

Malihe found this incredible. This journey was a feat in itself, but to hear such stories about this empty, barren land was making it more ancient, mysterious and magical for her. She looked around and tried to imagine it as a sea, a sea bed with strange fish and plants. In parts it did resemble something sea-like: the large sand basins looked like the bottoms of lakes, the pebble paths looked like sea coasts or the banks of rivers. The grey and white sandy beach was patterned, as if by the ebb and flow of a tide. Dry as stone, the desert might be with its thirst-killing air, but it seemed as if water had been there once, and a sea of it too. As the camel pushed its hooves in and out of the pebbled sand, rocking her gently, Malihe wondered what tured a sea into a desert and how through the ages the living and life-giving sources disappear, are transformed into the dust and sand, as if the coastal line, the beach, had gradually expanded and eaten up the sea. Could the process be reversed? Could this vast kavier turn into a sea again some time? And where would she be then?

The flat ground was rising steeply into a sand hill and the mountains were coming closer. Banoo said that they would be there soon. Malihe detected exhaustion and hunger in her voice. She was thirsty too. How precious was water! She did not dare to drink sufficiently of their meagre store, always only a mouthful or two, it's too rare here, she must not satisfy her thirst, must always keep a little in case. She had never before appreciated its value. How much of it is wasted in towns – they wash their arses with it – while the water shortage is killing people. The government's motto is, let them drink oil. In the kavier, she thought, they cleaned themselves with sand; and the *Republic's Voice* newspapers, which she'd put on top of her bag to distract the pasdars in their search on the journey, were becoming most useful.

At last the hazy green of the tiny oasis appeared in the distance. Banoo was pleased, Malihe relieved. Dreams of shade, coolness and rest, a long rest, filled her mind. The large gaz trees at the entrance of the village of Shurak protected it from full view, a well by the trees had a bucket hanging from a pole above it. Malihe was impatient for water. What a delightful sight, a well in use, a dangling bucket. She wanted to jump off the camel, run straight to the well and saturate herself with water. But Banoo reminded her that it was dangerous to drink too much, too fast when thirsty and hot. Malihe felt embarrassed at her impatience. She had been away from the desert too long.

The village was a small cluster of clay houses, hens, small patches of cultivated land and lines of pistachio and pomegranate trees. It had a population of three families. They rested for a couple of hours in the cool room of a house belonging to one of the inhabitants, and the woman who owned the house took care of their camels. Their bodies were stiff and aching, each muscle was as tight and hard as a bone. Malihe made a cosy corner for Banoo to lie down in and offered to massage her. Her awkward fingers opened up and spread out on Banoo's back. She found the tight muscles around the neck, at the top of the shoulder blades and on the lower part of her back, the thigh muscles which were sleepy from sitting on the camel, the most painful parts, and worked on them slowly and gently. Then all over her body. Banoo said she wanted to massage Malihe too but sleep overtook her. The woman who owned the house said that she didn't mind giving her a massage and Malihe soon fell asleep.

When they woke up, freshly baked bread, goat's cheese, dates and a raisin omelette, as well as a bubbling samovar greeted them. They had the luxury of a blissful cool wash from the well, combed their hair and dusted down their clothes, before they sat down comfortably at the sofreh. They ate slowly and gently appreciating every morsel. What a difference from a quick bit of a stale and sandy sandwich on the camel's back. After the meal and a sweet hot glass of tea, they went for a walk around the village. Malihe had never seen such a small village, with only a small road going through it and so few houses. She bought some fresh food and water from their hostess.

Banoo told her that the village had once had ten families living there but some had moved away and the desert was expanding, reclaiming the oasis. They could see dust piling up on the doorstep of the houses.

Malihe saw a young man digging in the sand and stopped to talk to him. He explained that he was planning a plantation of pomegranate and oil trees to help halt the encroachment of the sand. He also showed her a few local plants and their uses and she took a selection of leaves and flowers and put them in her pocket to study later. How did it feel to be one of a population of three, she asked him. He said, 'Lonely and a lot of hard work.' She questioned him about the plants, their watering systems, and he explained about some of the trees and bushes, their growth and their uses. It was an amazing place. This tiny family of people, trees and a cluster of houses living and thriving in the middle of wilderness, in the middle of this lifelessness. It felt like a country, like a tiny family of a nation.

When they set off again, high on their camels with their heads wrapped up in their heavy headscarves, it was early evening. The sun was lower, fading – hot, but getting cooler. Soon they were out in the open and the village like a green apple was miles behind them. Travelling at night was easier for the camels and if the weather held they could keep going as long as was physically possible. Banoo reminded her that as this was a salt desert it would not be completely dark at night. The salt reflects any light there is, providing enough to go on especially as the camels found their own way. The narrow path was becoming more and more salty and the camels' hooves turned it up and sprayed it around in different colours. The contours of the mountain range came closer. They were approaching the Thousand Mountains, an inter-locking range of mountains and hills, through whose narrow valleys their passage ran to the other side of the kavier and the village of Chopanan, which would signify the end of their third 'house'. They were hoping to get through those snake-like valleys to Chopanan without difficulty, and have a full day's sleep there.

Malihe often consulted her map of the desert to compare

their route and the landmarks on it. She could not find the mountains in front of her on the map; the relationship between the map of the kavier and the real kavier was as distant as that between an oasis and the false lure of a mirage. Banoo did not use a map, trusting instead her own sense of the land around her and the camel's judgment.

The dying sun polished the pebbles and sand around them as they zig-zagged through the narrow gorges, surrounded by cliffs rising to steep ridges, some with knife-edge crests. Limestone hills with varied, layered textures hugged each other. A broken dome, the ruin of a ghaleh, capped one of the peaks. It had been one of the old watch towers for the caravans that had plied the old trade routes. There were many such ruins in the kavier, reminders of its more active days. The explosion of colours – sepia, pistachio, copper – on the ridges and butts under the fading sun amazed her. In the midst of this desert, this lifelessness, such an abundance of colour and texture pleased her, gave her hope that even the desert was not completely bare and uniform. But soon the sight of dried shallow water courses at the base of the valley warned her of the danger of the desert.

As they wended their way through the gorges and sand hills a gentle, warm breeze touched them. At first it was refreshing, felt good on her skin but soon it gathered speed and hurled bits of sand at her. It moved in a circular fashion, creating dust devils and whirlwinds, noisier until it became a howl.

Banoo asked her to cover her face fully and poke her camel to speed up. They could be about to get caught in one of the kavier's sand storms. As they speeded up so did the sand, swirling, gathering speed and throwing its weight at them. Her hands, holding the reins, had no way of escaping the fury of the rough sand. The air became thick with it, the sunlight disappeared behind the wind and it became greyer and greyer, harder to see the path through the hills. The camels began to slow down.

Banoo shouted that they must find a safe shelter fast before they were buried beneath the shifting sand. They poked the camels harder and harder and kept a look out for a covered spot. They swung from side to side, the camels roared and grunted, refused to move on. Malihe dismounted, held the reins firmly and went forward pulling it after her. Banoo followed.

'Which way?' She went only where her feet stepped solidly. Nothing could be seen, the hills and the rocks, the dried bushes, all went blurred and out of focus. Only shadows remained. It was a struggle to move, pushing and pulling forward, eyes blind, powerless just like swimming against the current. Banoo tried hard to remember her knowledge of the terrain, of the kind of cover they could find. Ahead the valley was widening, and the wind deafened them, the sand blinding and exhausting them as they groped on. At last Banoo exclaimed that there was a cave leading into the rock somewhere near and they pushed on for it. Covered in sand, deeply afraid, dry-mouthed, with sand blocking their noses and throats, their camels exhausted, looking like moving sand knolls themselves, they reached the rocky entrance of the cave and crawled in, having couched the camels in the entrance to the caves.

Banoo was angry. It was a bad omen. God was angry with them. She was worried that if it went on through the night they would be stranded and lost. She was swearing under her breath, and calling upon God and his twelve Imams to help her. It was pitch dark and forboding. Malihe wanted to consult her map, but Banoo had warned her against using any matches or a lighter as the air in the confined space of the cave was too precious. Banoo wanted to pray but there was no room to stand up so she decided to do it sitting down. Malihe tried to calm Banoo, telling her that it was a natural event and that God was not angry. Why should God be angry with them – they hadn't done anything yet. Banoo was still anxious, tapping her knees, reading some prayers out loud, and begging for help from God. Malihe was also worried. What would they do if the storm changed the structure of the hills around them? What if more sand hills had formed, barricading the cave by the morning? What if it just went on, for twenty-four or forty-eight hours? The questions buzzed around her head. They were exhausted, tense, full of pain and stiffness, hunger and thirst. The temperature had dropped, as was common at night in the kavier. Mental anxiety overcame physical hunger as they leaned on the hard and uneven cave wall, sleeping fitfully.

When Malihe opened her eyes it was calm and the camels were grunting with hunger. Malihe looked at Banoo who was still half asleep. They looked like a pair of sand heaps. She shook herself free of the sand and ran out of the cave. Thick layers of soft white sand had covered the ground but there was no wind. The sun was up in the sky just behind the ridge of the highest mountain and the mountains and hills were there, not smaller or larger. She took a deep breath of relief and sang happily, looking for leaves on the sandy bushes to feed the camels. Banoo woke up, dusted herself down and then cleaned the camels, patting them, admiring their patience: in the heat of the kavier they were their best friends and guides and should be fed and watered first. She scooped a hole in the sand to see how deep the rain had gone, and dug out some possible sand holes which could lead her to water. After digging for some time she came to some greyish, salty water that tasted foul but was still precious. She managed to get a few bowls out to water the camels and with that, and Malihe's leaves they were content.

Malihe and Banoo had some water, fruit and nuts, and were soon on their way in the fresh heat of the early morning. Banoo noticed the changes that the wind had left behind: the soft sand crunching under the camel's feet was of a different colour and texture; the subsidence of the distant hills, and the blocking of some passages through the valley became apparent to her. As they went along Banoo pointed out the shiftings of the sand storms, the appearance of new mounds and the hidden dust-covered water courses.

Slowly and painstakingly they rode out of the valley into the open spaces, pleased to find easier paths, to go faster, pushing on to Chopanan and the end of their third house. They had no water left, very little food and lots of aches and pains, were dreaming of a soft, shady place for their afternoon siesta, as the sun moved in a straight line up into the heart of the sky.

The sight of the palm trees and minarets, the sleepy contours of the village, was a happy one. They had just about enough energy to smile and think of water and sleep. Malihe thought, desired water, a bath, to wash the sand off her skin, out of her hair. Would the village have enough water? More than anything on earth now she wanted to bathe, water dripping down her neck to the bottom of her spine, tickling her tired back and a massage from the washer woman afterwards.

The visitors were welcomed by a gang of noisy children. They gathered round them, looking, laughing, making comments and touching the camels. Malihe noticed that they were all boys. Where are the girls? she wondered. In the public hammam – how lucky that the village had one – afternoon sessions were women only, and Malihe and Banoo soaked themselves, revelling in the cool humidity of the dripping walls and floors. They were washed by a washer woman who gave them a thorough massage until Malihe felt good in every pore of her skin, imagining herself to be a queen, her heart's desire come true.

Malihe did not see any girls in the hammam either; it was unusual. There were lots of women, no girls. Out by the stream there were only women doing the washing, down the road in the local school as they passed at break time the playground was full of boys.

'Do they bury the girls in this village?' Malihe asked Banoo.

'Don't be silly. Girls are too useful to be buried,' Banoo answered.

Chopanan was a large village, home to 400 families, with a few water wells, a ghanat, a small stream and sufficient arable land outside the village. It produced wheat, cotton, grapes, pomegranates and onions. A run-down caravanserai was the only reminder of the glories of the old trade routes. Malihe collected some of the local plants and flowers, bought bread, dried fruit and cheese and chatted to many local women who were excited that two women were making such a journey on their own.

She noticed that people here had darker, stronger features; they looked more like Arabs and Indians – some of the men even had African features. She had heard that further south in Kerman there lived descendants of escaped African slaves, but she had not thought she would see them here. The people wore colourful costumes: the men had long jackets with a belt, a white or woollen hat and heavy scarves around their necks. The women wore long and very loose skirts which they had embroidered themselves each with a unique pattern, and plain waistcoats, heavy scarves around their waists and long colourful headscarves held in place by a plain smaller one wrapped around the centre of the head. It was elegant and graceful to look at, but it must be difficult to work in such a costume – with only their faces and their hands showing, on which the sun had left its mark.

Directed to the basement of a house to buy some goat's cheese, Malihe passed a half-open wooden door. Glancing in she saw many young girls sitting on low benches, all weaving carpets in a lightless, airless room. So here they were. They were alive after all. She asked the forewoman if carpet-weaving was a major industry and if there were such workshops in every house.

'Oh yes,' she said. 'Carpet-weaving is vital to us. It's the only work that brings cash into the village. Without that cash the village would not be able to buy tools, or anything from the town.'

So, Malihe thought, they do bury the girls alive after all.

For the next two days their ride continued over the sand hills, dried lakes, abandoned wells and the red mountains of Pozeh and Rebneh. They were climbing higher and it was cooler by day and night. One night they pitched their tent next to the Saroman sweet water spring, on the plains that spread before Saroman mountain. There was a small rock shelter built by the spring but Malihe slept out, in the open air, beneath the bright stars, sharpened by the desert air.

Their arrival in Jandagh was at night, and the last part of the journey, through the Jandagh mountains to the village, was frightening. Darkness, night's silence, the looming contours of the mountains and gorges, the exhausted camels and occasional animal noises in the distance, all combined to bring Malihe's heart to her throat. Her nerve was wearing thin, their way forward was unseen and Jandagh was far beyond the mountains. She felt uncertainty, exhaustion began to over-take her. She held the camel reins tightly, as if her life depended on it, her back stiffened with cold fear.

Arriving in Jandagh was therefore a great relief and their visit was made into a special family occasion. They were treated with the utmost generosity. The first few days were taken up in just visiting, chatting and lazing about. Banoo spent her time making family visits and catching upon who had been married, how many babies they had had and who had died. Left to herself, Malihe went around the village, talking to women and girls, finding out what they did in work and leisure, and what they grew in their gardens and why. She was fascinated by the diversity of local plants and their uses, especially by the use of the long date palms and tagh trees planted outside the village to keep the wind and the shifting sand away. The easiest trees to grow in this sandy, salty place were black, yellow and pink tagh and gaz, chij shoreh, mezvak, jaroo and pak. Some of these were small bushes which grew only when it rained, and were used for firewood and camel fodder. The village was green, vividly so in this yellow land with yellow mud houses. Malihe soon came to appreciate the growth in the village, even the fruitless and flowerless plants and trees were important, a part of the irrigation, the caring horticulture that went into keeping the kavier at bay.

When, after a restful few days, they set off to complete their last 'house', they knew that they were close, very close to their destination. They were riding in the direction of the local salt lake and the sand was getting whiter and grainier, smoother and drier. They rode over a few low salt hills, with sinuous white lines stretching across them, as if long snakes had wri-thed over the sand, leaving the mark of their movement behind. The camels' hooves broke the patterns of wriggling lines.

Beyond these stark hills a tiny oasis serviced by a lone well came into view. A shack, a few trees, a stream, a cultivated patch, made up the whole oasis. This was the end of their journey. Banoo and Malihe couched their camels and went to see if anybody was around. There seemed to be nobody there.

They decided to pitch their tent anyway as they needed to make this their base for a while. As they unpacked and put up the tent a strong-looking, middle-aged woman appeared with her dog, a pathetic, bony creature.

They exchanged greetings and she offered them her room but they said they preferred to be in the open air. She was living alone at the moment as her husband had gone to Jandagh a week ago to do some seasonal work there. The three women had tea and a long chat. The tea tasted especially fine and sweet unlike the bitter, salty tea that they had had so far. Robabeh said that the well's water tasted lovely, surpassing any other water in the kavier, and that it was the main reason why she lived there.

Banoo enquired about the area, what changes had occurred; Robabeh told them that the salt lake was expanding, that a small spring had been found, that she had planted bamboos around it to protect the spring from the desert. That in among the bamboos tiny flowers were growing, she didn't know their name or function. That she had enough dried branches for fire, and that she was extending her patch of plants by the stream, and that out in the desert all the traditional plants thrived. Banoo was pleased. This was going to be their base, from where they would make trips into the desert, to search for and gather their plants. They would make a start the next day. At last they were here. Malihe did not know what to think.

The small salt lake was not far. In the early evening, after they had cooled off by the well, Malihe decided to walk there, leaving Banoo to rest.

The sun was setting on the salt-rimed horizon – a huge blood-red disc, sinking. In the distance a flat basin sparkled white, tinged with the pink shadow of the sunset. That was the salt lake, Malihe guessed, striding on. Had it been the bottom of the sea? Now it was part of the kavier. So white, swan white, snow white, white as fear. There is no life there, no growth. Only layer upon layer of bitterness, flatness, lifelessness. Imagine having that much salt, being surrounded by it, eating it all. The image of the salt in that bloody, desolate sunset possessed Malihe. The space was infinite and she was standing in the middle of it, she and her shadow. The infinity frightened her. She returned.

Banoo was sitting by the well, resting, planning for tomorrow. Malihe sat next to her.

'It would be too much to want a cup of tea, no?'

'Yes. There isn't enough firewood.' Banoo disappointed her.

'All right, I'll have sweet water.'

She sat down next to Banoo on the soft warm sand, and drank the most delicious water.

'We're here at last. It's wonderful for me to be here – do you feel the same? Tell me what the pleasure is for you in using herbs, and why you stopped your work.'

Quietly, meditatively Banoo began to unfurl her life story into that void where stories are made, are told and are ended too.

'I liked plants and flowers, we all did, especially my grandmother and mother. As a child I played with them, took care of them and preserved them. Gradually I learned about them, grew them myself and used them. We all did in the village, except that I liked them more and preserved them.

'What was the village like when you were a child? It must have been a different world.'

'It was. Just a small cluster of houses and all your relations living in them – simpler, friendlier, a better place, but a lot of hard work. Places grow and usually get uglier. What can you do? It just happens that way.' Banoo placed her hands in her lap in a gesture of resignation. Her hands were as black and as wrinkled as her skirt, a yellow gold ring sat on one bony finger. Malihe tried to imagine Banoo's hands as a child.

'How did you manage to keep up your childhood interest in plants? Didn't you get bored or take up something more useful like sewing or needlework?'

'I did those too. Women can't do without needlework. What kept up my interest in plants was the illness of my first two daughters – both suffered from asthma. They were tiny little things, so weak, so tender. It broke my heart to see them suffer.' Banoo's eyes were sad, unshed tears hung on her lower eyelashes. Malihe kept quiet.

'I had to rely on remedies made from our local herbs. There

218

were no doctors around – the nearest one was in Yazd, and we had no transport, not even a proper road, to take a sick child on such a long journey. So with the advice of my mother and other older women I just kept up the treatment. The recovery was slow, but—'

'I'm so surprised to hear this,' Malihe interrupted. 'It sounds like a fable to me. In Tehran nobody believes in such medicine any more. It's just aspirin for every illness – you just buy them and swallow them.'

'It's like that in Anarak now too,' Banoo continued. 'Not many people use herbal medicine. But these plants saved my daughters. I was so pleased and thankful that, I suppose as a sign of appreciation and belief in the magical power of the natural remedies, I continued using them. By then most of the neighbours were surprised at my daughters' recovery and came to see me for their children's illnesses. It just developed from there, adults came, then even people from the next village came and so it went on till the city medicine man came to peddle his white tablets.'

'Tell me about some of your cures, the ones you were most satisfied with.'

'I enjoyed curing children's illnesses the most.'

'How did your old man take the streams of strangers coming and going and knocking your door down at odd hours?'

'He was ... God ... I don't remember very much. He would grumble and make jokes about it – he would call me a grass hakim, a village nurse. He thought my jars were in his way, took up too much space in the house and so on. You know. But whenever he coughed he ran to me.'

Robabeh appeared and Malihe invited her to sit down.

'Banoo's telling us about sick people she has cured.' Robabeh sat down next to them; three women by the well.

'Now ... Where was I?' Can't remember, oh yes, the cases I've been most satisfied with. The ones that I most enjoyed treating were when the medicine man's white tablets has been no use and the desperate mother came to me as a last resort. I asked for patience and tolerance from the mother while the child was under my care. I had to convince them that it took longer and that the cure was more gradual than conventional medicine. Once I had a boy gone yellow all over, nobody had any hope for him . . . And a young man who had dreadful rheumatism, nearly disabled with it . . . And many women suffering with all sorts of pains, back pains, breast pains, period or menopausal pains and, of course, those who had pains from their men.'

'What did you use for all these ailments?'

'I used a lot of seeds, leaves and roots. I remember walnut leaves and oil, orange oil, and varius pastes I made myself from various roots and oils. Oh, my girl, I wish I could remember things better . . . '

'Did you travel? Go to other villages or towns to find out more about the traditional medicine that existed there?'

'No. I mean, I never thought of it that way. But I heard from the visitors to the village and other patients that I wasn't the only village nurse, grass hakim. I had six children, I worked on the land. We had lots of animals and a big farm that needed caring and managing. But there is something I do regret. And that is what my daughter tells me, that I should have learned how to read and write properly, to write down everything that I have learned and to have kept a proper record of my discoveries, my experiences and of the people that I treated and their cures. I relied on my memory. Such foolishness. Little did I know of the worst incurable disease – of old age, that takes your memory away, your strength, your independence. I regret losing my health. Why can't we get old gracefully, still in control of our bodies and our minds, still relying on the power of our hands and knees and eyes?'

'But Banoo, you are still strong, you have physical and spiritual strength. You are still independent, more so than some younger people.'

Banoo lifted her aged hands and with her hard, strong fingers, she touched her face, lingering on her eyes and tapping her forehead. Her temples were hidden under a white tuft of hair, the middle fingers searched for them, her tired, throbbing temples and rested there, on both sides of her cheeks as if framing her face.

A face that was lined, the lines of a long lifetime. Her skin curled, overlapped and tucked in layer after layer on her forehead where her life story was written, on her cheeks beneath her deep eyes, around her soft lips and under the sunken archway of her chin.

Malihe looked at Banoo's crowded face, crowded with experience. I will learn, she thought, and I will write it all down. Robabeh's dog barked out into the open spaces. She got up and went to it. Night was falling. Banoo looked exhausted, she stood up leaning on her wooden walking stick and turned back towards her tent.

Beneath the far hills, around the salt lake, shining pearl white, under the infinite sky, the three women milled around, preparing for their rest. Tomorrow was going to be a very different day. Malihe went to sleep with a vision of the azure petals and the dry roots of the Shiroo plant in her mind's eye, and dreamed of the tomorrows to come.

221

# 20

Before her return to Tehran Malihe could not say why she stayed so long in the desert and then in Anarak. She lost track of time the longer she spent there, the more she learned from Banoo. Sometimes it felt as if she had been there for a century, sometimes no time at all. She was busy, her energy and curiosity focused on her studies, and news from the outside world rarely got as far as Anarak to distract her from them. Letters from her friends, in their prearranged code, came very irregularly. She had been waiting for their call for her to return, but the time had not been right for them, until just now.

A sense of forboding gripped her, waking her, as from a dream. It had been a long time, far too long, she had not expected to take this long. Leaving Anarak was not easy either, leaving the people she had lived with, the land of the sun and sand and nature that she had grown to love so much. She was leaving yet again. The last time she had left it had taken her nearly thirty years, three decades, to return. How long would it take next time? Would she ever return again? She was sad. She didn't want to dwell on that. But saying goodbye was difficult, going harder. She was leaving half her heart behind.

A couple of days before her departure she went around the village at its quiet time and looked about, at the dried uneven walls, hand-carved doors, narrow and dusty lanes and the empty streets. She sat by the old tree in the cemetery to say a prayer for her mother and father and stayed there for some time, absorbed in thoughts about her birthplace, her identity, her sense of belonging. She thought about the people she knew there, especially Banoo, and what she had taught her, a unique experience. Would she see her again? The cemetery made her feel sad and melancholy. She was reminded of all her dead, the dear ones, the precious and the distant ones. She wanted to be buried there, in that small familiar cemetery, not in a huge, crowded unknown one where you needed a map to find your beloved. And her children, where were they now? Her heart ached unbearably and she left the cemetery.

She went for a long, lonely walk in the melancholic peace of those narrow red-clay lanes. How do you say goodbye when you know that it may be the last trip? How do you leave when you know that your destination may be gaol? How do you leave the friendly and familiar for the unfamiliar and hostile? The question of leaving, the departure from her present comfortable life to the chaos of Tehran preoccupied her.

She reminded herself that she had an independent and useful life here, among people she trusted, who trusted her. It was a simple life – the bare necessities, no cinema or television, no parks or Lebanese apples. Only kindness, care, common sense, hard work on the land and happy co-existence among the women. She could stay, continue with her herb garden, take it seriously and make it into a life, write it all down and keep a comprehensive record of it, treat people, teach people, teach the young, boys and girls – especially girls – and help to make changes and progress that way. Her life had changed, why shouldn't she go on with it now, in the present? She envisaged her present life continuing, successfully and comfortably.

But what would she say to Goli, Zareen and Fatemeh? Do they still believe in a collective action against repression? Without a doubt? Had she changed her own mind? Did she now believe in individual salvation and reform from within? She believed in both these alternatives – collective action and individual salvation – but how long would her stay there last without trouble? When would the pasdars, with their secret agents, march in to patrol these streets and the minds of people here? The cosy communal life around her could be shattered, her peace could be invaded again.

'Good evening Malihe. This time of the evening and you're still out and about?' said Shams Baba, a neighbour, startling Malihe.

'Good evening to you. I have been out for a walk. I can't sleep tonight. I went for a long walk to see the village before I leave.'

'Don't fret, you will be back. It won't change much, we will keep it safe and sound for you.'

The single lamp flickered. The flies buzzed round it incessantly. The dark shadows of doors, trees and houses deepened. The air was hot, God was breathing heavily on them. The faint sound of distant animals echoed into and mingled with the night's noises. Darkness spread around the village. Malihe walked through the thick air and left the outside behind the wooden door to her house. She let herself in, closed the door and shut it, slowly but firmly.

She took an express coach back to Tehran. There were only two short stops. She did not want a slow journey. She wanted the distance to fly away and land her there, on her friends' doorstep. She was the only woman on the coach and this frightened her. Would she be questioned? Would she be stopped? She was travelling at night, hoping that she could spend the impatient hours in sleep and just wake up in Tehran. But one woman among fifty-four men, the sheer immensity of it took her by surprise and stole her sleep. She gazed out into the darkness, worried and tense, wishing she could sleep it away, afraid that the revolutionary guards would stop the coach and search bags and passengers. A neighbour advised her to put a prayerbook in on top of her luggage, so that if her bag was opened they would see how pious she was and search no further.

She was glad of the advice. The coach screeched to a halt, lights flashed on. The passengers jumped. She covered herself totally in her black chador for protection and pretended to be asleep. The guards walked in, asked a few questions and walked up the aisle. Her heart was beating so fast that she thought the guards would hear it. She felt for her pouch, the precious pouch containing her herbs; it was tucked safely in under the weight of her hair. The sound of the heavy army boots, sharp clicks, came to a halt beside her. She froze, her limbs stuck together with fear. The sound of breathing above her head, moments of silence, centuries of it, was she shaking? Was she too still? Would he read her fear from beneath the cover of the chador? No voice, no calling out, no search yet.

'The mother is asleep, she is very tired. Let her sleep.'

'Ouum.' The heavy army boots clicked on, the sound retreating.

She unfroze, and only when the coach started again did her limbs thaw and warm blood course again through her body. But still she did not move, she wanted to thank the man who had saved her from scrutiny, but she did not dare. He must have felt protective towards her, he must have known she was not asleep, he must be feeling pleased with himself to have saved her. How grateful would he expect her to be? She tried to sleep. The coach was stopped by the guards five more times. Each time she went through hell, but by the end she was used to it and prepared to challenge any search. She relaxed. She would challenge them. Nothing can happen to her. They would not find anything on her anyway. They would not know what to look for anyway. The herbs in her pouch were as safe as if they were still in the desert. They would not have the brains to know what they were or what they were going to be used for. They were looking for other kinds of enemies, with bombs, machine guns and grenades. They would never see an older woman with a pouch of desert herbs as their enemy. She was safe.

The coach shook, jerked, moved, speeded up, slowed down, climbed and descended, continued. On, with Malihe's eyes fixed on the edge of the road, skidding and disappearing lines. The last part was the hardest, the hope of arrival, the joy at reaching the end of the trip, getting to safety, escaping arrest – it all turned her stomach over and over.

Once the coach had stopped she was out fast, carrying her bag, walking out on the road, free, fresh early morning air on her face, it was a good feeling. She walked on for a bit. There were very few men on the road going to work and no women. She was the only woman again. Strange, so few people in such a heavily populated area.

Just before the crossroads at Shush shock hit her between the eyes. The blood shot to her head and solidified there. Four bodies hung in front of her, on wooden poles, dangling in the air. Hanging dead bodies with large placards on them. Her bags dropped to the ground, her hands felt lifeless, like hanged things. Two women, two men, their necks stretched, their legs dangling. Four hanged bodies and a small crowd of people on a corner watching. The bodies must have been left there as an example. She picked up a bit of courage, and her bags, and went forward to read the placards: 'Homosexual', 'Prostitute', 'Adulterers', 'Abortionist'. Malihe did not understand what was meant by abortionist. She went to one of the people in the watching crowd and asked her about it.

'That one over there was a bastard homosexual . . . He said he loved a man . . . This was a doctor, a gynaecologist, a criminal, performing abortions – you should have seen the beautiful baby boys he murdered, young and tender, only six weeks old, murderer.'

Malihe picked up her bags and her nerve and walked on. Men were going to work now, still no women around. The morning was mute, the streets bare and lifeless, so uncommon for this area, where there had been street markets, a centre of wholesalers and retailers, a huge shopping quarter. Walking down the dead road, she passed a closed baker's; a note on the door said, 'Sorry no flour, no bread'. Further away another shop had its shutters down, the notice said, 'No fresh fruit and vegetables in the market today'. So how do people manage then? What do they eat? The pavement life was dead too: no street vendors, cooking pots on the curbs selling breakfast to the workers, grilling kebabs, selling the delicious greasy kebabs and drinks to passers-by, sandwiches and snacks for lunch . . .

Don't people eat in the street any more? she thought. Have they all become health conscious? Don't they need to make money? Are there other kinds of eating places? Where are the children selling sweets and cigarettes? Have they got other, better-paid jobs? Or are they at school perhaps? They're not even playing in the street, no football, no fighting. Why is there no noise? No noisy children?

Straight ahead the streets were packed with small box-like houses, one next to another. But now there were no trees in those small gardens, no honeysuckle hugging the walls, no scent of jasmine wrapping around the morning air, no vine trellisses. And where are all the tall, heavenly Tabrizis lining the streets? Have they been uprooted. No naughty children climbing up them ? Where are the women? They can't be sleeping while the men go to work. Who buys the freshly baked hot morning bread, the breakfast cheese? Why are the streets so thin of people? So empty of life?

She saw a few people going in one direction and followed them. They came to a square where a large crowd had gathered. Malihe's heart started beating faster as she went closer. In the centre of the square was an area fenced about, with armed guards surrounding it tightly. Inside the fenced area four people were tied to wooden poles, a few feet apart. They were blindfolded, handcuffed, their legs tied, all dressed in white burial shrouds. They were bound to the wooden poles. Four soldiers, fully armed, were facing them, awaiting the orders of their sergeant. The crowd was gathered on all sides of the square, looking on passively at the condemned bodies. The soldiers were standing to attention, with their rifle butts at their feet, the barrels in their fists. The moments ticked away.

Malihe's mouth was wide open, she was numb, petrified. Why? How? Questions she could not ask.

The sergeant's voice echoed out. The soldiers knelt, aimed, fired. The shots poured out, plunging into the bodies. The crowd cheered. Malihe screamed, forgetting herself and her veil.

'What have you done! What have you done to this city! Tehran, the capital city of injustice!'

Nobody noticed her or what she had cried out, all were cheering. At the soldiers, at the bodies, the bodies that bent over, heads flopped on to chests.

Suddenly she was terrified of what she had said, of how she

looked and where she was, right in front of the soldiers. She put on her veil quickly, picked up her bags, straightened herself.

Was she insane? Was she deranged like everybody else? Had fear and sheer terror of this bullet-laden atmosphere flipped her brain out of her skull? No. She must not allow herself, even for one short moment, to lose her power to think. She must guard her sanity with her life. She looked around. Nobody had noticed her unveiling or her words. Everybody had been so enraptured by the public execution that they had not noticed her outburst.

She had better go to the railway station, not far now, and take a bus home. She had seen enough of city life for one day. Heart-broken and demoralised, she walked towards the square, eyes on the ground. She had no desire to see any other atrocities.

At the entrance to the huge square where the railway station was, she looked up and saw a long line of conscripts. The square was jam-packed with snaking lines of them, all different shapes, sizes and uniforms. A notice in front of one queue read: 'Conscripts for war against the foreign imperialist infidels queue here.' The queue stretched all the way to the marble steps of the railway station. Another queue stood in front of a different banner, 'Conscripts for war against Monafegheen here.' This was a word she had heard last when she went to Quran classes as a child, an ancient Arabic word which was only used when the prophet waged war against the non-believers in his own land, the internal enemy. There were thousands, all lined up in their green army suits, heavy black leather belt and boots. They were being counted, given a number and a ticket, led into the hall, beyond which long empty trains waited for them. Another sign read: 'War volunteers for ancillary work queue here', and there were crowds of women covered in black from head to toe, with a white shroud overall on top, being given a number and a ticket and directed in through a separate gate. A man, a sergeant, kept the women in line. They too were being posted to the war zone, but they were volunteers, not conscripts, for the cause. Another placard read, 'Volunteers for the war against drugs, alcohol, gambling queue here,' another, 'Neighbourhood vigilante groups against imperialist corruptive influences here'; 'Anti-make-up squad', 'Anti-fashion squad', 'Anti-unveiled squad', 'Children's squad – the eyes and ears of our society'.

A long queue of boys aged from eight to fourteen and another of girls stood silently in lines. So here are the children, thought Malihe. They looked like children until you looked in their eyes and at their posture, cowed and fearful. Is this their new game? She went up to one of them, a small skinny boy, pretending to be older than he was. She touched his arm.

'What are you lining up here for, what are you going to do?' The boy looked at her as if she was a nobody.

'We are going to be the eyes and ears of our country and expose the enemies of the state. We will maintain law and order. We are patriotic soldiers of the future. We will defend this land and its superior Islamic ideology with all of our might.' Malihe could not believe her ears; had she heard him correctly? She wanted to pinch him to see if he would react. She wandered on; feeling like a zombie.

A huge fire was burning somewhere. She moved towards it to get herself warm. Fear expanded under her skin, giving her goosepimples. Women clad in black veils, from head to toes, were gathered around the fire, in the midst of piles of books and magazines. As Malihe looked on, they began to grab handfuls from each pile and tossed them into the fire: women and socialism pamphlets, *The Role of Women in the Iranian Revolution*, books and leaflets belonging to every society imaginable – they all caught flame, covers resisting at first, then titles melting and pages blistering in the heat. The magazines burned faster, their colour pages mingling prettily with the colours of the fire. *Art and Society, Women in Persian Art, Musical Instruments and their Influences, Modern Painting* – the pages flapped in the breeze as they lit the fire, women's arms and legs shot into flames. Malihe hated the sight, she hated the fire and heat and the women around it.

Malihe stood there, surrounded by the crowd, green-jacketed official men, young and old civilian men, weary, but determined men, blank, mute faces and numb expressionless eyes. The women seemed even more resolute. They had willingly

offered themselves to the service of the war, both as combatants and as ancillary workers; and now they had to prove
themselves, they would try to prove that they were better
than the men. They would dedicate more, sacrifice more, take
greater risks – if only to be accepted, although inferior, by the
men. A woman is good enough to fight, good enough to service
men's needs and good enough to die – but she would never
be good enough to be one of them, to be a sergeant in a
commanding position.

ای زنان تاکی اینسان خموشید
تابه کی روی آتش بجوشید

چون زن ایلیائی بکوشید
جامهٔ بندگی رانپوشید
عزت بودای خواهران دری نیازی

Oh women till when so silent?
Till, when bearing and burning
try, like the tribal women
throw away the garment of slavery

There is pride in independence.

Malihe mumbled the old song under her breath. Her knees
gave up and she squatted on the ground, unable to move.
This is the new life, she thought, the new city. Vivid flashes
of other events this square and the streets around it had
seen during the revolution interrupted her resigned train of
thought, lifting her spirits an inch. These very same streets,
these very same people had demanded liberty, equality and
justice. They had marched for it, for miles, for hours, and it
had been snowing then. We had energy, imagination and a
lot of spirit. We carried banners of defiance – of protest, not
shrouds. Women were everywhere active, progressive and on
the side of time. We didn't give up then. What has happened
to these very same people? We helped to liberate the men, so
that they could liberate their bullets, with us as their targets.

Where is our power, pleasure and creative imagination? Our dreams? What have they done with our city? Images of death, martyred faces papered on the walls, hanged bodies, bullet-ridden corpses, the people's subdued posture and the atmosphere of resignation – all sank her further into depression. This square, what a sad circle of betrayal and deceit had been described here. It is not even snowing.

A rough voice shook her out of her thoughts and the warm security of her veil. She put her head out and faced the young, unshaven face of a soldier.

'Mother, you must move, you're blocking the way. There's no room to rest here.'

'All right, my son. I was so tired. There's nowhere to rest any more, and on such a sad day . . . I will move now.'

'Is your son gone? Don't worry, he will be blessed in the hands of the revolution.'

Malihe was reminded about her son, her daughter . . . Thank God they didn't return to this death trap, she thought. This land of corpse worshippers. But it wasn't much consolation. They too had been involved in battles against another holy faith, all might and right . . .

She stood up, feeling very tired and depressed with so many would-be corpses, so many death worshippers and cheap offerings to a cruel God. Men and women who were living their lives happily 1300 years behind their time. She turned away in anger, in hatred, in disdain, and spat on the ground. Avoiding people, walking by the wall and looking at the ground, she walked towards her bus stop. She could not, however, avoid looking at the walls. They were black with slogans for war and for the veil. 'We are men of war!' read the huge printed letters illustrating a mural of happy soldiers in trenches. 'Sister! Your veil is my honour!', 'Sister! Your veil is your trench!'. An advertisement for a magazine, *Zane-Rooz* (*Women of Today*), read 'Keep war alive in all its dimensions for future generations', printed in thick, black letters, a chilling message. Then came the posters of martyrs' faces and their names graffiti-ed on the walls. Dismal faces of dead youths, slogans and dead faces, more dead faces. A black flag, the sign of mourning, above every other house, a green flag, the colour of Islam, at intervals. Passers-by did not even glance at the dead faces, did not even bother to read the slogans. They passed by uncaring, unaffected. What has happened to the people? Where are their eyes? Their ability to read, to care? Where are their expressions, their kindness? What have they done to women? Who has stolen their kindness and warmth? Why? How?

She went back to her bus stop timidly, head bowed, eyes lowered, shoulders drooped. She got a ticket and waited among the other timid, numb people in a long queue, waiting for the arrival of a bus to take her home. She wished for a bus that was empty, so she could drop herself into a seat and rest till she got home. But a bus arrived packed with men: she didn't have the energy to push and her bags were a problem. Men rushed forward, getting to the seats first, then having got there, if they felt generous they might give them up for an older woman or a mother. She would be well squashed. A bus, running every five minutes, with a seat all to herself was another lost dream. How many revolutions do you need to win to get a seat on a bus?

She arrived at Seh-Rahe Jaleh square. Nothing looked familiar. The small roundabout had changed, there was no sign of the market stalls; instead a small shrine was built in the centre with black and green flags flying above it and a low iron chain all around.

She walked over towards Ziba Style, hoping to see Zareen and give her a big hug. Every few yards she noticed a demolished house or a burned one. The area looked like a war zone. Ziba Style was boarded up, broken glass littering the pavement in front of it. Graffiti was scrawled in red all over it: 'House of Sin', 'Whore House', 'From Here Straight to Hell' . . . The Ziba Style sign was half torn down.

Her heart sank. Why hadn't she been told? Where was Zareen? She tried to peep through the boards and broken glass. The interior was full of rubbish, broken mirrors and rusty driers and other hairdressing paraphernalia. She turned away and set off for home. Her street was unrecognisable. Nothing was in its place, everything was more dirty, broken, ugly.

Her house wasn't there. It had been demolished. She knocked on a few doors, looking for her neighbours, somebody, anybody who could tell her what had happened to her house. Knocking at one door, she met a young woman who had been a friend of Leila, her landlady's daughter. The young woman took her over to their house. Leila, also a young woman now, opened the door and called everybody. They all hugged, kissed and welcomed her. A little later, when they were alone together, Leila told her quietly that Zareen and the others were fine and would be in touch as soon as they could. The other news and the story of their compulsory removal would have to wait till she had rested.

Malihe sat down to tea. Cross-legged, she held her feet in her hands, massaging them and said, relaxing into the familiar, friendly atmsosphere, 'You don't know how far these tiny boats have sailed today, carrying this weary passenger, and against how many high and low tides.'

## 21

A few days later there came a message via Leila to meet the others at a Friday prayer meeting outside the university. Everywhere else was either bugged, or banned to women. Women on their own were not allowed in parks, restaurants or clubs. However, the Friday prayer meeting was different and women treated it like an all-day event, sometimes like a picnic. Women did need passes though to enter the streets around the university and were physically searched before they went in. The others would organise a pass for Malihe and meet her beforehand.

Every Friday, the Muslim rest day, the streets for miles around the university were closed off to traffic and passers-by unless they were going to the prayer meeting. Men gathered inside the university grounds, among the flowers, bushes and hedges of the gardens. Some were brought in from distant suburbs and workers were coached in from their factories or brought by company transport. Women were allowed to join in the prayer meeting, but only in the streets outside. Women and children sat on the hard pavements and streets and listened to the all-day sermons and prayers broadcast from huge microphones which were placed in trees and on the roofs of buildings.

As soon as the sermon began the sound echoed throughout the whole area for miles around. People had no choice but to listen, their only rest day invaded with a high-pitched booming and electronic shrieking that pierced right into their sitting rooms. The broadcast was designed to present the city as a united community, all conforming, all submitting to holy instruction on a Muslim rest day.

The friends arranged to meet in the early hours of the morning. Fatemeh was given the responsibility of getting Malihe a pass and it was she who Malihe found waiting for her outside the perimeter to explain the procedure of the day and the degree of the surveillance at the prayer meeting. Once entrance to the women's section of the prayer meeting was gained there was little external surveillance as women were themselves spied on by each other; and, in any case, such a gathering of women was not considered a threat to the regime.

They met under a tree, at a street corner near several families with noisy children who would camouflage their meeting and conversation. Zareen had bought some sweets, cream cakes and made some zolbia for the occasion. She was the first to arrive, and was soon joined by Goli, then Fatemeh and Malihe arrived together.

It was a nervous, fearful reunion – their surroundings dictated that – but they were apprehensive for other reasons too: would they have changed a lot? Were they still friends? How much did they have still in common? They were together, happy but a little shaky, hugging each other a little, kissing politely and restraining themselves with care. They could talk there, but they had to be very careful whenever somebody else came near to change the subject or stop. The noisier the children were, the better it would be.

Zareen put the sweets and cakes down, Goli got some tea from the nearby street vendor, they offered it around to the other women and children near them as was the tradition at such a prayer meeting. Then, as they ate and drank quietly they had a good look at each other. They had aged, truly, more than their natural age; lines and lines had been added to their faces and hands. But they looked well and in good spirits, as far as they each could judge from faces and hands. Malihe looked much darker, thinner, but livelier and in better physical shape than the rest.

'So lovely to see you after so many years. You've gone dark, a deep brown, nearly coal black,' Zareen whispered.

'Yes, it's so *good* to be with you all again. When I arrived in Tehran I thought I had landed on another planet.'

'Sometimes we wonder the same.' Fatemeh looked wiser, and not so shy. Malihe wondered if she and Zareen were still together.

'How come you haven't got a few kids?' Malihe asked Goli with a smile. 'Pass me the zolbia . . . oh . . . lovely . . . '

'I have made it especially for you. Changed a chicken coupon for a sugar one – everything is rationed here and sugar most of all, of course,' Zareen said.

'All the registry offices have been so packed with weddings, because the government now offers money for first-time marriages, that I couldn't get a look in. Do you think I'll be left on the shelf? Is there still some hope for me?' Goli asked mischievously. She still looked fresh-faced in spite of a few new lines around her eyes.

'Definitely. I will take you under my wing and be your matchmaker myself.'

'I had other options as well, you know. I could have left for abroad, as my parents did after the murder of my younger brother. I could have got married and had some pretty babies, as many of my friends did. But I didn't want that,' Goli finished off.

'Tell me what else has been happening,' asked Malihe. 'What happened to Ziba Style, Zari?'

'Oh that, like everything else it's become illegal, cutting hair is a sin. I can't do hairdressing any longer.'

'So what do you do now? How do you earn your living?'

'Women don't need to earn a living, financial independence is now against the law – women should depend on men. It's the new law – haven't you listened to the radio?'

'No, I didn't have it in the village, and I didn't miss it. But why have you all been moved around so much?'

'Each time there was a protest, the entire population of that area was moved. Quite normal now.' Zareen answered.

'We have seen so much, here in the city,' said Goli quietly. 'We have seen vultures, we have seen rats. The city is full of them, chewing at our spirit, on every street corner.'

'We have seen our childhood monster Dieve resurrected –

presented as a prophet, worshipped as God,' Fatemeh said. 'I have watched and listened to the silence of women, their griefs, their lost hope. We have been living under the barrel of a gun. I see women shrinking, shrinking to the size of a thimble, and then disappear. Years of it, long, bitter years.' Zareen said dully. 'Most hurtful of all, we've seen betrayal. Sisters telling on sisters, brothers cutting brothers' throats . . . the youngest, the most beautiful and the brightest comrades hanged at every cross-roads,' Fatemeh added. 'And Azadi Square was reserved specially for mass hanging of women, of prostitutes and adultresses.'

'We have had spies as neighbours, police as shopkeepers, friends sitting on fences, vigilantes teaching our children. We have been tongue-tied.' Zareen twisted her hands in her lap. 'I have seen women's faces,' she continued, 'from one week to the next, the lines growing deeper under their eyes, at the corners of their mouths, lines like sudden, deep cuts inflicted, like bruises, cuts—'

Goli spotted a plain-clothes policeman coming near, speaking into a walkie-talkie and, even though the sermon was loud, Zareen stopped what she was saying and chatted about the sermon, picking at a cream cake.

'I have seen women's faces,' she went on, after he had disappeared, 'like battlegrounds, poor women, their beautiful eyes that I used to make up, making them shine. I never got tired of looking into them; now their eye sockets sink deeper and deeper into their skulls, after endless crying, returning from prison visits, from torture chambers, from inquisitions. I don't ask questions, they don't explain. We just know.'

'How many prisoners have we got these days?' asked Malihe.

'Nobody knows the exact number,' Fatemeh replied. It reached such a high point a few years ago that they brought in new codes, and mass executions and mass graves became common.'

'Now it's difficult to know, because people are not allowed to talk about certain subjects – and that's one of them,' Goli said.

'So much has happened to us,' said Zareen. 'I don't know

237

where to start, or what to say. It reached a point, you know, when they didn't really need to ban hairdressing, because women didn't need it any more. They started losing their hair, overnight their hair turned white, as if they had aged thirty years on a single night, or with a single piece of news – usually after the disappearance of their daughters or sons. Sometimes I got so tense inside that my hands started shaking as I was washing their hair; I could see the shiny patches on their skulls, I could count the hairs, the skin so bare, as if – just as in medieval times – some torturer had pulled out half of their hair and left the other half as a reminder. My women's precious hands, which I so carefully manicured and varnished – you should see their hands now: coarse, neglected and dry as bones, as if they had been digging graves and digging them for centuries, for themselves, like the Mexican rebels.'

'And you should see how bent women's backs are becoming, how veiled and cramped their bodies,' Goli said sadly. 'Just like the Vietnamese war prisoners who were kept in cages. And the university turned into a place of prayer,' she went on, 'a national sermon station. It now takes ten years to get a three-year degree. We could climb up to the moon in that time. Half the books in the library are classified as forbidden; we are only allowed to sit at the desks, listen to the teacher memorise and repeat his lessons after him. No questions are allowed, no answers are given and doubt is sacrilege. We only went to the university because sitting at home was so boring.'

'My father is back in jail,' said Fatemeh. 'He's accused of being a liberal mulla, not revolutionary enough. And our house has been confiscated, too rich and too arty for a fundamentalist state. So my mother and I live in a small, bare flat, very basic, and we live on state hand-outs. Radical Islam has gone underground and now it's disappeared.'

Malihe was silent. She felt utterly overwhelmed and depressed by the dismal picture her friends' words had conjured up. Sensing her mood Fatemeh burst in upon her thoughts.

'But we have survived. We've survived many heart-wrenching situations, personal, collective and family traumas. And we are still here.'

'Yes, we are still here, still resisting,' Goli added.

'We have a plan,' said Zareen quietly.

'We weren't sure if we could survive for so long; and we weren't sure if you would either, whether you would ever want to return after so long.' Goli said to Malihe.

'Yes,' said Malihe slowly. 'It did cross my mind that I should stay in Anarak, teach the children, continue to learn the herbal medicine of Banoo and revive her profession. It felt safer there, a stronger community, not yet penetrated by the state and the rise of religious fanaticism. Perhaps because it was too far away and too poor an agricultural community. But in the end I could feel that the pasdars might come, might take over. I weighed up the decision to stay or leave many times, emotionally and rationally, but when your call came I finally decided to join you. I felt deep down within me that being a teacher or a doctor wasn't enough. The sickness of this state is gone beyond that sort of medicine. But I did feel very sad on leaving. I've got what I went for.'

'Good. You are with us then,' Goli said.

'Yes.' Malihe's voice was quiet but firm. 'How are your kids, Zari, well adults I suppose they must be, nearly?'

'Yes, they have grown up – and feeding on what, you may ask. Education these days is for producing and perfecting a subjected society, a subjected people. Unfortunately my children don't support my criticism of the government. There is a wide gap now between me and my daughter. We've stopped talking for fear of fighting each other. It's been a desperate time for mothers and daughters. But I will not submit. My children had to.'

'Islam means "to surrender" – to the will of God and his representatives on earth,' Goli said.

'I disagree,' said Fatemeh. 'Under a pure Islam, the word means to surrender, but not under force. It's a spiritual term, like when I pray, like meditation. To me it means to give up material attachments and to feel unity with my spirit. This is my Islam – don't you call this pure barbarism Islam.' Fatemeh looked angry. Silence fell. On that sad note their meeting came to an end.

'We can't sit here and talk for much longer,' said Zareen.

'We need to have another meeting – we'll let you know when and where – it's not as easy as it used to be, and then you will need to be taken to see our base and the other members of our group, but it will all have to be done gradually. We can't rush anything.'

Malihe left them and made her way home, remembering the first time they had all been together in that area. It had been at the demonstration, the Women's Day march, how it had snowed. They had become four that night. Something was missing between them now, she couldn't put her finger on it. She was more aware of a distance between them and of the changes they had gone through. This meeting had lacked the warmth and joy she had expected and hoped for. They too had been influenced by the austerity and cruelty around them. Had they too become colder, harder and devoid of love? It was good that they were still continuing to resist, to plan, to fight back. For that she was thankful.

Their next meeting took place in a park. They borrowed four childen from their neighbours and relations for the day: Goli and Zareen each brought one of their nieces, and Malihe brought two of her neighbour's children whom she often looked after. The four children were the right age, between three and five, below school age, and small enough not to be trained to spy.

At the entrance to the park, they had to show their passes, sign the register for themselves and the children. They had chosen a Wednesday afternoon, a time when most other women who had no small children would be at the mosque and it would be quiet in the park. They wanted, in this meeting, to brief Malihe on events since she had left. The best time to talk was when the children were playing on the slides, and they arranged themselves around the slides so that while Goli kept an eye out for the children, Fatemeh and Zareen briefed Malihe. They all had to keep watch for other people, especially the park attendants and gardeners.

Zareen began without much deliberation.

'Shortly after you left the civil war started. A small, strong élite force emerged from among the fundamentalists, the Party of God, and it grew very rapidly until it had become a mini government within the government. They advised and guided the elected members of the parliament and got rid of them if they dissented. They drew up a strict constitution based on four basic laws: there is only one God; there is only one holy book – the Quran; women will be mothers only; and non-conformist heretics will be punished by death. They – the Party of God – select God's representative on earth and reinforce his teachings. This representative – the interpreter of the word of God on earth – would be their leader. This constitution had a long section concerning women which was headed: 'Women shall not say no'. It included two hundred pages of directives for women: how to be mothers, and why they should submit to men for the good of society and mankind, why they should never say no. Women were banned from participation in sport, higher education, from inheritance of and ownership of property—'

She stopped abruptly, having spotted a young boy coming towards them.

'He's too old to be in the park,' she murmured. 'And look, he's got one hand in his pocket.' Turning to Malihe, she continued, 'That means either that he is handless or fingerless. Chopping off hands for stealing and non-obedience is very common now and there is at least one guillotine in every mosque. And then some boys are recruited into the services of the POG.'

The boy looked around, checking out the playground, watched the games the children were playing for a while and left, going towards the café in the corner of the park. Goli resumed Zareen's narrative, while she went to play with the children.

'Women were then barred from going out in public, men's spaces – streets, parks, cinemas, etc., except when they were with children or were doing the shopping. Women are allowed to wear only a few colours – black, grey, brown and blue. White can only be worn at funerals or for war. They have even decreed on which days women can go to the public baths, on which day of their periods, and which shade of their period blood signifies their readiness for intercourse with their husbands.

'It was a unique civil war. The POG had an elaborate plan to divide and rule all the opposition parties and thereby become the government, and nobody took them seriously. First they aligned themselves with the largest Marxist party, promising them an equal share in power if they would help the POG to get rid of the rest of the competition – the other left-wing groups. The Marxists agreed and so began the saga of alliances and betrayals till all the opposition parties, one by one, were decimated until the only party remaining was the Party of God. From then on there was no remnant of a civil society left, only a society of obedient believers. It didn't matter how many people were executed – a few million was nothing – so long as the ultimate goal was achieved: the creation of a country with a purer, cleaner population. They boasted of getting rid of one million disobedient women in Tehran alone. A holy society—'

She broke off suddenly. 'soz! Sisters of Zeinab!' she hissed. The way she said it made Zareen – with her hand on the swing – jump; the child she was pushing jumped too, and Malihe twitched as well. But they swiftly resumed the appearance of normality, chatting about the beauty of the park, and commenting on the cleverness of the children and their games. Two women, all in black, only their hands and faces visible, walking together, came towards them. As they drew nearer the women could see that they were wired up with small microphones.

'God's holy blessings on you,' said the two Sisters as they passed, checking out the playground.

Goli made a gracious bow in their direction while keeping her face well hidden. They went away.

'They are called the living martyrs, totally dedicated to the POG. They are the most dangerous women around. When you see them, be on your guard, fear for your life.' Goli shivered.

They all felt they needed a cup of tea, but wondered whether they should go to the café. The boy must have left by now, but would the Sisters of Zeinab be there? As the playground was still fairly quiet they decided to stay there just a little longer.

Malihe's soul was sinking. She could not believe the demands that conformity and subordination placed on women now. She felt just like a swing, pushed forwards and backwards with something else's weight upon her. She did not want to hear any more: it was soul destroying and she was surprised that they had survived at all.

Fatemeh began again.

'We haven't become the passive, obedient believers they wanted to make us, we have resisted, how is a long, too long a story. I can only tell you a fraction of it. We have fought on many fronts, but most of all we have fought tooth and nail to remain alive, alive if only to resist and disobey. At the time of the civil war when women were recruited to work outside their homes, we even worked *for* the system – I worked as a park attendant, Goli became a mosque cleaner and supplied us with invaluable information, and Zari became a tea woman and got to know some important women allies. Our object was mainly to infiltrate the system and provide a cover for our own activities.

'Women's groups too were caught up in the spiral of betrayal. One by one all those groups, the women, Marxist Women, Women Socialist Libertarians Group, Human Rights For Women, etc., they were all destroyed, both the openly active and the underground ones.

'One of the most tragic cases was that of the women's village. A rich Mojtahed died and left all her wealth to her only daughter. As it was forbidden for her to inherit it, she decided to dedicate it to a worthy cause. At this point we moved in: I knew and was friendly with her and I advised her to dedicate it to sick women and children, as most of the wealth was concentrated in land, in a small village. She agreed to the project but only if the government permitted her to be in charge of it. She made me her assistant and I took on the job of organising it with some of the other women comrades. We turned it into a beautiful village for 'disturbed women', as they called them. With facilities – clinics, sport and art therapy, everything to cure mentally and emotionally sick women, and protect their children.

'Our "patients" were mostly women who had been interrogated and sentenced for the offences of putting on make-up, wearing bright colours, disobeying their husbands and brothers, and so on. Of course, the number of women with mental problems had gone up so much, and the lack of resources was such a big problem that the government didn't mind at first, so long as they were kept somewhere out of reach and forgotten. They didn't want the burden or the expense.

'We organised it very efficiently with the help of unemployed women doctors, therapists, nurses, and a few other dedicated sisters. You don't know what a great source of power and independence it turned out to be, a small, self-sufficient women's space – it was fantastic!

'It worked just fine for five glorious months, until it was surrounded and attacked – twice we fought back, and repulsed them successfully. Our underground system of communication and our emergency living quarters in a bunker were effective protection. But we hadn't counted on the chemical bombing. It happened out of the blue in broad daylight, a few months after the second attack. Everything was wiped out and three hundred women and children, doing their daily work and play, were killed. I didn't live there myself, I just worked there. It all happened after we had done our shift and had left the base.

'After a period of hiding, we got together again and started the Alborz Women's Unit, which is still going strong. We have had to keep on the move and now we are a much smaller group, an élite force of women, strictly organised and highly skilled, working in complete secrecy. We have a secret base outside Tehran and we have equipped it with computers, weapons and communications. We have a communication network, a network of safe houses and a vital transport system. We are now a powerful underground movement, and now that you are back, you're with us. We need you and your knowledge, your medicine . . . ' Fatemeh ended.

It was getting late and the children were thirsty and wanted a drink.

The café was large. Women and children sat together at a few tables, at another sat a group of boy children with their table tennis bats and ping-pong balls, and a group of the Sisters of Zeinab sat at another table as if in a conference. Further along from them sat a couple of young men, with their hands in their pockets, looking like spies.

They got drinks for the children and tea for themselves and sat down at a corner table, holding on to their nerves tightly while the children sipped their drinks and teased each other.

Malihe went back home, to Leila's. She wanted to be taken to the base and meet the other women in the unit. She wanted to know how her herbal medicine was going to be used as part of their plan. But she had been told they did not know when the meeting could be arranged; it could take a while to organise it. She had to wait. And that was the hardest part, waiting and being alone.

She felt misplaced, homeless and friendless. The intimate, friendly atmosphere of Ziba Style and the life that they had known there had been blown away . . . only dust was left. Alone and lonely, depression overtook her sense of the urgency of their cause. She continued to float in this vacuum until, at last Goli was able to take the risk of visiting her, bringing with her a bundle of joyful surprise.

Which part of the house was the safest place to talk, they both wondered. Leila suggested the shower. She then took the rest of the family out to the mosque for the afternoon sermon so that they could be alone. Malihe felt relieved and she relaxed after Leila, her mother and younger brothers had all left. She and Goli sat in the bathroom, next to the shower, which they turned on full to mask their conversation. They made themselves comfortable, with tea and plain sweets, on the bathroom floor, knees touching and shoulders rubbing.

'What is Leila's role in all this?' Malihe started off. 'She's part of the unit, isn't she?'

'She is a "friend",' Goli answered. 'There are many of them in various locations and they pass on messages, and care for our members who are in transit or hiding, looking after them and making sure they are kept away from any danger. They are women who don't want to, or can't for a number of reasons, be directly involved in our struggle . . . But Malihe, tell me about yourself and how you feel about your return.'

'Oh Goli, I am dumbfounded. I don't know what to say any more. Why is this city so loveless now?'

'Hm, well, the Ministry for Guidance decrees that love should be confined to the family – as if you could build a wall around love, cage it in only to bestow it on your relatives!' Goli was scornful. 'Of course it doesn't work. Caged love becomes suffocated and is replaced by authority, fear and hatred. We are a people saturated in hatred now and not only the hatred of women.'

'But what has happened to you? Why are you all so detached and cold to each other? Why didn't you lot preserve some of the sparkle we once had?'

'I don't know.' Goli was uncertain, sad. 'Do you think we have changed a lot? I guess we don't notice it . . . we . . . have grown with it . . . it was inevitable . . . how could we keep our sparkle? How? After what we have gone through? What we have seen, witnessed? The death carnage in the women's village, a child's singed body hanging between the branches of what was once an apple tree, and pavements of burned women's bodies, their skulls blown apart and their memories turned to ashes – how could we, having seen all that? It seemed beyond hope. Why should we do anything? People have given up, women have turned into slaves. Why struggle? For what? For a defeated, will-less, and subjected people. Malihe, we lived and worked in such an atmosphere. Don't say that. Please don't blame us. If you knew . . . if you had seen . . . you would be surprised how we are still here, *and* have the will to live on, determined, with the same intentions. Don't blame us. Don't.'

The two women sat drinking tea, each wondering in their solitude. Goli wasn't sure if she had reached Malihe. She went on, eager to bridge the distance between them.

'Tell me about Anarak. How was it? How much had it changed? And your trip to the desert?'

Malihe was gently brought out of her thoughts, she smiled, the first in a long time, and started to tell Goli about her village and Banoo with warmth and ease. She relaxed. Goli was fascinated by Malihe's account of the herbal apprenticeship, of Banoo's age and experience and their long trek across the kavier, to find that most dangerous plant. She questioned Malihe for a little while about the properties and effects of the plant.

It's especially effective when taken with water,' Malihe responded. 'With this I can send two thousand men to their death, an instant poisoned death, a speedy departure to their beloved heaven. But tell me about your plan, about the Womens' Unit and your activities since the arson attack.'

'We went underground during the cultural revolution. The government closed the universities and colleges of further education and set up a committee of mullas to establish a new Islamic culture for the younger generation: to write new books, to devise a new history and rewrite the old one. In this period all the non-religious women's centres and women's papers were officially banned. We started training to prepare for firearm combat and guerrilla attacks.

'But the women's village opened up new avenues and we invested a lot of hope and energy there. Fatemeh was convinced that we would be safe there for at least six months because there was little that we did there that could be classified as un-Islamic. But then we had control over our affairs and protected it ourselves . . . I guess the ultimate destruction of that was inevitable.

After the chemical war waged on the women's village we couldn't do very much for a long time. The most political and subversive act in those grief-stricken months was to paint the town occasionally with one of the forbidden colours – yellow or pink.

Later we began again with a few small-scale attacks against a few particularly obnoxious mullas, but it wasn't enough. Since then we have been gathering a number of old friends and allies together, extending our communication networks and support groups further afield, even abroad, and have been planning our first major assault on the government.'

247

Malihe would soon join the underground unit and help its preparation for the attack, Goli told her, but she would have to wait a couple of weeks while her passage was arranged. In the meantime they would try to find her a job, as she couldn't go back to her old job, women's dressmakers were redundant now the government suplied women's clothing – uniformed sacks for all from the age of five onwards. Goli suggested that, if Malihe wanted, she could help out in the local mosque, where she could keep her eyes and ears open for news about the movements of the clerical establishment, until Zareen was able to escort her to their base. Goli left and Malihe thought of the heavy times ahead, the waiting and the tense pace of life.

The day arrived. A message had been sent giving a date and a time. On the allotted morning Malihe took the bus to the waiting room in the Sina Hospital, where Zareen met her dressed as a Sister of Zeinab, in a head-to-toe black veil with a short white overall. They were then driven in an ambulance by a woman driver, dressed just like Zareen, through the city centre right out to a mental institution in the suburbs. Here Malihe also changed her clothes, assuming the disguise of a Sister of Zeinab. They transferred to a soz's patrol van and drove for a long way to the foothills of the Alborz mountains.

They pulled off the road on to a dirt track where a rickety old shed held a motor-bike. They got out of the van and the woman drove off. Not a word had been spoken for the whole of the journey. In the shed they got changed again into men's peasant clothing, and Malihe slipped her shoes off and put them carefully into a bag which she slung round her neck. Zareen hauled the bike out of the shed, climbed on and helped Malihe to get on behind her.

They set off, riding uphill along narrow dusty, rocky tracks. After about an hour they stopped and Zareen hid the bike away in a cave. They then went on, climbing the rest of the way.

The entrance to the base was another cave. They were met there by two women who took them through a long, narrow rock tunnel to another cave where they sat down on stone benches to rest and talk. Malihe's head was dizzy with altitude and excitement. The two women introduced themselves as Azar and Bahar. Bahar turned to Malihe.

'It is good to meet you at last. I gather you have got a precious gift for us,' she said, smiling. Malihe was pleased to see that she was a tall, good-looking unveiled woman.

'I am one of the five women in this base,' Bahar continued. 'There are another five in another outpost base in the mountains. We move around all the time. We have been here, in this base, for two months. I am the head of the operations, with Azar's help, of course. Our maps and computers are in the next cave.' She pointed to the tunnel extending away into the mountains. 'If you are rested enough now, we will move on. We have much to discuss.'

Malihe stood up, Bahar led the way, the light of her torch darting into the darkness. The tunnel was narrow and tight. They walked about for two hundred metres before reaching a door which led into another cave.

'This first room is our planning and computer room, the second one through there is communications where we have our radio sets for maintaining contact with the outside world, and the third and last, also the largest, is our weapons and equipment room.'

Malihe could not believe her eyes and ears, so much sophistication, so much technnology right in front of her eyes. Amazing, she thought, not long ago the only technology available to women was the typewriter, and not their own either. She was thrilled inside but kept cool. Bahar continued.

'Come, I will show you my room and then we will go to Azar's room.'

Room was a grand word for the barrel-shaped place, like calling a bird's nest a palace, Malihe thought.

'Don't you have a table? Chairs?' she asked.

'No,' Azar replied.

'So where do you do your writing, drawing . . . maps.' Malihe persisted.

'Everything is done on the computer, sometimes even our thinking. It would be nice to have a table, chairs, or a bed.

It would be nice to have them one day, to stretch and roll over in a soft bed. I dream of it sometimes.'

On a small flat stretch of rock there was a red sleeping bag and a yellow pillow and next to them some books in English, one with a picture of the Aswan Dam on the front. A few clothes in a pile sat in one corner, a small mirror and a box of make-up next to it. They went on to Azar's room and they all sat down, close to each other, on the rocky floor. Zareen and Azar spread a map out in the middle.

'This is what we have been working on: Ershad.' Azar pointed to a red cross on the map. 'It is a large mosque built before the revolution and now the ideological seat of the government. It holds two thousand men, and in less than a month they will have the anniversary celebration of the revolution there. All the ministers, leaders of the Party of God, heads of the army, the police, the revolutionary guards, as well as many of the leading mullas will be gathered there together. We have got the day's programme, the list of the participants, speakers and the security arrangements. It is on that day that we will strike.'

'Before the revolution I worked as a civil engineer in Egypt on the construction of the Aswan Dam,' Bahar started to explain. 'Azar was a physicist working at the Sorbonne in Paris. We came back to help the revolution and women's causes. We met up in the high days of the women's demonstrations in the university and recognised each other – we had been school mates together. We worked together in the campaign against the sacking of professional women employees. We had to go underground for a long time. This group is only two years old – we joined up when Fatemeh and Goli were building it up. We called on a few other of our trusted activists and other skilled women. This is how we built up this unit for our purpose.'

Azar joined in. 'Our plan depends on the skills of our explosives experts who have had experience abroad in regular and irregular armies and, Malihe, on your herbal lore.'

Malihe thought of her children, not with pain, but pride. Azar pointed to the map again and went on.

'These are our targets, primarily Ershad Mosque, but also,

nearby, the Ministry of Injustice and the Centre for the Rehabilitation of Women, where they teach women obedience in matters of marriage and motherhood,' she added for Malihe's benefit.

Azar spread another map, a large-scale one and placed it on top of the one on the floor. Bahar took over.

'We are going to isolate the main water supply to the Ershad Mosque the day before the celebration and we will contaminate it with your herbal medicine. We have spies in the mosque – administrative staff, the tea lady and the cook – they will both be off sick that day. It will be the last thirst those men will need to satisfy.'

There was a pause. Azar renewed her part of the narrative.

'We have designated the three target buildings for detonation all at the same time, just after lunch time, when the herbal medicine should have taken effect. We want to make absolutely sure of their destruction.' She folded up the two maps. 'After the explosion our transport unit will go into operation and ship us all from the observation point to secure safe-houses. By two p.m. our attack will have been accomplished and we will be safe, free and away.' Azar folded her arms and leaned back, her long hair falling back on her shoulders, over her pink jumper.

Malihe was confused and overjoyed. What to say? What to ask?

'Malihe do you want to ask something?' Bahar said gently.

'I don't know how to say it.' Malihe let her surprise and appreciation pour out unreservedly. 'This is incredible, beyond me. I didn't expect any of it, any plans we made in the past were very basic, nothing as sophisticated as this complex system you have created. Zari, weren't they?'

'Yes, of course,' Zareen said, understanding her, 'but we had to move on. The state became more sophisticated, more vicious and we too had to become sophisticated in order to protect ourselves. We have also had to get help from outside, our contacts and comrades abroad, including the Iranian women emigrants settled in places as far apart as Vietnam, Mozambique and London, have helped us in many valuable ways, especially in guaranteeing the shipment of the latest equipment and weaponry necessary for guerrilla warfare.'

'What of your communication and safe-house networks? The ambulances, the soz's patrol car, and their drivers, are they reliable?' Malihe asked again.

'Through the women's village we made a lot of contacts with hospital workers in many parts of the city,' explained Bahar. Many of them became our messengers and then collaborators. After the destruction of the village we survivors kept up our contacts and developed them. We are helped by the increasing number of mental institutions and punishment centres for women and by the fact that the government cannot carry out full surveillance on them, their workers and inmates. And many doctors and nurses have been persecuted and executed for prescribing "imperialist" contraceptives, for performing abortions and so on, making them our natural and committed allies.'

'We have three groups of comrades: "facilitator", "messenger" and "friend",' added Azar. 'Facilitators are women who are well placed to get us things – especially equipment; some have contacts on the black market, others are outside the country. Messengers give us news, link us to the city and events there, some are radio operators, others are drivers. And then there are the "friends", women who don't want to be too deeply involved but who help us as much as they can within their limited family and home situations. Leila, for instance, is a "friend".'

On the uncomfortable rock wall Malihe leaned back, hope glowing like a beacon inside her. She enjoyed listening to and looking at these strong, beautiful women.

'It feels a bit like Ziba Style used to be, with that intimate atmosphere, doesn't it Zari?'

Zareen nodded. 'I had forgotten all that, we had to, the memories ached so.'

'I can't forget it,' said Malihe. 'I miss it so terribly, all those women, our endless chats, the friendship, intimacy, even the conflicts. And the make-up: you have some on now,' she said, gesturing towards Bahar. 'I haven't seen anybody with make-up on for so long, it's delightful to see some colours on women.'

'Do you know what she would get if she were caught in Tehran?' Zareen faced Malihe.

'I guess six months in gaol for the shade of her lipstick. No? Too short?'

'No, worse. The latest punishment carried out by the moral squads is morbid. They carry rats or spiders in cages in the separated section in the back of their patrol cars. If they catch a woman with make-up on they put her in the back, open the cage and leave her there as long as they see fit.'

'Spiders, rats . . .' Malihe covered her eyes and tried to shut her ears against Zareen's words.

'I hope we make it through this,' she said, after a while.

They sat in silence. Malihe broke it, as if remembering a forgotten question.

'You haven't said a word about any men comrades and supporters. Have no men, or men's groups, helped or been part of the struggle?'

'Which men? Do you mean members of the left? Our families? The intellectual classes? Which men?' It didn't sound as if Azar was asking, but stating, stabbing.

'Any.' Malihe said and moved her hands, open-palmed, in front of her breasts in a flash of request, still wanting to know.

'Well, it is a sorry sort of an affair,' Zareen said. 'We tried, as you know some of us still live with them, we tried to have them join us and support what we were doing – those on the left, the liberals, the intellectuals. But soon it became obvious that we had to join them, that they always have to be the initiators, they have to set the agenda for women. They would not follow or adhere to anybody else's, least of all ours.' Azar took over. 'Has a murdered prostitute, or a stoned adulterer ever moved a male poet to write a poem? Or has a male artist ever been moved to dedicate a story, a painting, a song, to his own mother or sister, for their anger and pain against the compulsory veil? Since Eshqi wrote that poem:

If two or three poets add their voices to mine,

The people will soon start humming this song.

253

Did they? That was over fifty years ago. Has there been any solidarity from the students and lecturers who filled women's places in the class rooms and universities, any one of them refused a position because it was taken away from a woman? Have you ever heard of any protest from history teachers, boycotting teaching of one-sided history? His own side? I think not. Iranian middle-class intellectuals, on the left and the right, are the most sexist and misogynist men in the world.' Azar finished bitterly.

'We have debated this for so long and I disagree with Azar, and her sweeping generalisation.'

This was still the good old Zari she knew, Malihe thought.

'It's a personal feeling, I just feel it inside me,' Azar emphasised.

'I see it like this,' Zareen went on, 'it is good that we have organised this all on our own, ourselves alone. They're a nuisance anyway – imagine if they were helping how many more shirts we would have had to wash!'

Malihe laughed. This was her old Zari.

'I don't mind their shirts. It's their enormous egos that I can't massage.' Bahar complemented Zareen's sentence.

A small electronic bleep interrupted their friendly talk.

'I am sorry, Malihe, but it's our shift now and we have to go. It is Mina's and Pari's turn to sleep.'

'Thank you for today. I'm pleased to have seen all this, and to have met you here.' Malihe took her shoes out of her bag as she spoke and, with a tiny screw driver, dismantled one of the heels, pulling out a tiny wrapper from a compartment inside.

'This is it. I had never in the whole of my life believed that I could get such pleasure from the murder of men.'

She passed it to Bahar who took it and said, 'We know. It's in safe hands.'

On the way back Malihe and Zareen stopped off in the cave that sheltered the bike and talked together.

'Tell me about yourself, Zari,' Malihe asked. 'What do you do here? And Goli and Fati? Are you and Fati still together? God, I have so many questions to ask you. Now at last we can talk as we used to.'

'Oh,' smiled Zareen, 'We, the three of us, are messengers. Of course we are still together, but I don't know what that means any more. So much has happened to us. you remember Goli's best friend Marjan? She died in gaol, unvisited by anybody for ten months, and her body was buried in a mass grave, nobody knows where . . . you knew Azadeh, the young woman who was disfigured by the revolutionary guards? She died in childbirth. I think she just gave up living. She wanted to die rather than mother the sickening baby of a brute. Who else?' she continued grimly. 'My regulars either worked for the system or disappeared or died . . . ' Zareen tailed off, her voice quiet and unemotional.

'I can't get used to it, Zari,' cried Malihe. 'The other day when I went to collect my widow's ration I saw that two women had been hanged from a very high wooden post. The placard said that one was a singer, the other her accompanying musician. Further on in the square, they were flogging men for drinking alcohol, their backs bruised and bloody. I was holding my hands over my ears, closing my eyes and trying to run away from the place, but other people were gathered there watching. I hated them. Like a gathering of bats. It seemed as if they had no senses left, no sensibility. Zari, what has happened to the humanity of man? Where are we going? Why and how did we come to be governed by this class of men, these mullas? We have got centuries of history about their ignorance, their opposition to science, about how money-grabbing they are – mulla-khor – about their manipulation, brutality and more. Our literature is full of stories, poems, proverbs on their dishonesty, hypocrisy and misogyny . . . Why!!! How could we have such a government?'

'Malihe, we are sinking. Sinking and there is no end to how low we can go. We are all used to those scenes now, they don't move us any more. Who cares about history or literature, when the ultimate aim is to go to heaven. We have become numb. A numb nation. Well, Goli would say that humanity never existed, least of all in this ancient land. Myself, I think it is God. He needs sacrifices, and women have always been first at the altar. Don't ask me where it will end. You know, it is so ironic, some people, and working-class people too, have started calling places by their pre-revolutionary names. People call out to cab drivers, "Shahyad Square", not Azadi Square . . . and call the Shah's period, "The Golden Age". Could we ever in our wildest dreams have believed that would happen?'

'A singer hanged, strangled by the throat, her music, her songs choked. This must be our witch hunt . . . another witch hunt . . . ' Malihe was mumbling to herself. 'Zari, what will happen to us? We are so separate, so isolated. It doesn't feel as if we will be friends again and keep our friendship.'

'I don't know. Perhaps that is part of the sacrifice, the hardest part. But don't be so low, we have kept our hopes high for a very long time and we must not give up now.'

Zareen took Malihe's hands and held them between hers, caressing them.

'We must not give up now.'

The day came. The anniversary of the revolution. It was a Saturday, decreed a public holiday. The whole day of official celebration was planned at the Ershad Mosque. Government ministers, heads of the army and the police and members of the clergy, they were all there together for the day of jubilation, for food, speeches and self-congratulation. The high point was to be the lunch at one p.m. with a speech given by Mojtahed Emami, the prime minister and the head of the clergy. The building and all of the surrounding area was being guarded by pasdars and the revolutionary guards.

At the base the women had been working meticulously and tirelessly for the four weeks leading up to the anniversary. Messengers, civil engineers and explosives experts, they had all been working long days and through sleepless nights to ensure that their tasks were carried out smoothly and successfully. The revolutionary guards had even played their part and had evacuated local residents from their homes the day before the celebration, as part of the normal security procedure for such occasions, thus making the task of planting the bombs easier.

Just before one thirty p.m. the four women met on a hillside some miles away, facing the Ershad Mosque. Each was disguised but underneath had dressed in bright, beautiful colours, and each carried a gun, except Malihe. She did not want to be armed and was, as usual, in her black veil, saying that she still did not dare to go without it. Goli had a man's suit on, a new one that fitted her perfectly.

It was nearly one thirty p.m. By now the herbal medicine would be on its way, travelling through their veins, settling in their nerves and, just when they were sitting back comfortably after their meal and checking their afternoon schedules, a sudden death, like a quiet heart attack, a silent, red explosion would envelop them, and then another, a final explosion.

They waited, trembling, fearfully excited. The ticking of their watches, of their hearts. The tiny twitches of their hands and feet. The tightening of the skin to goosepimples. Eyes racing, watching, checking. Malihe looked at Zareen and then back at the golden minarets rising to heaven, the holy hand on its pinnacle. Her fingers beat out a rhythm, an uneven tattoo. Zareen was twisting, pulling and even ripping out her hair. The sound of biting nails, chewing, tearing. Time crawling on, blood warming inside them, nervous, thin hands fluttering to, framing their faces, unframing them. Breaths, breathlessness, exhalations of anticipation hit the hot air. Fatemeh reached for Zareen's hand, squeezed it, dropped it. The ruffling of their trousers, skirts, tossing and turning of their impatient bodies. Goli leaned on Malihe, back to back, shoulder to shoulder. The earth around them was bare, an immense barrenness, a nakedness around them, except for the telephone lines which twittered in the air above. The curve of the hill at their heels, the golden minarets in their eyes. Their stomachs shrank, tightened, loosened. A salty feeling settled in. The lingering moments, the pain of suspense. Raw anxiety, raw nerves. The sharp cutting edge of the last few seconds.

A twitch of an eyelid later, the red explosion, the huge fire burst, a deafening noise. The hand disappeared. The golden minarets blew apart into a thousand pieces. Its bricks, cement, wood and golden tiles burst apart and the holy hand was blown away, in front of their eyes. The sound shrieked in their ears. Immense fear, immense relief gripped them. Flames shot up, whirled and twirled in endless circles of red and black. The debris scattered, thrown about, the matter whizzing around at the speed of light. The second and third explosions would follow but too far away to reach their eyes and ears. Soon they would know.

Smiles covered their faces. The pleasure of victory, like the flames that rose high above, circling ever larger and larger. The golden-black clouds formed and collapsed, formed and collapsed. The smoke, the dust, the debris and the soot reached the gates of heaven. The fire reached to the horizon beyond, the sky and the houses, blackened them, lost the horizon and hid the daylight. A patch of darkness, highlighted by the sun, glowed and shone: the flame of celebration.

Goli and Zareen jumped with joy, Fatemeh sighed with resigned relief, Malihe sat still, astonished at their triumph.

A messenger sailed by on a bicycle, along the road, with one hand up, fingers wide open, the sign of success. Zareen burst into tears, tears of happiness.

'We have done it!' she cried. 'Our women have done it!'

'Two thousand big-bellied, corrupt parasites, with their amamehs and abas on, are blown apart, into pieces, their rotten brains burned out,' Malihe said slowly, relishing each word.

'Victory,' murmured Fatemeh, 'for us, we did it. Congratulations to you all, to me . . . '

'A small favour for a sister. For Azadeh. I hope she can hear it,' cried Goli with passion.

'Some mothers will judge us, some will condemn us, some women will think of us, some will hail us and some will support us.' Zareen's voice was tinged with doubt.

'We haven't done it to be hailed. We have done it for our own pains and sorrows.' Goli looked as if she were remembering dark memories.

'I have done it for my grandchildren, so that they can wash their hair in the rain and dance with naked feet on the banks of the Karoon river and on the shore of the Caspian Sea.' Zareen glowed.

'We have proved that the state is not omnipotent,' said Fatemeh, 'just as we can create it, so we can dismantle it.'

'Let's say we have just shaken it, knocked down a few of its pillars. We may have to come back, there may be more to do.'

'Let's leave this mess and go somewhere safer and better,' Malihe said.

'Yes, the next step,' Goli said.

'Zari and I are going to Mashad for a while to stay with one of my father's friends. My mother will join us in a couple of months. We are just going to eat and drink and stay in bed. Zareen wants me to nurse her. She says it's my turn to do some housework. I have agreed, for now anyway,' Fatemeh laughed.

'What have you done with your old man and the kids?' Malihe asked.

'I told him it's his turn to look after them,' she replied. 'He said that he'd never done it. He can't imagine doing it. I told him to start using his imagination, it's about time.'

'What about the shrine there?' Malihe was curious to know why they chose Mashad, a holy city.

'I think it should be a museum. It is a beautiful building.' Fatemeh was still reverent.

'I think it should be demolished,' Zareen protested. 'It has huge grounds and a lovely garden. A spacious and beautiful hairdressing and beauty salon could be built on its site for women only.'

'I think you should fight that one through there. I am going to Anarak,' said Malihe. 'Goli wants to come with me, to learn about herbal lore. We will set something up together. If you don't agree on your future plans come and visit us.'

'Don't you go crossing the Gulf to the sands of Arabia!' warned Fatemeh.

'No chance!' said Goli. 'We still have a lot to do here. They don't need us.'

'No, most of all, we're going to enjoy ourselves and have a long holiday first,' Malihe added.

'Soon the transport will be here, haven't forgotten your codes?' Zareen reminded them. 'Have you? You took the rainbow colours and we are the igak [snow] terms, from autumn on.'

'We haven't,' Malihe and Goli replied together.

The beautiful mosque burned away, its golden minarets and its holy pointed hand having crumbled in the flames. Four women stood in twos, with veil and without the veil, stood waiting to go in two different directions.

'Take my harmonica and learn how to play it. I've got myself a new one – actually it's a very old one and was going cheap in the musician's black market.' Fatemeh handed the instrument to Malihe.

'I have got something for you too,' said Malihe to Zareen. 'I meant to give it to you earlier.'

She passed a silk Yazdi scarf to Zareen who shook it, admiring its bright primary colours. She wrapped it round her hand like a bracelet.

'We will share it between us,' she told Fatemeh.

They all looked at each other, all eyes, then shook hands. The meeting of the left and the right hands. The hands clasped, the last meeting points. The hands held on, the hands let go. The weight lifted. Goodbyes and best wishes, smiles, waves, walking away, the turning up of the red earth behind them. The arrival of the transport. The music of the new harmonica.

# Glossary

aba – brown surplice worn by Iranian Muslim clergy

addasi – a dish made with green lentils;

amameh – head cover of the Iranian Muslim clergy. There are two colours – black and white; black is said to be worn only by the descendent of the prophet Muhammed

ash reshteh – spaghetti soup – but a very complicated and elaborate one with many ingredients

ayatollah – an Arabic word meaning 'sign of God'; the title for a high-ranking Muslim clergyman

Baha'i – a Shia sect, with a progressive line on women. It originated in Iran in the nineteenth century and its members have been persecuted ever since, especially after the revolution

caravanserai – a staging post

chador – a long, engulfing piece of material that covers a woman's body from head to toe. The word means tent

dayereh – means round. It is a hand-drum played by women, beaten on by the finger tips of one hand at the same time as being held above the left or right shoulder

Dieve – is a mythological figure, a horrible monster who kidnaps naughty children

Farvardin – the name of a street, and the first month of spring, which comes in March and April

gaz tree – a desert tree

ghaleh – a watch tower in the desert

ghanat – an ancient system of underground water reservoirs in the Middle East

hammam – a public steam bath

Hejab – the Islamic term for the women's veil

'house' – a desert measurement, by which stages of the journey are measured

hoze – a small pond situated in the courtyard of the Iranian house

kafan – a shroud

kavier – the desert

Komiteh – the militia headquarters during and after the revolution

korsi – a traditional means of heating in winter

Mojtahed – a high ranking mulla

mulla – Muslim member of the clergy in Iran

mulla-khor – slang term used when lending money: the lender would say don't pocket it as mullas do

Nu-Rooz – it literally means new day, the first day of the Persian New Year on 21st of March. It is pronounced as 'No-Rooz'

Ordibehesht – name of a street, and the second month of spring, which comes in April and May

Qajar – dynasty ruling Iran in the eighteenth and nineteenth centuries till the advent of the Pahlavi dynasty in the 1920s

pasdar – local militia

poshti – the heavy, tough cushions with lovely rug covers for leaning on that are common in the traditional home

Rey City – an ancient city south of Tehran

rozeh – a sermon

sangak – a hand-long, large, flat and very popular kind of bread, freshly baked three times a day

shahpasand – a kind of flower; I haven't seen it in England

Shia – there are two major sects in Islam: Shia and Sunni, the Shia being the minority sect, except in Iran, the Lebanon and Iraq

sofreh – a cotton cloth spread on the floor to eat from

sohan – a kind of sweet, a speciality of Qum

Shah – the king

Shaheed – meaning martyr: Jaleh Square is now called Martyr's Square

tagh tree – a desert tree

Tabrizi carpet – one style of the many types of Persian carpets which is named after the city of Tabriz, where it is produced

Tabrizi tree – Italian or Lombardy poplar
Ulama – means learned and is a title for some Muslim clergy
vaugh! – an exclamation
Yazdi (scarf) – Yazd is a city famous for its silk industry and
   its silk scarves in particular
zolbia – sweet; in India it is called *jilabi*
ziba – beautiful (as in Ziba style)

For the benefit of the British reader I will explain a few of
the names of the characters and streets and their meanings.
Most Persian women's names are derived from nature: Goli
from the word for 'flower', Zareen from gold, Shabnam from
'dew', etc.; and men's names often come from religious figures
and saints. But I have not selected the names of the women
characters on the basis of their meanings, but mostly on that
of their class position, which is how in reality people are
named. Only two of the women's names have I chosen because
of their meaning. Most of the street names at the time of the
Shah were derived from that title: Shah-Abad, Shah-Reza,
Shah-Dokht, etc., but now most of the street names have
religious names after male martyrs. Here are some of the
names and their meanings:

Malihe – gentle one
Banoo – woman
Azadeh – free woman

An Iranian linguist brought it to my attention that the Farsi
(Iranian) words for man and woman are derived from the
words for life and death. Zan (woman) is the root word for
zendeh, zendegy – life, living, being alive, to live, etc.; and
the word for man – mard – is the root word for mordan, mord
– death, dying and dead, etc.

   I have also used some Persian sayings and proverbs trans-
lated straight into English: 'My eyes don't drink water' is a
very common saying and means that it is not possible, it won't
happen. 'Moving from foot to foot' means to delay. 'Don't put
your hand on my belly' is a common saying amongst women,
meaning I have a belly full . . .